THIS CURSED
CROWN

Books by Alexandra Overy
available from Inkyard Press

Middle Grade

The Gingerbread Witch

Young Adult

These Feathered Flames
This Cursed Crown

THIS CURSED CROWN

ALEXANDRA OVERY

inkyard PRESS

ISBN-13: 978-1-335-41868-5

This Cursed Crown

For questions and comments about the quality of this book, please contact us
at CustomerService@Harlequin.com.

Inkyard Press
22 Adelaide St. West, 41st Floor
Toronto, Ontario M5H 4E3, Canada
www.InkyardPress.com

Printed in U.S.A.

For Katie, the most glorious of starbeasts

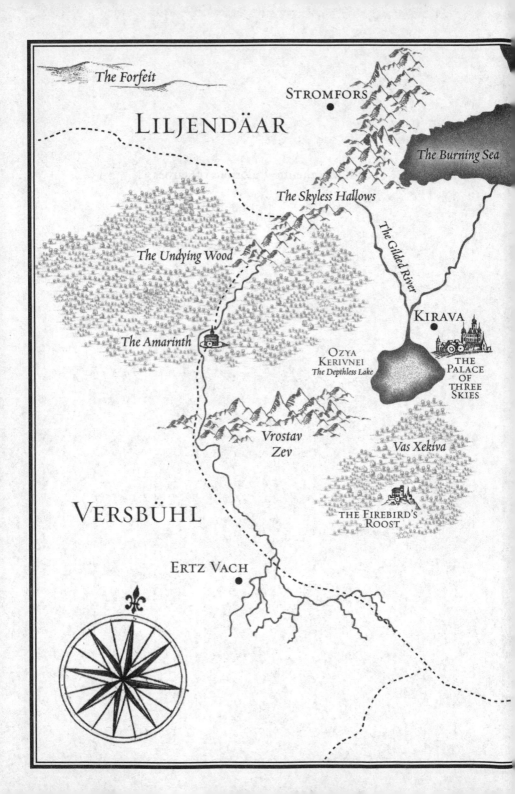

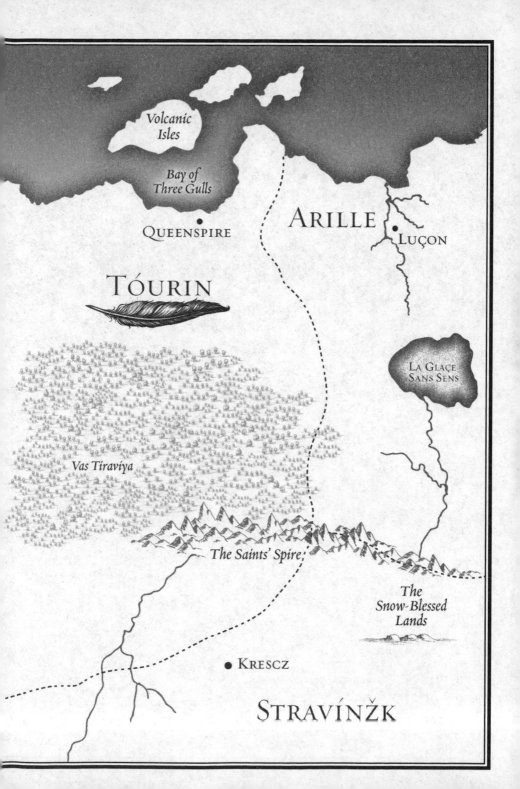

PART ONE:

FROM OUR RUINED ASHES

Once, in Tóurin, two princesses fell,
Torn apart for the price of a spell.
A mother's sins for which the land must take blame,
A sister's love, which neither can claim.
But now it has tolled, a bell cannot be unrung,
And the oldest foe holds a curse on their tongue.
For when all is taken and the fates unbound,
Who in this forsaken ruin is left to be crowned?

—The Ballad of the Firebird and the Queen

CHAPTER ONE

Asya didn't need the falcon circling overhead to tell her something terrible had happened here.

There had been one trailing her, as sure as smoke trails flames, every time she went outside the past six days. A scorch mark against the clear sky. But she didn't need the winged silhouette to mark her as a portent of ruin. She'd done that well enough herself.

She took a careful step forward, light on the uneven ground. Ash hung in the air still, thick enough to coat her tongue. Remnants of magic too. Like tattered shreds of silk caught in spindled branches.

Asya had never seen the Elmer in daylight. Not from this vantage point, anyway. Not without the thick bars of a cage tight around her and fear clawing its way out of her chest.

Daylight leeched the wonder from the Elmer's facade. Where shadows and pale moonlight gave the old church a sinister air, the feel of something ancient that stood against a rising tide, daylight washed that away. Smoothed its edges until Asya could see it for what it truly was: a ruin slowly being reclaimed by the earth around it.

A tomb.

She teetered on the threshold. Her muscles pulled against

her, even the Firebird's firm presence recoiling from the memory. Her sister's hands tight in hers, swallowed by unforgiving flames. But she had to go inside. Had to see for herself.

It was her last hope.

Tarya had told her not to come. That the past held only echoes with no bearing on what happened next.

But that was precisely why Asya had to come.

She took a breath—cinders catching in her chest—and stepped inside.

The Elmer hadn't changed in the past six days. Somehow, Asya had expected it to. As if the night that had torn her apart might have left its scars here too. But it looked just the same— save the fine layer of ash coating the wreckage.

The silence was the worst. It reminded her too much of the terrible silence of that night. The pounding storm and soaring song snatched away as soon as the price was paid, leaving her grasping at empty air.

Asya used to like the quiet. The soft hush of twilight, the moment when the earth held its breath between night and day. The hopeful silence of dawn when the forest still slept, all its potential standing in wait. But not anymore. She'd been left in an eternal, empty quiet. A lonely quiet.

As she moved through the ruin, eddies of ash whirled in her wake. Odd ghosts of the Firebird shadowing her steps.

The strashe had searched it, of course. Combed through the still-glowing embers and crumbled stone for remains. Thirteen bodies, all victims of the Firebird's wrath—all members of Fyodor's religious sect, set on destroying her.

But no hint of either of the people Asya so desperately needed. The scholars and cabinet and courtiers had any number of theories, whispered too loudly as Asya passed. Rumors of flames that blazed so hot they consumed even bone. Of the Firebird's anger that had turned on her own sister.

Asya had not indulged them, of course. Had refused to give them any more fuel to destroy her sister's memory. No matter how much they asked or demanded explanation.

She'd hoped it might be easier to see the Elmer in the light. Give her more chance to banish the sharp memories and suffocating nightmares. She was wrong.

There was no hiding here. No ignoring the ring of scorched stone where the cage had stood atop the half-crumbled altar. No tearing her eyes from the charred remains buried beneath piles of rubble and broken saints.

No way for her to stop her feet from walking toward that spot, in the shadow of the altar.

She knelt down, pressing a hand to the unmarked ground. It felt warm, still, despite the cold bite to the air. As if the stone held the memory of that moment just as close as Asya did. The stark change from before to after. Her sister slipping through her fingers.

Izaveta's strangled confession, shouted into the storm. The admission that her spell had killed their mother—that she'd been the one Asya had searched for all through the mourning days. Then Izaveta had paid with her life.

Asya bit the inside of her cheek, her eyes smarting. She couldn't cry here, not now.

So she began to search.

Methodically at first, pushing aside debris and carving a neat line through the ruins. Her movements slowly became more desperate. A frantic beat, increasing as she went. She tore her nails bloody, soot streaking her hands as she searched until finally there was nowhere left to look.

No sign of a body, no ash where Izaveta had been consumed. No remains the strashe might have missed.

Asya sank to her knees in the middle of the cavernous space, the falcon's black wings still visible through the collapsed dome. Its shadow flitted across the cracked ground. The only living thing here.

She didn't know whether to feel triumphant or despairing.

Nothing meant there was still a possibility.

She blinked back tears. This should feel like a triumph. It meant there was weight to her theory—it meant Iza might not be really gone. If she'd found a body here, there would be no denying it.

But *nothing* was also a blow. No hints she could follow or new information that might have given her answers. Just a blank, endless nothing. She was in the same place she had started.

Asya put a hand in her pocket, touching the rough edge of parchment that was the other reason she was here. Her eyes roved the hollow shadows. Where should she leave it?

The altar. Hidden from prying eyes, but she'd know to look there.

Yuliana had never returned to the palace. Asya had hoped, at first, that Yuliana didn't think it was safe. Or didn't know how to come back after all that had happened, not realizing Asya had long since forgiven her.

So Asya had left notes everywhere she could think of. Tucked between the queenstrees, among the bustle of the night markets in Kirava, near the strashe outpost in the thick forest of Vas Xekiva. Any place they'd been or talked about. Just a few words, enough for Yuliana to understand. To find a way back to her.

If she wanted to, that is.

Even with the resounding silence in return, Asya still left

the notes. Like all those unanswered letters she'd sent to Iza-veta in their years apart. Missives sent out to empty skies. A dying hope Asya couldn't quite let go of.

Perhaps that was Asya's destiny. To always be the one searching, reaching for something that wasn't there anymore.

To always be the one left behind.

Her fingers tightened on the parchment, sending deep fractures across her words.

Something fluttered in the corner of her eye. She whipped around. A presence, slow and trickling, that told her she was no longer alone.

"Yuliana?" she said softly, so quiet she could ignore the sharp pang of hope it ignited in her chest.

Nothing moved around her. Even the falcon had paused in its circling, its shadow vanishing. But Asya was sure she'd seen something.

She trod carefully through the debris, ears straining as she ducked through an arch—the same arch that she and Yuliana had tried to escape through.

A figure flickered up ahead and Asya's pace quickened.

"Yuliana!" That one came out closer to a shout, jagged in her throat. The name echoed back at her, amplified a thousand times by the low ceiling. A chorus of desperate hope.

She blinked. It was just trailing shadows and swirls of ash.

Her chest squeezed, tears pressing against the backs of her eyes again. It was foolish to believe anything could be that easy.

But she could still feel...something.

The person wasn't *here*, Asya realized. She'd just been so focused on what was in front of her that she hadn't recognized the soft pull of flames for what it was.

A Calling.

CHAPTER TWO

The Calling twined around Asya now that she'd named it. A harmony of flames forged into something more solid. She wished she could lose herself in its song, as she had done before.

But now it just made her think of Izaveta.

The notes ringing in Asya's ears, the strong pull toward magic unpaid, tightened around her like a noose. It brought the Elmer back to life. Darkening the skies, that unnatural storm filling her vision. Fire reaching for her sister.

Asya shook her head, squeezing her eyes shut. She forced herself away from that tangled melody and the memories it brought.

She didn't want to do this.

But *want* had very little to do with it.

She turned on her heel, hurrying out of the claustrophobic tomb of the Elmer. Gulping in clear, forest air, the Firebird fluttered its wings in her chest.

It was nearby, this Calling.

She hadn't had another one—not since that night. For one to blossom now, here of all places, sent a prickle of unease up Asya's spine. Too many tricks of fate to be a coincidence.

The notes spooled together to form a rope drawing her forward. Back to the frost-crusted branches, past where her bear, Mishka, was sleeping and into the dark tangle of the trees.

The Calling crescendoed as Asya stepped into a clearing.

The person was hiding behind a thick trunk, in a dip just out of the natural line of sight. The thin layer of snow around had been kept carefully free of tracks, undisturbed as the rest of the clearing.

A good hiding place. It would have kept them safe from anyone else.

She took another step forward. "I know you're here," she said, her voice softer than the rustle of empty branches above them. "Show yourself."

The words were oddly foreign on her tongue. An echo of Tarya that had somehow taken root inside her.

Asya hadn't expected that to work, but with a low scuffle of snow, a figure appeared from behind the nearest trunk, hands raised in surrender.

He was younger than her, with a crop of unruly, straw-colored hair. He wasn't dressed for the cold, in only a thin shirt and bare feet. A bruise was blooming on his cheek, matching the pale blue tinge of his lips.

Her breath pinched in her chest, sharpening to guilt.

"Firebird—please," he stammered. "It wasn't my spell."

Asya kept her hands carefully at her side, the Firebird in check. She could see the stratsviye on his wrist, feel the magic that unraveled toward him. But still she asked, "What do you mean?"

"I work on General Azarov's estate," he said, words tumbling over each other like scurrying mice. "He needed information on someone. Someone important. So he did a spell to hear a thing unsaid."

She nodded to the stratsviye, the sign of magic with its price unpaid. "Then, how are you marked?"

The boy took a tentative step toward her, a sliver of hope lightening his features. Perhaps it was cruel to draw this out. To dangle hope in front of him when she knew, in the end, it was for nothing.

"He has us complete the final steps of the spell for him," the boy finished.

"Us?" Asya repeated.

"He uses all the people in his household for spells. Making sure we're the ones to pay the price in his place."

Asya blinked, trying to take in what the boy was saying. It wasn't a possibility she'd ever considered, but she supposed it could work. If the general needed a spell done, he could prepare the ritual and ingredients, but have someone else recite the words. And then the burden would fall to them, even if he were able to reap the benefits. The Firebird would be none the wiser.

"But you ran away," she said slowly. "Before he could take the price?"

"I knew when I saw the mark that you'd find me, but..." He chewed his lip, his hands still visibly shaking. "But I thought maybe you could help."

The slight tremble, the fragment of hope in his voice made something twist in Asya's chest. It was the same fragile optimism she'd clung on to after her mother's death. The idea that anything Asya did might *help*.

But if she hadn't even managed to help the one person she loved most in the world, then what hope was there for anyone else?

"There's nothing I can do."

Any faint light in the boy's eyes snuffed out like a candle. "But he's evading the price. Evading *you*."

Asya shook her head slowly. She reached for Tarya, for that impassive calm. "The Firebird isn't a judge. I don't get to decide who pays."

"But that's not fair."

Asya clenched her teeth. Of course it wasn't fair. *None* of this was fair. But that didn't change anything. Didn't change that the earth was owed its price.

That for all the power contained inside her, she was still powerless to help anyone.

The low thud of bear paws on crisp ground made her turn.

"Makzen." A jovial voice rang out. "There you are."

The boy scrambled back, eyes widening. Apprehension shivered up Asya's spine. Her senses sharpened, hand reaching instinctively for her shashka.

Two snow-bears padded out of the trees. Their riders both wore dark red, like spots of blood against the pale landscape. Their dress could have been matching uniforms, but Asya had been in court long enough now to recognize the fine work. Much too detailed and ornate for livery.

The first rider inclined his head to her in greeting. "And the Firebird." He exchanged a smile with the other rider, as if sharing some private joke. "Strange, isn't it, how magic works?"

Asya didn't reply. Her eyes darted from the bears to the boy—Makzen—who was somehow paler than before. The rider smiled, and something in that look was familiar. Perhaps someone she'd seen around court. "I'm General Azarov's son, Kyriil." He gestured to the other rider. "And this is my sister, Tsiviya." The girl didn't smile, her gaze fixed on a spot somewhere to Asya's left.

"We're just here to ensure Makzen gets back to my father's estate safely," Kyriil finished. "But please," he added, with a grandiose gesture in her direction. "Finish your work first. I wouldn't dare stand in the Firebird's way."

Asya felt the Firebird's wings flutter against her ribs, irritation mirroring her own. The way he spoke made this all feel worse. Like a performance she was being pushed into, doing someone else's dirty work.

"Do you use all of the people on your father's estate to cast spells in your name?"

Kyriil canted his head with an easy smile. "The terms of my father's employment do not seem relevant to the Firebird."

Asya moved instinctively, a slight shift of her body that put her firmly between Makzen and the two bears. "It's relevant when he is using people to evade the price."

Kyriil's careful expression didn't falter. "He's marked, is he not? Does the method of casting matter to you?"

It shouldn't, Asya knew that. It didn't to the balance of magic, nor the world. She'd said it only moments before: the Firebird wasn't a judge, she didn't get to decide anything here. And was it worse to draw this out, when there truly was nothing she could do for this boy?

Tarya would say her actions were a kindness. That to move swiftly was a mercy.

But it still mattered to Asya. She raised her chin. "Who are you to question what's important to the Firebird?"

Kyriil's smile widened, as if Asya had said something deeply amusing. "An unusual creature who would question taking the price from a stranger, but took her own sister's heart with ease."

Asya gritted her teeth, unable to stop the image flashing

in her mind. Izaveta's face, somehow trusting despite everything, before flames devoured her.

Asya took a slow breath, willing the world to fill back in around her. Trying to pull herself out of that night. That had been happening since then. A slight remembrance, a scent or word and she would plunge back into the memory. A stone sinking to the bottom of a lake, unable to surface.

From the expression on Kyriil's face, that had been his intention.

Asya suddenly needed to be away from there. From the smoldering ruins of the Elmer, from the oppressive hold of all her failures.

She turned back to Makzen. His wide eyes were flitting from her to Kyriil, a cornered animal.

But there was nothing she could do about the mark on his wrist. She'd seen what an imbalance of magic could do.

"I'm—" She swallowed the apology—it wouldn't help, and it wasn't truly hers to give.

She closed her eyes and let the Firebird rise. It was easy now, the way the creature lifted itself from her bones, stretching free. An extension of herself.

"No—" Makzen shrank back. "Please—"

He stumbled, falling hard to the frozen ground. Asya could see herself reflected in the strained whites of his eyes. The Firebird's wings spread behind her, sparks trailing down to her feet like fallen feathers.

It wasn't the sight that sent nausea rolling through Asya's stomach. It wasn't even the fear threaded through Makzen's features—that pure, primal terror she still remembered. It was her memories again, too sharp and too close to the surface after returning to that ruined church.

But she couldn't hesitate, not now. That would only prolong the inevitable.

Her fire stretched toward the boy, unrelenting, even as he tried to scramble back, his fingers desperately raking the unforgiving earth. The bright reds and golds leeched the color from the forest as they coalesced into a burning rope that twisted around the boy's neck.

He clutched at the flames as if they were something he could pry off himself, something tangible. He was screaming now, mouth wide and gasping. But Asya couldn't hear it. Blood rushed in her ears, in tune with the Firebird's lilting song.

And then, it fell away. A last shuddering note that said the price had been paid.

Painfully familiar again. The resonating quiet the Firebird left in its wake. The empty church.

Asya blinked, forcing herself to focus on the forest. On the snow-flecked trees and the boy in front of her. Sound seemed to be the last piece of the present to return. The boy's mouth was open in a scream, yet Asya still couldn't hear it.

No—there was nothing to hear. His voice was gone. An unusual price, almost ironic. As if the gods had a sense of humor. The spell had given him information, and now he had no voice to relay it.

That stirred something in the back of her mind. The idea of the price taking what had been given.

"Fascinating."

The word jolted through Asya, too loud in the sudden quiet.

"I've never seen the Firebird exact a price before." Kyriil watched with a vague interest as Makzen clutched at his throat. "Cleaner, this way. It always makes a terrible mess in the manor." His eyes darted to Asya. "All the dismembered limbs, you know. Perhaps we should let you come more often."

That cut through the cold in Asya's chest. An angry welt as red as her flames.

"The Firebird isn't at your beck and call," she snapped.

"Aren't you?" He arched an eyebrow as if genuinely considering the question. "If I cast a spell now and forewent the price, would you not be bound to come and take it?"

Asya clenched her jaw. Some of the anger and frustration of the past six days bled out, a reopened wound. How dare he stand there and make light of the prices people paid? How dare he use magic for his own gain and pass the burden on to someone else?

"I will not let you keep doing this."

He raised a brow in apparent confusion. "Am I breaking any laws?" he asked. "Either of this queendom or of magic? If so, I shall of course answer for any crimes."

The anger crested in Asya's chest, a boiling wave of fury that had nowhere to break. "I won't stand for this," she said, some of the Firebird lacing through her words. "And neither will my sister."

Asya caught herself. That crashing wave inside her collapsed, sucking the air from her lungs. Past tense. *My sister* would not *have stood for this.*

Kyriil's expression hardened. "Well, she doesn't get much of a say in anything anymore, does she? You made sure of that."

Asya opened her mouth, wishing she could find that anger again. But her insides were hollow, a gaping chasm ready to swallow her whole.

Tsiviya nudged her bear forward, perhaps fearing Asya's retaliation. "We should go."

Asya stood frozen, teetering on the edge of that abyss as they turned their bears away, already disinterested in Asya and her suffocating grief.

Kyriil gestured over his shoulder. "Come, Makzen."

That jolted Asya back. Sparks lit at her fingertips, a belated protection. "No—you can't take him."

Kyriil glanced back at her with an acquiescent smile. "Of course, he's welcome to go with you. I already have the information from the spell."

Makzen's eyes widened like a rabbit in a trap. He jerked back, banging into the snow-bear.

"I doubt I could stop you," Kyriil went on. "So please, go ahead."

Asya let her flames extinguish with a low hiss. "I don't mean— Just let him go." Her words were meant as a command, but they came out more like a plea. A desperate need to at least do this for the boy who'd thought she could help. Who'd been unlucky enough to look for mercy where there was none.

"Is that what you would like?" Kyriil asked Makzen in a tone of exaggerated politeness. "To forfeit your pay and position?"

Makzen shook his head vehemently.

"I didn't think so."

Kyriil shrugged, as if that decided the matter. Tsiviya pulled Makzen onto her bear without protest—not that he could have said anything if he wanted to.

"You can't..." Asya tried, but her own voice gave out.

She just watched as the bears vanished back into the trees, slowly merging with the snow.

Once they were far enough away, less than blots in the distance, she sank down to her knees. The frozen ground bit into the exposed skin of her palms. Her breaths felt sharp in her chest, tears burning against her cheeks.

It was only then, her empty hands pressed to the ground, that she realized she wasn't holding the note anymore. The one she'd meant to leave for Yuliana. Had she burned it along with the boy's voice? Or dropped it in the confusion of the sudden Calling?

It hardly mattered. The notes were an act of desperation. A pretense at doing something.

All this power inside her and there was nothing she could do. She hadn't been able to help her sister or Yuliana, and she couldn't help that boy. Couldn't even stop him from returning to the very people who'd done that to him.

Asya was as helpless as she'd ever been.

CHAPTER THREE

In the days following the would-be coronation, Asya had all but taken up residence in the library. A desperate search for something that might help, the slightest mention in an old text that her hope wasn't completely unfounded. It also hid her from the stares, the whispers, which had taken on a vicious hiss. The endless questions she couldn't answer.

Today she'd taken a back entrance into the palace, leaving Mishka to roam free instead of returning through the busy thoroughfare of the bearkeep. She was still too jangled from that Calling, from the memories of the Elmer, to have to face the glaring strashe and courtiers.

The library could hardly be called a refuge, as it held so much frustration, but her muscles still loosened a little when she crossed the threshold.

A pile of books awaited her, holding that same promise and defeat of the Elmer.

But her tomes and notes didn't sit abandoned on a table as they had when she left. Nor was Izaveta's cat, Lyoza, the culprit of this disturbance—in an unusual show of restraint. Instead, the Amarinth scholar leaned over them, brow furrowed in concentration.

It was not a surprising sight. Along with Lyoza, Nikov had

been her uncertain companion in the library these past days. He offered her smiles and idle chatter, as if everything were normal. None of the probing questions or accusing glares Asya had been expecting from him.

A kindness she wasn't sure she deserved.

She hadn't dared ask why. Izaveta's name was an unspoken thing between them, a soft whisper that hid in the recesses of the shelves. Asya thought Nikov was waiting for her to explain, giving her the time she needed. But Asya *couldn't* explain. Not without ruining his memories of Izaveta too.

But she didn't want him looking through her work—there was a reason she hadn't asked for his help. She couldn't face the note of pity when he had to let her down.

Asya hurried over to the desk. "Nikov?"

He jumped at her voice. "I forget how quietly you move." But he didn't say it like an accusation, the way other members of court might. Just an interesting observation.

Even though he'd already seen, she began closing books and pulling her notes toward her. If she could even call them that, they were embarrassingly sparse.

"Sorry," Nikov said, noticing Asya's expression. "A scholar's interest, you know. I can't help my curiosity sometimes."

Asya didn't look up. "It's fine."

She could feel him watching her—could feel the way her fingers shook and the color in her cheeks. All signs Izaveta would say gave too much away.

"Are you all right?"

Asya almost dropped the book she was holding. She wasn't sure she could remember when someone had last asked her that. In the spiraling grief and unending pressures from the court and the cabinet and her great-aunt, no one had once thought to ask her feelings.

Something tightened in her chest, her ribs squeezing. "It's nothing." She wasn't evasive for the reasons most would be in the palace, out of mistrust or the hope to earn a returned favor. She just didn't think she could voice how she felt without falling apart again.

Before Nikov could push it, the concern evident on his features, Asya asked, "Why are you here?"

As soon as she said it, she realized how rudely that question might come across. She hurried to correct herself. "I mean— not that I mind. I just wonder why you stayed at court."

What was it that kept him trapped here? Asya knew what bound her here. A duty to Izaveta and Tóurin, a hope that Asya might be able to rectify all their mistakes. But couldn't imagine why someone would choose to stay otherwise. There was a slight undertone to her question too, the thing she and Nikov had been avoiding all this time.

She still remembered his face when she'd returned from the Elmer. He hadn't said anything—none of the accusations or questions of everyone else. But his expression remained branded into her memory. The loss that said Izaveta meant far more to him than just as the future queen.

"I came here as an envoy from the Amarinth to pay our respects to the new queen," he replied. "And a queen has still not been crowned."

Asya bit her lip. Of course, the expected answer. She didn't know why she'd thought she might get more than that.

"I went to the Elmer." The words jumped out almost of their own volition. As if they'd been building in her chest, desperate to escape.

Nikov's eyes widened. "You went back there?"

Asya sank into the chair, the weight of it all pressing down on her again. But there was a relief in saying it out loud. "I wanted to see what was left."

"Asya—" He put a gentle hand on her shoulder, sitting down next to her. "That must have been hard."

She nodded, tears constricting her throat. "I had to see."

"You don't have to blame yourself, you know—"

"It's not just that," she interrupted. "I had to see if there was still a chance."

Nikov's brow furrowed and Asya was suddenly unsure. Hope was such a fragile thing. She didn't want to hold it out only for it to shatter—not when she would shatter with it.

"A chance at what?" he said slowly when Asya didn't go on.

She swallowed hard. She cast her eyes around the library, the towering shelves and ornate woodwork swirling a little through the burn of tears. She'd combed her way through the books in here in the past six days, desperation fueling her through all hours.

But she was no scholar and there was plenty she didn't understand. Texts in languages she didn't even recognize.

If she truly believed in this possibility, then maybe she had to risk this hope. Had to voice it aloud. "I have a theory." Her voice came out so quiet she was surprised Nikov could hear even in the hush of the library.

His mouth quirked into an encouraging smile. "You know I always like a good theory."

"There was no body."

He looked at her in confusion, and she realized that for any of this to make sense she needed to make her thoughts more coherent—always a challenge for her. "In the Elmer," she added quickly. "The order acolytes—" bile seethed in her stomach at the memory of them, turned from living beings to something unrecognizable "—they left behind remains. Even though the Firebird…even though *I* burned so hot, there were still remains. But there was no sign of Izaveta. Of her body."

Asya clamped her mouth shut, tears threatening to choke her again. It had been easier not talking about it, not having to voice the jagged grief that now lived inside her.

But Nikov wasn't looking at her like she was taking leave of her senses, or with the soft pity she'd feared. The gentle reminder that grief could make you believe many things.

"You think there's a chance she didn't burn?" Nikov asked, his intonation light and scholarly.

It made it a little easier for Asya to reply, for the coiled anguish in her chest to loosen. "When Tarya— When the Firebird has taken prices before, it never leaves anything behind. As if they don't burn, but maybe just…" She trailed off, she didn't have a very concrete way of describing her theory. "As if they go somewhere else. Same when you throw a price into the flames. It doesn't burn, it *vanishes*."

Nikov leaned back on two legs of his chair, one hand absently running through his hair as he considered.

"I know it might be impossible," she said quickly, preempting his disbelief, as if that could lessen the pain of it. "And perhaps it would be no different to her being dead. But I have to try. I can't just give up on her."

"No," Nikov said slowly, understanding seeping through his voice. There was something in his expression that Asya couldn't quite catch, some sadness she was not privy to. "I suppose you can't."

He let the chair fall abruptly back to the ground with a solid thump. "We have work to do, then." His brown eyes were gleaming, the idea of research immediately igniting that spark. He paused, glancing back at her. "If you want my help, of course."

Asya stared up at him. She'd been so prepared for his immediate denials. For him to remind her that there was no actual evidence, that her theory was built on desperate hope and grief.

"I—" Asya cleared her throat. "Yes, I would."

He turned to examine the library, as if he already had every location cataloged. Perhaps he did—he'd spent most of his time at court in here. "We should start with the recorded histories. You already have Perenius's *Kingdoms* here, but we should widen the net. And then there's *The Formation and Defamation of the Early Empires...*" He trailed off, a little sheepish as he glanced back at Asya. "Not to say your work so far hasn't been extensive, I'm sure."

She shook her head, something close to a laugh bubbling in her chest for the first time in days. "It's definitely not been extensive."

"The untrained eye can see many a thing a seasoned scholar cannot."

Asya wasn't sure that was true, but she appreciated his kindness. Appreciated that he didn't care how his helping the Firebird might look.

"Thank you," she said, trying to impart as much of the true weight into those two words as she could.

"Never tempt a scholar with a daunting task," he said, waving off the importance.

She met his eyes. All the things she'd avoided saying this past week, the words too guilt-laden to look at, rose in her mind again. Questions and justifications she'd wondered at. But all that came out was, "Why?"

Even without the whole question, she saw Nikov understood.

Some of the excited academic glimmer faded from his eyes, an uncharacteristic seriousness shrouding him.

"Because I know what it's like to have something you don't want forced upon you," he said. There was a quiet urgency to his words, as if he suddenly needed Asya to understand. "And to want more than anything to fix it. You and Izaveta deserve at least a chance to make things right."

Asya watched him, not daring to let her hope creep through. The fragile wish that she did deserve another chance. That one could still be possible. "You really believe that?"

He huffed out a breath through his nose, spreading his arms wide to the tower around them. "Well, if we're going to do this, we have to believe in it, don't we? A scholar does not do research without belief." He paused, amending, "That's actually not entirely true. We do a lot of useless research. But in *this* case, I think you have a good place to start."

"Even without knowing the truth of that night?" she asked.

He ducked his head, torchlight gleaming gold against his brown skin. "I do know. Most of it, anyway."

Asya's eyes widened. "She told you?"

He nodded. "The night before the coronation."

"Oh."

Asya clasped her hands together, curling her fingers around each other. She couldn't ignore the slight sting that brought, even now. That Izaveta had told Nikov, someone she barely knew, before she'd told her own sister. But Asya swallowed it down. Any lingering hurt didn't help now.

"It's my fault too," he said suddenly. "What happened, I mean. I should have told her to be honest with you at once. We could have tried to find some other solution before…" He trailed off, but Asya knew what he meant. Before it was too late. Before magic had reached its destructive peak. Before the only path left was to take the price from her own sister.

"That's not your fault," Asya said, her voice a little strained.

"Probably more than it is yours."

Asya was so taken aback by that, she couldn't speak. Tarya had said the same, of course. Reminded Asya over the past days that she had only done her duty, as if that was some comfort. That she couldn't be held at fault for what the earth required in exchange.

But it was different to hear it from Nikov. Not spoken with the detached certainty Tarya always held, but with a raw thread of emotion.

Nikov's throat bobbed, shoulders squaring as if steeling himself. "I told her not to go after you," he said softly, in a tone of confession that Asya recognized. "When she realized someone had taken you. I told her she should be crowned first. That she shouldn't go alone. Even if it meant risking you.

"I—" he finally looked up at her "—I'm sorry."

Asya couldn't find the words to reply. She was fairly certain *she* was the one who should be apologizing; Nikov had been right to warn Izaveta. Her sister should have stayed away. It might have been better for the order to succeed. For all Asya knew, their theory had more weight than hers, and the Firebird's death might have undone the Fading. Might have allowed magic to flow through this land freely again.

Nikov watched her, as if expecting admonition.

But guilt was a weight Asya understood well. She could feel it now—the way that guilt bound the two of them together. Perhaps that was why Nikov was the only person who seemed able to bear being in a room with her.

Maybe there was nothing they could have done differently—or maybe everything. Asya would never know. But they could at least try to do something now.

CHAPTER FOUR

Asya's hopes that she could hide with Nikov in the library until they found an answer were immediately dashed the following morning. She awoke to a full complement of strashe at the door, bearing a written request for her to appear in front of the cabinet.

Tarya had seen the letter arrive, disapproval etched into her features. "The Firebird will dance at the cabinet's request, will she?"

"I want to help, if I can," Asya said. A pointless thing to say, as that would never be reason enough for Tarya.

Her great-aunt simply bowed her head and retreated. Her disappointment always worse than her anger.

It had been like that since the Elmer. Tarya no more than another ghost around the palace. Not involving herself with anything and spending most of the time in the frozen confines of the Sunken Gardens. When asked about what had happened with Izaveta or to consult on matters of court, Tarya merely returned to her impression of impassive stone.

Though that didn't stop her from cautioning Asya every day that she should leave. That the Firebird had no place here and she was risking her duty.

But Asya couldn't leave. If she did, she was turning her back on Izaveta. On any chance her sister might still have. Not to mention she'd be leaving Izaveta's legacy to burn—all at the cost of the people of Tóurin.

So whether Tarya believed it was the Firebird's duty or not, Asya wasn't leaving.

But now, on the ornate threshold of the cabinet room, the idea of running off into the woods without a glance back was more and more tempting. She just wanted to be done with all of this.

The cabinet sat around the grand table, two seats noticeably empty. One on the left where Conze Vittaria, who had died during the mourning days, would have sat. And the other at the head, the queen's seat.

Bishop Deryev spotted her first. He'd been standing in for the disgraced Vibishop Sanislav in the Church's seat and had made his dislike of Asya clear from the beginning. She had played a role in his forebearer's downfall, of course, but she couldn't say she regretted it.

"Thank you, Firebird," Deryev said acidly. "For gracing us with your presence."

Asya didn't bother to point out that she'd come as soon as she was called—as good as a trained dog for risk of upsetting this careful balance.

Stood before so many seated figures, Asya felt the focal point narrowing in on her. She clasped her hands together, tugging at a loose thread on her sleeve.

"We have an important matter to discuss," Bishop Deryev went on.

Yes, the cabinet was very good at finding *important matters* that demanded Asya answer invasive questions or help pander to their power—with the unspoken threat that her stay at the palace would be over the moment she didn't comply.

She was beginning to understand Izaveta, more than she ever had. Asya had not even been here a month and there was already the temptation to burn it all in her wake.

Vada Nisova, a woman with a pinched face and perfect posture, leaned forward. "We wanted to give you a last opportunity to tell us the truth of what happened."

Asya stilled. "I've already told you all I can."

Nisova pressed her thin lips together and pulled a piece of parchment toward her, reading from it. "All you've told us is this supposed Order of the Captured Flame kidnapped you in an attempt to end the Fading. That for some reason your sister abandoned her coronation and followed you on a ridiculous lone rescue mission, then helped you escape, only for you to feel one of your apparent *Callings* and have to take a price from her."

Every one of Asya's muscles was taut. She didn't want to hear it recited back at her in this airless room. Especially not with the qualifying words of disbelief. "Yes."

"Yet no explanation," Bishop Deryev added. "Or evidence, as to the spell Lady Izaveta cast or what price she owed. And no witnesses to confirm any of this. So the only account we have to go off is yours."

He didn't expand, watching Asya as if waiting for her to break down and confess some treachery.

Commander Iveshkin, the brusque leader of Tóurin's military forces, took the opportunity to interrupt. "We are wasting our time on these details," she signed. Her interpreter, Mila—Asya had seen her in the training grounds, clearly as formidable with a znaya as the commander—relayed the words aloud to the ringing ceiling above them. "The question of the Firebird's role in Lady Izaveta's demise—" Asya flinched at the sharp slash of Iveshkin's hand that formed that word "—is irrelevant in the grand scheme of things. We have been almost a month without a queen. That is more than enough time for our enemies to make moves against us."

She took a steady breath, looking around at each of the members before finishing, "Therefore, with no apparent heir or wishes from the former queen—or any way to determine the nature of Lady Izaveta's death—we must set a trial of succession."

Asya frowned, suddenly adrift in this conversation again. She'd never heard that phrase before, but Iveshkin signed it as if it held some great weight.

"I agree," Deryev said sagely.

Everyone stared at him. Asya was still finding her footing in the intricacies of court, but even she knew it was unusual for him to agree with Iveshkin.

He used the momentary surprise, his posture straightening as if giving a sermon to an awaiting chapel. "The gods are displeased. We have upset the balance so long set out, put power in the hands of queens who have abandoned us."

Asya's fist clenched. *Abandoned* wasn't fair to either her mother or Izaveta.

"A trial of succession is the only answer," he finished. "Each cabinet member may put forth their candidate and the gods will decide."

Nisova narrowed her eyes. "Are we ruled by them now, as well as the Church?"

"Do we not trust the gods to show us who is the queen and who is the Firebird?" Deryev asked. "This ritual is the same conference with the gods. Perhaps you merely fear your preferred candidate will not be found worthy?"

Nausea roiled in Asya's stomach again as she began to understand. The easy way they all talked about this, about replacing Izaveta, who might not yet be truly gone. She took a half step back, judging the distance between herself and the door.

"The decision must still be ratified by the cabinet," Iveshkin signed, her eyes cutting to the bishop.

"Of course." He smiled, stretching his hollow cheeks. "We shall start preparations at once. The night of three full moons would be best to commune—"

Iveshkin frowned. "We cannot wait another three months for a queen."

"The First Snows, then," Conze Bazin suggested. He was a member of the cabinet Asya rarely noticed, always hanging back in the bishop's shadow. "That is a day for renewal and the snows shall come soon en—"

Asya spun around, the Firebird aware of something a breath before the high arched doors swung open.

The light beyond the windows was muted, thick gray cloud darkening the day to twilight, so Asya could not at once make out the newcomers. Only the fluttering orange of a burning torch caught the features of their leader.

An unfamiliar man with a neat beard, graying slightly at the edges, and a stern expression that reminded her of Iveshkin. Gold gleamed across his clothes, adorning each of his limbs, more than could possibly be comfortable—or necessary. He was flanked by two people Asya did recognize. The brother and sister from the forest. The ones who'd found a way around the price.

"General Azarov," Bishop Deryev said, eager to be the first to greet him. "Welcome."

Asya wracked her brain for some memory of how he fit into all of this. His family used to hold a seat on the cabinet, though they'd been disgraced for some reason, so they held no position in court. It definitely made no sense for him to be here now.

Boots echoed against the marble floors as guards fanned out behind them. It seemed excessive that a single family would need that much protection. They looked far too much like an army for Asya's liking.

Commander Iveshkin seemed to agree, judging by the way her eyes had narrowed with each word Mila relayed to her.

"I am pleased to finally return to the palace," the general said with an overly grandiose wave.

Iveshkin raised her chin, taking the general's measure with her careful gaze. "You sent word ahead that your arrival was urgent. We have even allowed you into the cabinet room for this *private* matter," she signed. "Yet you seem in no great hurry."

Azarov inclined his head to her. "As I said in my letter, I bring with me someone of great importance." Everything about him unsettled Asya. The way he strode in here ready to perform, as if they were all just players who existed to reflect off him. "Someone who may shed more light on the tragic absence of our late princess."

Something in his voice made the hairs on the back of Asya's neck prickle. A dread she couldn't quite name, as slow-moving as a glacier, crawled through her veins.

He gestured to his entourage, all no more than dark smudges in the vast shadows of the room. "We caught her trying to steal from our supplies on our journey here—" two of the guards moved forward, dragging a figure between them "—and noticed she bore the mark of the treacherous Order of the Captured Flame."

Asya's mouth was dry, a strange buzzing in her ears. Her heart couldn't quite settle on a rhythm.

They pushed the figure to her knees in front of the cabinet's grand table, close enough for the candlelight to glint off the chains at her wrists. Off her tangle of dark hair, so far from her usual neatness that it might have been impossible to recognize her.

But Asya would know her anywhere.

Asya stepped forward, drawn almost without volition—as if the Firebird's Calling had urged her on. A name echoed in her chest, so sudden Asya didn't even realize she'd uttered it aloud.

"Yuliana."

CHAPTER FIVE

Being pieced back together was much harder than being torn apart.

Perhaps it was poetic. After all, destruction had always come easily to Izaveta. Looking right down to a person's core and pulling at weak threads until they unraveled.

She had thought that would be it. An abrupt undoing and then…nothing.

But gathering all those tattered threads and trying to weave them back into a tapestry—that was almost impossible. Each dropped stitch tugging at her essence, breaking her apart all over again.

The first few days—Izaveta thought they were days—passed in a muted blur. Remembered flames clawing at her, ash-charred threads of being crumbling at her touch.

She held on to one point of clarity through it all. Asya. Izaveta's counterweight, the string that kept her from toppling into that gaping chasm.

But remnants were still missing, as if some pieces had been lost in the making and unmaking. A veil that had been drawn between the self she remembered and the self she was now.

When Izaveta felt enough threads of herself had coalesced, more a fragmented whole than scattered remnants, she was able to take in her surroundings in more than blurred smudges. Not that it helped much, as all she could see was a circular stone room. It rose high above her head, windowless and shadowed.

It was freezing here. Izaveta's slowly strengthening breaths hung in the air in small clouds. Sometimes frost fissured across the floor, creeping cobwebs that numbed her hands. She might have been able to use that to work out more of her surroundings—or at least the time of day—if her mind weren't still so tangled.

That's what she would have done, before. She'd have cataloged every tiny detail of the room, trying to catch any hint as to where she was. But there wasn't anything to see, or at least her tired mind could not grab on to anything. It was like trying to keep water cupped in her hands.

It kept her surroundings a little hazy, distorted memories merging with the endless, silent isolation.

The rough stone of the walls was unfamiliar, a kind of veined and unhewn mineral Izaveta didn't recognize. No light filtered from above, or even snuck in through cracks in the stone, no outline of a door. A perfectly sealed tomb.

As soon as Izaveta had that thought, the day when she was able to stand and run her fingers along the impenetrable wall, she wished desperately that she hadn't.

Because this *did* feel like a tomb, suffocating and claustrophobic, a place where she had been left to rot.

CHAPTER SIX

Asya's heart stuttered in her chest, Yuliana's name skittering in time to the beats. General Azarov was talking, but she couldn't hear him. All she saw was Yuliana, on her knees and bruised but wonderfully alive.

Heavy chains at her wrists trailed back to two of Azarov's guards. Her eyes traced over Yuliana's form, taking stock of her injuries. Dried bloodstains where the metal had rubbed the skin raw. A healing bruise on her chin. Her left hand was wrapped in a thick bandage, traces of blood darkening around her missing finger.

Asya wanted to run forward and—

The thought petered out in her head. She didn't know what she could do. Force all the guards back and pull Yuliana free? It might be worth it. Just to feel that Yuliana was real. To touch her cheek and see the storm in her eyes that said Yuliana was alive.

But Asya stood frozen, just out of the pool of light cast by Azarov's guards. Yuliana's eyes were downcast—had she seen Asya? Or heard her say her name—the muttered utterance that undid everything inside her?

Those burrowed down to a deeper question: Did Yuliana *want* to see her?

She'd clearly not been brought here willingly. Asya knew Yuliana had seen all her fears confirmed in the Elmer, the burning vengeance of the Firebird. Asya didn't even know who she'd killed. She had no way to tell if Yuliana's brother had been among the dead.

Some things were too terrible to forgive.

"This traitor may be able to tell us the truth of that night."

Azarov's voice finally burst through the buzzing in Asya's mind. With it, the sounds of the room crashed in around her, hushed murmurings that were suddenly far too loud.

"She's not a traitor." Asya stepped forward, all other thoughts forgotten. "Let her go."

Everyone's eyes flicked to her, though she only saw one pair. Storm-gray ones that snapped to Asya like lightning.

"Let her go?" the general repeated with a vague air of distaste.

Bishop Deryev took a languid step forward, eyes alight. "Afraid she won't corroborate your story of what happened in the Elmer?"

"No, of course—" Asya dragged her gaze from Yuliana, forcing herself to address the cabinet. "Yu— Strashe Vilanovich wasn't involved with what happened that night." She winced internally at that not-quite truth, but pushed on, "Fyodor was the traitor. We don't need anyone else to suffer. She didn't see anything that could help you." She tried for that imperious air Izaveta had held so easily, as if she could persuade them all the Firebird wouldn't be questioned. "So let her go."

"This order was working against the good of the queendom," Iveshkin signed. "If there are any more members left, they must be snuffed out."

"Yes," Asya replied, a ragged edge to her voice that she

was sure did little to convince any of them. "But she's not a part of it."

"She bears their brand," Azarov supplied.

"That doesn't mean— She does, but—" Asya tried, unable to find the words to properly explain. She wasn't ready for this. For *any* of this. In all her imaginings, she hadn't thought when she next saw Yuliana it would be like this. An unwilling reunion, forced upon them both. Too many emotions swirled through her mind. Sharp colors and scheming voices, a maze Asya was suddenly trapped in the center of.

Izaveta would have been able to fix this. She'd have Yuliana freed in two sentences, and have all the cabinet convinced it was their idea.

But Asya couldn't do that. Couldn't make people listen to her, even with the fire that burned beneath her skin.

"She was trying to help," Asya finished, looking down at the floor so she didn't have to see the amusement dancing across their faces. The all-powerful Firebird unable to form a coherent sentence.

"Yet you did not mention that in your account."

The breath huffed from Asya's lungs. No, she hadn't. An attempt at keeping Yuliana out of this mess that clearly hadn't worked.

"She deserted from her post." Pity crouched in Iveshkin's features—somehow worse than the derision, as it spoke of something far deeper—but her gestures were still firm. "The strashe must have a formal hearing for that."

"And a full investigation into any other treachery," Bishop Deryev added with barely concealed relish.

"I—" Asya's hands twitched, words failing her again. Looking around, she realized she had fallen right into a trap. She was showing too much, exposing a weakness that shouldn't have been there.

She remembered Kyriil's words from the woods. *Strange, isn't it, how magic works?* And that boy, Makzen, had said General Azarov cast a spell to get information—information on someone important.

Could it have led them to Yuliana?

Asya blinked. Her thoughts were racing too fast. She pushed past the lump of fear in her throat, gesturing to the guards. "Can't you at least unchain her? She's not a threat to anyone."

"She maimed one of our guards," Kyriil said with a disinterested calm. "So the chains are certainly necessary."

Strashevsta Orlov nodded to Azarov's guards and they handed the chains on to two waiting strashe. "Lock her up."

As the strashe started to pull her away, Yuliana caught Asya's gaze again. Asya saw that lost look then. The same one from the Elmer—helpless as Fyodor raised his blade.

Embers sparked at Asya's fingers, unbidden. She went to step forward—to *make* them listen. She couldn't be helpless in this too.

A hand grasped her arm. Tarya. Asya hadn't even noticed her enter, though she stood now at the spymaster's side. Still watching over her foolish niece.

Tarya shook her head. "Don't let them see this part of you."

Asya clenched her jaw. What if she didn't care what they saw? Perhaps she was done with pandering to these people and this palace that had destroyed so many things she loved.

Tarya released her arm, slipping back to impassivity. "It would not be safe for the Firebird. For *either* of you."

That quashed Asya's flames.

Tarya was right on that. Asya might be immortal, but Yuliana was not. And even if the Firebird were able to burn through an entire company of strashe, turning the palace to a crumbled ruin, they would still be hunted for the rest of their lives. She would lose any chance of finding her sister and doom herself to an immortal life as an outcast. Always running, always the monster that stalked the dark.

Yuliana might not even want that.

Asya didn't say any of that to Tarya—didn't bow to her aunt's warnings. But she still forced herself to turn away. The small movement wrenched something in her chest, another piece of herself torn loose. She didn't let herself glance back to see Yuliana's expression—to see if she was even looking.

This wasn't Asya giving up. She simply refused to be the monster again. She'd find another way.

Yet as she walked out, she couldn't help but think of how this palace had a way of taking things and never giving them back.

Of how Yuliana could be the next thing it took.

CHAPTER SEVEN

It took Izaveta a long time to realize that the last gnawing emptiness inside her was hunger. With time passing in juddering whirls, she didn't know how long she'd been there. She only knew her head had started to spin whenever she stood up and walked the small perimeter of this room. That weakness was beginning to work its way into her newly reformed muscles, an exhaustion that had nothing to do with the frigid temperature.

She'd found water, on a closer inspection of the space. A small trickle that ran down from a crack in the wall, too high for Izaveta to see its true source. Not much, but enough to keep her alive. If this In-Between state could be called that.

A coincidence, or careful design? Keeping her conscious but weakened, allowing only the smallest glimpse of hope. That was how her mother would have looked at it. A good strategy to impair one's opponent, to make them vulnerable.

But this was more than one of her mother's games.

When Izaveta awoke from a trembling sleep, her head ringing and fingers numb, to find the short walk to the water too much to make, she knew she had to do something.

She wasn't quite sure what drove her, with no real hope

for salvation, but there was one small, stubborn seed inside her that was not ready to surrender.

Supporting herself against the rough stone of the wall, she dragged herself to her feet. She inspected every inch of this cell she could reach, crawled on the floor to examine each crack and dig her nails into any possible weaknesses. It got her nothing.

When she gave up, she slumped in the corner, the cold of the floor barely registering against the icy sheen of her skin.

What would her mother say now?

It was hard to conjure her image, so out of place in this tomb. Queen Adilena would never have found herself here, except perhaps to look down at Izaveta in disappointment. That expression shone bright in her mind, the arched lip and artful look of disdain. Izaveta had thought she'd outsmarted her mother with that spell, played her final card and won at last.

But Izaveta couldn't even find peace in death.

She knew vaguely that she had to keep trying, that she couldn't just curl up here and give up. But all her thoughts and feelings were slippery, falling through her fingers to scatter on the floor.

"You need to do something." The words were more thought than voice, her tongue so disused it came out as little more than a wheeze. Not something solid to grasp on to, but another thing to dissipate into the ether.

Her mind turned then to Nikov, of all people. The smiles he gave away so freely and the easy way he could turn a problem into a simple academic discussion. He'd have some poorly timed remark to make about this situation, a comment to lighten the crushing weight of isolation.

She wasn't sure how he'd managed to sneak into her mind

and find purchase where so many others had failed, but he seemed to materialize before her. Leaning against the wall, he examined the space with a grimace. "Not much for interior design, are they?"

Izaveta blinked, her swirling head somehow taking this in its stride. "Who?"

He shrugged. "The gods, your enemies, the fates... I know as much as you."

"What use are you, then?" she ground out, the usual bite missing from her words, stolen by exhaustion. "Why are you even here?"

Nikov grinned, a useless expression that he tossed out with such ease. "I'm not." His brow furrowed, considering. "But perhaps you're thinking of me because I'm the only one you can face."

Izaveta couldn't argue with that, even inside her own head. Nikov had known the truth about the stratsviye. She'd managed to tell him before anyone else. Not necessarily for sentimental reasons, but because it *was* easier to face someone who didn't know her inside and out.

She couldn't bring Asya's memory here to this dark prison of her own making. Izaveta almost recoiled at the image, interposed with that memory of betrayal, of the sadness cracking across her sister's face when she realized what Izaveta had done.

Should she feel guilt about that—about how she still didn't want to face the truth of what she'd done?

She wasn't sure, but there was a space where she imagined that feeling might be, a small corner of self left to rot, just beyond her reach.

"Why do I feel like something's missing?" She almost hadn't realized it until she said it, but then she knew it was true.

Nikov raised his eyebrows. "Perhaps because you died."

Had she? Death should be an end, not a dragged-out existence. Yes, the Church had spouted their theories about evildoers cast out into the eternal skies, but Izaveta had never believed that. It was supposed to *end*. All the uncertainty, all the fighting against what she wanted to do and what she should do. Her final heroic act, something to blot out the rest of her sins.

But if the Firebird had not taken her life, then what was the price?

She could feel herself growing weaker, the threads of her mind unspooling as cold and hunger gnawed away at her. "If I'm hungry, does that mean I'm alive?"

Nikov, her imagined version of him, who knew no more than she did, shrugged. "We're on to philosophical questions already, are we?"

The real Nikov would have probably expounded on that, run off along a tangent about the merits of different concepts of existence. But this Nikov was born from her fractured mind, so he just watched her, waiting for answers neither of them had.

She slumped back against the wall. She was too tired for this, too much a sum of broken parts to begin to untangle anything.

Nikov looked down at her. "Giving up already? Is that not unbecoming of a queen?"

"I am not queen yet," she snapped. "And I'm not giving up."

Useless to argue with him, a mere reflection of her own thoughts back at her. But that small spark of anger forced her mind to refocus, to pull back from the teetering edge of despair.

Izaveta had never entertained ideas of the gods before, never bothered to turn to them for guidance when they were ther long gone or uncaring. So there was no use in looking to them now. No use in confusing her addled mind further.

She had to hold on to what she *knew*, the things that were solid and tangible. There was water here, and there was cold and fear and pain—all very living things.

And if this was somehow the work of mortals, each choice careful and intentional, then there had to be someone nearby. Guards or a smug captor, either to make sure she stayed inside or to watch her die slowly.

And if she was wrong, if she was just reaching into a frozen void that would never answer, then what did it matter anyway?

"I have to eat, you know." She'd meant to shout, to raise her voice up to anyone who might listen, but her words came out tattered, a ragged edge of cloth worn far too thin.

There was no answer.

"If you wanted me dead, then I would be," she yelled, her words bouncing back at her in a hollow cacophony. Even her imagined Nikov had vanished, just her own voice left. "What's the point of keeping me here only for me to starve?"

Though she refused to let it show, she didn't entirely believe that. She'd seen plenty of cruelty—caused it too—and it was well within her realm of belief that someone did want precisely that. For her to suffer as she deserved. A slow death in this icy tomb.

CHAPTER EIGHT

Asya had never been up to the dungeons. They were hardly used anymore—throughout her childhood, she didn't think there'd been a single prisoner. Only people accused of treason would be kept here. Those who were considered a direct threat to the Crown.

The entrance was a simple wooden door, so out of place in the ornate grandeur of the palace, at the base of Zmenya's Tower. Asya and Izaveta had found it on one of their many explorations, Izaveta coming up with increasingly gruesome horrors hidden in its depths. There were other entrances, she was certain. Hidden doors and secret passageways that a queen could use if she wanted to enter undetected.

But her mother had never shared those with Asya.

Two strashe stood guard, their uniforms another bitter twist in Asya's gut. She missed that silver shadow.

She shook her head, focusing on the solid figures in front of her. Tarya's warning flickered at the back of her mind. *Don't let them see this part of you.* All the strange traps of court she still didn't know how to navigate.

But this wasn't in front of the entire cabinet. This was just two strashe. A risk Asya would happily take for a moment with Yuliana.

She squared her shoulders, reaching for her best impression of Izaveta. Asya was the Firebird, that was all people saw her as. So she may as well use it.

The two strashe visibly paled at her approach. The younger one put a hand on his znaya, clearly uncertain how they should react. The older, with snow-white hair, stilled like a wolf caught on a scent.

"I'm here to question the prisoner," Asya said with as much authority as she could muster.

The younger one squared his shoulders. "We were told not to admit anyone."

Asya raised her eyebrows—wishing she had Izaveta's ability to raise just one in scorn. "By who?"

"Strashevsta Orlov."

"Does the strashevsta have more authority than the Firebird?"

The strashe exchanged a glance, caught between two impossibilities.

"I—" the older one said. "I'd have to check with—"

"I am helping the cabinet in their investigation," Asya pressed—not entirely a lie, which she hoped made it sound more convincing. "We must find the truth of the events in the Elmer as soon as possible."

From the dark expression that flitted across the strashes' faces, they both thought they knew precisely what had happened that night.

Asya tried to push past it. "You can always explain to the cabinet why you have delayed this investigation."

She held their gaze, leaning on their desire to be as far away from the Firebird as possible and not wanting to displease authority.

The younger one broke first, eyes darting to the other

strashe. A silent conversation passed between them, one that Asya hoped fell in her favor.

"Very well," the white-haired one said. They pulled a key from their belt and unlocked the door with only the slightest hesitation.

Asya forced herself not to pause, not to consider what she was doing before she stepped through the doorway. She didn't want to show any sign of uncertainty after the story she'd just given. And she didn't want to give herself the chance to back out.

One of the strashe moved to follow her and she held out a hand. "I'll go alone," she said. "Unless you think you can be privy to the Firebird and the cabinet's secrets."

The imperious tone worked, because she was alone as she stepped onto the tightly wound staircase. It was brighter than she would have thought. In all her childish imaginings, she'd pictured a dank hall dusted with cobwebs and cloaked in shadow. But it wasn't so different from the rest of the palace. Plainer, certainly, but not horrifying.

The staircase wound tighter and tighter as she ascended, and with it came a creeping apprehension slithering around her neck. There were no windows here, the only way out was the way she'd come in.

It reminded her of that suffocating cage. Trapped. Firestone and helplessness clawing at her—

She blinked hard, trying to get her stuttering pulse under control. Not bothering with subtlety, she pushed her feet to move quickly. To propel her out of this tightening noose. The steps ended so abruptly Asya almost tripped.

Her stomach swooped. It would have been a very long fall. Only a small platform stood between her and a sheer drop all the way back down to the bottom of the tower. She wasn't sure if even the Firebird could have saved her from that.

She turned her eyes up, away from the dizzying height, and let out a soft gasp.

She'd never realized the tower opened out to the sky.

Although there was a dome—the same one that she'd so often seen silhouetted against the skyline—the very top had been cut open. Allowing Zmenya's realm to look down on the tower's occupants.

Thick chains snaked down from the dome, ending in the twisting metal of cages. At least fifteen, all at slightly different heights around the tower. Held suspended off the ground so the prisoners could not seek comfort in Dveda's realm, left instead in the emptiness of Zmenya's wide skies.

Asya reached up to touch the wooden icon around her neck, more habit than anything else. As if that could stave off this sight.

The platform spiraled around the edge of the tower, reaching right to the uppermost cages. As far as Asya could see, only two were occupied. She hadn't spared Vibishop Sanislav much thought since Saints' Night and Izaveta's plan, but she now realized he must be here too. A flicker of guilt curled in her stomach. Even he didn't deserve this.

But Asya's eyes caught on another cage, a little higher and almost obscured. Black hair that shone even in the clouded light. Her back was to Asya, head tilted up like she was watching the sky.

There was a terrible irony to seeing Yuliana trapped in a cage, Asya now unable to free her.

Asya moved quietly, almost reverently, up the last set of stairs. Past Sanislav, who spared her only a cursory glance before returning to apparent prayer, past several empty cages, until there was only one left.

Suddenly faced with this, Asya found she couldn't speak. Yuliana's back was still to her. Perhaps asleep or too distracted to notice the footsteps.

Asya could still turn and leave. Could run from this truth she wasn't sure she wanted. But that would leave her even more alone than before.

"I know you're there." The words were faint, yet they resonated in the domed tower.

Yuliana made no move to turn around, to so much as glance back. Asya blinked, her eyes stinging.

"I—" Asya choked on the word, so futile against everything. She had no right to ask for forgiveness now. "I'm so sorry."

Yuliana turned, the movement sudden and jerking in the tiny space. Her expression was unreadable, gray eyes boring into Asya. "Why are you sorry?"

"Because it's my fault," she managed to say. "You wouldn't be trapped in here if it weren't for me. You wouldn't..."

Asya's gaze dropped to Yuliana's hands. To the bloodstained bandage that twisted around her left wrist, dirt-stained and graying. Guilt pressed in tighter around her, that moment in the Elmer branded into her mind.

"All of...all of *this* is my fault," she finished softly.

Yuliana was staring at her, a kind of gritted resolve tensing her features. A determination Asya didn't understand.

"There are plenty of people I could blame," Yuliana said firmly. "But you aren't one of them. I've only got myself to thank for this mess. Because I couldn't see past revenge, because I couldn't find a way to stand up to my brother. And it could have killed you. I...I could have lost you." Her voice hitched now, a slight crack in the raw certainty. "I suppose I did lose you, in a way."

There was a hollowness to those words. A pain Asya understood, and—finally—she saw it wasn't anger that pulled the line of Yuliana's shoulders tight. It wasn't fear or distrust of Asya that kept her from meeting her gaze. It was shame.

A guilt-laden silence hung between them as Asya struggled to find her voice again. "I've already forgiven you, you know that—don't you?"

Yuliana's eyes flicked up to her, hooded and darkened to a sharp flint. "Should you?"

Asya didn't quite know how to put into words if she *should* forgive or not. Just that she had. She wasn't even sure when she had made the conscious decision. It was an irrefutable truth in her core. One of the threads that pulled her toward Yuliana.

"I…" Asya started, trying to find some way to explain that, but a commotion on the stairs made her whip around.

"You lied to us." The two strashe burst onto the platform, the younger one at the front, accusation dripping in his words as he leveled his znaya at her. "The cabinet didn't give you permission to see the prisoner."

Sparks flew to Asya's fingertips, more out of frustration than anything else. "Leave us," she said, trying for unquestionable command, but her voice was still caught in that conversation. Her words fraying at the edges.

Before she could press her point, Strashevsta Orlov emerged from the twisting staircase, followed by what Asya really felt was an unreasonable number of strashe. They couldn't even stand in formation on the narrow walkway, forced into a strange uneven line that somewhat defeated the purpose of superior numbers.

But it was still too many. Too many for Asya to even try

forcing them to listen without fracturing the fragile truce that allowed her presence in the palace.

"Firebird," Orlov said with more confidence than she'd ever heard from him, now that he had an army at his back. "I believe you've taken a wrong turn. We can escort you out."

"I—" Asya was too jumbled up now, too many emotions coursing in her chest to formulate a rational response. "I won't be much longer. I just need…" She trailed off. She had no idea precisely what she needed.

"You can stay if you must," she said instead, an attempt to placate them, though she really didn't like the idea of doing any of this with an audience.

"We cannot allow that, I'm afraid." The words may have held a hint of apology, but Orlov's tone ensured otherwise.

"What am I going to do with all of you here?" Asya asked, annoyance finally searing through. "Execute a sudden and daring jailbreak?" Though the idea was more tempting than she could admit.

"Perhaps you're planning collusion," Orlov said. "Or maybe you're here to kill a witness who could disprove your story. Whatever your plans, they end here."

Asya flashed a look back at Yuliana, a desperate missive. Ever so slightly, Yuliana shook her head.

Asya didn't know what that meant. If Yuliana was digging in her heels, determined that she didn't deserve Asya's forgiveness, or something else.

Asya was lost either way. There was nothing else she could do here. Powerless again, even with flames igniting in her blood.

She took a half step toward Yuliana's cage, prompting the low *shrik* of drawn blades. But Asya didn't turn, whispering,

"I'll find a way." Only four words, but the best she could manage.

Then she faced the assembled strashe, hands raised. "All right," she said. "We can go."

Strashe pressed in on either side, but as she passed the other occupied cage, pale eyes caught hers. Sanislav was certainly watching—maybe he had been all along, but only now chose to show it. "Perhaps I'll be granted the honor of a visit from the Firebird soon enough," he called after her.

Asya didn't reply. She pressed her lips into a thin line, forcing her hands still at her side. She hated this. Hated that she still couldn't do anything to protect the people she cared about.

Tarya's warning resonated in her head. *Don't let them see this part of you.* It was far too late for that. She could feel that care etched onto her face—written into the tight coil of her muscles.

Strashevsta Orlov stayed at Asya's back, adding to the awkward procession that made its way down the spiral staircase.

Asya blinked as she stepped out into the brighter light of the grounds. It took a moment for her eyes to adjust—for her mind to pull from Yuliana and focus on the present—so she didn't quite recognize the figure waiting for her.

She took in his uniform first, then the array of crimson guards at his back. And finally, the too-friendly smile on his lips.

"I believe it's high time we were properly introduced," he said with a joviality that grated against Asya's skin. "My name is General Azarov. And I think we can help each other."

CHAPTER NINE

Izaveta had not realized she'd fallen asleep until her eyes opened and there was the slightest change to the monotony of the cell. Her head felt a little hazy, drowsy tendrils still clinging on, but she could clearly see the rye roll left in the middle of the room.

She lunged for it, unable to hold on to any dignity or caution. Caution seemed redundant anyway, given the situation.

The bread was dry and hard to swallow against her parched throat, but it was enough. As she ate, a question crept across her mind, one that left trailing cold in its wake. She hardly slept heavily on the freezing stone floor, so how had someone managed to enter and leave this food without her so much as stirring?

She finished the bread too soon, nausea rolling through her at the abrupt addition to her diet.

"Not dead then, it would seem," her imagined Nikov said, now sitting against the wall with an ease completely at odds with the dismal room. "Unless we've been entirely mistaken on what constitutes mortality, which is always possible."

"A scholarly answer," Izaveta scoffed, her voice stronger now.

"What else would you expect from me?"

"The answer to why I'm here would be a good start."

"Why are you here?"

An eerie reflection again, her thoughts echoing back to her tenfold.

But with some food in her stomach, her mind was a little clearer and she finally had something she understood: information.

Not more than a scrap, but after the vast nothingness of this cell, she clutched it close to her. Her only weapon.

Wherever she was, whoever held the keys, they didn't want her dead. Not yet. And that gave her a slight advantage—not much, but Izaveta was grateful for even the smallest glimpse of power.

The next time she fell asleep, she clearly tasted the sweet powder in the air and felt as it pulled her down into darkness. And she wasn't surprised to wake to another offering of food.

Time passed strangely in this room, in fits and starts that Izaveta couldn't quite get the measure of. If only she could grasp some kind of pattern, perhaps she could find a way to evade it and discover the truth of how someone else was entering this room. And maybe a way she could get out.

"It's almost a riddle, isn't it?" Nikov asked, now sitting as if perusing a book in the library. "The dead girl locked in a tomb of her making, not quite here and not quite there."

"A dull riddle if you have no idea of the answer."

Izaveta wasn't sure she could quite call him a hallucination anymore, though the cold still distorted her thoughts a little. He was more intentional now, a way to pretend she wasn't entirely alone in this.

She didn't want to examine it any further than that—didn't need to.

"Why're you here?" Nikov asked again, staring at her as if sure she held the answer somewhere.

Izaveta intended to find out.

She sat alert now, ears tuned to even the slightest sound, so when she heard a soft *hiss* from above her head, she reacted at once. She stilled her breathing, tipping her head forward a little to let the ragged fabric of her bodice cover her mouth. Hair spilled across her face, hopefully obscuring her ruse.

She waited, air trapped in her lungs, her ears straining. Her subconscious was screaming at her to breathe, but she couldn't give in yet. She might not get this chance again.

There it was, the low *click* of a door and a narrow shard of light that pierced through her eyelids.

Her body finally protested, her mouth opening and gasping in a breath. She tasted a lingering hint of that powder on her tongue. Cursing herself, she threw aside all pretense and pulled herself to her feet.

Part of the wall had swung back and a figure stood in the arch. If not for the sliver of torchlight, they might have looked like they were floating.

"Nikov?" she mumbled, half-worried she was imagining again, projecting something where there was nothing.

But the person moved, light glancing off their unfamiliar features. They dropped the bread unceremoniously to the ground and Izaveta caught a glimpse of a shining sword edge.

Izaveta steadied herself against the wall, sleep clawing at the edge of her vision already. "I know you're there!"

It didn't come out with the accusation she'd intended, more a soft whimper against this darkness. But the figure paused, ever so briefly. Enough to give Izaveta a slightly better view of their outline.

And as they turned away, taking that last glimmer of light

with them, she saw something else. A crest adorning the gilded hilt of the sword. A crest she remembered well.

Sleep was grasping for her now, hands trying to drag her down. But she'd seen it clearly, she was sure of that.

"I know who you are," she called, her voice weakening but still threaded with that imperious note. "Stop playing these games. Tell me what you really want."

There was still no answer, but as she slid down the wall and back into the blackness of sleep, she was certain they had heard.

CHAPTER TEN

Asya did not return the general's smile. In his glinting eyes, she saw the boy in the forest, cowering away from Kyriil and his sister. She saw Yuliana brought before the cabinet in chains.

"There's no help I'd want to give you," Asya spat.

She was sure this was flouting some etiquette of court, but she didn't really care. She might be forced to adhere to some of their rules. To be part of their performance of power. But courtesy didn't play into that.

Azarov didn't waver. "Would you like to join me for tea?"

Asya blinked. Had he not heard her? Or was he just so used to this forced politeness that he didn't understand when someone refused him?

The strashe still stood at her back. Orlov hovered in the corner of her vision, torn between ensuring Asya left and not disturbing the general. Asya didn't know much about the hierarchies and alliances in court, not like Izaveta, who could guess them from a single glance. But for someone who hadn't been there for the mourning days, General Azarov seemed to hold a lot of sway. Even the cabinet had acquiesced to him—other than Commander Iveshkin, that was.

All the more reason for Asya not to spend a moment longer in his company.

She reached for Tarya's supreme disinterest, her easy dismissal of anything not directly relating to the Firebird.

"I have important matters to attend to," Asya said, managing to keep her voice steady. Right now, those *important matters* involved going and hiding in Mishka's stall until her pounding heart had settled.

Azarov stepped forward, lowering his voice to the soft cadence of a psalm. "If you want your strashe to stay safely in that cage, I think you'll be inclined to accept my invitation."

The air rushed from Asya's lungs. There was no venom in his words, but the underlying threat hung in the air like incoming snow.

But surely, for all his posturing, Azarov couldn't truly find a way to get to Yuliana—could he? Not now that she was under the guard of the strashe.

"I brought her here, didn't I?" he asked, as if reading the question on Asya's face. "I have more influence than you may know."

Again, she remembered Kyriil's smug expression in the cabinet room. His offhand comment on how magic worked in strange ways. A chilling certainty settled over her—*this* was the information that spell had given them.

"Come find me tomorrow, so that you can attend to those important matters first," Azarov said, light as a friend arranging a dinner. "In the east parlor. I think you'll find we have much to discuss."

CHAPTER ELEVEN

Much as Asya tried, she couldn't convince herself to ignore General Azarov's summons. Not when so much was held in the balance—not with his threats to Yuliana.

That was how Asya found herself sitting in the east parlor, clutching a steaming cup of clove-infused tea. It was a room she tended to avoid, even in childhood. Too full of fussy and delicate furniture, yet somehow still hollow. Drained of color like the rest of the palace.

The cup was too hot, even against the flames under her skin, but she wanted something to do with her hands.

The room bustled around them. Courtiers and strashe moving between small knots of people, unsubtle glances and whispers thrown over their shoulders. Hardly the place to discuss a subject Azarov had deemed so important. But Asya understood now. It wasn't *what* he wanted to speak to her about, it was that Azarov wanted to be seen talking to her.

It was probably why Azarov had set this time, to ensure he had an audience.

It made her skin prickle, too aware of the onlookers. The caged bird again, here for the court's amusement.

Azarov took his time with his own tea. Mixing the spices

with a careful precision, refusing to look at Asya as though deeply engrossed in this simple activity.

But Asya's patience quickly frayed to nothing. "What do you want?"

Azarov sprinkled a little cinnamon into his tea, tutting under his breath.

Asya was tempted to throw her own cup at him, just to see if she could break through his unshakeable calm. It reminded her too well of Tarya. Of moments where Asya felt too much and all her emotions crashed against the immovable wall that was her aunt.

He sat back in his chair, flanked still by his scarlet-clad guards. Bloodstains against the pale snow of the palace.

Asya didn't know why he deemed them necessary instead of the strashe, but it felt like something her sister wouldn't have allowed. Her mother certainly would not have. It gave him his own pocket of influence here, separate from the palace-controlled strashe.

"Please," he said, gesturing to the cup clenched in her hands. "Do drink up."

Asya took a small sip. Anything to end this interaction sooner. It burned down her throat, the strong spice of cloves warm in her chest.

Azarov finally finished fussing with his own tea and sat back to survey Asya. "Did you know my family used to hold a cabinet seat?"

She kept her mouth shut. She didn't know that. Political history had hardly been a part of Tarya's education and Asya couldn't see how it was relevant now.

"Up until about half a century ago," the general went on. "As you know, the Karasova queens had reigned more than five hundred years by then. It seemed their line was unending." He canted his head toward Asya, an odd smile on his lips. "Until now, of course."

Asya gripped her cup. Her knuckles shone white, bones pressing against skin. She was surprised the porcelain didn't crack.

"But my grandfather believed all things should have an end. How could there be balance when the scales were always tipped in favor of one family? So he tried to change things, to end an unquestioned—unearned—eternal reign."

Asya still didn't say anything. She was sure if she did that she'd give too much away, if she hadn't already.

"It cost him his life and our family's seat on the cabinet," Azarov finished. "All in his quest for greatness. A tragic story, I suppose."

The general took another sip of his tea, staring out the arched window to the canopy of forest beyond.

The sudden silence pressed in on Asya. It gave too much space for her thoughts to run. For her fears to accelerate her pulse. But speaking felt like it would be a concession.

She thought of Izaveta and her zvess games. The way she could predict a person's actions before they'd even made up their own mind. She would find a way out of this. Meet the general on his battlefield and force his hand.

But Izaveta wasn't here.

Asya broke first. "And why should this story matter to me?" she asked.

"I suppose it doesn't, not in the specifics. I thought you might like to know the reasons." He shrugged, waving an elegant hand. "Perhaps unnecessary for me to give rationale to the Firebird. A creature who must follow any basic instinct without independent thought."

Asya bristled. "What do you want?" she said again, a hard

edge to her voice. She hoped it sounded determined, when the truth was it took every ounce of her strength to not let her emotions all come spilling out.

"I suppose I can cut to the point." His demeanor didn't change as he took a sip of tea, regarding Asya over the rim of his cup, despite the weight of his next words. "I need you to kill Commander Iveshkin."

Chapter Twelve

When Izaveta awoke, she was no longer alone.

A figure leaned against the far wall of her cell, far too casual against the sharp lines of her imprisonment. A single torch burned above them—too high for Izaveta to reach but enough to illuminate some of her prison. Enough to cast flickering light over the familiar shape across from her.

Not Nikov and not another product of her increasingly weak mind—or so she hoped. But he looked real enough, real and substantial in a way her hallucinations had not.

Izaveta tried to keep her eyes half-lidded, her breathing the slow rhythm of sleep. She needed a few moments to collect herself, to plan.

But the figure spoke first, catching her off guard. "You're awake, excellent."

Throwing aside all pretense, Izaveta pulled herself upright. Even if her legs shook and her muscles ached, she refused to greet him kneeling at his feet.

The torchlight glinted off the crest on his shoulder, the same one Izaveta had recognized before. The rooster with blood-tipped feathers, surrounded by a halo of light. It had always struck her as an odd choice for a family crest, taken from one of the more bloodthirsty stories from the life of Saint Dyena.

But then again, perhaps that was the Azarovs' intention, to state their clawing desire for power so clearly.

Kyriil stepped toward her, his golden hair and immaculate clothes a shining contrast to Izaveta's filth. She hated him for that, for being able to set the terms here, for trying to knock her off-balance. All tricks of manipulation her mother had been far too good at.

He held out a bowl and the scent suddenly hit her. The warm spices and heady promise of food. Her entire stomach lurched.

He smiled. "Stroganov was always your favorite, wasn't it?"

She wished desperately she had the strength to refuse. But pride would be her undoing here if she allowed this weak hunger to spread, and she found her hands already reaching for the bowl. He handed her a knife and fork along with it, a surprising concession. She'd expected him to force the indignity upon her—but then again, perhaps this was an attempt to be the savior after so many days of darkness.

She ate quickly, not bothering to hide her need. When she was finished, she set down the bowl with as much poise as she could manage, given the situation, before turning her gaze on Kyriil. He hadn't spoken as she ate, merely watched her. Unusually quiet for the boy who so liked to hear the sound of his own voice.

But even as her stomach tilted, unbalanced by newly rich food, she felt some of herself settle. She couldn't see the logic here, the long game Kyriil had to be playing, but at least she was on familiar ground.

"I didn't believe even you could be this ridiculously foolish," she said, opting to needle at his arrogance from the start. "To kidnap the queen and hold her prisoner."

Even as she said it, the strangeness of it struck her. The Azarovs had always wanted power, yes; they had always strived to claim their cabinet seat back. But they had kept to the delicacies of politics, never stepping beyond that.

Kyriil didn't flinch at her accusation. "Though you are not the queen, are you?"

It was disconcerting for him to echo her own words back to her. Izaveta clenched her hands behind her back, pushed all her tension into that movement so her face remained serene.

"Semantics," she said. "And hardly likely to save you from burning as a traitor."

"To threats already," Kyriil said mildly. "I am curious where this will go."

She'd hoped to rattle him more with that. On the day of the coronation, when he told her how his family had funded the Order of the Captured Flame, how he already knew of her stratsviye, he'd been emotional. He had wanted her to understand, had convinced himself that he was helping her.

Where was that now? She didn't know how long she'd been in here, but in that time, what could have wrought such a change on Kyriil?

Izaveta took a breath. She only had moments to decide which way to manipulate this conversation, usually she relished that—the power it gave her. But the conversation had never been quite as crucial as this. She'd never been in such a precarious position.

"I know your father has always drawn you into his schemes," she said, making her choice. "But you don't have to be blamed for this. You can still make it right. You can still get all that you've wanted."

"Is that so?"

He spoke with a disinterest that almost dislodged Izaveta's resolve, but she forged on, "I know of those who would still be loyal in the palace. I'm sure if we got a message to them, we would be able to arrange safe passage back for myself." She leaned forward, matching his posture. "Of course, once my crown is assured again, I would be eternally grateful for all of your help, and we could return to the question of the cabinet seat."

Kyriil didn't reply, watching her with a curious expression that made her stomach twist.

"Or more," she went on, hating to be the one pushing the negotiation, but unable to think of another route. "The hero who saved the queen would certainly be rewarded with the highest accolades."

He still didn't react. None of the familiar fire of ambition in his eyes, none of that greed she'd anticipated. Without any reaction, she didn't know what strings to pull, what weapons to try. There were rules to this game, and he couldn't simply ignore cordiality even if they were in a prison.

"Remarkable," he said finally. "You truly are all the same."

Izaveta tensed, unable to keep the edge from her voice. "What do you mean, Master Azarov?"

"Izaveta—" no title, no pretense at reverence "—do you know why we are here?"

She gritted her teeth. He knew perfectly well that she didn't, forcing her to admit ignorance, so instead she kept silent.

"You aren't curious why you've been kept here, in isolation?"

Izaveta raised her chin. "I assume because you do not want news of my presence to get back to the palace. Not unless you're the one controlling it."

"That's part of it, yes." He nodded, almost like a scholar

lecturing on moon phases. It was disconcerting in this already unsettling location, all Izaveta's expectations tilted on their axis. "Because to everyone else, you're already dead. Which means, you have no power to offer me anything." He angled his head, the light catching in his eyes so they shone almost translucent. "Which means, we may do what we want with you."

Izaveta felt as if the air had stilled around her. A crack worked its way through her bones, through her carefully placed armor, through all pretense at certainty. A crack that could make everything inside her collapse.

She'd felt real, all-consuming fear only a few times in her life. When she'd first seen the Firebird rise, the night when Asya killed the banewolf. When her sister had been trapped in that cage, about to die.

And a trickle of it now, creeping through her veins like a slow frost.

Izaveta tried to keep her voice strong, even as everything was crumbling. "You cannot treat me like this. I demand to speak to the general at once."

"Demands mean very little from a dead princess."

For the first time, she felt suddenly naked. Her armor peeled away, her carefully hoarded weapons useless. She had never been a fighter, but she found herself wanting something physical, a real weapon to grip in her hands, even if she could not use it.

He'd given her a knife with the food—

"I wouldn't bother," he said, his tone not changing. "That one's blunt."

Izaveta swallowed. She hadn't let her gaze slip to the knife on the ground, but something in her posture must have given her away. *Careless*, her mother's voice reprimanded.

He pulled another knife from his belt with a low screech of steel. A bird's wings spread to make the grip, its sharp beak open wide in a hunting cry. Not a rooster, and not a weapon she had seen him carry before.

He held it out to her, hilt first. "This one would work better."

Izaveta did not take it. She knew a cursed offering when she saw one.

He gave a little shrug, as though to say he had tried, and returned the knife to his belt.

"You don't want to kill me," Izaveta said, her voice low and frustratingly shaken. "And you won't be able to keep this secret forever."

"I don't need forever," he replied. "Just long enough for you to fulfill your purpose."

"Asya will find me before then." Izaveta wasn't sure where that certainty had come from, the fierce belief in her sister that never abated. It shone through the thick veil that kept her separate, through the numbing effects of tiredness and cold.

"Are you so sure she'll want to?"

A shard of fear dug into Izaveta's stomach, momentarily cutting off her breath. Some of that certainty began to ebb away as she scrabbled to hold it close.

"She's my sister." But even she could hear the desperate thread in her voice, the fear that Kyriil might know something she did not. Izaveta was letting him get to her, letting him under her skin in a way no one should be able to manage. "Nothing changes that."

"You'd be surprised how much can change."

Izaveta did not want to ask the question, didn't want to be forced to look to him for answers. But she couldn't stop the words flying from her lips. "What do you mean?"

"You haven't worked it out yet?" he asked. "Perhaps there's too little of a difference for you to see it."

Izaveta gritted her teeth, hands clenched at her sides. "To see *what*?"

"The price, of course." He took another step toward her and she made herself stay still, not cower away from him even if he held all the power here. "You didn't think this was it, did you? Not for the dark magic you cast."

He reached for her, pressing his palm against her chest. "You don't feel it?"

But as he asked, a pooling dread began to settle over Izaveta. She *didn't* feel it. Didn't feel what should be thrumming just below Kyriil's fingers.

"After all, it's only fair." He smiled again, the long shadows carving deep hollows in his face. "A heart in exchange for a heart."

CHAPTER THIRTEEN

Izaveta might have thought her heart was racing, her pulse accelerating her thoughts into a whirlwind. But there was no beating in her chest, no steady rhythm, nothing to tether her here.

She'd never heard of a price like this, not outside fairy tales or the vibishop's talk of saints. She thought of Saint Dyena, who'd torn out her own heart to save the woman she loved, of Saint Restov, and the absurdity of him somehow surviving a knife in his chest and keeping it there for the rest of his life. Stories, nothing more.

Yet that same knife had worked on Asya, so there had to be some truth to it. Perhaps there was some truth to all of it.

Izaveta remembered that feeling of being torn apart, of being pieced back together. The fear that something might have been lost and the veil drawn between her and her emotions. That place where her guilt had been left to fester, somewhere she couldn't quite touch.

She refused to ask him more questions, to beg information of him like a child, so instead she said, "This is a tomb, then."

A statement that invited him to expand, putting the power back in her hands. Not that she truly had any power here, no matter how she tried to maneuver these conversations.

"So dramatic." Kyriil sighed, exasperation suddenly making him look so much older. "You're still very much alive, Izaveta."

"My anatomy tutor would be shocked to hear it," Izaveta said, managing to suppress the shudder as she realized she was talking about Fyodor. When she'd last seen him he'd been barely recognizable, engulfed in flames. "He was always so certain hearts were what kept us alive."

"Hearts aren't so simple as that." Kyriil spoke as though he had great authority on the subject, as if this were a well-known weather pattern rather than the impossibility it was. "Your mother would be proud. You'll be just like her soon enough. It doesn't take long for your last memories of humanity to fade. Especially when you hardly had much to begin with."

She didn't have anything to say to that, no way to manipulate this situation or try to leverage more information.

"Enjoyable as this chat has been," Kyriil went on, "none of this is why I came to speak to you today. Since you decided that sitting and waiting quietly is beneath you, I'll give you an immediate problem you can solve."

Izaveta stilled, everything tensing as she anticipated another blow.

"Tell me where the crown is."

With everything thrown at her, Izaveta couldn't hide her surprise at his question. She assumed it sat in the cathedral, as it had during the mourning days. She couldn't think why they would have moved it or why Kyriil would be interested in it. He could hardly grasp hold of the crown and use that to claim the throne.

But the question shifted the dynamic, it gave her back some shred of control. If he thought she had something he wanted, then she could use that.

"What will you give me in exchange?" she asked.

He sighed and turned away, again not engaging in the conversation. As if somehow he was beyond that, beyond the mere politics and machinations of the palace.

"I'm sure you're missing life at court, are you not?" With that abrupt change, he leaned down and swept a hand across the grimy floor, as if wiping back a layer of frost from a windowpane.

The floor rippled and light sank into it like liquid into fabric, creating a pooled mirror beneath her. But it showed no reflection, no hint of the gaunt-faced girl she must be. She stepped closer, curious despite herself.

It was not so much a reflection, she realized, as a window. It looked into one of the parlors of the palace, busy and vibrant as Izaveta had ever seen it. Like nothing had changed.

Then her eye caught on a flicker of red hair and her lungs constricted. Asya looked as exhausted as Izaveta felt, deep grooves carved under her eyes and a strain to the way she held herself.

Izaveta scrambled forward, hardly realizing she fell to her knees in front of the strange pool, desperate to reach out to something real. But her hand touched only the cold ground, immovable and unchanged.

What was this—a trick, some kind of magic?

"Don't worry," Kyriil said. "The price is paid. The Firebird isn't going to appear."

The reflection shifted a little to reveal General Azarov, talking pleasantly to Asya over a delicate cup of tea.

"What is this?" Izaveta's voice came out raw, less substantial at the sight of her sister.

"This is a problem for you to solve. As soon as you give me the answer I need."

He bent down again, one finger reaching for the shimmering window. Ice spread from his touch, cracking across the image like dark veins. But they didn't spider across the ground toward Izaveta, spreading through the cell as she'd expected. Instead, they sank into the image, corrupting it.

Izaveta could do nothing but watch as those icy veins slowly circled her sister.

CHAPTER FOURTEEN

General Azarov's words rang in Asya's ears, reverberating like a struck bell. *Kill Commander Iveshkin.* She looked around. Over the gathered crowd, it was unlikely anyone would have overheard, but she still couldn't believe he'd discuss something like that so openly.

She reached for her immediate instinct, for the response Tarya would have given without hesitation. "The Firebird plays no role in the affairs of mortals, not unless there's a price in question."

"Oh," Azarov said with a twitch of his lips. "There's a price involved. But of a sort you're not so used to dealing in."

Asya's grip on the teacup tightened, her fingers heating before she even realized it. A trail of steam rose from it, bitter and swirling.

"You cannot make demands of the Firebird," she said again, relieved that her voice sounded more determined now. More the powerful Firebird than the scared girl.

Azarov propped an arm on the back of his chair, his every movement languid. It was odd that he was a general, yet he didn't move like a soldier. None of Yuliana's sharp precision and grace. There was a laziness to him—the kind of surety that came from being able to order others to die in your place.

"Oh, I think I can," he said, that surety laced into his every syllable. "You may be the Firebird, may have all that power at your fingertips, but you are also a child. One who makes their emotions far too plain."

He reached into the folds of his fur-lined coat, extravagant even by the standards of court with its gold embellishments. He pulled out a small piece of paper. Discolored by dirt and a little crumpled at the edges, Asya still recognized it at once.

She took it and crushed it in her fist, as if she could protect it now. Something that personal, that small piece of her. The note she'd intended to leave for Yuliana at the Elmer. The one Asya had thought she'd lost or burned. One of the Azarov siblings must have picked it up without her notice, dropped in the distraction of the Calling.

This was precisely why Tarya warned against making connections. Against ties to the mortal realm. Because the Firebird couldn't have those and be impartial.

But it was much too late for that. Asya couldn't sever the tie between her and Yuliana now even if she wanted to. What had started as the most fragile of threads had somehow formed into an unbreakable chain. Forged in pain and fire and loss— strengthened by all of that into something indestructible.

A tether Asya knew she would always follow.

"Do not test the Firebird." It wasn't hard to inject anger into her voice, searing sparks across her vision. Her hands were shaking with it.

Azarov didn't seem moved. "Or what?" he asked simply.

Asya opened her mouth to reply, but hesitated. That moment of hesitation cost her. It was too plain in her slight pause that, just as he'd said, for all of her power, she still let her emotions get the better of her. Her draw to humanity.

"I doubt you'd kill me." Azarov shrugged, mulling over his

tea. "Your conscience is your downfall. But even if you did, that wouldn't help you. Kill me and your strashe dies too."

"I care for Commander Iveshkin as well," Asya said, choosing her words carefully—so carefully they came out a little stilted. "I care for the safety of this queendom. My *conscience* also keeps me from wanting to harm anyone. If that is what you're relying on to keep you safe, then you should know it makes this bargain impossible to fulfill."

Azarov laced his fingers together in front of him, leaning forward like a parent addressing a confused child. "I'll keep it very simple for you: there are no ways around this. I have something that you hold dear to you, which means all of your actions now carry a potential price. You can decide if your idea of humanity is worth the loss it will bring. And ultimately, it makes no difference to me. Is that plain enough for even you, Firebird?"

Asya tried to breathe, to force her mind to stop racing long enough to think. She bit the inside of her cheek. What would Izaveta say?

"Though if you're quite adamant," Azarov added. "We can always execute Strashe Vilanovich now. Save us from any future bother."

"No!" The word flew out before she could stop it, as much an admission as anything else. "I—" Asya tried, but there was nothing else to say. He had her at sword-point and he knew it.

Azarov got to his feet, dusting down his jacket as if to brush off any stray traces of Asya. "I'm not a gambling man, Firebird," he said. "And this is a risk I'm willing to take. That should tell you I like my odds."

The worst part was that he was right. Asya was too much the monster to refuse, too human to fight back. Not when the only way to victory would be killing. Likely more than just the general—any strashe who got in the way, innocently trying to protect what they thought was right.

Azarov turned to leave, gesturing to the assembled guards. Over his shoulder, as though this was an afterthought rather than a calamity, he said, "I'll give you some time to consider. I can stay the executioner's blade until the First Snows. No later. Then we will see how much leverage I have."

"The First Snows," Asya repeated. "The same day set for the trial of succession."

He raised his eyebrows innocently. "Is it?"

Frustration was so sharp in her vision she didn't notice the movement behind her until too late. Out of place in the calm conversations of the parlor, even the other courtiers didn't react at once.

A sword slashed down into the arm of her chair, narrowly missing where her hand rested. The silver uniform of a strashe. Yells sparked across the room, courtiers scattering.

Asya leaped to her feet, ready to confront whatever new foe this was.

But even as she did, the strashe faltered. There was something not right in his eyes. Some glint that felt inhuman.

He was raising his blade again, arcing it toward Asya, when he was consumed.

Not by Asya's fire, as the watchers might have expected— as she herself might have expected. This came from inside him. Spreading from the strange glint in his eye, caustic veins tracked across his face.

He dropped his znaya, corruption swirling around his throat.

Asya opened her mouth—to call the voye or more strashe, anyone who could help. But before she could, the strashe stopped moving. Frozen as a statue. A corpse somehow still standing in front of her.

She couldn't sense magic in the air, no hint of a Calling, but he clearly was dead. Destroyed by a magic she couldn't feel.

PART TWO:

A HEART FOR A HEART

A young queen, afraid of losing her crown, turned to a demonya asking to ensure no one could ever question her rule. He offered aid, for a price: he could do as she wished, but the queen could never leave her land again.

She was young and foolish, so she agreed at once and the demonya granted her wish. He let cold creep across the land, and into her heart too, destroying any dissidents until there was no one left to question her rule. So she ruled eternally, a queen carved from ice, presiding over a dead and frozen land.

—"THE FROZEN QUEEN," AN OLD FOLKTALE

Chapter Fifteen

Night had long since seeped across the sky, darkening the leeched color of the parlor to uncertain shadows, and the frozen corpse still stood unmoving.

Asya couldn't tear her eyes from it. Strashe surged around her like a river around a stone, buffeting but not quite engaging. The accusation was thick in the air. The courtiers had been hurried out, nobles and attendants slowly morphing from shocked silence to almost excited whispers of scandal.

The cabinet had looked to Asya then, as if hoping the Firebird might shed some light.

But the truth was Asya couldn't even begin to guess what had happened here. She'd never seen magic like this—magic that could twist through a person in mere moments.

And there were no signs of the order on the strashe's body. Asya hadn't looked, but she'd heard the strashevsta say as much. Though, the number of people who might want to attack the Firebird was not necessarily limited to them.

General Azarov had been more than happy to provide his side of the story, somehow framing himself as heroic. Asya just kept seeing the strashe's face. A terrified anger that he didn't seem to understand.

It took her too long to realize someone was speaking to her—the spymaster.

"Firebird," Zvezda said again. "There's nothing more for you to do here."

"I should…" Asya trailed off, not quite sure what she *should* do. She'd always thought of the spymaster like Tarya, like her mother. Immovable and impassive. But Zvezda was looking at her now with a slight crease of concern. Not worry for what Asya might do—but worry for Asya. In the heady plunge of adrenaline following what had just happened, it made her feel a little unsteady.

"Get cleaned up," Zvezda said softly. "There's nothing more to be done tonight."

Asya felt like she should disagree. This wasn't something that could wait, she didn't have the luxury of time. But she couldn't quite get her voice to work.

So she simply nodded.

It was a relief to turn and walk away. To finally step back from her vigil, no longer staring at the strashe's lifeless face.

Another voice called her back only a few steps from the respite of the passage beyond.

Commander Iveshkin's face was grim as her interpreter waylaid Asya. The commander carefully placed herself between Asya and the commotion of the rest of the room, using her height to ensure no one else would see Asya speak.

"Leaving already, Firebird?" Iveshkin's face wasn't accusatory, but it felt like there was a test in her words.

"Uh, yes," Asya replied. "Not a lot more I can do tonight." She echoed Zvezda's advice, relieved again to have that way out.

Iveshkin stepped a little closer, hands moving in small, careful gestures to not be obvious to the rest of the room. Mila matched her stance, voice a low murmur. "What were you speaking to the general about?"

Asya's stomach turned over. She was sure her face gave away too much, Azarov's demand etched into her features. She'd been trying not to think about it. One horror eclipsed by another.

Asya should tell her the truth. Find a way to speak in private and tell her Azarov wanted her dead. She didn't know much of the court but she certainly trusted Iveshkin's stoic leadership over Azarov. Trusted that Iveshkin truly wanted the best for Tóurin.

But that would mean Asya's choice was made. That she'd accepted the risk to Yuliana.

She swallowed, her throat dry. "Nothing," she said, not very convincingly. "Nothing at all."

Iveshkin fixed her with a careful look, appraising. "I had hoped you would be above the sort of games your mother and sister played. That path leads only to ruin."

She strode away with that remark, the words echoing in Asya's mind. She wasn't trying to play games. To get involved in the nuances of politics that meant nothing to her.

But maybe Izaveta hadn't *wanted* that either. Want and need meant very different things in this palace, Asya was coming to learn that.

Asya felt someone following her when she made her first turn away from the main thoroughfare to the quieter passage that led back to her chambers. Not the usual strashe who'd been shadowing her since the would-be coronation, but an unfamiliar presence.

She didn't glance back—didn't need to give them any sign she knew they were there. But she wasn't going to run this time. She was done with being hunted by people like Fyodor or Azarov. Now she was getting answers.

She thought back, trying to remember somewhere that might provide cover without attracting too many people. She didn't want an audience again.

Asya adjusted her footsteps, trying not to walk with obvious purpose as she turned in the direction of the Voya Wing, not too far out of her way. It had first been built in a time of plague, when the palace had opened its doors to try to heal as many people as possible. There were far more rows of rooms and empty beds than could possibly be needed in peacetime. That left plenty of unoccupied space in winding corridors lined with dedications to Saint Xishin.

Asya took one flight of stairs up, moving a little quicker to give herself a head start. She couldn't hear any footsteps, but she was sure they were still there. As soon as she rounded the corner at the top of the stairs, she ducked back into the alcove that protected a towering statue. There was one on each floor here, saints to overlook people in their darkest times.

It would only give her a moment of cover, but that was all she needed.

A figure emerged from the stairs. They hesitated, eyes scanning the corridor, and Asya lunged. In the blur of movement, she caught only the bloodred of his uniform—one of Azarov's guards. But even with her moment of surprise, the guard was stronger. They pushed free of Asya's grip, forcing her back against the wall, a knife to her throat.

But Asya's fire was ready. A thick rope of crimson and gold that—

Then she took in his face. She froze, so surprised that the flames slid from her hands, cinders scattering at her feet.

"Dima?"

CHAPTER SIXTEEN

Dima Vilanovich looked just the same as he had that night in the Elmer. A face that shared the same sharp lines and storm-gray eyes as Yuliana but held none of her warmth. None of her electric possibility and steadfast loyalty.

They were the impassable gray of stone. Of someone who would choose revenge over his own sister.

Asya shoved him back with a burst of flame. He stumbled, slamming into the statue. One of Saint Xishin's fingers broke off with a crack.

"I don't want to harm you," he said, a stark contrast to the blade still ready in his hands.

"I find that hard to believe."

But she didn't advance and he didn't lower the knife. A strange stalemate between two foes. Asya's eyes caught on the blade. It was plain steel, no dull edge of firestone. A symbol was etched into the handle, one Asya recognized well. Three lines encasing a flame.

Fury ignited easily then.

"You still carry their weapon?" Her voice reverberated through her teeth, every inch the monster of legend. Was that the same one he'd used in the Elmer too, the one he'd held to Yuliana's throat as they forced Asya to surrender?

She took a step forward. She didn't know what she planned

to do, but Dima moved too quickly for Asya to react, throwing the knife in a swift arc. It buried in her left shoulder, a staccato burst of pain.

Asya felt the Firebird's cry in her head. Its anger twined with her own. The creature that had struck down all the order members without so much as a second thought. It would only take a moment to set it free—

Fear flashed in Dima's eyes, sudden and bright. It eased some of Asya's fury, tempering it with shame.

This was the boy who had watched the Firebird take his father's life. Who had been scarred by those flames just as much as Yuliana. Could Asya really blame him?

But that didn't mean forgiveness came easily. She wouldn't soon forget that Dima was the one who had dragged his own sister to Fyodor and left her at his mercy.

"Please." Asya could see that word cost him something. "I just want to help my sister."

She moved her hands and he flinched back, the image of unyielding soldier shattered.

But she only reached for the hilt of the knife. She wrenched it out with a low growl. He'd aimed well, even in his fear. Striking right into the muscle. It would be another hour at least before the Firebird had her arm back to normal.

She lowered her hands to her sides, the sparks subsiding from her eyes. She remembered someone else with a blade like this, someone who had moved with a careful precision.

She glanced up at him. He'd drawn another dagger now, one shining with the Azarov crest. "You were the one who attacked me in the palace gardens, weren't you?"

He blinked, surprised by the question, then nodded stiffly.

"I spared your life that night," she said. She could still remember it as sharp as the blade in her hands. How the Firebird had wanted to burst free, to destroy all of them. If it had, perhaps that would have stopped so many of the terrible things that happened later. If she'd shown the order she was a strong Firebird, not to be trifled with, then maybe there could have been another way.

"And yet you still wanted me dead," she finished.

He shrugged, his every movement tightly coiled. "It's not my fault you missed your chance."

"Why are you here?" Asya asked, tiredness beginning to leech into her. She pressed a hand against the wound in her shoulder, blood now staining her jacket pitch-black. It didn't help her muddled thoughts, the painful twist of emotion in her chest.

"I want to help my sister," he repeated, as if he had memorized the line and now had to stand by it no matter what.

"By becoming one of Azarov's soldiers?"

Dima shook his head. "No. We went to Azarov for protection."

We.

"You and...Yuliana?" Asya asked, the name catching in her throat.

"She lost so much blood," Dima said quickly. "I took her from the Elmer as soon as things started to go wrong."

Asya didn't let herself ask if it was Yuliana's choice.

"She needed help," Dima pressed on. "And at the palace she'd be executed as a traitor. So I took her to Azarov's estate. I knew he had funded the order, so I thought he might be sympathetic."

"I suppose you were wrong about that?" Asya let herself lean back against the wall. It didn't really matter what weakness Dima saw in her, or how much she held up her guard. Even in this diminished state, it was a fight they both knew she would win this time.

"He was mostly disinterested. Told us to stay out of his way and not trouble him," Dima replied. "Then something happened. He and his children locked themselves away for days, planning. That was when he came back to us. Yuliana was still healing—his medic kept her on something for the pain, it made her confused."

Asya swallowed, trying not to let her mind imagine it, to think of Yuliana that vulnerable among enemies.

"He said we were returning to the palace, that it was some triumphant moment. He promised we wouldn't be harmed." Dima ducked his chin, shadows shifting across his features. "It didn't sound like a request. When we reached the Depthless Lake, his guards bound Yuliana. He told me I had to keep playing my part or she'd die."

Asya's throat constricted. She had to bite back her accusations, the sharp retort that he'd gambled with his sister's life before. But she'd hardly done any better at protecting Yuliana, had she?

"But I took this," he said, lifting something from a loop on his belt. Light sloughed off the dull metal like water from a leaf. An ancient, rusted key.

"It opens one of the old queens' passages into Zmenya's Tower. You enter just by the carving of Queen Teriya. You'd be able to free Yuliana and be gone before anyone realized."

Asya stared at the key, making no move to take it. There felt like some unspoken catch here. "Where did you get that?"

"I stole it from Azarov." Asya didn't have a moment to take in the ramifications of that—the fact Azarov had secret access to Yuliana.

"You've decided you don't hate me anymore, then?" Asya asked.

"I've decided to choose my sister," he replied, squaring his shoulders. "And you happen to be useful to that. She matters more to me than any revenge."

Asya let out a low huff, something too hoarse to be called

a laugh. "I wish you'd decided that sooner. You would have saved us so much trouble."

His fingers tightened on the key, knuckles whitening against his skin. "Yes," he said quietly. "I probably would have."

Asya didn't know what to say to that. Her shoulder was aching and her head was spinning with all the possibilities of the day—all the impossibilities. Too many enemies circling her, too many people she couldn't trust.

And Yuliana right in the middle of them all, weapons held to her throat.

"Why don't you free her?" Asya asked. "You have the key."

Silence pooled between them, so long that Asya thought Dima might give up and stab her again. Then finally, he said, "Because I can't protect her. You can." There was a frayed pain to those words, an admission he didn't want to share.

Perhaps that, more than anything else, made her believe him.

"Take it," he pressed, holding the key out to her like a divine offering.

She kept her hands at her side. "No."

"Why?"

So many different reasons clamored in her mind. Firstly, she didn't trust him, even if she thought she believed him. Then, there was the chance she still owed Izaveta. And the risk of Azarov's reprisal, his own power in Tóurin. Freedom this way would never truly be freedom. It would mean condemning herself to a life in exile, always hunted. There'd be no going back.

Asya just shook her head. "I can't."

Any trace of fear vanished from Dima's face, his features hardening. "Then, what use are you?" Asya rocked back on her heels, the sudden venom in his voice striking her unguarded. "You have all this power and yet you won't even try?"

Asya had nothing to say to that. It was the same thing

she'd felt all this time, ever since the Firebird had first risen inside her.

He surged forward, anger flashing until he was staring down at her. His eyes were smoothed stone again, just as they'd been in the Elmer.

"You pretend to care about her, and you'll leave her there to die?" he hissed. "You made her turn against the only people who ever cared for her—you *killed* what had come to be our family—and you can't even do this? You can't be bothered to try?"

Asya couldn't speak. Caged in again by her choices, options narrowing around her to nothing. Each path led to a greater monster. Kill Iveshkin and save Yuliana. Stop Azarov and doom her. Try to escape now and risk losing her anyway—while certainly losing Izaveta. No matter which way Asya went, she still lost.

Dima leaned in and Asya expected more anger, for him to reach for his knife again. She probably deserved it. But instead, he took her right hand and pressed the key against her palm, folding her fingers over it.

"You owe her this," he said, voice low and shaking.

He took the knife from Asya's loose grip and strode away without so much as a backward glance.

She was left staring down at the key. Like a two-sided coin, where one half could never truly be apart from the other, it was one part damnation and one part shining possibility. One that came with much too high a price.

Chapter Seventeen

The Celebration of First Snows was a festival held every winter on the day that the three domes of the palace were all covered in a thick layer of snow. It was a celebration Asya had always enjoyed. There was an excited anticipation to it—guesses and wagers made throughout the palace as to when the snow would truly fall.

But the uncertainty held no excitement now. It was sand running through an hourglass, yet Asya had no idea how much was left. She could wake tomorrow and find a new wind had brought a storm with it, blanketing the palace already.

Azarov's deadline and a new queen, all at once.

She suddenly, desperately wanted her sister. For everything they'd been through, for all the lies, Izaveta was still the one person Asya felt she could turn to about anything. The one person who would make all this feel manageable.

Two days had passed since Azarov's threat, since that strange magic had burned through the strashe. Two more days of hoping to find some scrap of information in this library, and two more days of disappointment.

Asya blinked back against the sharp sting of tears, refocusing on the skies beyond the narrow library window.

Kill Commander Iveshkin.

The demand circled round and round in her head like a

falcon. She should have refused him at once. The fact she hadn't was damning enough. Another of her shortcomings brought painfully to light.

Then, there was the question of what had happened after her conversation with Azarov. She kept seeing the frozen body, branded into her mind. Another attempt on the Firebird, like the order members from before—or something else?

And the key still burned in her pocket. She'd taken to walking past Zmenya's Tower whenever she had a moment. She wasn't sure if she was trying to bring herself comfort, to tell herself Yuliana was still alive and snow did not obscure the domes yet, or if she was setting out some kind of test for herself. Seeing if she would break and free Yuliana despite the consequences.

Asya hadn't, not yet anyway. The inaction of it all made her want to burst out of her skin.

The almighty Firebird, no use without a Calling.

She turned, leaning back against the window and its threats of snow. Nikov sat at the only lighted table, flicking through another ancient tome.

A thought caught in her mind, almost too fleeting. Tarya had always said the Callings were the earth's way of keeping balance. They pulled on the strings that held the Firebird connected to magic to ensure the price was always paid.

Her feet were moving before the thought had entirely coalesced. She hurried to the nearest desk, pushing it aside to create a small space in the middle of the room.

Nikov looked up from his books with a puzzled frown. "What are you—"

She moved aside another chair, almost knocking it over in her haste. "If the Firebird—if *I* know when a price is owed, then I must have some awareness of magic. Of the harmony it's meant to create."

"I suppose—"

Asya didn't wait for him to finish, new energy finally coursing through her. "Then, the Firebird must know what Izaveta owed—where she went to satisfy the price." *And*, she added inside her mind, *it should know if there's any way around that.* "So why don't I ask?"

"Ask the Firebird?"

"I've had visions before," she went on. "Not just when there's a Calling." They'd plagued her during the mourning days, not only searching for that imbalance but also in those burning dreams. Scorching and too bright to fully comprehend.

"I did set fire to my chambers," she conceded. "But that was then. I understand the Firebird now. And she's helped me before."

"The Firebird *is* you. Can it know something you don't?"

"Let's find out."

Nikov stood up slowly. "A solid theory, but shouldn't we test it first?"

"No." Asya sat herself in the middle of the cleared space, hoping it was enough. "I don't want to wait anymore." After all, she wasn't even certain how much time she had.

"I would prefer if you didn't burn down the library, though."

Asya glanced over at him. "If the fire spreads too far, wake me up."

Nikov's eyes widened, but she didn't give him another moment to protest.

Asya closed her eyes and the Firebird reared up out of her, as if it had been waiting. Even through her lids, the golden red of the power shone bright.

"Svedye," she heard Nikov murmur through the flames.

Asya remembered the days following her mother's death. When the power had been too scalding, so many threads tangled into something incomprehensible. But the Firebird spread out around her now, comfortable and familiar.

Show me, she thought. *Show me what I need to know.*

She reached for the notes of a Calling. Not the crescendo of a price that needed to be paid, but the subtle melody of magic around her. The undercurrent that was always there. She was so used to it already that she barely noticed it. Like honing in on dust motes in the air.

Show me.

Asya was standing on the banks of the Depthless Lake.

Its waters gleamed, luminescent against the night. Asya had to wait for her eyes to adjust to its brilliance, the rest of the scene slowly painting itself in with soft brushstrokes of color. The night sky was cloudless, but no moons glimmered against the black, leaving it starved and empty. The lake truly shone like the fourth moon of Tóurin.

There was no sign of Izaveta, no hint of that night in the Elmer.

A queen stood on the bank, resplendent even in a simple robe of white. She wore no crown, but there was no question of her position.

There was something familiar in her features, a slight hint of Izaveta. Or reminiscent of those stone carvings that dotted the palace. Small jars sat in front of her, the pale white of queenstree bark, what looked like everroot and something far less substantial.

Two larger bundles lay nestled in the snow next to her, wrapped tight in furs. Asya might not have known they were babies, silent and sleeping, if not for the luminance of the lake. In her hands, the queen clasped a book bound in twigs and leaves— though the leaves had no edge of crispness, no beginnings of decay creeping across them. Impossibly, they seemed alive.

A falcon swooped low overhead, the ink-dark feathers coalescing into the figure of a man between one blink and the next.

The queen looked up at him, as if she'd been expecting this obstacle. "Koschei."

The name rang through Asya's mind. The sorcerer who had created falcons and sent them out to steal children's hearts.

His eyes were flat in the reflective light of the lake, but his voice was cutting as the wind. "You took the book."

"It was hardly yours to begin with."

He advanced on the queen. Asya's feet tried to move, to invervene, but they seemed to have forgotten how. She was only able to watch.

"You truly believe you can succeed with this?" he asked.

The queen stood, a protective barrier between the sorcerer and the infants. "I refuse to continue to be beholden to the price," she said, every syllable ringing and regal. "If I can undo all of that pain, then I shall."

"Arrogance," Koschei hissed. "You think you can—"

"I'm doing the ritual. My children will not suffer for this too." She turned her back on the sorcerer—the foolish surety of a queen. Fire kindled in his hands, ready to strike.

"Watch out!" Asya tried to yell, though no sound came out.

The flame gusted at his fingertips, rearing up and—

Asya came back to herself with a stuttering gasp.

She blinked, unsure what had pulled her from the vision until she felt water drip down her face. Nikov stood over her with an apologetic grimace, an empty pitcher in his hand.

"Why did you stop me?" Frustration punctuated her words. She'd been so close, *so* close.

Nikov gestured around them and Asya pieced together the rest of the world. Scorch marks, deep and gouging as burning claws, spread from where she sat. They reached toward the nearest shelves, leaving burning cinders of books behind.

One window had cracked and a fine sheen of soot hung over the space.

And Nikov was clutching his hand. "Did I burn you?"

He waved her off. "I'll be fine."

She clenched her jaw. So much for being able to control it now. Even searching for answers managed to have a price.

"Did you see anything?" Nikov asked, eyes eager despite the angry burn.

Haltingly, she recounted what she'd seen as best she could. It sounded stranger voicing it, much less substantial. But one part stuck out—the queen had talked about a price. About a ritual and *undoing* that pain.

She'd been poring over that leaf-bound tome. Asya had only heard of a book like that in stories of the saints—a book that could cause fresh grass to spring up, even in the harshest winters. "What do you know about Saint Korona?"

Nikov tilted his head quizzically but didn't question the subject change. "She really liked trees, people paint her all the time because it's supposed to bring them good fortune—" he counted off on his fingers as he spoke "—and she died tragically young. Fairly expected saintly duties."

"Anything about her book?"

Nikov shrugged, apparently used to being interrogated about random bits of knowledge. "Not that I remember, but I didn't study the saints in much detail. I've never been one for so much needless self-sacrifice."

Asya bit her lip, willing herself to make the connection. "No stories of her interacting with the Firebird? Or a queen who tried to undo a price?"

"Not that I know of." He paused, as if not wanting to break bad news. "Is it possible you were just seeing the memories of another Firebird's Calling? Perhaps it isn't related at all."

Asya stood slowly. That *was* possible, but why else would the Firebird show her that specific moment?

A different memory nudged at the edge of her mind. A crowded room and a desperate search for the remnants of another saint.

She drew in a sharp breath. "Vibishop Sanislav told me they have her cloak of leaves in the cathedral. Perhaps they have the book as well."

Nikov looked skeptical. "That's assuming it's real. The majority of saints' relics are just cheap imitation."

Asya was already moving. "Saint Restov's knife was real."

Nikov hurried after her. "Or it was a normal knife that bled the firestone out of you, and then the Firebird's power healed you."

She knew Nikov was right, of course. But Asya's choices were narrowing around her. Her time in the palace—her time to find some answer about Izaveta—could be cut short at any moment. A dusting of snow and her hand would be forced: Iveshkin or Yuliana. Risk escape or cave to Azarov's will.

Either way, she was running out of time. Already there was a bite to the air, the slight edge that foreshadowed deeper winter.

But if this could be a way to bring Izaveta back, then that problem would solve itself. With the queen at her side, Azarov would be powerless.

Asya was about to voice that, when the door opened. The movement was sudden and sharp but somehow soundless. The spymaster stood in the doorway. Her eyes swept over the room once, over the destruction Asya had left in her wake, but she didn't linger on it.

Zvezda looked right at Asya, a grim set to her mouth. "It's happened again."

Chapter Eighteen

Only a spattering of light illuminated the cabinet room, nearly all the elaborate candelabras left empty. As if they were determined to keep this shrouded in secrecy. Or so they didn't have to look too closely at the bodies.

The cabinet weren't seated at their ornate table tonight but instead gathered in a tight knot in one corner.

Bishop Deryev turned at the sound of the door, his displeasure evident even in the near dark. "Firebird," he said—that was the only greeting Asya got now. "You were not asked to join this discussion."

"I invited her." Zvezda slipped from the shadows. "The Firebird is uniquely positioned to help on matters of magic. It would be unwise to overlook her for petty personal squabbles."

Her voice was soft, no notes of accusation, but it still made Deryev's expression darken.

He looked to Asya. "Well then, do you care to explain this?"

He stepped aside and the rest of the cabinet moved with him to reveal the macabre display.

Two bodies this time. Bile rose in Asya's throat, sharp and burning.

"You don't have to look," Nikov murmured, a reassuring presence at her side.

But she couldn't look away.

There was a wrongness about the corpses that Asya could see at once, even before she was close enough to take in their gaunt faces. The frost that spiderwebbed across their skin, like newly carved veins. No—not across their skin, but *beneath* it. As if the magic had somehow remolded them from the inside out.

And just like the first strashe, their eyes were open wide, all color leeched from their irises to leave pinpricks of black pupils in the midst of the whites.

"Well?" Deryev prompted.

Nikov gestured to the frosted veins. "The Firebird tends to do the opposite of that." His voice was harder than usual and Asya was relieved again to have someone by her side. "And not to mention that the Firebird was not even present."

"Magic," Strashevsta Orlov growled from behind Asya. "Just like my strashe who was killed by that falcon. Magic that *you*—" he jabbed a finger in Asya's direction "—won't do anything about."

"We cannot determine the cause yet," Zvezda said, her tone unchanging. "It's unlike anything we have seen before, and we would be foolish to rush to judgment."

Asya nodded gratefully. This was why she liked Zvezda best of all the people in these meetings. She was the only one who didn't play to the audience. She spoke with a calm certainty, not trying to twist information to her will.

But everyone was still waiting for Asya to say something. Izaveta would use that—and maybe Asya could too.

"I—" Asya paused, trying to collect her thoughts. She didn't want to give them any ammunition against her. "I haven't seen magic like this before. And the price would be more than one person could pay." She thought of Makzen, his desperate voice as he'd described the Azarovs' neat work-around. "Though I have seen people who use others to pay their prices. That method might work here."

"Who?" Iveshkin signed.

Asya took a breath. This might risk Azarov's ire—risk him taking it out on Yuliana—but she couldn't stay silent. "General Azarov."

The effect was instantaneous. Scurried whispers and loaded glances exchanged between each of the cabinet members.

"Ridiculous accusations from an untrustworthy source," Deryev said.

Vada Nisova sniffed. "It's hardly uncommon for those who run large estates to use people in their employ to enact the smaller details of a spell."

The momentary inspiration pushing Asya forward deflated. "They do?"

"Of course," Nisova went on, as if Asya were very slow. "A conze can't be expected to deal with the minutiae. The price *is* paid, so what difference does it make?"

The ground tilted a little beneath Asya's feet. They spoke about it as if it didn't matter, as if it made no difference to the lives they played with.

"We are distracted from the true problem here," Bazin said. "This is all for us to address when the new queen is crowned."

"The problems are not so disparate," Iveshkin signed, her eyes piercing into Asya. "Which is why the Firebird is my nomination for queen."

"No." The word burst out of Asya at once, an instinctive reaction.

"There is no precedent for such a—" Bishop Deryev sputtered.

But Iveshkin's decisive presence cut through them both. "The trial of succession means I may recommend any candidate, and the gods will decide." She raised an eyebrow to Deryev. "Unless you doubt they will make the right choice."

"No," Asya said again, more determined. She had no desire for a crown and the weight that came with it—the Firebird's burden was more than enough. There was a reason the two roles were separate.

Iveshkin shrugged. "I suppose I cannot force a candidate. Though you'd do well to consider."

"But I don't want it," Asya murmured, her words doing little to call back the arrow already unloosed.

Iveshkin was still watching her carefully. "*Want* means little to the needs of a queendom."

CHAPTER NINETEEN

Izaveta kept trying to feel her heartbeat, pressing a hand against her rib cage, searching for the steady rhythm she knew should be there. Poking at it in her mind like a child that had found a dead bird.

There was still something. An echo, or the remembered sensation, of a heart in her chest. She tried to wall it in, a dam to protect this last trickle. But she could feel it would not hold forever.

Though she refused to dwell on it now, not when Kyriil had given her what she so desperately needed: an idea.

The price is paid, he'd said. *The Firebird isn't going to appear.*

Izaveta moved over to the thin stream of water, the only re-source she had. Water was used in plenty of basic spells, she'd used it herself during the mourning days to contact Conze Vittaria. Though she'd had far more assets then. Moonlight for one, which steeped the water in its power to help speed any message through the In-Between. This tomb was per-fectly sealed, not so much as a hint of outside light. No cracks for the gods to peer through.

But Izaveta didn't truly need to *send* a message, she did not even need to do more than the smallest of spells.

All she needed to do was not pay the price, then Asya could find her.

A scrap of fabric served as the closest replacement for paper, and Izaveta's cupped hands were the best she could manage for a bowl. She wasn't sure it would be enough—even if she did not need the spell to succeed, she needed *something* to happen. Some slight shred of magic so that the world would know she owed it a price in return.

She took a shaking breath—it seemed unfair that if she had to be heartless, fear was one thing that remained—and whispered the incantation. There was no great shimmer of magic as there had been when she'd done this before, more a sputtering candle than a blazing furnace. But it should be enough. It had to be.

Izaveta held her breath as the fabric swirled across the surface of the water, resolutely present.

Then, with the slightest ripple of air, it vanished.

Relief sagged through her, water falling from her hands as she pressed her forehead against the cool stone of the wall. She hadn't realized how desperately she needed this to work until that moment. How much she needed someone else to know she was alive.

Asya would know where she was. Asya would find her.

And Asya would know how to keep Izaveta on the right path, to not let her become the heartless queen she'd once aspired to be.

Izaveta gripped her right wrist, turning it over to trace the lines of the stratsviye. The faint scar of the first one still remained, soft as distant moonlight. A mark she'd never quite be free of.

As she watched, the lines slowly darkened again. A swirl of ink moving through water, serene and placid even as it marked her fate.

It was different to the first time she'd seen the mark. That night had been one of panic, terror at the realization of what she'd done. This one was relief.

"I think that's about enough, don't you?"

Izaveta jumped, banging her forehead against the rough stone of the wall. She hadn't heard footsteps—hadn't heard anything other than the faint drip of water—but Kyriil now stood behind her, a torch held aloft.

From the way his eyes narrowed with careful calculation, he knew precisely what she had been doing.

CHAPTER TWENTY

Kyriil lowered the torch, its flame sending shadows skittering across his face, and leaned it against the wall. "I must admit, I was hoping for something a little more creative."

Izaveta wanted to put her hands behind her back, to hide the stratsviye already forming there. But if she did that, it would be tantamount to telling him there was something to hide. So she kept her hands carefully casual, hanging at her sides—something she'd become accomplished at the past few weeks. Though gloves had made it easier.

Izaveta raised her chin, drawing on her mother's most imperious expression of disinterest. "I could say the same of you. Keeping me trapped in here certainly lacks imagination."

His hand flashed out, fingers fastening around her right wrist like a vise. He twisted it so the pale inside caught the light, along with the stark lines of the stratsviye. The burning feather branded on her skin once more.

His lips curled into a smile, almost impressed. "Back here again, are we?"

His grip tightened and Izaveta was suddenly acutely aware of how alone she was. Abrupt, suffocating fear clawed up her throat again. No amount of pretty words would help her here.

He pulled a knife from his belt—the same one he'd offered her. She wished she'd taken it, even if she would be no use with it. At least then she wouldn't feel quite so debilitatingly helpless.

He pulled her over to the torch, but instead of tearing some hairs from her head and tossing them into the flames as she'd expected, he bent to put the tip of the blade into the glowing embers. Fear kicked in her chest and she tried to wrench herself free, but her movements were too weak—even before all this time down here, she doubted she would have had the strength. Her mother had never bothered with actual weapon training, only the metaphors of court.

Kyriil lifted the knife out, now a gleaming amber in the dark room. "The heat will make it cleaner," he said, as if in answer to her question.

Ice spread through Izaveta's veins, accompanied by a burning, nauseating terror.

"It should only be a few hairs," she blurted, unable to keep the desperation from coating her voice.

"Magic is a temperamental thing," he said, in a measured tone that felt so out of place. Even in his worst moments, Kyriil was usually one for grandeur. "And we want to make sure the lesson is learned."

He adjusted his grip, forcing her index finger out. "I think a fingernail should suffice."

He positioned the burning blade under the nail, just where it met flesh.

"I'll do what you want." She scrambled for words, for anything that could stop this. But for all her practice at manipulation, even her mother had never pushed her like this. The conversations may have been full of traps and pitfalls, but those were never literal.

"Let the Firebird find me," she pressed, hating how close

her voice veered toward begging. "And I'll show you where the crown is."

"You'll *show* me?" Kyriil asked, apparently amused by the notion. "How kind of you, offering to take me back to the palace, where you believe you could somehow control the situation. I think not." He held her gaze, but she couldn't read anything in the smooth lines of his face, her usual keen eye failing her. "Besides, why would I bargain for what I know I will get?"

The blade dug in with a sharp, blossoming agony that made darkness cloud the edges of her vision. A scream wrenched from her lungs as the nail tore free. This wasn't like the flames that had unmade her—this was present and terrifying and *real*. He let her go and she stumbled back, thudding into the wall. Each shuddering breath drove the hammering ache deeper into her. He tossed the bloodied nail into the eagerly waiting flames, the price paid.

She clutched her other hand around her finger, teeth gritted so tightly she thought she might shatter. "You won't get what you want," she said through gasping breaths, trying to reach for anger through the spiraling pain.

He slid the knife back into its sheath. "I think somehow you still don't understand."

Her breath was jagged in her chest, her shoulder pressed against the wall—the only thing keeping her upright.

"I have time. That curse will continue to spread through the palace and either you will give up and tell me or you will forget to care and share the information without regret. You don't have any choice in this. Tóurin has moved on without you."

"I am still the rightful heir—"

"The heir who killed the queen. The Tóurensi don't take

too kindly to traitors, do they? There's no place left for you there. No place anywhere for a heartless, powerless girl who betrayed anyone who was foolish enough to trust her."

He turned to leave, and she reached for another thing to say—some way to pull strings as her mother had. "You weren't always like this. You don't have to do what your father wants."

He let out a low, scoffing laugh, eerie in the cavernous space. "General Azarov has nothing to do with this beyond the use he can serve."

"What happened to you?" she asked, almost surprised at the question. This wasn't the Kyriil she had known those years ago, and it wasn't the Kyriil who had returned to the palace with his half smiles and promises.

When he looked back at her, there was something heavy in his gaze. A strange burden that she found she could not name. He rapped his knuckles on his breastbone as if testing wood for a hollow. "I could ask you the same thing."

CHAPTER TWENTY-ONE

For the briefest moment, Asya saw her sister. Not the lingering phantom that had followed her since that night in the Elmer. But whole and real—though she didn't look as Asya had ever seen her. Izaveta's clothes were in tatters, her hair hanging lank and her eyes bloodshot. Asya thought there was someone else there, another voice speaking—

Then the doors snapped behind her and the image was gone, crumbled to cinders in her mind.

"Asya?" Nikov was watching her with that troubled furrow between his brows again. She'd managed to bring that expression out a lot the last few days. He tried for a smile. "Don't look so worried. I think that went very well."

Asya let out a surprised huff of laughter. It was an exhausted, dwindling sound, but somehow a comfort still. It felt odd in the wake of the horrors they'd just seen, but also something she needed. Something to pull her back from the edge of despair.

"Well, I haven't been exiled yet," Asya conceded. "Or forced into a cage." *Or given Azarov what he wants*, she added in her head—a thing she'd not yet mentioned to Nikov.

"Definitely both positives."

Nikov's optimism in the face of everything really was remarkable. She'd had some of that once. An unwavering belief that somehow everything would work out, as long as she had her sister.

"Do you—" She broke off, almost afraid to voice the possibility aloud. "Do you think it's connected, somehow? Izaveta being gone, this curse. All of it."

Nikov's expression grew wary. "I'm not sure we have enough information to hypothesize."

He always spoke in grand words like that, in a way that somehow managed to circle past condescending. It was probably what Izaveta had liked about him.

"But we'll find something," he said, an odd inflection to his words that Asya couldn't quite interpret. "We have to."

"I just feel like it comes back to Saint Korona's book," Asya said. "That it'll pull together all the missing pieces. I know it's not logical or scholarly…"

"I could try asking the bishop. I can be quite persuasive," Nikov suggested without much conviction. He knew as well as Asya that Deryev wouldn't help anyone vaguely connected to the Firebird. "Oh, or we could try a heist!" he added, eyes gleaming. "I've always wanted to do that."

"A heist might be difficult without any inside information. We have no idea where they keep the book," Asya pointed out, and Nikov looked a little crestfallen.

But as she said it, something sparked in her mind.

Asya still knew of one person who might have that answer—for a price, of course.

Dima's instructions led her exactly where he claimed. A narrow alcove adjoined with a pillar carved in honor of Queen Teriya's coronation. Asya knew she should take her time, examine the entrance and keep an eye out for anything untoward.

But she found herself moving toward the door anyway. She'd already made up her mind.

The key fit into the lock easily and clicked open with a fluidity that suggested it had been used far more recently than Queen Teriya's time.

It led into a tight space that could hardly be called a passageway. For once, Asya was grateful for her shortness, as the top of her head only just brushed the low ceiling. She didn't dare conjure any flames, instead feeling her way along through the darkness.

The tunnel narrowed the farther she walked and she forced herself to keep count of her breaths, to remind herself that there was still a way out behind her.

Then it ended abruptly in thick metal bars.

For a sickening moment, Asya thought she'd walked right back into her own cage.

But these bars weren't gleaming firestone, they were rusted iron, and they gave way under her touch. A small grate in the wall, one that led right out onto the winding platform of the dungeons.

Despite the rust, it moved just as silently as the first door had.

It put her in a different place than she'd come to the other day. Rather than at the base of the wooden platform that wrapped around the interior, she was already part way up it, in line with one of the swinging cages.

An empty one—to her relief. She could see Yuliana's cage above her, the outline of the strashe's body against the light. But she didn't go that way.

She wasn't quite ready to face Yuliana yet. To show her

this bright possibility of freedom she couldn't take. Asya had her hood raised and hoped that from this distance Yuliana wouldn't be able to pick her out, wouldn't sense any of Asya's betrayal.

Instead, she turned right, down the winding platform and toward the only other occupied cage.

Vibishop Sanislav sat as if receiving worshippers after a particularly devout service. His expression was serene, hands gently folded in his lap. Completely at odds with the dungeon around them.

"An honor indeed," he said with no hint of surprise. Either Asya was still that easy to predict or Sanislav was so used to the turbulence of the court that he let nothing faze him.

She hoped it was the latter.

"So," he went on, taking command of the conversation even in this strange circumstance. "To what do I owe the pleasure?"

Asya swallowed, deciding not to bother with forced niceties and get straight to the point. "You told me that there are several saints' relics in the cathedral, including Saint Korona's cloak of leaves."

"Yes." He didn't expand, didn't ask why Asya had come all this way for such a benign question. It set her a little on edge, as if he knew far more than he was letting on.

"Do you know if the cathedral also holds a book of hers? Bound in leaves, just like her cloak."

He held her gaze steadily. "I believe so."

"Where is it?"

"In the cathedral," he said, in that same frustratingly placid tone.

"*Where* in the cathedral?"

"I'm sure—" Sanislav broke off, catching Asya's expression. "Ah yes, Bishop Deryev is not a friend of the Firebird, is he?" He inclined his head to her, as if they shared some great secret. "Not like me. I was always happy to work in the Firebird's best interests."

Asya didn't point out the obvious lie in that. The court certainly had very different ideas than she did on what constituted a person's best interests.

But she jumped on the opportunity. "You'll tell me, then? As it is in the Firebird's *best interests*."

"Of course." His thin lips curled into a smile. "But I would ask for something in return. You, of all people, know all things must have a price."

She held up the key. "This will open your cage."

He wrinkled his nose in distaste. "To live my life as a criminal."

"I could exonerate you," Asya added quickly, anticipating this request. Izaveta wouldn't be best pleased to have to go back on her accusation, but she'd find some way to spin it. Besides, without this book Izaveta might not *be* anything ever again. "I'd tell the truth of what happened on Saints' Night."

Sanislav didn't reply. Asya clasped her hands together, the key digging into her flesh as she willed herself not to fidget. She'd expected him to leap at that chance, but instead he was considering her as if he'd found he had overestimated her and was disappointed with the reality.

It reminded her too much of Tarya.

"Isn't that what you want?" Asya pressed, unable to stand the waiting silence.

"If the gods desired me free from this cage, then I would be."

Asya didn't know if he truly believed that or if it was simply his way of not telling her the whole truth, but she didn't like the slight slant to his words. Another meaning she felt she was missing.

"Though, I would be happy to tell you where Saint Korona's book is," he went on, "if you tell me what spell your sister cast."

Asya felt her mouth go slack. She'd thought she had anticipated what he'd ask for—at least vaguely guessed. But why in all the gods' names did he want that?

The one thing she had refused to share with anyone. The one piece of Izaveta she still felt she could protect. The one piece that no one else was owed.

"She's gone," Asya said, not quite managing to keep the tremor from her voice. "What does it matter to you?"

He raised an eyebrow. "I could ask you the same question."

Asya held his gaze, too many thoughts flying through her mind. Did it matter? It was giving ammunition to someone who certainly held no love for Izaveta. But then, what did any of that *matter* if Izaveta was truly dead?

But it was still her sister's memory. And Asya hated to think of Izaveta remembered only for that, for one disastrous act of desperation.

Asya didn't want this choice. It veered far too deep into politics and lies and manipulations, territory where she could never find a sure footing. She could claim it was all in the name of making things better—but hadn't her sister thought that? Every time Izaveta had done terrible things, she'd had that justification. She'd told Asya as much. Even the spell that killed their mother was to keep Asya safe.

Perhaps this was just how it started. With all these good intentions, then one small step and you couldn't stop yourself from falling.

That was when the screaming began.

CHAPTER TWENTY-TWO

Asya didn't hesitate to think how it would look, for her to come careening down the stairs from the inside of the dungeons when no one had admitted her. She simply moved on instinct.

The first thing she took in was the blood. The second was the acrid burn of magic in the air. Mingling with the metallic blood, it was so sharp it almost made her stumble back.

A body lay on the ground. It was immediately obvious that it was a *body* and no longer a person. A deep gash in their neck had turned the frozen ground a too-bright crimson. Judging from the clothes, it was a member of court. Someone who should never have been in harm's way.

A few paces away, the silver-gray uniform of a strashe lay facedown.

A sick wave of nausea rolled through Asya. She took a step forward, hands reaching out to turn them over, to see if there was anything she could do, when she saw what was different about the strashe.

There was no blood there. No piercing wound or slumped corpse, but ridged lines cracking across their skin.

Another scream rent the air and Asya whirled around.

Close to the line of the trees, she could see several figures.

They were cowering against trunks, only holding up hands against a blade. And the person bearing down on them also wore that silver-gray uniform.

Even from a distance, the strashe's movements were wrong.

She ran toward them, the frantic beat of the Firebird's wings pounding in time with her heart. She stepped quickly between the strashe's weapon and the would-be victims—the Firebird had far less to fear from steel.

"It's all right," Asya said, trying to keep her voice low and soothing. "We can help you."

The strashe looked just as those corpses had in the cabinet room, yet he was clearly still alive.

That same strange frost creeping through his veins, the color siphoned from his eyes to leave only a pinprick of black. For an instant, she thought she saw something else—the sharp edge of something catching in the light. But it was gone too quickly for her to be sure.

It was nothing like the whirling magic that had consumed the banewolf's eyes. Nothing like the chaotic release of that storm above the Elmer.

She took a slow step forward, positioning herself between the strashe and the two courtiers. The strashe matched her, his movements strangely fluid, so at odds to the ice spreading through him.

"We can take you to the voye," Asya said, still soothing. "We might—"

He didn't even register that she'd spoken, raising his znaya with a look of mingled terror and rage contorting his features.

Asya only just drew her shashka in time. Their blades clashed together, perilously close to the exposed skin of her throat.

He attacked with a ferocity she hadn't been anticipating. Even in moments when she'd been fighting for her life, she hadn't faced an opponent who flung themselves into a battle with so little self-preservation.

It put her immediately on the back foot, forcing her to defend against the barrage, with no openings to rebuff.

"Go get the strashe!" she yelled over her shoulder, not able to turn enough to see if the courtiers were even listening.

She used her retreat to get out of the open and into the tangle of trees where she could get better cover and slow the strashe's advances.

He followed, his blade plunging into the bark of a tree where her head had been only moments before. It took him precious moments to pull it free and Asya seized her chance. She dodged around him, aiming for his legs as her breath sang in her lungs. She caught him behind the knees and his weight went out from under him, sending him crashing to the ground.

It was almost a relief to fight—to *do* something, instead of being forced into strange conversations that doubled as battle-grounds. Though Asya began to rethink that as the strashe lashed out at her from the ground, somehow still holding his znaya. Not even trying to regain his feet, he slashed at Asya's ankles. Almost animalistic in his movements.

She danced back again, skipping over roots to provide cover. Her best chance was to disarm him—but he wasn't giving her breath to go on the offensive.

Nothing held him back. Not the sting of sharp twigs snapping against his face or the threat of Asya's blade.

She let out a burst of flame, but he barely noticed the sizzling fire as it flared past him. She let out another, white-hot and close enough to singe his skin. Blisters seared across his left side, angry and exposed beneath the charred fabric of his uniform.

Still, he pressed forward.

What was this magic that had consumed him—this curse or imbalance that no one had ever seen before?

Tarya had always said there was no such thing as evil magic and good magic, there was only magic and the various ways it could be used. But this *felt* evil. A wrongness in the strashe's staring eyes and twisted anger.

He lunged again, blade slicing through the air. There was a wildness to his movements, a desperation that drove each blow.

She ducked, using the trees to shield herself. Branches and twigs cracked behind her with terrifying ferocity as the strashe kept coming.

There was only so much Asya could do when she was holding back. Just like when those order members had attacked her in the gardens, she still wasn't using her full power. Still the weak, afraid girl.

No, she wasn't afraid this time. She was careful. They needed him alive. The bodies had shown them nothing, but this might help them discern a cause. Perhaps even a cure.

This wasn't weakness. It was far harder to control this fight without resorting to death. And no more innocent people needed to die from this.

But the Firebird could still help without resorting to destruction.

The thought had barely crossed her mind when the Firebird rose, as if it had been waiting for just this moment. It was a tight space, trunks pressing close on either side. But fire didn't need space the way a solid thing did, the way the arc of a blade needed room to find its mark. Fire could carve its own path.

The strashe's expression didn't change, none of the mingled wonder and horror that mortals usually showed when first faced with the Firebird.

With the Firebird roaring through her veins, she could reach out with its senses too. Not overtaken by the flames, but working in tandem. She felt rather than saw where the strashe's znaya would fall, the slightest ripple in the air. She swung round and the blade missed her by a hair, its momentum sending it toward the knotted roots of a thick tree.

It gave her the briefest opening. She reached out, not for the strashe but for the znaya, the sharp metal biting into her palms. The Firebird reached out too. Flames licked along the blade, eager, as if the metal were kindling. Blood seeped between Asya's fingers, but she didn't let go. The Firebird did the rest for her. It knew what she wanted, understanding her as easily as she now understood it.

The rope of flame—almost solid against the strashe's arm—twisted at the same moment Asya kicked out. The znaya flew free, its gleaming blade now tarnished black. In the same breath, Asya let the Firebird's wings stretch out farther. They curled around the strashe to form a burning wall of brightest gold. Protection for the strashe, more than for Asya.

Weaponless and caught in a fiery cage, some of the strashe's desperation ebbed away. As if now that he could not quite see Asya—could not see anyone—he no longer felt the need to attack. He looked almost entranced by the flames, though they did nothing to ease the spread of frost across his cheeks.

Asya was breathing heavily, her hands slick with blood even as the wounds already knitted closed. She saw now there were people all around. Silver flashes of strashe along with curiously scared courtiers and even some of Azarov's crimson guards. There'd be no stopping the rumors now, the panic, as clashing accounts of what had happened here got out.

Through the golden flicker of flames, she saw the cursed strashe's lips were moving. He was saying something, so soft it was barely audible over the spitting fire. Asya took a step forward, careful to still keep her distance.

"You can fix this." The strashe's voice was an anguished hiss, the same quality as extinguished flames. "Will you pay the price? Did you—"

It happened so quickly it almost seemed frozen, each moment separate rather than part of the whole. The slash of a blade. A thin line of red—so insignificant. Then the strashe's head tumbled to the ground.

The flames that had surrounded him faded, Asya's shock swallowing them too.

She stared up at General Azarov, his sword raised, streaked now with the strashe's blood.

"Why did you do that?" she yelled, adrenaline still bursting from the fight. "We could have helped him—he could have helped us!"

Azarov wiped his blade on the grass before neatly returning it to his waist. "He was a threat."

"He was unarmed and captured," Asya sputtered, still staring at the place where the strashe had stood only breaths ago.

"We cannot risk the Firebird's life," Azarov said, his voice raised to ensure all the onlookers could hear. "Even the most minor of threats cannot be ignored."

A convenient moment for Azarov to decide he cared about the Firebird.

Asya couldn't speak for the rage clogging her throat. Not only had that been a lead—a possible answer to whatever this magic was or proof it was Azarov's doing—they had been a person. A victim as much as anyone else.

Strashe were moving in now, examining the body and the scorched earth around it. All giving Asya a wide berth. She didn't see why, given it was Azarov who had just murdered one of their number.

Despite that—despite the spots of blood still shining on his otherwise pristine blade—they still looked to the general as a hero.

The general looked just the same as he had only days before when he'd insisted she join him for tea. As if the beheaded body at his feet were no more than a felled tree.

Asya suddenly felt sick. Bile churned in her stomach, the air around her too hot to breathe. Was this how it would always be? No matter what she tried, monstrous things would still follow her. This was the role in which she'd been cast and there was no undoing it. No railing against her fate.

She'd barely paid attention to the morbid audience that had gathered, horror-struck courtiers unable to look away, until Bishop Deryev pushed through their midst. He bowed to Azarov, drawing everyone's eye with the unnecessarily grand gesture. "General, you saved us."

Asya let out a choked sound, a hollow laugh. Deryev hadn't even been here, and Azarov was still the person Asya thought most likely to have caused all of this.

"I only did what was right," Azarov replied, performing for the waiting crowd.

"The gods smile upon you in our hour of need. You have always done so much for Tóurin even without recognition."

Asya felt it coming then. An already-rehearsed line, the actor ready for their part. But she couldn't tear her eyes away from the bloodstained grass. The patch of blond hair that could have still been alive and breathing.

There was no more for her to feel. No space left for surprise. Even when the bishop declared Tsiviya Azarov his candidate for queen.

Chapter Twenty-Three

The passage of time was difficult to mark in this tomb with no changes to the dingy light. Food appeared in the wake of that sleeping powder but at such irregular intervals Izaveta couldn't begin to gauge the gaps.

When Kyriil returned, Izaveta should have been ready for him. She should have used the time—however long it was—to prepare a new line of attack. She knew what he wanted, at least partly, and should have been able to work out some strategy.

But what did she have left to fight with?

The throbbing pain in her finger, the empty nail bed, was a constant reminder that she had no power here. Nothing to bargain with when the world believed her dead.

Or perhaps it was as Kyriil said, and the hollow space where her heart had been had finally decided to give up all pretense.

She didn't even bother getting up this time, didn't bother to engage in the fruitless cordiality of it all.

"I trust you've had some time to think," he said. She didn't reply, her one weapon had already proved useless.

Kyriil bent down to the floor again, sweeping his hand across the grime to reveal that shimmering window. Izaveta braced herself, but the view of the palace did not knock the air out of her as it had before. She was so separate from it here, it hardly felt real.

It didn't show gleaming marble walls and bustling courtiers this time—it didn't even show Asya, though the place was instantly familiar. The walled area of the gardens, where Izaveta had first cast that spell, desperately scrambling with the saint's bone as magic slipped through her fingers.

It was not empty in this shining window as it had been then, though it was clearly full dark. The glint of strashe and soft colors of winter furs were all Izaveta could catch.

"I don't know what use there is in showing me this," she said, defeat weighing down her words.

"Consider it motivation. It's tiring watching you wallow."

Despite herself, Izaveta leaned toward it. There was something not quite right about the scene, but from this angle it was impossible to tell what.

Then her eye caught on a lone figure, at the base of one of the towering statues. The slant of their body wasn't quite right. The realization hit Izaveta in a wave of slow-building horror. It wasn't the red of fabric that speckled the snow, but blood. And the image was not frozen or slow-moving—the people were.

She stared up at Kyriil. "What did you do to them?"

"*This* is not my doing." He almost sounded offended at the accusation, ridiculous amidst all his other wrongs. "This all ties back to you. To the selfishness of the Karasova queens."

"A convenient lie to absolve any guilt," Izaveta spat, a little of that anger resurging. "If you know so much about this all, then why not fix it?"

He smiled. "There we are, that's more like it."

Izaveta's jaw clenched, that smile cold and unpleasant against her skin.

"And I am trying to fix it," he went on, with a magnanimous glint. "You're the one standing in the way of that."

"You must *know* where the crown is," Izaveta snapped. "I doubt it has vanished since my coronation. Not that it would help you and whatever ridiculous ambitions you have."

"Not the ceremonial crown." Kyriil spoke as if explaining something very simple to a child. "The real one."

"The—" Izaveta broke off, catching herself before she could give anything else away. She wasn't taking the time to think, to calculate each response, and it could very soon cost her.

But Kyriil read the ignorance from her face. "Your mother never explained it to you? You never wondered at the unyielding rule of the Karasova queens?"

The answer to both was no, but Izaveta did not voice that aloud. It was a ridiculous question in any case. The Karasova line had ruled for so long because of their political prowess, the way each mother passed their scheming to their daughters.

Kyriil turned to leave, hand reaching for the sleeping powder. "Think on it."

Izaveta pulled herself to her feet, relieved at least for the fuel anger gave her. "How do I know any of this is real?" She gestured to the now-fading window beneath them. "That this isn't all part of some ploy to manipulate me?"

Kyriil watched her for a moment, considering. "A fair question." He moved more quickly than Izaveta would have thought possible, too fast for her to react. A ring gleamed on his hand, an unnatural light in this dark, as he grasped her arm. "How about I show you?"

And he dragged her into nothingness.

CHAPTER TWENTY-FOUR

The past few days, ever since Azarov's demand, Asya had been actively avoiding her aunt—sure Tarya would be able to read her shortcomings in an instant.

But tonight, after everything Asya had seen, she couldn't put it off any longer. Tarya was still the former Firebird, and if anyone might know more about this magic, it was her. So Asya had left a note in her aunt's chambers. She hadn't explained the details of why she needed to speak to Tarya—if her aunt realized what this was about, she might refuse to come.

She might refuse to come anyway. Asya wrapped a loose thread around her finger, pulling it taut as her nerves. She and Nikov stood in the darkened passageway, a few paces from the arched door that led out to the western-facing grounds. The bodies had been left there, this time, as if they feared that bringing them into the palace might invite in more of that magic.

At precisely the time Asya had requested, Tarya emerged from the shadows.

She didn't greet Asya—the formal *Firebird* would have felt strange from her aunt's lips and Asya's name had always sounded like an admonition. She didn't even acknowledge Nikov at Asya's side.

"I suppose we'll have to go outside," her aunt said simply. "To examine these bodies."

Asya's lips parted in surprise, then snapped shut as Tarya's gaze snagged on her. Asya should have expected that. Tarya had always known everything going on around her, even if she chose to keep herself out of it.

"Yes," Asya said, as if that hadn't just thrown her carefully rehearsed explanation out the window.

Tarya stepped toward the door, though she hadn't come alone. Zvezda trailed in her wake, a dark scarf tied around her braids to obscure any hint of the glinting gold threaded through her hair.

Tarya answered Asya's wordless question with a raised eyebrow. "How else were you planning on opening the door?"

Asya twisted her fingers together. She hadn't even thought of the locked door, of the strashevsta's command so many hours ago to keep everyone inside while they searched for any perpetrator. Asya hadn't thought much beyond getting her aunt to agree. Any other problem seemed small compared to that.

Zvezda stepped forward, before Asya could even ask why the spymaster had agreed to help them, and unlocked the door.

CHAPTER TWENTY-FIVE

It took Izaveta three staggering breaths to come back to herself, to begin to undo the tight clamp of fear that had seized around her throat. She wasn't coming undone, not again. She was whole—well, almost.

She forced herself to straighten, to take in her surroundings and not let that edge of panic cloud her mind.

For all her questions of illusion, this certainly felt real.

They stood close to the tree line, and in front of them, the Palace of Three Skies speared through the night. It looked so unchanged, the gleaming spires and whorls of ornamentation just as they'd always been. A lump rose in her throat, a feeling she found she could not quite name.

How? floated on her lips, swallowed by shock and confusion.

Kyriil adjusted the ring on his finger. "You know the power of a saint's relic, don't you?"

"Saint Ilyova," Izaveta murmured. The woman who had asked the gods to grant her passage through the stars. Another impossibility. Though Izaveta likely had to reconsider that word—so many impossibilities had built around her since her mother's death that they could hardly be called *impossible* anymore.

Kyriil kept a tight grip on her arm as he led her forward, but her mind was already racing ahead. If she was *here*, then there had to be a way to get a message to someone—anyone. If they knew she was alive, then so much of Kyriil's power over her would dwindle.

She had nothing beyond the ragged dress she wore, even her feet were bare, already numb from the cold of that tomb. Surely there was some way she could leave a mark, any hint that could give her hope.

But all thoughts of that evaporated as they stepped through the trees to a manicured clearing. The saints stood round in silent vigil over the massacre. Izaveta had never seen anything like this.

Those standing were clearly dead, but not in the absent way of corpses Izaveta had seen before. For one, they had a feeling of momentum abruptly cut short. Dolls discarded by an invisible hand at the last moment. Frozen veins gouged across their skin, as if the statue of Saint Lyoza had sprung to life and torn at them with her claws.

Beneath the frozen strashe, blood dappled the ground. Izaveta remembered what she'd seen in that parlor, how the strashe had turned on Asya before their abrupt halt. The same had clearly happened here, with passing courtiers caught in the violence.

She turned slowly to Kyriil. "What is this?"

"You wanted to know if it was real."

She had, in the hopes she might call his bluff. Not so she'd be trapped in this horror too, unable to turn away.

"Do you want to put a stop to it now? Do you want to tell me the truth?"

She *had* told him the truth, much good that had done her. She was in the dark here too. Whatever crown he imagined, she'd never heard of it. Her mother had never so much as mentioned it.

"You're supposed to be so clever, aren't you?" he asked. "So what's the answer?"

She was, wasn't she? That was the thing she'd always relied on. She'd enjoyed the challenge of a problem to solve, the way the intricate threads could be untangled. It wasn't quite the same when she was caught at its center.

A noise drew her attention and her head snapped around. Soft footfalls against the frozen earth, slowly drawing closer.

"It's through this way." A voice that was achingly familiar.

Izaveta lurched forward. *"Asya!"*

But the cry never left her lips. Kyriil struck first, one hand tight around her throat, the other twisting her arm back. Izaveta kicked out, thrashing against his grip. Nothing had felt this clear since she'd awoken in that room, but now the fierce need to get to her sister pierced through the veil. Torment and desperation bouncing around the hollow space inside her.

Izaveta got the barest glimpse of her sister, the edge of her red hair, before she was torn away again.

The stone walls of the entombing prison slammed around her and she staggered forward as Kyriil released her, still reaching for the thing that was no longer there.

"No!" She whirled on Kyriil, a storm crashing in her head. "Asya—Asya was there—you—"

She launched herself at him, no plan in mind beyond frantic retribution. She barely landed a single blow before he caught her wrists, easily holding her in place.

"Interesting," he said, infuriatingly calm to the torrid anguish in Izaveta's veins. "You must be trying so hard to hold on to these emotions for your sister. But don't worry, they'll fade soon too."

Izaveta let out a huffing breath, somewhere between a yell and a sob. She didn't like this pain, the agony of being so close to Asya and then ripped away again, but the idea of it going was infinitely worse. Of watching all that love wither away as her mind forgot how it felt to have a heart.

"What are you?" Izaveta wasn't quite sure where the question came from: the sudden and disconcerting way shadows shifted across Kyriil's face, or the changes wrought on him, or this magic she could not explain.

He tilted his head, his usually bright green eyes oddly colorless in the dark. "Finally asking the right questions, Izaveta."

But he didn't answer, didn't give her anything more than an appraising look as he threw the sleeping powder into the air. The last thought Izaveta was able to grasp was a fragment of hope—no bigger than the scrap of her dress she'd managed to leave in the clearing.

CHAPTER TWENTY-SIX

Everything was eerily quiet, no wind rustling through the grass even as clouds gathered overhead. The three moons were obscured, only a trickling of their light seeping through, as if the gods couldn't bear to look down at this destruction. Asya could see why.

The bodies had been left to the open air. They should've been covered in a shroud. Something sewn with blessings, like Asya's mother's had been. That would ensure their souls were already resting in Dveda's embrace, prepared to return to the earth. Instead, they had been left here. Abandoned, as if they didn't matter.

Asya lit a small flame in her palm, bright against the muted moons. It cast ghastly light across the corpses. They looked worse, somehow, in this flickering darkness. It twisted them into something inhuman, as if they'd never been mortal beings at all. Demonye stepping out of a children's book and into this world.

Tarya cast an eye over them before looking to Asya. If her aunt was surprised or horrified by the sight, she didn't show it.

"We—" Asya caught herself "—*I* wanted to work out what happened to them. The cabinet thought it might have some connection to the Firebird, or those strange instances during the mourning days. I think people blame me—blame the Firebird.

"And…" Asya's resolve was flagging. The certainty in her voice ebbing away in the face of her aunt's disapproval. Before, she would have let her words fade away. Let Tarya stare her into silence. But Asya pressed on, "I want to help if I can. I want them to see that the Firebird can help."

"You cannot," Tarya said flatly, turning away from the corpses as if they were no more interesting than the surrounding trees. "It does not concern you, or the Firebird's duty."

Asya gaped for a moment. She shouldn't have been thrown by her aunt's immediate dismissal, not after years of Tarya intoning the importance of duty above all. The importance of casting aside any mortal ties, any weaknesses. Asya glanced at Nikov, who gave her a small nod of encouragement.

"But what if it does?" Asya caught Tarya's arm, turning her back toward them. "And what if there's something I can do? The Firebird should protect, shouldn't she? Isn't that what you've always said?"

"You can't protect people who are already dead." There was a weight to her words, an inflection that implied she didn't just mean these strashe.

"Then, why did you agree to meet me here?" Asya threw out, frustration thrumming in her veins. "If you knew what this was about, why did you bother?"

Tarya fixed her with a look. A familiar, long-suffering expression. "I made my thoughts clear when you decided to remain here. I had hoped you might change your mind."

"I won't leave when there's still a chance I could help." Help stop this happening again, help Yuliana, somehow help Izaveta—*anything*.

"Even at risk to the Firebird? At risk of shirking your duty?"

"Yes." The Firebird was Asya's power now, hers to use in

the best way she could. And she wouldn't use it as a reason to abandon people in need.

Tarya sighed, reading the rest of Asya's thoughts in her silence. "You have always cared too much."

Asya rocked back on her heels. She couldn't hide the sting of that—of course she couldn't. Because she *cared too much.* Izaveta had said as much in their fight. That last real conversation they'd had before the price.

To Asya's surprise, Zvezda saved her from answering. "I remember someone else who cared too much."

An expression shuddered across Tarya's face—such an unusual crack in her stone facade that Asya was sure she'd imagined it. "And look where that got her."

But Zvezda held Tarya's gaze, some unspoken thing passing between them.

When Tarya turned back to Asya, the intensity of her expression had simmered down to nothing. The usual weathered marble Asya was used to.

"I don't believe this is a spell," her aunt said, her tone measured and even. Asya wasn't sure if she imagined the slight strain in Tarya's neck. Holding herself a little too carefully. "It could not have been cast by an individual."

"Even someone using others to complete it?" Asya asked, thinking of Azarov.

Tarya frowned. "The caster would need to be nearby, so unless those bodies are hidden among these, then it is unlikely. And you haven't felt a Calling or sensed any magic."

Not quite a question, but Asya nodded anyway.

"Could it have been disrupted?" Zvezda asked. "Or somehow obscured from the Firebird?"

"No." Tarya kept her eyes fixed on Asya. "Therefore, it is of no concern to the Firebird."

But Asya wasn't listening. "If it's not a spell," she said slowly, turning the words over in her mind. "And it's not an imbalance. Then, what is it?"

Only blank faces looked back at her. No answers in the wake of this destruction.

"We should go before the strashe patrol again," Zvezda said with a glance over her shoulder.

Asya nodded, her throat stuck. She was about to walk past the statue of Saint Lyoza, back into the trees, when something snagged at the corner of her vision. The opposite of the thing she'd found last time she was in these gardens—that scrap of bone connected to a spell. This was dark, only standing out against the pale frost.

Asya bent down to pick it up, letting the others move on ahead.

A small scrap of black velvet, not that uncommon amidst the grandeur of the palace. But it held a familiarity. Instantly conjured the memory of Izaveta in her black coronation dress surrounded by flames.

That wasn't possible. This fabric had lain above the layer of frost, untouched by the forest beneath. It couldn't have been preserved like that ever since the coronation. But black was an unusual color for a courtier to wear.

Asya turned slowly, her sister's name rising to her lips. But the surrounding forest was just as empty and quiet as before.

Asya told her fingers to let it go, to drop it to the ground as no more than the debris it was. But she couldn't quite bring herself to. Instead, she slipped it into her pocket. A reminder and, perhaps, a promise.

When Tarya and Zvezda were a little way ahead, out of earshot, Asya caught Nikov's arm. "It's time we get Saint Korona's book."

No matter the price.

CHAPTER TWENTY-SEVEN

Asya didn't return to her chambers. Instead, she picked a quiet path through the palace back to Zmenya's Tower. To the same secret passageway the key opened. But this time, she did not turn right along the teetering walkway down to Sanislav.

She had to go speak to him, she'd made her decision already, but there was something else she wanted—*needed*—to do first.

The key felt heavy in her hand as she reached Yuliana's cage. Weak moonlight filtered through the open dome, weaving silver into her dark hair like a spattering of stardust.

Asya hesitated, entranced by the way that light danced across Yuliana's skin. The sharp planes of her face and curve of her back as she hunched against the bars. Asya had only ever seen Yuliana like this in glimpses before. Brief moments between her stone-sure precision.

It made Asya's heart twist. A painful lurch in her chest to see Yuliana laid so bare—so vulnerable.

Asya must have made a sound, because Yuliana's head snapped up, an immediate caution in her eyes. Their last conversation flickered between them, Yuliana's certainty that Asya shouldn't forgive her.

Asya didn't wait for Yuliana to stand up, instead lowering

herself onto the edge of the platform. Her feet dangled down into the nothingness of the tower, but it felt more familiar. It put only a little space between them, even if that space were a freefall. She could almost pretend they were somewhere else.

"I brought you a fresh bandage."

The corner of Yuliana's lip hitched. "Better than a torn shirt, I suppose."

Asya's cheeks heated as that memory hit her. A strange reversal of now, when the strashe had offered to bandage the wound in Asya's side. The first moment she'd seen something else in Yuliana, the first spark of something *more*.

Asya pulled out the bandage—slipped from the Voya Wing while the medics were on their rounds. Yuliana reached out her uninjured hand for it. "I can do it."

But Asya shook her head. Yuliana watched her for a long moment. The slight gleam of humor was gone from her face and that caution was back. Asya hated that—hated the doubt trembling between them.

Then Yuliana held her other hand out through the bars. With Asya perched on the very edge of the platform, she only had to lean forward a little to close the distance. The chain that held the cage creaked, swinging closer as Asya clasped Yuliana's hand.

Carefully, like cradling a newborn bird, Asya began to unwind the bandage. It had obviously been done hastily, likely not changed since the wound was fresh. She kept her eyes down but felt Yuliana's gaze on her bowed head.

The final pieces of bandage fluttered free and Asya froze, her hands still gently encircling Yuliana's.

The fourth finger on her left hand was entirely gone. Dried blood caked the skin around it in thick rivulets. A scabbed mess closed over the wound, perhaps branded to stop the bleeding but still seeping scarlet drops. The svash had been sharp, but the cut was clearly not clean. Jagged and tearing to get through flesh and bone.

Asya's lips parted, her stomach swooping. She saw the flash of the knife in her mind. Remembered the Firebird pressing against her skin, screaming to break free.

Yuliana must have read her thoughts on her face as she said, "Don't you dare apologize."

Asya swallowed the apology already working its way up her throat. She glanced up at Yuliana, but she couldn't read the expression in the strashe's shadowed eyes.

Asya reached for a small vial of water and a cloth—also courtesy of her trip to the Voya Wing. Her touch was gentle as she cleaned off the blood, yet each brush of their bare skin tingled up her arm. When she'd finished with that, she drew out her final bit of plunder from the voye: a salve of chamomile and ashwing feathers.

"It should help with the pain," she said, still not quite looking up.

There wasn't much else she could do about the wound itself—Asya was far from a medic—so she smoothed the salve across Yuliana's palm and around the angry red of the wound.

Pitifully little in light of the severity, but it was the best Asya could do.

She wound the fresh bandage back around, trying to keep it in neat rings that would allow for some movement. When she finished she couldn't quite bring herself to let go of Yuliana's hand. A protection that came far too late.

But Yuliana didn't pull away. She reached out with her other hand to cup Asya's cheek, tilting Asya's face up toward hers. There was still so much holding them apart, but in that instant, it all vanished. As intimate as they'd been on Saints' Night, before everything had gone wrong.

"Is that better?" Asya asked, tentative.

Yuliana nodded, her right hand sliding down to join the other, clasping tight around Asya's fingers. "Thank you."

Just two words—two very simple words—but so much more was threaded into them. So much more that Asya didn't deserve.

This time, Asya pulled away, curling her arms back around herself. "You didn't ask me how I got in here."

"No." There was no accusation in that word.

"Your brother gave me a key," Asya said, "and showed me a way in that the strashe don't know about."

Yuliana let out a soft exhale. Asya didn't know if it was in relief or surprise, but she didn't want to give Yuliana a moment of false hope.

Yet Asya still couldn't meet her eye as she forced the words out, bitter on her tongue. "But I can't help you escape."

"I know."

Asya looked up at her, lips slightly parted.

"I was a strashe, wasn't I?" Yuliana asked. "And I'm not a fool. There are too many moving pieces. Even with the Firebird, an escape may not work. Besides, you can't leave any hope of your sister behind. I wouldn't want that."

Asya stared at her. At this girl who had somehow put Asya's thoughts into words, who had read Asya's true meaning and still not turned away from her. There was no hint of fear or anger in Yuliana's eyes. Asya had imagined her eyes so much these past days, imagined the storm brewing in them.

But now they were soft and vulnerable, looking at Asya as if Yuliana were the first person to understand both parts, the monster and the girl.

"Asya." Yuliana grabbed her hand through the bars again, her grip firm. "You know I wouldn't take it back, don't you?"

Asya didn't move, not quite sure what she meant.

"My father, the Elmer, *this*." Yuliana gestured at the bars over her head. "I wouldn't take any of it back. Perhaps that makes me the monster, because I'd be willing for all those terrible things to happen again. Because in the end, it all led me to you."

Asya pulled Yuliana's hands closer, the chain of the cage tilting. The bars were too close together to truly reach Yuliana, but Asya pressed her forehead against them anyway and Yuliana mirrored the movement.

"I wouldn't either," Asya murmured.

She didn't know how long they sat there, encased in a strangely warm silence, each anchoring the other in ways they didn't quite understand. But when the pale gray of dawn began to creep across the open dome again, Asya forced herself to her feet.

The time they'd had felt like stolen minutes—and Asya couldn't risk more. There was still a bargain she had to strike, a piece of her sister that she would give up for a slim chance.

"I'll be back," Asya said softly. "I promise."

Yuliana smiled then. Tired and strained, a little frayed at the edges, but the expression still sent sparks surging through Asya's veins. "I know you will."

As she walked back down toward Sanislav and his waiting price, she tried to hold on to some of the warmth Yuliana's smile had left with her.

But even that couldn't overshadow the betrayal of telling Sanislav the truth of what Izaveta had done.

CHAPTER TWENTY-EIGHT

The heist—there really was no dissuading Nikov once he set his mind to something—was simple enough in theory. The difficulty lay in the number of moving parts. It wasn't as simple as following a Calling to the single person who owed a price, it was a hundred Callings moving in discordant symphony. One small misstep would ruin it all.

According to Sanislav and the information Asya had bartered for with Izaveta's secret, they had to enter the cathedral in daylight, as it was locked every evening when the sun passed the silhouette of the palace and only reopened once light hit the domes once again in the morning. That meant they couldn't avoid clergymen and other acolytes, or likely Bishop Deryev with his disapproving frown.

But if Asya had learned anything from her time in the palace, it was that gossip would always draw attention. All it took was some letters sent the night before, some left in obvious places where a curious strashe might glance at them. Some sent in very loud whispers by Nikov, making it clear who the recipient was.

The letters didn't even say much more than a few lines of pleasantries. But the content didn't matter so much as the intrigue around them. All sealed with Tarya's crest and sent to entirely contradictory factions. Asya knew how much people wanted Tarya to fall in with their ideas of what a person *should* do, and this made it seem like she had. Like the former Firebird was finally engaging in politics—and that could hold great sway.

Sure enough, when soft smudges of dawn drew across the cathedral the next morning and the doors were flung open, Deryev was already ensconced in deep discussions with Conze Bazin. It wasn't long before the two of them headed back toward the palace, several acolytes in tow.

Asya and Nikov waited behind one of the manicured hedges, hidden well enough by the foliage that no passersby would spot them. Once the two cabinet members had vanished into the distance and the path seemed clear of any prying eyes, Asya nodded to Nikov. "I think we can go in."

Nikov didn't seem to hear her. He was running a thumb over the back of his knuckles in an unsteady rhythm, unusually agitated—especially as stealing the book had been his idea.

"Are you all right?" Asya whispered.

Nikov jumped, as if only just noticing his twitching hands. He clenched them firmly at his side. "Yes, I—" He shook his head, in contradiction to his words. "Yes. Let's go."

He hurried off in the direction of the cathedral before Asya could ask if he was sure. She didn't want to push anyone into doing something they didn't want to. She was fine taking the risk for herself, but she would not drag anyone else into danger with her. The cabinet had made it clear that their patience was running thin and his presence here could easily be revoked. Asya didn't want him sent back to the Amarinth in disgrace. Partly a selfish want, a need to not be alone in this.

But by the time she caught up with Nikov, he was already striding through the high-arched doors of the cathedral.

Asya didn't follow him. Instead, she skirted around the side of the towering building, past the stained-glass window of Dveda. It cast multicolored hues across the grass, his judgmental eyes reaching for her.

But there was no room for doubt now.

She walked along the right-hand wall of the cathedral, opposite the smaller building that contained the school for initiates. At the very end, in line with where the altar would be inside the cathedral, Asya stopped. If she hadn't known where to look, she'd never have seen the thin outline of a door, almost hidden in the ivy-clung wall.

According to Sanislav, it served as the acolytes' entrance and only opened from the outside—some symbolism for the acolytes taking their fate into their own hands and entering the cathedral of their own free will. Asya still thought it was a strange design.

But it would help her this morning. As no one could leave by that entrance, there shouldn't be anyone around to see the escape path she had laid. From what she'd seen in her vision, the book was too large to slip easily under a coat, and they couldn't risk someone spotting Nikov with it on the way out.

She pulled the door open a crack, relieved it gave easily under her fingers. No matter his assurances, she didn't trust Sanislav in the slightest. Peering inside she saw a narrow, plainly decorated passage that led straight to the altar. If she strained her ears, she could just hear Nikov's voice.

"It truly is wondrous how much you can see Yerstova's original stylings in the carving, even though they were finished after her death."

"Her apprentices worked without sleep," another voice replied, evidently excited to have someone to talk to. "They used reliefs of her previous works to match the woodcuts exactly."

Nikov had promised he could expound on any subject well enough to engage a member of the clergy, and it seemed he was right.

"I'm impressed," Nikov replied, earnest as ever. "You know more than many of the Amarinth scholars."

"We do a lot of good work here. We even have some of her original designs."

"Oh, I would love to see those," Nikov said, somehow not sounding too eager at the acolyte offering exactly what they needed.

The other voice paused, a little unsure. "They're kept in the cloistered archive. I can't allow anyone else back there."

"Could you bring them out?" A slight hesitation, then Nikov added, "I would love to hear your thoughts on them as a fellow scholar."

That seemed to do it, because the acolyte replied, "I don't see why not. Wait here."

Through the crack in the door, Asya watched as a man in cream robes strode past the altar to the right wing of the cathedral. As soon as he had disappeared down that passage, Nikov moved into view.

He knelt down behind the altar, feeling around. Sanislav had said Saint Korona's book was kept with the other saints' relics in an ornate, concealed box. Where worshippers could imbue the holiness without knowing the relics' true hiding place.

Nikov should be hidden enough from any lurking people in the cathedral. Usually there was only one acolyte tasked with overseeing the altar, and Nikov had got him out of the way. Unless Sanislav had been lying. About any of it—the location of the book, the number of acolytes preparing for morning prayers, the door.

Any number of discordant notes that could throw all of this off.

Something made Asya turn around. Not so much a sound as a feeling, as if the Firebird's senses were reaching out again.

She couldn't abandon the door, otherwise Nikov would be trapped inside with an incriminating book. But if someone walked past now, they'd see anyway.

Adrenaline forcing a decision, she pushed a stick into the crack of the door—enough that Nikov should be able to push it open—while she crept forward to peer around the corner to the back of the cathedral.

She caught a flash of red and gold among the pale grays of dawn. Colors she recognized at once as General Azarov.

He was meant to be off dealing with Tarya. Asya had specifically sent letters to people around him, made sure that his guards overheard. Had he seen through her ploy that easily? Or had Sanislav double-crossed her? It wouldn't be entirely surprising, given their history, for him to go to Azarov and tell him what Asya had asked.

Either way, as soon as he walked around the corner he'd have a clear line of sight to Asya and the slightly ajar door. Not to mention any moment now, Nikov would be emerging from that doorway with the stolen book.

Asya had to redirect the general.

So much for her part not involving dealing with people.

She stepped forward quickly, blocking off his path. "General Azarov," she said, as loudly as she could in the hopes Nikov would hear if he was near. "Good morning."

Azarov stopped, only a few paces from the cornerstone of the cathedral. He didn't seem surprised to see her, more curious at this turn of events. Asya forced her breaths to steady. She couldn't put Nikov in Azarov's path as well.

"Are you not looking for Conze Tarya?" As soon as the words were on her tongue, she knew it was the wrong thing to say. But she couldn't take them back.

"It seems everyone is," the general replied, with a lightness that made Asya sure she'd just given herself away. "And what is the Firebird doing skulking behind the cathedral at this hour?"

For an instant, Asya's mind went blank. She couldn't do this, not with Nikov emerging at any moment and giving them away. Not with this man who held so much over her. She glanced around, desperate for a way out. Perhaps she could let out some trailing sparks, set a bush on fire or—

No. The smug set of Azarov's mouth said he assumed this from Asya, assumed she would be unable to hold her own in this arena. He expected her to feel too much, to cave to his will. So she would just show him what he expected to see.

"I wanted to talk to you," she said quickly.

He raised his bushy eyebrows. "And so you looked for me behind the cathedral? How unusual."

Asya's mouth was dry but she forced out, "I know you're always at morning prayers." She swallowed, trying not to let the ragged edge into her voice. What was it Nikov had done to deflect that bishop? A compliment to draw the attention back on them. "Always so devout," she added. "A worthy quality."

Azarov looked more confused by the statement than flattered, but it worked either way. "Why did you wish to speak with me?" he asked, bored of Asya's awkward attempts at politeness. "Have you done as I ask yet?"

"You would know if I had," Asya replied, unable to keep the irritation from her voice. The death of a member of the cabinet would be enough to wake the entire palace, no matter the hour.

"Then, what is it you want?"

"I want you to let Yuliana go." She probably shouldn't have used Yuliana's name like that, so intimate. But it worked, any hint of suspicion wiped from his expression, replaced with a calculating smile.

"Are you resorting to threats already?"

"No," Asya replied. It was easy to let the shaky edge of fear into her voice, anxiety hummed beneath her skin as it was. "I'm asking you. She's been through enough as it is, she doesn't deserve this."

"Interesting to hear you speak of *deserving*. I thought the Firebird was not in a position to judge?"

He looked like he might walk away then, leaving her with that remark, so Asya hurried on. "Please." It took a marked effort to not glance back and give away what she was protecting. How long until that acolyte returned? If Nikov still had the book then, there'd be no explaining it away.

"I'll be in your debt either way," Asya pressed. "Just... please. Let her go. She has nothing to do with any of this—with politics or magic."

Asya could tell Azarov was enjoying this. Perhaps that was the true secret to all these twisting words and politics: let the other person think they're right about you.

"How unexpectedly polite," the general said, jumping on the chance for a speech—he clearly loved the sound of his own voice. "But you're wrong. You see, she has everything to do with this. You made it so when you marked her as someone important to you. You know all about marks, don't you, Firebird? A stratsviye cannot simply be wiped clean. Neither can this. If anyone brought her into this, it's you."

That caught Asya off guard, a crack of something real through her attempted act. She hadn't thought about it like that before.

He held a hand up toward the sky, as if he could sense oncoming snow in the air. "I doubt you have long, you know. Especially as the cabinet has now ordered her execution."

Asya stared at him, her stomach swooping in very real fear. "What?"

"They decided yesterday, you hadn't heard?" he asked, in a

tone that very much implied he knew he was delivering this news himself. "No other fitting punishment, really, for a traitor."

Asya couldn't fill her lungs enough to speak. As if all the air had suddenly been drained away, leaving her choking. "But—you said you could stop them from sentencing her. That—that was the whole *point*. If she's already been sentenced, then it's too late."

"No," he said evenly. "I said I could keep her safe. And I can. *If* Commander Iveshkin is no longer in the way of my daughter's bid for the throne."

The ground felt like it was tilting beneath Asya's feet. She had read this entirely wrong. She'd thought Azarov already had the power to stay Yuliana's sentence. That was what he had implied—more than implied. That would have left some room for Asya, some fragile hope that there was a way around it.

But if Commander Iveshkin's death was the only thing that would give Azarov that power…then there were no loopholes. No appealing to anyone else or hoping the cabinet might change their minds. It was a simple cause and effect. Kill Iveshkin or Azarov couldn't help her—even if he wanted to. Even if Asya had hoped there was another way to persuade him.

"You said I had until the First Snows," she said, clutching desperately at anything. "You said I had time to decide. But if they've sentenced her—"

"The sentence won't be carried out at once. Though, I suppose, it does add a little pressure to your schedule." Azarov tipped his hat to her, mocking, as he turned back toward the shadow of the palace, his job apparently done.

"Always a pleasure, Firebird," he called over his shoulder, and strode right around the corner before Asya could even try to push him off in a different direction.

Her heart stuttered as she turned to follow, to find some way to distract him again before he saw the door ajar.

But the stick was gone, the door closed, and its seam hidden again by the tangled ivy. Asya could just see a slight protuberance where Nikov must have stashed the book before slipping back inside to await the acolyte's return.

Azarov vanished around the front of the cathedral without another glance back. Satisfied to have left Asya reeling.

She sagged against the wall, caught between defeat and relief. She hadn't had many choices before, but they were narrowing around her with each day. Her fate never truly in her hands but always forced upon her by others.

A few moments later, Nikov hurried around the corner, grinning from ear to ear. "We should do that again." His smile faded as he took in her expression. "What happened?"

Asya just shook her head. She didn't want to think about that now, certainly didn't want to talk about it.

"You got the book—it all worked?" she asked instead, wishing she didn't still sound so ragged.

Nikov picked it up, dusting it off. A solid tome that certainly would not have fit into his breast pocket. "Exactly where he said it would be."

Asya wanted to tear through it at once. To see if it really did hold the only way out of this tightening cage. But they couldn't do it out in the open.

Nikov must've been able to tell from her expression, because he added, "Why don't we continue our crime spree and steal some syrnyki, then go look at this in the library? Everything's better with food."

CHAPTER TWENTY-NINE

Syrnyki didn't make everything better, but their warm sweetness did make Asya feel a little less hopeless. Even when confronted with the immediate obstacle that Saint Korona's book was written in old Tóuren. Nikov explained dutifully that it was one of the dialects from the region before it was unified into a single queendom. Hints of it had filtered through to Tóurensi, but not enough for it to be understandable.

To Asya, it mostly meant frustration, as they'd have to go through the painful process of translating the entire thing before they knew if they had any more answers.

Now the sun was spilling its last light through the library windows, and they were still on the first section. Between the faded quality of the paper and the fact that they had to refer to several different dictionaries for each sentence, it was slow going.

"I can finish it, if you like?" Nikov offered when Asya couldn't suppress her third consecutive yawn. But she shook her head. In all honesty, she knew Nikov would manage this far more quickly than she would, but she felt useless enough as it was. She couldn't just sit back and wait. Not with Yuliana's life in the balance.

That scrap of fabric burned in Asya's pocket—impossible, yet somehow she was still sure it connected her to Iza.

"There has to be *something* here." Impatience spurring her on, she flicked forward a few pages, scanning the words for some kind of sign even if she couldn't catch their meaning. Her eyes were beginning to blur despite herself.

"I'm sure if we—"

Asya barely heard him. She'd turned another page, almost at the back of the book, and her heart constricted. A piece was torn from the bottom, neat and intentional. It cut right through the curling script—different to the hand the rest of the book was written in.

"There's something missing," she breathed. Her thoughts skittered ahead of her, falling over a slope she hadn't quite seen yet.

Nikov took it from her with a slight crease of his brow, running his fingers over the tear as if he could somehow sense what had been there. "It is old," he said. "At least six hundred years, I'd guess. And even if it's well-preserved it's not entirely surprising it has some damage."

"When the rest of the book is perfectly intact?"

"It's not much," Nikov said. "It might not be too important."

Asya thought of Sanislav, of every reason the vibishop had to betray her and Izaveta. Had he not only told Azarov where she would be this morning but also warned him of what she was looking for?

She flipped back to the beginning, this sabotage igniting something new inside her. If someone had gone to the lengths of tearing a piece out, then surely that had to mean there was something important in this book. It meant it could finally hold answers.

★ ★ ★

By the time the first rays of dawn splayed over the distant horizon, Asya thought she had it—written and rewritten, and scratched out, and fixed—but *there*. Nikov had fallen asleep on the floor a few hours before, head pillowed on what looked like an ancient prayer book. She couldn't blame him. The only thing keeping her awake was the fear of falling asleep. Too many painful things lurked there.

Saint Korona's book was more a collection of writings than a single story. Some musings on the gods and the nature of magic, some hints of fairy tales Asya knew, but told with slight differences. But it wasn't difficult to work out which piece she needed, which part the queen had been looking at in Asya's vision.

It told the story of Iaga and how she had first brought magic to this land. Asya had heard it before, from her nursemaid, from the illustrated tomes she'd pore over before sleep, more interested in the elaborate drawings than the text.

In the story Asya remembered, Iaga was a young princess who wanted to bring prosperity to her land. She'd known the tales of the ancient heroes who first brought snow, the youngest soldier who'd fought the sun for the right to the moons, and Iaga wanted that same greatness. So she went in search of the one thing they did not yet have: magic. The gods saw her dedication as she traveled from the mountains to the seas, through storms and floods, and so they granted her a single drop of magic. Not wanting to keep it for herself, Iaga let the drop fall into the Depthless Lake so that magic could seep from there and spread through the lands.

The gods did not appreciate her deception, and so they created the Firebird to ensure there would always be a balance between gods and mortals.

Asya had never thought of the story as true. Iaga was not a saint, not one of the real fixtures of this world. She was something mothers told their children to explain the ways of the world. Besides, there were numerous folktales of how the Firebird came to be.

But this version was a little different. Instead of a benevolent gift from the gods, this version said Iaga had stolen the drop of magic from Vetviya. That she'd sought advice from the falcons, and they helped her craft a spell to allow the magic to permeate the land.

Then, the final page—the torn page, written in a different hand—Asya assumed was an addition from someone who'd owned this book since. Perhaps the sorcerer, Koschei, as she'd seen in that vision. It took aspects of Iaga's story and crafted it into a spell. Asya didn't know much about spells beyond the few basic ones Tarya had shown her to help her understand magic, but she'd never seen one like this.

Her heart accelerated as she went through the translation. All things she had easily on hand—everroot, bark from a queenstree, light from the three moons, the memory of a saint. The same ingredients she'd seen in the vision.

And then the final line, right before the rip: the blood of the Firebird.

The spell almost felt like kindling. The small start of something—like that first whisper of a Calling. The smallest inkling that this was the path she was meant to follow.

But the last steps were cut off, torn away right through the middle of an illegible word.

Asya was too tired to move, a deep exhaustion that even the Firebird couldn't fix, so she threw the nearest cyclopedia at Nikov's chest. She winced as it hit him—it was heavier than she'd anticipated.

He woke with a start. "Diye, what time is it?"

"It's light out," Asya said by way of an answer.

He then noticed the cyclopedia, half-open across his chest, and looked over at Asya as if she had just committed the greatest sin. He carefully righted it, smoothing down the pages as he set it to one side.

Only then did he turn to face her, scrubbing a hand through his tousled curls. "Are you all right?"

She held up the leaf-bound book, a slight smile tugging at her lips despite everything. "I finished it."

Even with the missing piece, she felt closer to an answer than she had in days. Felt a little less overwhelmed by her fate. No longer the scared girl who let the flames consume her, instead allowing them to forge her into something new.

Nikov blinked, as if still trying to disentangle his thoughts from sleep. "You translated it?"

"Yes," Asya said, ignoring the slight hurt at his tone of surprise. She might not be entirely comfortable around books, but she'd managed this.

The last tendrils of sleep fell away, his eyes bright as he joined her at the table. "Show me."

Words scattering in her haste, she explained the story as best she could—its important differences. The ritual written out in someone else's hand, the possibility it held, even with this missing piece.

"It's a story," he said slowly, as if breaking bad news. "And not one I've seen supported anywhere else."

"It's more than that." She tried to find the words to explain how the Firebird's feathers ruffled at this, a strange shiver of energy that made it feel *right*. "It requires the blood of the Firebird," she pressed. "It's like this spell was *made* for me."

Or she was made for it.

But her fervent belief wasn't reflected on Nikov's face.

"Even if we were to take it as real," he said, turning to the final pages. "This ritual is unlike anything I've seen before. It's dark magic, nothing good could come of it. Besides, the last part is missing. Incomplete, it wouldn't do anything."

"But isn't it a chance? We could work that final part out," Asya said, her voice dwindling. "It's more than we've had so far."

He pointed to the penultimate line of the ritual, the one the Firebird should understand more than anyone else. "Have you considered this?"

A magic this profound will demand the price.

Asya shrugged, pretending at composure. "All magic demands a price. I'm willing to pay it."

"That doesn't mean just any price," he said, running a finger under the word. "That phrase, *kosvenyen*, means *the highest price*. It means a life."

Asya's fluttering hope, that fledgling bird, fell to the ground with a heavy thud.

She hadn't considered that—hadn't thought how easily the magic could demand so much. It seemed foolish now, given all that she had seen. All that she had done.

Hadn't she said she'd be willing to pay the price, no matter what? If this could bring Izaveta back, then her sister would be in a position to stay Yuliana's sentence. It could answer both of Asya's problems, protect the two people she cared most about.

"You couldn't sacrifice yourself," Nikov said instantly, seeing the thought flicker across Asya's face. He pointed to another word, *vosroya*. "It has to be *taken*. A life forcefully taken from someone else. It's an act of cruelty. The true price here isn't even that life, it's the loss of yourself."

Asya stared down at the page. Through the fresh sting of

tears the ink spread across the paper like poison. She'd never seen a spell like that before, never heard of her aunt having to take a price like that.

But she'd also never heard of a way to undo a price, so it shouldn't surprise her there wasn't an easy solution.

Asya had blood on her hands already. The stained and blood-soaked history of the Firebird, however necessary those actions were. But also her own. The things she had done in the Elmer—all those people she had killed. The life she had taken from her own sister.

But taking a price from someone wasn't the same as this. This would be murder.

She hadn't realized until this moment, until the failure was laid out in front of her, how desperately she'd wanted this to work. To finally have a solution, a way for her to fix all of this. To get to speak to her sister again.

Nikov put a gentle hand on her arm, jogging her from her twisting thoughts. "Izaveta wouldn't want that for you."

Anger, hot and burning as tears, rose in Asya's throat. "And how would you know?"

Not that Asya would know, either. It was increasingly clear she hadn't known Izaveta nearly as well as she liked to believe.

When she looked up, Nikov was watching her carefully. Not with the fear most people held, but with some understanding she didn't want right now. "There are things you can't come back from," he said.

Izaveta had done it. Turned down a path from which there was no return.

Would Izaveta do this, if it meant a chance to save Asya?

Asya wasn't sure the answer helped her. All it brought with it was a sickening guilt.

She stood up, sucking in a breath to try to stop the tears

from falling. Nikov was right, she knew that. She thought of that boy in the forest, the one Azarov had used. No matter what Asya became, she couldn't be that. She couldn't see people around her as tools to help further her own goals.

"Asya," Nikov said, his voice painfully gentle. "We might find another way, still."

All her choices were narrowing down around her again, constricting like a cage until only one path spread before her. One she didn't want to take.

Out of the tower window, beyond the library's soft halo of warmth, snow was beginning to fall.

PART THREE:

THE IMPOSSIBLE BARGAIN

The fox had always wanted the crown of the forest, so oft taken by the wolf or the owl. The wolf praised for its strength, the owl for its wisdom, with no thought for the importance of a fox's cunning. But rather than bend to them, rather than change his nature, the fox laid a different plan. He burned down the forest and crafted a crown from its ashes. The undisputed king after all.

—"The Twice-Cunning Fox," an old folktale

CHAPTER THIRTY

Izaveta still remembered the exact moment she had realized she wanted to be queen. Not just that she was destined for it, that it was a path she'd been pushed along with no real volition, but a deep and all-consuming *need*.

She'd been just shy of thirteen, old enough to believe she understood the games of court but still far too naive to play them adeptly. It had been such an inconsequential day, Izaveta could hardly remember what it was she'd been so desperate to talk to her mother about. A new song she'd learned on her flute or perhaps an interesting bear sighting.

But at the time it had felt colossal, an achievement that had prompted her to run to her mother immediately—a clear sign of naivety in itself. Queen Adilena had been in the gardens, on no apparent official business. Surrounded by a knot of people as usual, petering out to distant eavesdroppers, Izaveta had been unperturbed as she pushed through them.

"Mother—" But the word was barely out of her mouth when Adilena met her eye and shook her head before turning away to some conze or other.

That was all it had taken. A tiny shake of her head and Izaveta was dismissed, all her excited pride extinguished. Because it didn't matter, she didn't matter.

As Izaveta had walked away, her eyes smarting, her mother had lapsed into silence, contemplating some question too important for anyone else's ears. But no one else had left, no one had dared interrupt her silence or even tried to reignite conversation.

They'd all just waited. These people who were supposed to be the most powerful in Tóurin, all at her mother's whims.

Izaveta needed that—had desperately wanted that. A way to ensure she could not be overlooked, could not be turned away with a simple snide glance, could not be told she didn't matter. A way to ensure she was truly in control.

And when she became queen, she finally would be.

Sitting in this tomb now, everything in tatters around her, it felt like such a faraway want.

A selfish one, she supposed, not that it mattered now. She had no power here, despite all the lengths she'd gone to.

Looking back, especially with the hollow resonance in her chest, she knew that selfish want had even driven her toward the spell. She'd managed to carve out power for herself, yet there was still one person who she could not move. So Izaveta had got rid of her. Consciously or not, worry for Asya had certainly not been the only reason Izaveta had done it.

She squeezed her eyes shut, dropping her head back against the unforgiving stone. Perhaps being heartless made her see more clearly now, made her able to look back with an unflinching honesty.

"Deep contemplations for so late at night."

She didn't jump at the voice, her eyes fluttering open to the imagined silhouette of Nikov. He sat a few paces away from her, a book open in his hands as if she'd just interrupted his reading.

Her mind really was unspooling, delirium and hopelessness getting the better of her.

She glanced down at the green-covered book. *"Meditations on the Course of Time in the Stars?"* she remarked, as if they really were having an unimportant conversation back in Vetviya's Tower and had time to discuss the merits of a centuries-old text. "That's certainly deep contemplations for late-night reading."

"If it is night, you mean." He shrugged, fingers lacing and unlacing. "Besides, it helps quiet my thoughts. Medvedev had many interesting ideas."

She let out a low scoff of laughter. "The ramblings of a definitely disturbed monk pondering on how we all came to exist help to *quiet* your thoughts?"

His mouth hitched into a shadow of a smile. "It reminds me that there are always other ways of looking at something. In this case, the belief that one day soon, the stars will fall to earth and devour us all."

He held her gaze, entirely serious, and she was suddenly struck by how much she had missed this. The person whose words became an elegant dance with hers.

A seriousness creased across his expression. "Are you all right?"

She was a little taken aback by the question. It was not a thing anyone ever asked her, let alone something she let her own mind contemplate. So irrelevant in the grand scheme of the world.

She opened her mouth to say as much, but instead a single word fell out. "No." Apparently lying to her imagined subconscious was pointless.

She wrapped her arms around herself, suddenly untethered.

All those fragmented pieces of herself that she'd worked so hard to pull back together threatening to shatter again.

The last time she'd sat with the real him—the last time she'd let these vulnerabilities show—she'd told him she was marked for the Firebird. That she had killed her own mother. She hadn't deserved to ask for his sympathy then and she didn't deserve it now, but she couldn't stop herself reaching for it.

"I've made such a mess of things," she whispered. She looked up at him, adrift in this emptiness of her own creation. "I don't know what to do."

One of the few truly honest things she'd ever spoken aloud. Vulnerability came easier in the dark.

All of her fears came creeping out then, heavy stone pulling her down. The curse tearing through the palace that she supposedly had the answer to, Asya exposed and unprotected, the Azarovs digging their claws into the court, these walls towering around Izaveta, inescapable.

A vital secret about the Karasova queens and their crown that her mother had never bothered to mention.

It all came back to Izaveta's mistakes. Her pride, her shortcomings. She couldn't even blame her mother for secrecy, when the queen could hardly have expected her death so soon. Certainly not at her daughter's hands.

Izaveta glanced over at Nikov, a fragile desperation fracturing through. "What do I do?"

Nikov's expression reflected some of that despair back at her. "I wish I could give you the answer."

"I thought scholars always had the answers," she said, a hollow echo of humor.

"Scholars always *search* for answers," Nikov corrected, face still grim. "We rarely find them."

Silence ticked between them, each empty beat a reminder of time Izaveta did not have. Yet she still didn't move.

"Are you giving up, then?" Nikov asked.

She shot him a glare, but it didn't have quite the same venom as before. "Why do you keep asking that?"

"You could," he went on. "It would probably be easier. Let this place truly become your tomb. The Karasova line and all their burdens would die here with you. A neat ending."

"You speak as if I have other options," she snapped—a fruitless argument with herself.

"You always have options."

"What else am I supposed to do? I was never prepared for this," she ground out, nails digging into her upper arms where she clutched too tight. Asya could have burned her way out— even without the Firebird, Izaveta could imagine her sister finding some way, as she always did.

Asya had stood against the legendary banewolf with barely more than her flames. She'd survived attackers armed with firestone, and betrayals from every side.

But Izaveta wasn't made for that. She'd been crafted out of lies and cunning, neither of which were any use now.

"There's no way out of here for me," she finished, her voice shriveling with the painful truth of it.

"There is a way *in* though, isn't there?"

Izaveta stared at him, sitting up a little straighter as her mind turned that over. He was right, of course, there was a way in. Why did that suddenly feel so important?

She went over the past few days, the times when food had been brought or Kyriil had appeared at her side. They'd always used the sleeping powder, disorientating her so she never truly saw the entrance.

But why would they bother to drug her, unless that entrance held some other possibility?

Izaveta had thought she'd scoured every inch of this cell in her first days of awareness, but there could have been something she missed. Especially when she hadn't known what to look for.

She glanced up at the teeming darkness above her. There could be someone watching her, that was likely how Kyriil knew she'd been attempting that spell, but there was little room for subtlety here. She had to hope that her actions didn't matter to them for the very reason she wanted to give up: because the likelihood of her managing anything of consequence was so low.

She forced that thought away. It brought too many of the claustrophobic fears crowding back in. This was not a sealed tomb. There were living people around her and there were ways in and out. And she would find them.

Either way, she could not be too obvious in what she was doing. She would only get one chance.

There were plenty of secret passageways in the Palace of Three Skies, a whole network of hidden doors and winding tunnels known as the Queen's Doors. They must have once been extensive, another way for the queen to spy on her own court, but now many of them had collapsed and even more were lost to history. The former queens had not been forthright in sharing information, even with their own daughters.

But Izaveta still had experience of doors that blended perfectly into wood paneling, of latches that only turned a certain way and edges of doorframes only visible in a particular light—even if most of them no longer led to anything.

There were plenty of cracks and creases on the unhewn

stone of this cell that could hide a door. The only question was if there was a way to open it from this side.

The Queen's Doors were all two-way, it would hardly be helpful for one to enter and then be trapped inside and forced to rely on someone else to let one out. And Izaveta could not imagine why they would need a hidden entrance into a prison cell, unless this had not always been a prison cell. Unless it had been repurposed for her. Which meant this had to have been a room, and a normal room would have exits.

She turned slowly, adding a tremble to her movements as if she was unfocused, still caught in her hazy confusion—which was not hard to do, given everything. If there were a hidden latch or handle, then it would be well camouflaged to the stone. Another part of the illusion of this tomb, another way to make this all feel impossible.

That was the point of all of this, for Izaveta to feel hopeless. The setting, the impenetrable dark, the sleeping powder… All of it was just another part of the appearance. And if something *appeared* strong, rarely did anyone look beyond that.

Slowly, she closed her eyes. If all of this was designed to make her feel more trapped, more isolated, then her vision would only serve to trick her other senses. To play into the narrative they wanted her to believe.

Eyes shut tight, she began to feel her way around the edge of the room, still swaying, murmuring to herself as if delirious. She ran her hands over the uneven surface, catching on anything that felt even a little out of place. The pain in her finger helped, jolting through her if that nail bed hit the smallest inconsistency.

It was slow work, far slower than Izaveta liked, given the risk that she could be interrupted at any moment. But she kept going, focused only on the feel of stone against her skin.

Then—a slight indentation, the smallest shift beneath her fingers.

Her eyes flew open, and sure enough, she would not have managed to see the small latch. It was no bigger than a thumbprint and blended perfectly into the join between two blocks of stone. A little higher than her head, she had to stretch to hook her fingers into the crevice.

With a soft *snick*, like a puzzle piece finally fitting into place, a door swung open.

CHAPTER THIRTY-ONE

Izaveta's first steps through the door were into darkness and she couldn't help but fear she had been mistaken. That this passage would only lead her farther into the bowels of her prison, playing into her opponents' hands once again.

Then the ground beneath her feet began to tilt up, the rough stone smoothing to a polished sheen, and the bright burn of light seared ahead. She hesitated, listening for any sign of guards or servants, or perhaps Kyriil himself. But it was unnervingly quiet—a smothering kind of silence, as if the walls swallowed the slightest sound.

Izaveta squinted as she stepped into the light, her eyes so unused to it after all the time in that cell. For a few blinks, everything was limned in gold, divine intervention shining down on her. She half expected guards arrayed in front of her, swords aloft to drag her back down. But as her eyes adjusted, the room she found herself in was quite ordinary and empty of people.

There was only a single window, still too bright against her vision. Unpolished wooden shelves lined the wall, piled with an odd assortment of items. A heavy desk, too big for the rest of the room, like an adult crouching to a child's height. Fire crackled in a grate, barely warming the icy chill. None of it was ornate, none of it spoke of wealth or power in the way Izaveta had expected of the Azarovs.

More than anything, that unnerved her. She kept coming up against warring truths, trying to take the measure of the people who held her here only to find another contradiction.

What are you? she had asked Kyriil, and the question rose again now.

She went to the window first, rough-hewn as if it had been blasted out of the wall and with no glass to protect from the vicious wind. Far below, snow blanketed the ground, spotted with frost-tinged trees with oddly pale leaves—not the towering firs or mountain-ash trees found in the forests of Tóurin. Not the grand manicured gardens of the Azarov estate.

Though Izaveta had surmised as much herself, it would be a foolish risk to keep her anywhere obvious. But it still dashed any lingering, ridiculous shreds of hope that she might gain an upper hand by at least knowing where she was—or having an easy way out.

She turned to take in the rest of the room. If escape wasn't an immediate option without risking that frozen wilderness, then she would have to bide her time. As long as she could hide the fact that she was able to leave her cell, she could gather information and try to find an escape. Or at least a way to send word to Asya.

The piles of paper and quills on the desk could have been haphazard, but there was an order to them. A careful precision. Apparent chaos was a good way to hide things—as well as proving a challenge for anyone who wanted to search through the mess without leaving obvious signs. Several scrolls had fallen to the floor, and even more letters with unbroken seals teetered at the edge.

Izaveta knelt to examine the fallen ones. The crimson

rooster of the Azarovs shone bright on several and her fingers hovered over it, eager to slip it open. Was this a letter that had just arrived, not yet read, or one about to be sent out? But breaking the seal would signal her presence at once to anyone returning to this room, and gathering information like this required she maintain the upper hand of secrecy.

She turned away and sifted through the rest, pausing at crests and seals she recognized. Several familiar noble houses and conze, though Izaveta couldn't think of a clear connection or alliances between them.

The desk was much the same, precarious piles of parchment that she dared not touch for risk of toppling them, a few notes in a shorthand she couldn't even begin to decipher. A small blade—a glorified letter opener more than anything else. Then her gaze snagged on a drop of brightest crimson. A knob of red wax and a gleaming, gold-handled seal.

Her heart should have been hammering, but instead there was a strange stillness inside her. She could use that to reseal the scrolls on the floor, as long as she moved quickly enough. She had no idea how much time she had, when someone might see her cell was empty, or when the owner of this room might return.

She had established they did not want to kill her, at least for now. That was her one bargaining chip, the one thing that made this risk acceptable.

Decision made, she snatched up the two Azarov-sealed scrolls from the ground and carefully pried them open. The first was only two lines long, with no salutation or signature for Izaveta to tell if it was being sent or received. There was something vaguely familiar in the looping letters, the neat and steady lines, but Izaveta couldn't place it.

Hope everything settles now outside. They know you require immovable, immutable loyalty.

That had to be coded, because Izaveta couldn't fathom a direct meaning.

She flicked to the second one. Again, it was not signed but much longer than the first and in a different, spikier hand. One word jumped out at her, burning and familiar: *Firebird*.

Movements, Izaveta realized as her eyes flew down the letter again and she began to catch on to a pattern. *Asya's* movements.

A slow-crawling ice slid through Izaveta's veins. She'd seen her sister in those terrible visions, caught a glimpse of her in the grounds, but she hadn't considered that someone might be watching her this closely.

What did Kyriil want with her?

Fear pierced through her—fear for her sister that she somehow managed to hold on to even as her other emotions fell away.

It wasn't much, but it was more than she had started with. There was a spy in the palace, someone watching Asya.

Having that information made Izaveta feel surer of herself, more certain she had made the right choice in searching for information rather than trying for a harried escape.

She had always been more certain when it came to her sister.

Ironic, when some of her worst decisions concerned Asya.

Izaveta shook herself free of those thoughts, grasping the crimson wax as she moved over to the guttering fire. The small sparks of flame gave off so little heat, she wondered why they'd even bothered to light it.

But as she held the wax toward it, she realized that was

precisely the thing. They had *not* bothered to light it. Even though she could see dancing flames and the soft glow of coals, there was no burn.

Izaveta did not know how it was possible—if it was some kind of spell or a cleverly placed illusion, like the ones traveling magicians cast at festivals. But the *how* was not important here, what mattered was *why*.

And she could think of no reason one would go to the trouble of making this, except to keep something hidden.

Discarding the wax without much thought, Izaveta reached into the flames. It was disconcerting to watch her hands engulfed in the burning reds, her mind screaming at her to pull back, certain that pain would follow.

But it didn't.

She pushed aside the dark coals, as smooth and cool under her hand as stone, to reveal a small wooden box. The surface was painted in intricate detail, the kind of rare craftsmanship one would pay dearly for.

The lid opened easily, dislodging a layer of dust. Inside, tucked protectively among silk like invaluable treasure, sat several folded pieces of paper.

Izaveta lifted them out gently, though even that slight movement sent a small trickle of flaked parchment onto the floor.

These were not like the letters at the desk. These pages were worn thin, ink faded and parchment so delicate she was almost afraid to touch them. They looked far older than anything else here—more ancient even than the illuminated prayer books kept in the cathedral.

Footsteps made Izaveta's hands jerk. The sound shivered up her spine, far too close. A little below her, but unmistakably drawing closer. If she was found here, any hope at advantage was gone, any meager weapons she'd managed to gather around herself would be futile.

The two opened letters lay discarded behind her, and with no real fire, she had no way to reseal them. Even if she did, the footsteps were nearing, neat and purposeful against the stone.

There was nowhere to hide in here—she refused to crouch under the desk and wait for Kyriil's inevitable arrival. She couldn't even run back to her cell as the footfalls echoed from that passage.

Her eyes fell on the window.

Unguarded and viciously inviting. She hurried over to it, leaning out to examine the drop again. It was sheer stone, no vines or obvious crevices that could ease the descent, only smooth, frost-dusted rock. There was another window, a little farther down, but still well out of her reach.

It was hard to tell, but she thought it looked glassless too, as roughly hewn as this one.

She thought of the saint's relic Kyriil had used to take them to the site of the curse. That could be hidden somewhere in this tower, a possible way back to the palace. Not a thoughtless, frenzied escape attempt, but a feint with a conscious objective. And that window could be her way back in.

She turned back to the room, reexamining. But there was nothing that could help her descent—even if there was, it would be madness to attempt it.

But perhaps that was the one reason to try it, to do something Kyriil would never expect. Something that couldn't be predicted or manipulated.

The footsteps rang closer, sand trickling through an hourglass until the decision was made for her.

She grabbed the letter opener from the desk, a crude tool but at least something solid in her hand, pocketing the parchment with little thought. Slowly, even her body protesting, she lifted herself onto the windowsill. The icy wind bit into her skin, tearing through the tattered remains of her dress. She looked back at the door, teetering as her subconscious battled against her. Even considering this was ludicrous, probably a sign that her thoughts were becoming too unemotional. So removed from humanity that they no longer held reason.

But once again, she was the one at risk here. Her life was something she could gamble with.

With a last reckless thought of her sister, Izaveta lowered herself over the ledge.

CHAPTER THIRTY-TWO

Asya stared up at the slow-falling flurries already consuming the ground around her in glistening white. They hadn't stopped since the previous night when she'd stared out of the tower window, the ritual she could never complete crumpled in her hands.

Frosted white was encroaching over the three domes of the palace now. People were already cheerfully celebrating the oncoming First Snows, anticipating a night of fun after so much hardship. Not only a new beginning, but also an end to all this confusion, as it would bring the trial of succession with it. Acolytes and clergymen moved around the cathedral with a bubbling enthusiasm, preparing the ceremony for when the three moons were high in the sky.

When the gods could look down on them all in judgment.

Asya touched a finger to the scrap of fabric in her pocket, one tangible thing. It would be all she had left of Izaveta if she went through with this, no more chances to return to the palace and search for answers.

The same two strashe stood guard at the prison entrance at the base of Zmenya's Tower. Asya didn't bother to sneak around this time, to offer them a way out. She just walked straight up to them.

"Stand aside."

Something in her voice, or the way sparks were coiling around her irises, made both strashe wilt. They didn't even reach for their swords as Asya stepped between them and into the tower.

There was a certain satisfaction in finally getting what she wanted. And it *was* easier just to let her power out. To let it do all the work for her.

That vindication propelled her up the twisting tower stairs, thrumming in her veins like the Firebird's song. Almost as soothing. Certainly as good at blocking everything else out, letting her forget.

She hurried out onto the juddering wooden platform, her eyes darting to the cage Yuliana had occupied the day before.

It was empty.

Asya knew her feet had stopped, that the wood had not splintered beneath her and tossed her down into the darkness, but it might as well have.

They couldn't— They wouldn't have—

The thought didn't want to form in her mind. Too much to even glance at.

"They haven't executed her yet."

She whipped around to where Sanislav was reclining in the lowest cage, comfortable as ever.

"Are you sure?" She didn't care that she was giving him leverage in asking that, didn't care that her voice cracked so sharply she could feel it down to her bones.

"It's the sort of thing they would ensure everyone knew," he said simply. "They have just moved her. Prisoners don't remain here after they are sentenced."

The falling sensation was back, a swooping relief that pummeled into her just as hard as the dread had. She still had time. Yuliana wasn't gone. Not yet.

"Where have they taken her?"

Sanislav shrugged. "I imagine General Azarov has secreted the girl away somewhere by now, with the trial of succession looming. She's far more useful like that."

"How do you—"

"I hear things through the bars of my cage."

Asya narrowed her eyes. Even a trapped snake could still lash out. And she hadn't forgotten that Sanislav had intended for her sister to abdicate so the Church could take over the Crown. "Just not the things I need to know," she snapped.

"He's not a very creative man, General Azarov." Sanislav leaned forward, long fingers curling around the bars. "You, on the other hand, are full of possibilities." Asya didn't like the way he said that, like a soothsayer eager to see how a bad omen played out. "You have the advantage. A blank slate with no preconceptions yet."

"They think me a fool."

Sanislav smiled. "Then, be a fool."

Asya blinked, her tumbling emotions momentarily dislodged by the strangeness of that statement.

"After all," Sanislav added. "Wasn't that how you tricked me? By playing the fool?"

No, Asya thought. *I tricked you because Iza was the one to come up with the plan.* And because her sister had hidden some of the details from her.

She turned to leave but Sanislav's voice snaked after her. "Best of luck with the trial of succession. I would offer a psalm, but it hardly seems the place."

Asya paused, one foot on the next step. Her rational brain was screaming at her to leave. Listening to Sanislav and his poisonous words wouldn't help her. But she looked back, unable to ignore that tug of curiosity.

"What do you know about the trial?"

He smiled, the spider enticing the helpless fly back to its web. "I am still vibishop, am I not? No one has been appointed in my stead. So matters of the gods are of great importance to me. I hope they judge you fairly."

"Me?" Asya echoed.

"You are Commander Iveshkin's candidate, are you not?"

"No—" Asya sputtered. "I refused her nomination."

"Probably for the best."

Asya's teeth clicked together, her anger looking for a path. "Because the gods would never find *me* worthy?"

"The gods have little to do with it. I imagine General Azarov and that upstart Deryev will be pulling the strings here."

Asya stared at him, his meaning permeating too slowly into her mind. "They would manipulate something like that?"

Sanislav smiled again, the endearing look of a parent whose child had done something innocently amusing. "Oh, Firebird. Did you truly believe it is always the will of the gods? That they care about the minutiae of mortals, the comings and goings of queens who will always die?"

"You're the vibishop, aren't you meant to believe that?"

"All the more reason I know better." He waved an airy hand. "A little smoke here, some special powders there, and it's very easy to ensure the decision goes the way one wants."

Asya felt as if she was teetering again, about to plummet over the edge. She ran her thumb along the scar on her palm, the remnant of another ceremony. A flash of sparks that chose her fate and Izaveta's.

"Did you…? Did they manipulate *our* ceremony? The one that made me Firebird?"

Sanislav shrugged. "That was before my appointment as vibishop. Though I doubt your mother would have left anything to chance."

A low buzzing chased Asya back down the stairs of the tower. Like a subtle hum of magic saturating her mind, speeding all her thoughts.

Could it have been as mundane as that? Not a divine decree, not great destiny laid out for them, but simply the whims of a mortal? Their mother's opinion falling one way or another and deciding how to divide Asya from Izaveta forever.

A throw of the dice and their positions could have been reversed.

Asya had imagined her duty as chosen by Dveda. Imagined it had some greater meaning, even when her legacy was blood and ruins.

She reached for the wooden icon that hung around her neck, the familiar comfort it had always given her.

What did I make you for? That was what he'd asked her in those burning dreams. Unless that was not Dveda at all, just her mother's manipulations again.

Asya hadn't known where she was walking—running—to after she left Zmenya's Tower, but her feet decided for her. They stopped in the mercifully empty waste of the Sunken Gardens. An appropriate place for the Firebird, devoid of life and yet still eternal.

She pressed her back against one of the dead spruce trees, the leafless branches reaching down toward her like claws. Snow was still falling, mockingly cold against the searing burn of tears behind her eyes.

The great silhouette of the palace rose at her back, as mocking as the snow. Yuliana could be anywhere in that vast expanse. Or even beyond that, sent to some nearby safehold to await execution. Far too many possibilities for Asya to even begin to search through when the domes of the palace were already thinly veiled in white.

As Sanislav had said, Azarov had probably been the one to suggest they move Yuliana in the first place. He wanted to ensure Asya had no choice but to abide by the deadline he'd set.

And that seemed to be working. All the options charring to cinders around Asya until there was only one choice left.

She could take Azarov's deal. Kill someone undeniably good and help a man like Azarov gain power, all while risking indebting herself to him for the rest of her immortal life.

Or Asya could walk away from it all now. Accept what Tarya had always told her and let Yuliana be executed. Leave the court to its petty squabbles and truly become the Firebird as she always should have. Separate and unemotional, uninvolved in the affairs of mortals.

She wrapped her arms tighter around herself, a hollow sob trapped in her chest.

Was this it?

The end of the path she had been pushed down that day in the cathedral. All that hope only to find it ended in a plunging drop. All this fighting to hold on to herself only to end up in the exact same place. The ties to her humanity would be severed. As alone as she'd seen herself in the banewolf's eyes.

And there would be no changing that. No going back. No new Firebird to take her place, not with the Karasova line broken. Just this.

No matter what she did, she lost.

It all spun through Asya faster than the falling snow. Words that laid traps at her feet, deceit scattered around her. She needed Iza for this. Or, diye, even her mother. Asya had never been the clever one.

Always playing the fool, just as Sanislav had said. Just as Azarov expected.

She had a sudden flash of memory, of the way Izaveta had laughed all of them off. The way she would never have stood for this. And the way she knew to use her apparent weaknesses as an advantage.

A light dusting of snow had settled in Asya's hair. It shook free with her sudden movement, a new iron purpose gripping her.

She grabbed parchment and ink as soon as she entered the library, not pausing to offer Nikov an explanation as she scribbled. The note to Commander Iveshkin was longer than she'd intended. A lot of rambling explanation that was probably unnecessary, but what really mattered was the last line: *Meet me at the Celebration of First Snows and I will be your candidate for queen.*

CHAPTER THIRTY-THREE

Izaveta had always liked heights. If her mother pushed her too far or the suffocations of court were too stifling, Izaveta would climb to the very pinnacle of Vetviya's Tower and stare out the window at the palace below her. All its twisting paths and hidden corners laid bare, the people fluttering between the courtyards no bigger than insects.

None of it mattered from that height. Izaveta could see everything, could piece it all together as dispassionately as a zvess game.

It always calmed her breathing, gave her back some semblance of control.

But staring down the sheer stone face of the tower wall—unforgiving as the ground far below—she could hardly fill her lungs.

One move at a time, she told herself. Simple as zvess. There was a terrible irony to that, of course, the false simplicity of the game that could easily turn back and destroy the player.

She gritted her teeth, one hand knuckle-white on the windowsill while the other reached down with the letter opener. Her first attempt to dig it into the wall, the blade merely bounced off, so sudden it almost flew from her fingers.

She moved slower the second time, carefully etching a

small hole with the tip of the knife before trying to press it in. Yet still the stone would not move. She didn't recognize the grain or composition of it, had no vague ideas of how malleable it could be. It was possible the knife would break before the stone, and with it, all her chances.

Her balance slipped as she pushed her weight against the blade, willing the hard surface to bend beneath it, and for a terrible instant, she thought she might just go tumbling down.

Then the stone gave way, the blade of the knife sinking in and flutters of debris falling to the ground far below. So far she couldn't hear the soft crack of them hitting the frozen snow.

She was breathing hard already. She had her first foothold in place, the slight advantage against this impossible swooping stone. She refused to let herself consider how this would only get harder as she went, the knife possibly a hindrance if she couldn't get the leverage to pull it free.

But even as she tried to push herself down this first step, out of reach of the safety of the windowsill, her body refused to move. If anything, she clenched tighter to the sill, fingertips already going numb.

She couldn't do this.

Izaveta did not scale impossible heights. She schemed and manipulated and pushed other people to perform impossible tasks for her.

But there was no one else here. No one left for Izaveta to risk in her game except herself.

No longer the unseen hand but now one of the pieces. Breakable. *Vulnerable.*

She should just pull herself back onto the sill into the relative safety of the room and try to think of a way to trick Kyriil or manipulate his game. That's what her mother would counsel: make the pragmatic choice. Just as Izaveta had always done. When she'd cast that spell against the queen, desperate to wrench back some control. When she'd twisted Nikov's words against him. When she'd used Asya as a bargaining chip.

Izaveta wasn't sure which of those thoughts propelled her to move, but somehow she released the ledge, her hand dangling into nothingness.

She reached down with her foot, feeling for the knife, her toe scrabbling for purchase on the smooth surface.

It only took five stumbling heartbeats for Izaveta to decide this was a very bad idea. The wind that had felt bracing from the window ledge was a buffeting gale, now she was clenched on the tower face, each gust desperate to dislodge her. The few cracks and handholds that had seemed manageable from above were actually much farther apart, each one a staggering drop down. The window below looked impossibly far now, a mountainous plunge away from her.

That was the thing about heights: they lied.

Seeing the palace from far above, neatly cataloging its twists and turns, did not actually mean it was easier to navigate. And it did nothing to alleviate the constant fear of maneuvering through those lies, all those twisting secrets. It just let Izaveta pretend, for a moment. And a pretense did not help in the long run.

Perhaps that was the real reason the frozen queen had stayed in her tower. Not because she could not leave, but because it was easier to stay there. To survey it all from a great distance, where she could pretend her actions did not have true consequences, where she could ignore the extent of the damage she'd caused.

Sharp, icy tears froze against Izaveta's cheeks, more from fear or frustration she didn't know.

But Izaveta couldn't climb back up and hide in the tower now. Though there was a part of her, louder than she cared to admit, that desperately wanted to retreat to that safety, she couldn't. The ledge was out of her reach anyway and pulling herself back up would be near impossible.

One way or another, the only option was down.

So that was what Izaveta did, one heart-lurching handhold at a time. Even as her fingers scraped against sharp divots, the sting soon eclipsed by a numbing cold, so deep she could barely feel her hands. Even as every breath felt like it might not be enough, like at any moment the gods would tire of her display and pluck her from the wall themselves. A small annoyance in the great tapestry of the world.

Her toes scrabbled for some kind of purchase as she bent down to place the knife again. There was no rhythm or ease to the movement, if anything, it got worse the farther she descended—the drop no less perilous than before. With her fingers numb it took a concerted effort to get them to obey her and clutch onto tiny crevices, even more to dig the knife into stone again.

She fell more than navigated the last few feet, scraping her palms bloody to slow her descent and just managing to catch herself on the window ledge. The knife fell from her hands, forgotten in her sudden need to grasp the sill. She heard it hit the ground below her, still so far away.

She heaved herself up onto the ledge, not even bothering to check inside first. She'd used any semblance of bravery on the climb down so far, she had none left now. Even if it meant straight back into captivity, solid ground was all she cared about.

CHAPTER THIRTY-FOUR

The plan was far from simple, but perhaps that made it most like something her sister would've done. Asya hoped it meant this would work. A small deception to expose Azarov for what he really was.

The Hall of Lost Moonlight appeared to have been frozen, frosted over with a soft dusting of some bright substance to herald the First Snows. Delicate lights hung glinting from the high ceiling, burning the bright blue flame of renewal that the snows symbolized. Spun silk adorned the windows, all the panes flung open to allow Zmenya's blessing to permeate through the hall. The real snow beyond mingled with the fabricated inside, a dizzying convergence that shone against the dark sky.

Asya would have once thought it beautiful. A scene lifted from one of her childhood fairy-tale books, brought to life in shimmering brushstrokes around her.

But now it made her think of those people, veins turned to ice and skin frosted over, just like this celebration.

She shuddered, twisting the loose thread of her sleeve around her fingers. She had changed from her everyday clothes into one of the less over-the-top jackets Izaveta had given to her, because playing a part felt necessary tonight. Asya hadn't even brought her shashka. The court saw her as hostile enough without wearing a weapon to a supposed celebration.

Excitement zipped through the air. An almost giddy joy that she hadn't seen since her return to the palace—perhaps even before that. She supposed they needed something to celebrate after the horrors of the past weeks, and tonight was precisely the outlet for that. A chance to move on. The world cleansed in snow and a new ruler chosen. The tragedy, or scandal, of Izaveta put behind them.

The room felt suddenly too loud. Stifling and vast all at once, whirling around Asya as uncontrollably as the snowstorm outside. A dizzying hysteria. Celebrations at what would be an execution.

Nikov put a hand on her arm and she jerked back so violently she almost upended a waiter and their sparkling tray of svode. She hadn't heard Nikov approach—hadn't realized she'd come to a stop in the middle of the room, drawing the attention of the gathered guests.

"Don't forget to breathe," he said gently, nudging her forward.

Asya nodded, trying to steady herself. Trying to steady the whirling room around her.

"Don't mind them," Nikov murmured, steering her away from the dense population surrounding the open windows. "They've all been at the svode long enough that I doubt they'll even remember seeing you."

When Asya's lips didn't so much as twitch, his voice softened again. "It will be okay, Asya. I promise."

She forced her mouth into a very unconvincing smile. "I'm all right," she said. "Let's get this over with."

Nikov nodded, but she felt his eyes lingering on her as he moved away through the crowd. Off to prepare for his role in all of this—more challenging than hers, as it involved actual magic, but she still wished they could switch.

Commander Iveshkin was easy enough to spot, even with her back to Asya. The commander had a certain presence to her that drew the eye. A way of filling space with her brusque manner and unshakeable certainty.

Cutting through the crowd, Asya caught sight of Azarov—also easy to find as he was looking straight at her. A steady gaze that said all she needed to know. *I'm waiting.* But she pulled her eyes away from him, focusing on following Iveshkin's brisk pace.

"Good evening, Commander Iveshkin," Asya said in greeting, her voice a little hoarse—she'd never been good at this. "And Mila." She nodded to the interpreter. "I'm glad you both came."

Iveshkin's face was grim, despite the surrounding celebrations. "Firebird," she signed. "I would hardly have missed this, regardless of your note."

Asya's cheeks felt hot, fumbling embarrassment and her surging flames mingling together. "Of course."

"And I do not take kindly to being manipulated," Iveshkin went on. "I did not consider you a candidate for queen so that you could take up the same mantle as your mother, or your sister."

"No games," Asya said. The first proper lie, but she couldn't help it. She knew if she told Iveshkin of her real plan, she'd never go along with it.

"Good. You know how well those manipulations ended for them."

"I—" Asya swallowed, her throat too dry. "I wanted to talk to you about something important." Iveshkin didn't move, so Asya added, "In private."

"Very well," Iveshkin replied. No hesitation, no hint of the threat Asya posed to her. The commander was one of the few people in court, in fact, who had never flinched from her.

Asya didn't trust herself to speak, so she just gestured for Iveshkin to follow. There was an antechamber only fifty paces away, one that Asya had scouted that afternoon to ensure it fit her needs. One that wasn't quite visible from the main hall, with a thick stone wall that kept any sounds muffled.

Iveshkin fell into step next to her, her interpreter following behind. Asya almost tripped over her own feet. How could she have been so stupid? Of course Mila had to come too— Asya had promised an important conversation and she didn't know the Signed Language.

She couldn't have more people there. Anyone else would make this messier than it already was. But there was no way for her to dismiss the interpreter without garnering suspicion.

Asya caught sight of Azarov out of the corner of her eye. She had no doubt he'd be close behind them.

So she forced her steps on, out of the echoing hall and into the muted quiet of the antechamber. The snapping of the door cut off the sounds of celebration. Nothing more than a distant storm, one that could not reach them in here.

Azarov expected her to be weak, to cave easily to his demands. So that's what she would show him. *Play the fool*, just as Sanislav had said.

"I didn't want to do this," she said, nerves adding a convincing tremble to her voice. "But I have no choice."

Iveshkin tensed, her body coiling toward action.

Asya swallowed hard, pushing on with the rehearsed reasoning. "Commander Iveshkin, you owe a price."

She looked to Mila, silently imploring. "You cannot interfere with the Firebird's duty. This is beyond any mortal matters."

But Mila didn't shrink back either. "This is ridiculous," she snapped, her eyes darting between Asya and Iveshkin. "The commander does not practice magic and you can't pretend otherwise."

Iveshkin was unmoved, the coiled tension releasing to something else. A kind of disappointment as she watched Asya. She signed something, though Mila took a moment to relay it, her voice uncertain when she did, "I thought you would have a higher price, Firebird."

She trailed off at the end, some kind of understanding cresting on her face. She wasn't looking at Asya now, but having a furious conversation with Iveshkin. Asya didn't need to know the Signed Language to guess at the meaning.

Mila spun on her heel, striding back to the doorway—a factor Asya hadn't counted on. The yell was already on the woman's lips when a golden tongue of flame surged toward her, almost solid. It sent her staggering into the wall, head cracking against the stone.

Asya winced at the hollow sound, the heavy thud as Mila fell to the ground. The whole point of a ruse had been to not hurt anyone.

Well, it made it look all the more convincing.

Iveshkin's expression darkened and she whirled on Asya—apparently more concerned for Mila than for herself. That just made Asya feel all the worse.

But she couldn't hesitate now.

The Firebird rose in a single swift motion, easy as a breath unloosed. Flames filled the room, slick and dripping as rain. They engulfed Iveshkin in an eager wave, leaving nothing but smoking remains behind.

Chapter Thirty-Five

Izaveta's knees hit the floor hard, the impact jolting up to her teeth.

She couldn't get herself to move. Lying there, her head against the floor and the window above her, she could just make out the sheer stone she'd somehow descended. A bubbling laugh rose in her chest, high-pitched and veering toward panic. What would her mother say if she'd seen that—what would anyone at court say? They wouldn't believe it. Izaveta herself hardly did.

She gave herself three more shuddering breaths before forcing herself to sit up. The last of her jagged laughter echoed against the thankfully empty room. She pulled herself to her feet, still leaning heavily against the wall as she turned to take in the space.

Lit only by a single guttering candle, it looked like a workshop—one of those book binders Fyodor had taken her to visit in Kirava. But rather than rolls of leather and the scent of paper, there were rows and rows of jars and a strange heaviness in the air.

It was a heaviness Izaveta knew, the same feeling of the queenstrees or the cathedral. Old magic, something ancient and long settled suddenly disturbed. There was no order to it, bowls scattered across a large workbench, interspersed with shattered glass and knotted ingredients. Dried rosemary and waterwillow mingled with chamomile sprigs and what looked like pale white shards of bone and teeth.

A prickling disquiet settled over Izaveta.

Why did the Azarovs have a tower in the middle of no-where, full of these strange, disjointed rooms?

The question fell from her head, eclipsed when she saw a quill and ink nestled into one corner.

With all these ingredients around, she could find a way to send a message to the palace.

There was no parchment in the assorted mess, but more than enough supplies for Izaveta to cast a simple message spell—that same one she'd done all those weeks ago to get her letter to Conze Vittaria immediately.

Izaveta had reached down to tear another scrap of fabric from her skirt when her fingers brushed against something else, tucked into the folds of her dress. The old letters she'd found in the room above. The backs of them were blank, cracked and faded, yes, but a far better medium than a scrap of fabric.

Her eyes caught on the front sides, the pages she had not yet had the chance to read. They didn't look like the coded letters of spies or the usual political correspondence. They looked like...stories. *A piece of yours to tether you here*—that was about the queen and the sorcerer who tore out his own heart. The next page was Ivan and the Arrow, where a foolish young man charmed an arrow to lead to his true love, only for it to run her through.

A drowning ecstasy, our love now eternal—that called back to the tale of the vodyanoy who had fallen in love with a human and dragged her down to the depths of his lake, not caring if she drowned.

But these were not written as folktales or poetic declarations, they seemed more personal than that. All tales of destructive, sacrificial love.

Something Izaveta understood more than she cared to admit.

The next page was signed at the bottom, the ink too faded to make out the shape of the name. Not just stories—these were letters, *love* letters, all circling around a great and terrible love.

She flipped through them slowly, flakes of the paper sloughing off under her touch. They all went much the same, until the final page. Three words had been inked at the top, an afterthought or an added note: *remember the price.*

The pieces of this swirled at the edge of her mind, so close to a coalescing tapestry. The crown and the Karasova legacy. Izaveta's price and the strange magic in the palace. They just missed one thread to tie them all together.

She shook her head, focusing on the solid thing in her hands.

It was only then that Izaveta noticed a third workbench, draped in a thin silk-spun sheet at the edge of the room. Another piece of this tapestry?

Yet as Izaveta moved toward it, a cold weight of dread settled over her, as if her body had realized something her mind had not. A sudden desperate need to know coupled with a screaming voice telling her to stop.

But her hand still reached out to pull the sheet back. The silk slipped easily across the smooth skin, more marble than human now.

Izaveta's mind was falling, dropping off an interminable ledge and unable to find anything to catch on to.

Lying before her, very clearly dead, was Kyriil.

CHAPTER THIRTY-SIX

Asya barely had a moment to catch her breath before General Azarov strode through the doorway. There was a certain satisfaction in knowing she'd been right that he had been watching. He was followed by Tsiviya, another piece of this play as the candidate for queen. Asya had counted on that.

No guards followed them yet, not when he still had to play the hero.

Horror was carefully painted across Azarov's face, far too artful to be real as he looked between the blackened remains of Iveshkin and Asya. "Firebird," he said with a low tremor, "what have you done?"

The performance seemed unnecessary when the only other people here already knew about his demands—and Mila was barely conscious. A sort of theatricality that Azarov enjoyed. Playing the part he always wished to be.

"You have to let her go," Asya said, her voice steady now.

Azarov did not drop his false concern. "You know you will have to face judgment for this." Azarov gestured to the ashes where Iveshkin had stood, as if Asya might not have noticed them. "You cannot use the Firebird's duty as a shield to allow you to take lives as you see fit."

Asya didn't look. She didn't need any slight crack to give

herself away. "I don't care what happens to me. I did what you asked. Now let her go."

"I would never deign to ask the Firebird anything—let alone an act as appalling as this. The murder of a cabinet member within the walls of the palace." Azarov took a slow step forward, exaggerated caution. He dropped his voice so only Asya could hear, a spark of triumph in his eyes. "And even if I had, I would remind the Firebird that I warned her it would take time. How long it takes—if we are able to stay the execution—well, that depends entirely on you. On how cooperative you continue to be."

Asya didn't know why she was surprised. A man who would order someone's death, who would hold a loved one hostage, was not a man who honored his word. But still, having him admit so openly to that dishonor felt like a slap. A sharp, ringing reminder of everything she hated in this palace.

This was the moment it could all fall apart. Yuliana paying the price of Asya's gamble. The very real cost of all of Izaveta's manipulations.

"You've already made me a murderer," Asya said, her voice so low—so threaded with anger—that she almost didn't recognize it. "I won't let you take any more."

He tilted his head, looking down at the scorched remains with casual interest. "I believe you made yourself a murderer when you decided whose life was more important." He raised his voice to call out, "Guards!"

It wasn't the palace strashe who streamed in, but the red-clad soldiers Azarov kept under his personal command. They must have been waiting—presumably the audience Azarov was performing for. Asya recognized one of them, but she forced herself to keep watching Azarov. To not let anything slip.

The guards raised their sabers, the muted light shone off not metal, but something darker. Firestone.

Azarov had planned for this.

Again, she shouldn't be surprised, but even seeing it all in front of her, this felt hard to believe. The lengths people would go to for power, for their idea of control.

The guards raised their blades, but Asya moved first. She didn't bother with the doorway or attempts to escape, she went straight for Tsiviya. The Firebird moved with her, flames reaching out to twist around the girl's throat—not quite close enough to burn, but the trailing sparks singed across her skin.

"Stop," Asya said, eyes on Azarov.

"You're surrounded," he said.

Asya's knuckles were white, every bit of concentration going into that ring of fire. "And she'd still be dead before any of them touched me."

Everything felt frozen in this moment, a bated breath of anticipation. The guards waiting for their orders, as still as the statues that surrounded them. Tsiviya caught in a bright web of flame, only her eyes moving. And Azarov, trapped by the monster of his own making.

"Tell me where she is." It was easy to lace the warning into those words, to let the Firebird burn through them.

The single, suspended moment spread between them. A thin layer of ice ready to crack.

"No."

"You've seen me kill once tonight," Asya growled, with each word her voice becoming more and more foreign. Someone else speaking through her tongue. "Do you doubt I would do it again?"

Azarov's tone didn't change, even and mild as if they were commenting on the weather. "Do it, then."

Asya blinked. "I—" She swallowed, trying not to let her eyes slide to Tsiviya, though she could feel the girl's shock as sharply as her own. The bluntness of his words, the casual way he discussed his own daughter's death. "You would gamble your daughter's life that easily?"

Azarov nodded, as if to say it should be obvious. "If this is truly the tactic you're choosing, then you need to make a compelling case. Kill her and perhaps I will take your threats seriously."

There was a challenge in his words, a gauntlet thrown.

"Father—" Tsiviya's voice was a thin thread, tears pricking at the corners of her eyes. "Father, please, I—"

Asya's heart accelerated, thundering in her ears. The flames tightened and Tsiviya's words cut off in a choking sob.

"Do it!" Azarov yelled. The words bounced around the small room, the harsh bark of a military leader.

Asya clenched her jaw. Did he truly not care about the fate of his daughter?

Or did he not believe Asya would go through with it? Of course she didn't want to. She'd thought Iveshkin's burned corpse would be enough proof of her ruthlessness. Enough for him to take this threat seriously.

Looking at the infuriating calm on his face now, Asya almost wanted to do it. Just to prove that she couldn't be so easily toyed with. To prove that he shouldn't gamble with other people's lives.

To make him feel some of the constant pain burning beneath Asya's skin.

It would only take a moment. Just a flicker in her careful control and the flames would consume Tsiviya. It would be over quickly.

One simple act to prove her word. If she waited much longer, the decision would be made for her.

But her flames didn't tighten.

"Go on," Azarov snapped, his voice the low guttural hiss of extinguished flames. "Prove to everyone what you are. There is no point in making threats you won't fulfill."

"Father," Tsiviya tried again, sweat slicking down her forehead.

A brief stab of guilt at the real fear in the girl's voice. None of this was her fault either.

"You can't, can you?" he sneered, not sparing his daughter a glance. "That's why you won't succeed, Firebird. Because you are not willing to pay the price."

Her hands were shaking, trembling as her will battled against her conscience. She'd spent all that time wishing people wouldn't see her as the Firebird. Wouldn't flinch at her approach. Now the one time she needed the monster, her opponent could see right through her.

And he was right. She wasn't willing to pay that price. To do the thing she could never come back from. She wasn't like her sister.

The thought twisted through her insides, unpleasant and bitter. She wasn't sure if that was a good thing or not.

Azarov opened his mouth, presumably to command the guards to action, but a crashing sound from the corridor outside cut him off.

Nikov careened around the doorway, out of breath and sweating. "I'm sorry," he gasped, "I couldn't keep her away—"

No sooner had the words left his lips, than the blackened corpse behind Azarov twisted in on itself. Fading to nothing more than a whisper of smoke.

Asya was out of time.

Commander Iveshkin, very clearly alive and unburned, strode in after Nikov, fury carved into every line of her face.

The general was staring back at her, face pale as if Iveshkin's corpse had truly just walked through the door.

Azarov whirled, finally finding his voice again. "A trick?" he spat. "And here I thought you knew better than to test me."

"I learned from the best," Asya said, finally understanding some of the satisfaction Izaveta found in outsmarting another person. "Have someone else complete the last part of the spell for you."

Nikov waggled his fingers with a slight bow. "Some of my finest work, I think."

Iveshkin advanced on Azarov. "The strashevsta and the cabinet are on their way. It seems you've finally shown your true colors. No weaseling your way out of this one." With Mila still on the ground, Nikov relayed the commander's words. She turned her glare on Asya. "Firebird, you know how I feel about these sorts of ploys."

Asya nodded, a little sheepish. She hadn't wanted the deception, but it was the only way to make it seem convincing enough. The flames had provided cover while Nikov snuck an unconscious Iveshkin back into one of those hidden queen's corridors, leaving behind the illusion of charred remains.

Ensuring Iveshkin's safety while exposing Azarov's treachery in one fell swoop.

"But perhaps you do understand the importance of the queendom before yourself," Iveshkin added, looking at Asya with a new appraisal Asya didn't want.

She blanched, glancing down. A small part of her had hoped this would dissuade Iveshkin of her misplaced belief.

Asya reached for Tsiviya. "Are you all right?"

Tsiviya backed away, eyes still wide. Asya raised her palms, perhaps offering assurance far too late.

Around them, Azarov's guards seemed uncertain what they should do, unwilling to stand up for the general but also unable to stand down.

"Will you keep this peaceful, Azarov?" Iveshkin asked.

Azarov didn't reply to Iveshkin but turned his thunderous expression on Asya instead. "Your strashe will pay for this."

Asya couldn't stop the flinch. She knew that was the risk, the real thing she had been gambling with all night. The true hypocrisy that Asya was the one willing to endanger someone else's life for this.

But she couldn't let Azarov gain any more influence than he already had. Couldn't let his poison spread.

And with Azarov's treachery clear, she might still be able to convince the cabinet to free Yuliana. Once Iveshkin's anger at not being party to Asya's plan had faded, she was sure the commander could be reasoned with. So much of this depended on Asya's fragile certainty that they were better off keeping Yuliana alive, that the leverage she offered was worth more than her death.

Even thinking it made Asya's gut wrench. She sounded very like all of these courtiers—like her mother and Izaveta. Playing games with a person's life.

Azarov turned in a slow circle, taking stock of the tight space around him. The anger had ebbed from his features now, replaced with an unsettling composure. "I had hoped to do this more cleanly," he said. "But you force my hand."

He drew a weapon with a high shriek of steel, leveling it at Asya.

Her hand jumped instinctively to her waist, but of course, her shashka wasn't there.

Yet still she reached for it, even knowing it was impossible for it to be there. Because there was no denying that the blade in Azarov's hand was hers. The carefully shining bronze, the slight nick on the pommel from a training session with Yuliana, the frayed edge of the grip that Asya hadn't got around to replacing.

She was so caught up in that confusion, the surprise at being threatened with her own weapon, that everything moved far too slowly. The Firebird lurched inside her, realizing something that Asya did not. But even its flames were too late.

Azarov turned with a speed Asya wouldn't have thought possible of him—a reminder that whatever else he was, he had been trained as a soldier. The blade cut a wicked smile in the air, a sharp betrayal as it arced down to Commander Iveshkin's exposed back.

Just as Asya had imagined it, just as Azarov had ordered her to do.

But there were no illusions now. No Nikov hiding in the shadows to ensure the trick was believable. The shashka speared through Iveshkin with a brutal, terribly real, finality.

Chapter Thirty-Seven

Flames leaped from Asya's fingers—far too late. They dissipated to a soft shower of sparks that shone in the blood pooling around Commander Iveshkin. Illuminating the fine engraving on the hilt of Asya's shashka.

Bile rose in her throat. Other bodies swam in front of her eyes. The blackened corpses of the Elmer, Conze Vittaria's staring eyes as the Calling cut off abruptly. The people who had knelt before her aunt as the Firebird and not risen again.

Tarya had told her once that she'd get used to it. It seemed her aunt was wrong on that too.

"Asya—" A hand gripped her arm, jolting her back to the present.

Nikov was staring at her, eyes wide and worried.

She gulped in the tainted air, the small room painting itself back in around her. She turned to Azarov, standing over Iveshkin's body with little more than distaste creasing his features.

"How—" Asya choked. "How could you do that?" For all of Azarov's posturing, she had still seen him as a member of the court. As someone bound by their rules. He couldn't just assassinate cabinet members as he saw fit.

She looked to Tsiviya, to see if the general's daughter had

any more understanding at this. But Tsiviya was just staring down at the body, paler than the marble behind her, one hand on the wall to keep balance, the other pressed to her lips.

Azarov took a careful step away from Iveshkin's body, keeping his polished boots clear of the seeping blood.

"*I* didn't do anything." He gave an exaggerated shrug. "You are the one who lured her in here. We all saw you leave the hall together. And you're the one trying to convince the cabinet to stay an execution. Perhaps you thought Iveshkin was your way in. Then when she disagreed, you decided to take matters into your own hands. After all, that's your blade, is it not?"

Asya stared at him, too many things tangling together in her chest for her to form words. The story fit so perfectly. Just as she'd known all along, these games were not worth the price of playing. These sorts of schemes had killed Asya's mother, had destroyed her sister.

What gave Asya the right to think she could do any better?

She caught hold of the one solid thing, the last scrap of rope. "All of these people saw you," she said with a frantic gesture around her, to Tsiviya, to Nikov, to Azarov's own guards. "They know you did this."

"It doesn't matter," Azarov replied, with an almost pitying smile. He pointed back to the hall, to the still more distant sounds of celebration slowly morphing to hushed whispers of fear. "Because they *want* to believe it was you."

No sooner had he spoken than he dropped to his knees, hands raised in a mockery of surrender. Again, Asya was so caught off guard by this, so many steps behind in whatever plan Azarov was concocting, that she didn't move fast enough.

Nikov understood sooner than her, as he began to pull her back toward the door. But there was no undoing this now.

No going back. A new beginning, just as the First Snows had foretold.

"Please," Azarov begged, his voice pitched high and rasping. "Please, don't hurt me, Firebird. I won't tell—"

Strashevsta Orlov burst through the door as if on cue, gleaming silver strashe fanning out behind him. Absurd in the small space. Courtiers peered in through the gaps, as if trying to get a better view for the entertainment. This absurd farce.

All of this was absurd.

They were all looking at Asya, waiting for something she didn't know how to give.

Nikov stepped forward, angling his body so he stood between her and the strashe. "Arrest General Azarov," he said, and Asya had never been so thankful to have someone at her side who was able to make their thoughts coherent. "He has been conspiring against the cabinet and attacked Commander Iveshkin."

Asya could feel the weight of their gazes, the suspicion as they looked from her raised hands to General Azarov, still cowering in supposed fear. He'd done very well at making her the instigator here, the one with something to prove.

"The Firebird did this," Azarov said, slowly getting to his feet. His scarlet-clad guards were all at attention now, their firestone-edged blades held ready.

"No—" Asya started to say, but Azarov cut her off, in his element.

"How many have died since she returned to the palace?" he pressed. "She believes consequences do not apply to her. Commander Iveshkin stood up to her, and she paid the price."

"No," Asya said, the only word she could summon. "No, I—" But she couldn't manage to rein in her thoughts. Her futile attempts at a plan had been torn to shreds and she was still trying to understand how this had gone so wrong.

Conze Bazin clutched his carved icon, knuckles shining white as he peered out from behind the strashevsta. His eyes were on Asya, vague suspicion slowly transmuting to accusation. "You argued with her about the trial of succession."

"They were arguing again tonight," Azarov supplied. "Their raised voices were what drew me here. Arguing over the traitor the Firebird wants freed."

"No, that's not what—" was all Asya managed, her chest tightening with every breath. Because of course she *did* want that supposed traitor freed and she had argued with Iveshkin over the trial of succession. This was the thing she hated about the palace. The way it twisted truths into lies. Snaring her with her own good intentions.

Nikov put a light hand on her arm, a soft touch of reassurance. "This wasn't the Firebird," he said again. "Why would she kill someone with a blade when her powers would be so much more efficient?" A very good point, but not one the gathered crowd seemed to appreciate. It did nothing to change the dark looks, the raised sabers. The unquestioning certainty that Asya had finally done what they'd all been expecting her to do.

The courtiers had backed away now, watching from the tightly packed passage. The other cabinet members too. Safe behind the line of strashe. Bars between them and the monster.

No one was listening to her. No one cared about the logic of Nikov's explanation or the gloating smile curling Azarov's lips.

The truth didn't matter.

Asya could see it reflected in their collected faces. They did not want her here, an uncontrollable entity. The First

Snows offered them renewal in more than one way. A new ruler and a chance to be rid of the underlying threat of the Firebird, all at once.

"We have to show that we will not be held hostage by this creature any longer," Azarov went on as if Nikov had not spoken. As if this matter were already decided.

Murmurs of assent rippled through the crowd. They had all been waiting for an excuse, and Azarov had been happy to oblige. Waiting until the moment most convenient to him, when she could no longer be used.

He'd cheated, but it didn't matter. He was a murderer, willing to do what Asya had not.

And he would win. Either with Asya in a cage or forced to flee as a fugitive, an immortal outcast. Yuliana would be executed and Izaveta would be lost forever.

Anger flashed through Asya's veins, white-hot and unanticipated. A burning fury at all of this—the gods, the palace, this man, all determined to control her. To twist her fate to their ends.

In all of these things that had happened, all the ways she had been forced into something else, she'd never felt angry before. Not like this. A consuming kind of rage, one that twisted her vision and begged to be released.

No matter what she did, what paths she tried to take or good she tried to do, she always ended up here.

Before she could act, someone else moved first—too smoothly, a jagged knife through snow. She heard shouts of alarm as someone broke ranks with the strashe, but Asya caught only the glint out of the corner of her eye, not a blade but the shining edge of frost.

Destructive veins tearing through their face.

Azarov lunged, znaya slicing across their chest with ease.

They collapsed to the ground, blood and cursed magic mingling around them.

Silence crashed across the room, strangled breaths as everyone stared down at the second corpse to adorn the marble floor. Violence brought right to their feet, no possibility of looking away.

Deryev broke the silence first, from where he crouched behind Orlov's protection.

"This is the retribution of the gods for such terrible atrocities." He turned to Asya, eyes burning into her. "*She* has caused this. Arrest the Firebird!"

CHAPTER THIRTY-EIGHT

Izaveta took a stumbling step back, knocking into one of the other tables and sending a pile of jars cascading. The shattering of glass resonated in the quiet. The ground felt like it was shifting, everything realigning beneath her in a way she didn't yet understand. Bile churned in her stomach, something caustic and bitter.

Kyriil's skin was pale, blue tingeing in at the edges. It was not a body just killed, certainly not in the short space of time since Izaveta had last spoken to him.

Izaveta vaguely knew she should be listening, making sure no one was coming, but she could barely hear through the rushing in her ears. The game board upended and pieces scattered at her feet. This was nothing she had seen before, nothing she could predict or manipulate. This was something impossible—an impossibility Izaveta could not have imagined.

What are you?

She took a shuddering breath and then another. She had to focus, find some way through this. She turned away from Kyriil, from the cold presence that seeped from him.

Information, she needed to narrow it down to just that certainty. And information only held power in how it was shared.

Hands shaking, she reached for the feather quill—the same

void-black of falcon wings. Her first thought was to write to Asya, the instinctive reaction the memory in her chest reached for. But logic chased swiftly after. The power Izaveta held here came from exposing that the Azarovs had been holding her captive, that they were dabbling in some dark magic.

Information the palace would already want to ignore, especially from a biased source. Even with proof of a letter, Asya could easily be dismissed. A grieving or desperate sister.

Izaveta needed something indisputable, more corporeal. She had one move here and it had to be decisive.

Her hand hovered over the ancient parchment, ink dripping as nothing beat in her chest.

A sound made her jerk, ink spattering across the table. Footsteps, more distinct than they had been before.

Svedye.

She only had a split second to decide, to weigh the risks. She had to get herself some leverage here, something to claw herself back into existence. And that meant reaching for the person who had most to lose—the person whose immediate action she could be assured of. Who no one would think could be swayed to her side.

Azarov—I know about your son and what you've done. You've gone too far. My next letter will expose your treachery. This is your last chance.

—Izaveta Karasova

Something in writing her name eased the screaming tension in her chest, even if it was echoed by the fluttering memory of guilt. Asya would find out soon enough. This was the only choice, the best choice—wasn't it?

Izaveta grasped a bowl of water, sparkling moonlight already held in its depths. She placed the parchment on the surface, the familiar words leaping to her lips.

Hardly breathing, she tore a handful of hairs from her head, hoping it would be enough, and tossed them at the dying candle. She wouldn't risk foregoing the price, not this time. They caught at once, just as the door swung open.

She could have tried to run, tried to skulk under one of the tables like a child, but she wouldn't face this while groveling on the floor.

Kyriil—or *not* Kyriil, an imposter wearing his face—stepped inside, the sharp angle of his features and gold gleam of his hair both familiar and foreign. He took in the scene slowly, eyes dancing from her hasty spell to the uncovered corpse, to finally rest on Izaveta.

"Well," he said mildly. "It seems we have a lot to discuss."

CHAPTER THIRTY-NINE

Movement burst across the room in jagged swirls. The strashe leaping to follow Deryev's order, like flames eager to fly free. Courtiers dispersing in their wake. But most terrifying of all, more of that frozen curse spread from person to person, a ruination that added to the clamoring chaos.

But Asya had only one goal now.

She'd been caught unaware by firestone before, but she was ready this time. She spun, releasing a whirl of flame that forced the strashe back.

One of the hanging tapestries caught fire, searing gold eating through the fabric and sending sparks flying.

There was something freeing in watching them all scatter. The strashe diving away in fear. They'd all held their breath for so long, been tensed for this blow, that it was a relief for them to act on it. They could all stop pretending.

In the small space, their attempted retreat from the flames sent them stumbling over each other. Blades and bodies all clattering to the ground as some tried to surge forward while others fled, hampered again by several strashe in the clutches of that frozen magic.

She didn't wait for any of them to recover. Didn't even pause to offer Nikov some hint at explanation. That time was long past.

With another rush of blinding flame—so bright it burned behind her lids—she launched herself out of the window. The falling snow sizzled against her skin, burning footprints smoldering in her wake.

Only Azarov, carefully out of the path of the roiling chaos, managed to follow. A mistake, though he didn't seem to realize it. She'd been sure she could count on him wanting to play the hero.

Asya ran only far enough to be out of sight of the still-burning room. She stopped beneath the looming shadow of Zmenya's Tower, the only protection from the thick flurries clogging the air. She turned to face Azarov, his ornamental sword drawn and ready.

Asya didn't need the faint gasp of moonlight to know that it would be edged with firestone. It didn't matter.

Anger burned beneath her skin again, a living thing beside the Firebird's steady pulse. That this man could play with people's lives and still get what he wanted. Asya let the flames reach out, curling around Azarov in warning. "Show me where she is."

Azarov didn't flinch. "I think we both know that if you were going to kill me, you would have done it by now."

He was wrong about that.

The thought crept along Asya's skin, bringing a shuddering realization with it. She wasn't searching for reasons to act. She was holding back a burning desire to do it. Kept in check by all the walls she'd built up, slowly being chipped away with every word he spoke.

She wouldn't even be going against the Firebird's duty. After all, Azarov had long found ways to escape the price. It would have to catch up with him one day.

"Drop your weapon," Asya said.

"You've already proved you won't make the hard choices." Azarov's grip on his saber tightened, even as Asya squeezed the coiling flames around him. "Threats are useless when they hold no weight."

Azarov went to advance, perhaps planning to call Asya's bluff—but a blade at his back forced him to freeze.

"How about my threats?" Dima asked in a low growl. Dressed in the livery of Azarov's guard, Asya had still not been sure if he'd help. Just as likely to disarm Azarov as he was to run her through with that firestone blade. That was probably why he'd waited so long to act. He wanted to see which side to pick to help his sister.

A strange truce built on the fact that they both cared for the same person.

Azarov's mouth twisted, fury flashing through him. "I knew I shouldn't have bothered keeping you alive."

He dropped the saber into the fresh fallen snow.

His acquiescence now, the way he listened to Dima without hesitation, prickled at that anger in Asya's chest. Azarov was wrong. She wasn't weak.

There was a brief moment, a flicker of uncertainty when Asya thought Dima might take up the firestone weapon himself. An assurance of Asya's loyalty, another vestige of vengeance still knotted inside him.

But he didn't.

Instead, Dima took a firm step forward, shoving the general on. "Show us where my sister is."

"This won't get you what you hope," Azarov said, as he haltingly led them across the snow-struck grounds. "You've shown your true self, Firebird. You'll be running forever."

Asya ignored him. She didn't need his words worming their way in.

"And you would trust the Firebird?" the general asked Dima, his performance sliding back into place. "Your father would be so disappointed."

Dima's jaw twitched. Asya could feel him forcing himself not to look at her. To find a way to keep this as separate as he could.

"Don't waste our time," he said to Azarov, pressing the saber into his back.

Azarov kept his mouth shut as he led them to the west side of the palace, though Asya doubted that meant he was done sowing discord. Just beyond the view of the training grounds stood a disused strashem, its roof damaged from a past winter storm. Devoid of strashe, with whirls of snow caught in the fractured moonlight, the guardhouse felt strikingly unreal.

Asya paused at the threshold, glancing at Dima with slight apprehension. But he just pushed Azarov ahead. Asya followed the two of them down a wide passage lined with doors. A small holding cell stood at the far end, bars rusted with disuse.

The perfect place to keep a prisoner they didn't want found.

A figure sat hunched against the bars, arms wrapped around herself, dark hair curtaining her face.

Asya's heart ricocheted against her ribs. She pushed past Azarov, feet drawing her on as certainly as a Calling. A glowing wave of relief that she was really here and alive.

Yuliana looked up at the sound, those light flurries of snow radiant around her. It reminded Asya of that day in the cathedral, the moment she'd thought Yuliana had first seen her as more than the Firebird.

The moment Asya had first seen Yuliana as beautiful.

"Asya?" Yuliana leaped to her feet. "How are you here?

I—" Then her eyes fell on Dima, still holding Azarov at sword-point. She took a step back, suddenly guarded.

"Dima?"

"We're getting you out of here," he said.

Yuliana looked like she wanted to say something, but pressed her lips together. A resolution passed across her face that Asya couldn't quite reach. Though the shift in Yuliana's posture was clear. She didn't trust her brother or the general to keep to their word any more than Asya did.

Dima shoved Azarov forward again. "Open it."

"I don't have the key," Azarov replied, a challenge in his voice. A challenge Asya thought she understood.

It was harder to forget you were helping the Firebird when she burst into flames. But she didn't have time to care about Dima's feelings. Even with the chaos left in their wake, the strashe would follow soon. Not to mention Azarov's own guards, who likely knew where Yuliana was being kept.

Asya turned to the bars, white-hot flames building at her fingertips. The Firebird surged out of her before she'd even formed the thought, as eager as her. The bars melted beneath her touch, molten metal spattering around her feet like snow. She heaved and the last bolts fell away. It was amazing how easy it was when she wasn't holding back. When she didn't bother with trying to be less.

Asya could feel Dima watching her, feel the misgiving trembling in the air.

But it didn't matter. Not when Yuliana was in front of her with no restraints—nothing to keep them apart—for the first time since the coronation. So much had happened since then and she wasn't quite sure where she stood.

Suddenly, Asya felt very shy. The greater fears shriveling to just this moment. Yuliana had not seen her like this before. Had not seen the way the Firebird rose out of her, terrible and breathtaking.

But Yuliana didn't balk at the flames that still curled around Asya. Didn't pause to take in her brother or Azarov. Yuliana just flung herself forward, arms wrapped tight around Asya—as if she wasn't burning. As if she wasn't scared at all.

She pulled away slightly, still clinging to Yuliana's comforting presence. She pressed her forehead against Yuliana's. Nothing between them now, no secrets or lies. No knives or locked doors.

Then Yuliana straightened, her eyebrows furrowing. She smacked Asya's arm, ignoring the trailing sparks. "What in all the stupid, reckless things do you think you're doing?"

"Saving you," Asya said with a small smile.

Yuliana stepped back, worry creasing across her face as she glanced at her brother and Azarov.

"We'll have to run," Asya said, the brief moment of relief dissolving. "I'm sorry. There won't be any going back."

That certainly summed it up. Decisions Asya couldn't come back from. No going back to the palace, no going back for Izaveta.

Yuliana grasped her hand, pulling Asya into that tight space where only the two of them mattered. "I told you before. I wouldn't change anything."

Asya opened her mouth to reply, but then their small refuge shattered. A sharp movement at the corner of her eye.

Both she and Dima had been too focused on Yuliana to notice Azarov had retrieved one of the fallen bars. Asya raised her hand instinctively, sure the arc of his swing was meant for her.

But Azarov feinted at the last moment, cutting around Asya to Yuliana's unprotected side. The bar cracked against Yuliana's knee with a sickening crunch.

Yuliana's tattered scream tore through Asya.

Dima was on Azarov in the next breath, Asya's sparks already dancing at her fingertips. Too late again.

"That might make your escape more challenging," Azarov said, smiling even as Dima dragged him back.

Asya knelt at Yuliana's side, her fingers skimming over her shattered knee. The weight and jagged edge of the bar had ensured a messy break, a shard of metal still sticking out. That was intentional too. No quick fixes, too much danger of infection, too complicated to even risk magic for.

Asya didn't know what to begin to do with this. It went far beyond her aunt's rudimentary explanations on bandaging wounds and staunching blood. The Firebird didn't have any real need for those anyway.

"I'm fine," Yuliana said through gritted teeth, a blatant lie that Asya couldn't bring herself to contradict. She put a hand on Asya's shoulder, trying to pull herself to her feet. Yuliana only managed halfway, her leg buckling beneath her. Asya caught her weight, steadying the strashe against her body.

They couldn't run, not with Yuliana like this. They wouldn't even reach the bearkeep before the strashe were on them. And there would be no standing to fight—no allies left to them in the palace.

She felt Yuliana's eyes on her, felt the thought sparking in her mind. "Asya—" Yuliana started.

"Don't say it. I'm not going without you."

"Of course we aren't," Dima snapped, still pinning Azarov to the ground. That strange *we* again, enemies who had somehow become bound together.

"I can always offer you other options," Azarov said, negotiating even with a blade at his throat. "I can reason with the cabinet, ensure your strashe is well cared for and kept alive."

Asya gritted her teeth. "As long as I do whatever you want?"

Azarov grinned, apparently oblivious to how close Asya was to letting the Firebird consume him. "Nothing comes without a price." He paused, appraising the damage he'd done. "And you really should get that looked at," he added. "Nasty wound like that, it could get infected."

"*Quiet,*" Dima growled.

Yuliana gripped Asya's shoulder again, her face growing paler by the moment. "You know we can't trust him."

Of course they couldn't. But who *could* they trust?

Forced to a crossroads again, each path promising more hardship. Each path pulling her further away from the people she loved.

Something flickered in the corner of Asya's vision.

A low sizzle of magic in the air. The slightest thread, reaching for her from somewhere far away. Like a hand tapping her on the back. She whirled around, but the passageway was just as empty as it had been.

No—a scrap of parchment floated down between her and Azarov.

Asya snatched it up, recognizing the curling handwriting at once.

Everything slowed around her. Or perhaps she was the one that stilled, clutching this precious thing in her fingers. It was only three lines, ink-splattered and hurried. But three lines that proved Izaveta wasn't truly gone. For all the searching, Asya wasn't sure she had truly believed it. A last desperate hope, a fantasy she'd clung to through all of this.

This was more than a scrap of fabric, it was tangible proof her sister wasn't gone forever.

It took a moment longer for the meaning to hit. She read it again, a tight pain squeezing in her. Izaveta hadn't written to her.

Asya turned it over, squinting in the darkness. There had to be more—something else her sister was trying to tell her. The writing was fainter on the back, certainly not in Izaveta's hand, yet still familiar. In a language not quite Tóurensi but with similar roots. One that Asya recognized as well. How could she not?

"What is that?" Yuliana murmured, leaning heavily on the wall.

Asya didn't know how to answer that. Far too much contained in something so small. She'd stared at Saint Korona's book long enough it had seared itself into the back of her mind, certainly enough to know that writing.

All of that searching and now the answer was right there. Conjured out of thin air at just the moment Asya needed it most.

She didn't understand it, didn't know how Izaveta's note played into it. But Asya couldn't ignore what this was.

A sign. A warning.

Or, perhaps, an entreaty. The gods nudging her forward.

"I say we kill him and get moving," Dima said, too focused on Azarov to notice what Asya held.

"No." The word rang out with the sharp cadence of a command, unfamiliar in Asya's voice. "Don't kill him."

Dima glared at her. "This isn't time for your moral quandaries. He's a liability, he—"

"No," Asya said again, still staring at the paper in her hand. "I'm not taking orders from *you*."

"Dima." The one word caused Yuliana far more effort than it should, her voice tight as she looked at her brother. She couldn't seem to form the rest of the sentence, but Dima didn't argue anymore. Perhaps his attempt at reconciliation.

Asya kept her eyes on Azarov, watching his slick certainty begin to slip away. "I think I have a better use for him alive," she said. "For now."

Chapter Forty

Izaveta should have grabbed some kind of weapon—shards of the broken glass or a heavy jar, anything to hold between them. With her back to the wall, the only exit blocked, fear came back again. It brought an astonishing clarity, far too late as the letter was long gone. She should've sent it to Asya. Her scant hopes here rested on it—rested on the question of if Izaveta had read this situation right and could force Azarov's hand.

If she'd sent it to Asya, at least there would be one person who cared, even if there was nothing she could do to help.

"Sneaking around seems unbecoming of a princess," Kyriil said simply.

Izaveta studied him—the voice was Kyriil's, but now that she looked at him, he did not look like…anybody. As if she were trying to catch hold of his reflection in rippling water. Even the deep green of his clothes shifted as she watched, so imperceptible she couldn't be sure they had ever been a different color.

"How long have you been him?" Not quite the question she'd intended, but she needed to know how long she'd been such a fool.

"Since after the coronation and your pitiful attempt to save your sister," he replied. "His father was desperate for some way back in, so I offered him a bargain." He canted his head to the corpse behind them, a mere piece to be traded. "It's so easy to manipulate someone who thinks they know everything."

There was a double meaning in that, a barb at Izaveta too. Another question rose to her lips, one that solidified some of her fear. "How did I end up imprisoned here?"

He smiled, a baring of teeth. "A neat trick, no? I have a certain *affinity* with magic, so I knew what the price would be and how to manipulate it. How to get the magic to bring you here at just the right moment."

Bile coated Izaveta's throat as she reached for any kind of weapon. "You cannot play with this kind of magic. The Firebird will not stand for it."

But Kyriil—the imposter in his place—was unruffled. "The Firebird will play her part soon enough."

Something painful resonated through the empty space in her chest, a remembered guilt. Izaveta had made the wrong choice again.

"You can't hope to kill the Firebird," she said, her thoughts now far away. How soon would Azarov act? Was there some plan in place already, or was there still time to protect Asya?

"So small-minded," he said. "Why would I want to kill her?"

Izaveta ground her teeth together, the frustration of not knowing building. "You want the Firebird and you want this mysterious crown," she snapped. "Neither of which will be much use to you." She nodded to the bowl of water still balanced on the table behind him, the guttering candle she'd used for the spell. "In a matter of minutes, the palace will know I'm alive."

"It's not the Firebird I want," he replied, entirely glossing over Izaveta's threats. "It's what she can do for me."

He bent to the stone floor, sweeping his hand across it just as he'd done in her cell. It revealed a brightly lit hall of the palace, sparkling decorations for the First Snows strewn across the floor in tatters as people fled. "Things are not going well at the palace. I think we can be assured it will push your sister to act."

Izaveta almost didn't hear him, her eyes not on the destruction as they should be but instead caught on something glinting on Kyriil's finger. As he straightened, the dying light snagged on it, a small burst of starlight. The ring he had used to take them to the palace gardens, the relic of Saint Ilyova.

A way out of here. A way to get to Asya before this all careened out of her grasp.

Izaveta let some of the fear sink into her, the very real terror of being trapped here alone, her breaths choking. Surging forward, she grabbed his hand. "Please—please, don't do this."

He didn't speak, but he didn't stop her either.

It didn't matter if he believed her or not, didn't matter if he truly entertained this possibility. She just needed to direct his attention for a moment.

"I know there must still be some of Kyriil in there," she said. "Please—we could be on the same side here."

She tightened her grip against his, her skin touching the cool bone of the ring. All she had to do was pull it free, then hope that the magic in it was simple enough to whisk her away at once.

Her thumb and forefinger snagged around it—

He stepped back, a smooth movement that took any hope of the ring with him.

"Such a waste, all your theatrics." His voice held little memory of Kyriil's now, instead something with a great resonance to it. A far older power. "But your sister will finish her part soon."

Pretense broken, Izaveta glared, voice unwavering. "Asya is better than me. Selfless. Whatever you have planned, she won't do it. You played your cards wrong."

"I think you underestimate my hand." He smiled then, an expression that split his face into something else, an inhuman mask. "Once, your sister would have never even considered this. But you ensured that changed. Being betrayed by those closest to you can twist you into something else. It makes a person so *easy* to manipulate."

CHAPTER FORTY-ONE

Even with the whirling snow and thickening mist, the glow of the Depthless Lake was easy to pick out ahead. A soft gleam, paler than moonlight. Not yet fully frozen as it would be in the depths of winter, solid enough for grown bears to walk on. But thin layers of ice frosted across the surface, a small promise of what was to come.

Dima still led Azarov at sword-point, while Asya supported Yuliana across the uneven ground. Even this short distance was probably too much for her, but Yuliana refused to be left behind even with Asya's promise of return. And, in all honesty, Asya didn't want to leave her.

Yuliana hadn't questioned what Asya was doing, possibly too preoccupied with her leg to be able to voice any misgivings. But when Asya gestured to Dima to halt at the edge of the lake, Yuliana finally spoke, leaning hard against one of the spindled trees. "What are we doing here?"

Asya took a step back, counting her paces from the ice-spun edge of the lake. "I think I can still fix this."

"You know this isn't your mess to clean up." A statement, but it rang like a question in Asya's head. "You don't owe them anything."

"Maybe not," Asya said, drawing a thin circle in the snow.

Not the ideal surface for a ritual, but her flames helped. Searing through the newly fallen snow to carve into the ground below, twisting whorls that she had seen drawn out in that book. As imprinted in her mind as the rest of the ritual.

The one whose price had seemed too high to pay.

"But I won't let him win," Asya finished. "I won't let him take you too. Not if there's something I could do."

"And what is that?" Yuliana asked, her eyes tracking the whirled lines with none of the suspicion Asya felt she deserved.

"I'm going to make up for what I did. I'm going to bring my sister back."

"Asya," Yuliana said, gentle as the soft snow. "What happened was not your fault."

"It was." Asya had thought the words, but they were spoken by General Azarov. He didn't look calm now. Dirt streaked his face, gray hair flecked with snow and his mouth a snarl as he tried to pull away from Dima's grip.

Yuliana's head snapped to him, all gentleness vanishing. "You don't get to talk," she spat. "We all know the things you've done."

"Yes," Azarov said, no hint of apology on his face. "To protect Tóurin from *her*."

Asya paused, the burning lines of the ritual receding a little. Of all Azarov's jabs, his attempts to distract her, this one worked. "To protect it from me?"

Azarov wrenched forward, spittle flying and feet slipping against the snow. There was no reserved statesman in him now. This was hatred. Something embittered and rancorous, an old wound left to fester. "From *you*," he spat. "From all of the Karasova line who felt entitled to their power at whatever cost." His features contorted, rage bursting as bright as any fire. "My grandfather found out the truth and it cost him his cabinet seat. Sent our family into disgrace. But I refused to stay back and let you continue to ruin Tóurin. You can't live on this stolen power forever. The past will catch up to you again. You still have much more to pay for, Firebird."

Asya stared at him. He really believed that. It wouldn't be a useful act at this point, and besides she could feel it. In the fervent buzz of his words, the anguished twist of his face. He really saw himself as the hero of that story.

Perhaps he was. Perhaps that was the truth Asya had been avoiding all this time.

"What did your grandfather find out?" Asya asked.

Azarov let out a vicious laugh. He seemed to be coming undone, as if speaking all of this aloud had unraveled some part of himself. "Don't pretend not to know, Firebird."

She opened her mouth, trying to form some response to that, but Yuliana grasped her arm. "Asya," she said, warning in her tone as she looked up at the slope behind them.

Asya followed her gaze to the pinpricks of torches, drawing closer by the moment.

She didn't have time to entertain whatever it was Azarov was trying to do. Once Izaveta was here, the rightful queen returned, they'd be able to sort all of this out.

There was still that doubt. Nikov's words echoed in her mind. *There are things you can't come back from.*

But weren't there also some things that were worth the price, no matter what it was? Wasn't it worth being the monster Azarov thought her if it saved the people she cared for most?

Asya looked to Yuliana, her anchor against this raging storm. "What if I'm making the wrong choice?"

"I trust you."

Yuliana said it so easily, as if it were obvious. Trust Asya wasn't sure she had earned, that she certainly did not deserve. Not with what she was about to do.

But she didn't have time to consider. Those torches were bobbing closer. And if she waited too long, she might change her mind.

She remembered every other detail of the ritual from that book, all the symbols and incantations. There had just been that one piece she was missing.

The fire rose up around them, a burning wall of searing scarlet. Asya barely felt the heat. A slight warmth at the ends of her fingertips, though she knew it must be blistering. But she wasn't worried. She could control it now, and it would only burn what it needed to.

"Whatever you're doing won't help," Azarov yelled, his words almost lost to the roaring fire in Asya's ears. Dima had let go of him now, too distracted by the dancing flames. Asya thought he was yelling too, voices all torn away in the rushing of the night around them.

Azarov didn't dare come closer now, though. He was not looking at her with that smug expression, not looking at her as if he knew what she would do.

"Is your sister worth this?" he asked—Asya only made out the words from the shape of his lips, illuminated by the warring light of the flames and the Depthless Lake. "Would she do the same for you?"

The answer stuck in Asya's throat. What she thought she knew of her sister had shifted so much since their mother's death. An ever-changing tapestry. She still didn't quite know which threads were real. The girl who had murdered their mother. The sister who would do anything for her.

It didn't change Asya's decision.

She grasped the sharp stone she'd found, holding the jagged edge over the pad of her thumb. The blood of the Fire-bird. This spell that had been made for her. Or she had been made for it. The end of the path the gods had set her on all those years ago.

She pulled the scrap of fabric from her pocket, the one she'd found in the forest. The last piece of the spell that had been missing, written out on the back of Izaveta's letter. *A piece of yours to tether you here.* The part of Saint Korona's book that had been torn out.

Asya placed the fabric in the middle of the burning symbols. They seemed drawn to it, leaning in to watch the performance.

Dima pushed forward, lighted by the trailing sparks. He held the firestone blade in his hands now, that old look from the Elmer alive in his eyes again. The deep, inherent fear the Firebird drew out. "Don't do this."

Yuliana stepped in front of Asya. Her body was angled carefully between them, protective and defensive on both sides—unsure which of them needed the safety.

"Stay back!" Asya yelled. Or she thought she did. The yell came out as another flash of fire, slipping around Yuliana to push Dima back. The ritual couldn't be interrupted now. An arrow already let loose from its bow.

Turning back to Azarov, Asya tore a piece of blistering crimson from the circle around them.

He looked small now. Tired and desperate in the way everyone did when faced with the Firebird. And a little defiant. The hero standing against the monster.

In the end, he'd been wrong about her.

Killing him was unnervingly easy. As if the Firebird had been waiting for her to do just that. A discordant Calling rang in her ears as a keen glare of flame consumed Azarov and he became a part of the spell. It rose up around her, spreading beyond the drawn symbols and down into the dark roots of the land.

The price was paid.

The symbols melted away, as if they'd been no more than snow to start with. All the Firebird's flames sputtered out, the world suddenly darker for their absence.

"Asya?" Yuliana said slowly, a grim hesitation seeping through her voice.

Asya looked around, waiting for the searing tingle of magic. For Izaveta to materialize in front of her. Or for a flashing lightning bolt or a shifting of the ground. *Something* to show what she'd done had worked.

But nothing happened. Everything was silent and still as a grave.

Dima lay pushed up on one elbow, his hair singed and expression afraid. Only a few paces away lay what had been General Azarov. And Yuliana was still at her side, face pale even against the snow.

A strange sensation crawled over Asya's skin. An abrupt loosening of her breath. Like a knot long tied had suddenly been cut. But there was no relief in the feeling. Just a terrible foreboding that resonated through Asya's bones.

Something that had been leashed—that *should* be leashed—set free.

She froze, trapped in that instant. In a heart–stopping fear that had clenched hold of her. So complete, she almost didn't feel the knife bury itself in her side.

PART FOUR:

THROUGH FIRE OR BLOOD

Does it make a difference to say I tried?
That I had the best intentions for my queendom,
that I truly thought my motives were pure. I
suppose it makes little difference in the end.
All history will remember is my failure, another
heartless queen who put herself first.

—FROM THE PAPERS OF QUEEN TERIYA

CHAPTER FORTY-TWO

Izaveta had never felt magic before. She'd read about how people had once been able to feel it in the air, how it had flowed through the land like a second wind. Asya had told her how she sensed it as the Firebird, the searing burn and calling notes.

But Izaveta had never truly understood it until this moment.

The way the hairs on the back of her neck prickled, a jarring thrum of anticipation that trickled across her skin. This strange sensation of *possibility*.

Then it was gone. Slipping through her fingers like trying to grasp hold of water. And, just like water, she could see where it flowed away to.

She did not know what had happened—if this was the plan Kyriil had intended. If it meant Asya had made the wrong choice.

He didn't look any different, not on the surface. But just as Izaveta had felt that tingling cascade of magic, she could feel the change in him too. A slight sharpening to his features, as though she hadn't realized that his edges had been blurred until they'd shone into focus. And that same sense of possibility. Of power.

Kyriil—the imposter wearing his face—tilted his head back as if basking in the sun. He looked less and less like Kyriil as Izaveta watched, features shifting and smoothing into something else, something still not quite recognizable, yet somehow familiar. An old portrait long fallen to disuse, reparations forgotten but a form still visible.

He wasn't looking at her, too preoccupied with this newfound power.

Izaveta took a slow step back, her mind only managing to process one thought: *run.* There was nowhere to go in this tower, she knew that already, but even the barren and unforgiving landscape beyond the window could offer more mercy than this. More possibility of survival than this raw and vicious magic before her.

She'd barely gone two paces when the floor in front of her shivered, transforming until its surface rippled like water. A shape rose, sculpted from the stone itself, the figure of an armored warrior. It towered over Izaveta as it lurched forward, a little unsteady on its feet. She felt something burn against her arm, a searing pain, but even that was not enough to force her body to move.

Each footfall vibrated through the floor, solid and *real.*

Magic like this should not be possible. It was the sort of thing she'd read about in ancient stories, not something that could truly exist. The realization crept over her too slowly, a dawning horror that she could not hold back.

The stone warrior grasped her arm, its grip immovable and strong enough to bruise.

Behind her, Kyriil—*not* Kyriil—flexed his fingers with a sense of wonder that turned Izaveta's stomach cold. He still crouched by the shimmering window to the palace, even as it shuddered closed. "The Firebird played her part," he said, so soft he might've been speaking to himself. "Fitting that she should repay what was owed."

Izaveta's left hand was going numb, the blood supply dwindling in the stone warrior's grip. She felt like she was dwindling too. Pieces of herself eroding. All the things she'd thought were stable beneath her feet torn away.

"Do you feel it?" The imposter looked up at her, an imploring adulation lighted in his gaze. *"Do you?"*

She gave a short nod, not much point in lying now. "Magic."

He rose, still reverant. "This was what it used to be like."

"Before the Fading?" Izaveta asked, curiosity piqued even through her fear.

He let out a faint laugh, the remembered impression of humor. "The Fading," he repeated. "Such a pretty way of describing a terrible tragedy."

He spoke about it as if it was some human event, not simply the natural course of magic as they'd always thought—some celestial change or slow-moving tide, the way lands re-form over the centuries.

She looked at the empty air, still so brimming with magic she imagined she could see it. A sickening thought crossed her mind, sharper than the acrid burn around her. The order had thought killing the Firebird would reverse the Fading. The same order Kyriil had funded to help provide firestone and weapons.

"What part did Asya play in this?" she asked with renewed effort to move the unmovable stone. "She didn't—you've not—" Izaveta was choking on the words, on this fear inside her so gaping it might wrench her apart. "Killing the Firebird would not end the Fading," she forced out, falling back on that logic. The same logic she'd thrown at her mother the night of her death.

"Of course it wouldn't," he said with the air of stating the obvious. "The Fading was never the fault of the Firebird. That responsibility falls squarely on the queen."

"I..." Izaveta trailed off, breath huffing from her chest. She might have dismissed that as mere taunting on his part, but there was a heaviness to him that spoke of truth. She'd never imagined a theory like that—had no idea *how* the queen could have such influence.

"Besides," he finished, as if she hadn't spoken, "this is not a reversal of the Fading."

"Then, what is it?" As soon as the words left her lips, she was sure she didn't want to know the answer.

He took a deep breath and the sharp tendrils of the magic drew back into him, not running freely but channeled through a source. "This is a debt long since owed," he said. "The retribution has finally begun."

He turned his back on her then, searching for something on the long workbench. Izaveta's heart should have been slamming in her chest, but instead the cold fear just seeped through her every orifice. The paralyzing terror of someone running out of options.

Her eyes danced around, a fluttering insect caught in a jar and banging uselessly against the sides. If there was nothing she could say in the face of this, surely there was something she could do, some trick left to try.

The knife at Kyriil's belt—the same one he'd offered her all those days ago, a bird's wings spread wide. The thin light in here was brilliance compared to the darkness of that cell, and it picked up the subtle details she hadn't noticed then. The sharp points to the wings, the way its beak hooked up over the blade, the inky black shine. A falcon.

He turned to face her and she forced herself to meet his

gaze—she didn't want him to glean what she was thinking, the ridiculous measure she was contemplating. He held something carefully between his thumb and forefinger, so insubstantial light traveled through it like ice on the surface of a lake.

He inclined his head. "Time to speed the process."

He took a step toward her, too close when she had nowhere to back away. But it also brought his dagger within reach of her free arm. All she'd have to do was grasp it and run him through.

A crude answer, deeply improper for a future queen, but she did not care. Her vision had tunneled to the immediate, to the present terror and threat. To her frantic need to run as far from them as she could.

He leaned forward, raising that insubstantial glimmer to her eye—

Fear kicked in her gut, propelling her hand to move, to grasp the hilt of the knife. It was lighter than she'd expected, warm against her fingers as she pulled it free.

She drove it into his throat with a sickening ease, flesh parting beneath the blade.

But Kyriil didn't stagger forward in pain, no blood burst from the wound. He merely turned his head toward her. A buzzing fly to swat away, a serving boy who had interrupted an important conversation, not a knife plunged into his jugular.

No more consequence than if Izaveta had driven the blade into a cushion.

He held her eye as he pulled the blade free, the low scrape of bone and tendons loud in the suffocating quiet.

Whatever this imposter was, he was not mortal.

CHAPTER FORTY-THREE

Everything was moving very fast around Asya. The swirling of the storm, the harsh yells of strashe closing in, Yuliana staggering to her side. But Asya was completely fixed. A single point of still among the rushing disarray.

It took a moment for the pain to pierce the numbing cold spreading through Asya's insides. The deeper cold of the firestone blade. Her foot slipped in the snow, one hand going to the bright splash of red on her side. Almost the exact mirror of where the order member had stabbed her.

The strashe's silver uniform blended into the snow, but their face was bright and clear. They looked almost as surprised as Asya to see the knife in her side. A last burst of flames pushed them back into the snow, another flare of scarlet against the pale backdrop.

Asya didn't need to look around at the thickening blizzard or squint through the shadows to know her sister wasn't there. Whatever the spell had done, it hadn't brought her sister back to her. Izaveta was her other half, the other side of the same coin. If her sister was here, Asya would know it.

The remains of the ritual lay strewn around them, Azarov's body splayed at an unnatural angle. *Something* had happened. A spell to restore something lost. But what Asya had lost was still long gone.

She'd paid the price. Had succumbed to cruelty. And it hadn't worked. She fell to her knees, biting cold sizzling against her dwindling flames.

The crushing weight of this grief was suddenly too much. It mingled with the creeping pain of her wound. The shame of what she'd done—what she'd let Yuliana see her as. A vortex that was dragging Asya down, down, down.

A hand grasped her arm, tugging her back from the lapping dark. "Asya—Asya, we have to go."

Shapes coalesced around them, like ghosts stepping out of the In-Between. More strashe moving closer with each shuddering breath. They must have seen what had happened. Must be able to at least guess at who the burned corpse had been.

But Asya couldn't get herself to move. She wasn't even sure why she needed to. Flames were leaking from her side, bright splashes against the snow. It couldn't be fire though—could it? The firestone had stolen that already, clamping down on the Firebird.

Yuliana cupped her hands around Asya's face, trying to force her to focus, storm-gray determination piercing. "We have to run, okay?"

Even through the haze that had settled around her, Asya knew that wasn't possible. Not without the Firebird. Not with Yuliana's leg and the growing stain of scarlet on Asya's side.

The only reason the strashe weren't on them already was the spinning confusion of the thickening snow. It hardly felt like it mattered.

They still might die here tonight.

But Asya's body listened to Yuliana, forcing herself up, even when her mind thought it was pointless. Even with the pain and blood ebbing down her side. Even with the hopelessness at their heels.

Even with her sister long gone.

CHAPTER FORTY-FOUR

The shock permeating through Izaveta, solidifying the air around her, came in waves. She'd dealt what should have been a fatal blow, yet he stood as poised and unbothered as ever.

He wiped the clean blade on his sleeve, as if dusting it of any traces of her, before placing it carefully onto the bench. He looked up at Izaveta, one brow raised in bemusement. "Does that satisfy your futile attempts to find a way out of this, or need I remind you how power works?"

Izaveta's throat constricted, the fading ache in her nail throbbing again. She'd thought she knew how power worked, how she could bend it to her will.

Yet this was another beast entirely, an untamed and uncaring creature that didn't adhere to the rules she'd always held close.

"I thought I could be more patient," he mused, conjuring that glinting shard between his fingers again. "Hundreds of years of waiting for the perfect chance, what's a few decades more? But now that I'm so close…" He took a step closer to Izaveta and she tried to pull back, her skin tearing against the immovable stone grip. "I find I grow tired of waiting on a queen's whims."

Izaveta grasped for something—some advantage she could spin here. The only vulnerability she'd managed to find.

"I know who you are," she said, pretending at a confidence that had long since slipped through her fingers. "The sorcerer who fell in love with the queen so deeply it became his undoing."

As soon as the words were out of her mouth, she knew they were a mistake. She saw it in the predatory slant to Kyriil's posture, the slight sharpness in the air.

"You talk of love as if you could possibly understand it." The words came out in a snarl, inhuman. "Love is a destructive, vengeful creature. You know *nothing* of who I am."

She'd made the mistake now, so may as well tear down this path. She reached into the tattered folds of her dress and pulled out the parchment, still brittle beneath her touch. "I know enough."

His face contorted, a flash of anger so deep it carved across his skin. The stone figure holding Izaveta in place flickered briefly, a lapse in the imposter's concentration allowing her arm to slip free.

"A thieving princess too," he spat, "though I suppose the queens have always been thieves, just not so crudely."

Izaveta took a small step back, gauging if the stone figure would halt her again. But the imposter's concentration had been drawn away, the stone figure useless in his absence. She tucked that away in her mind—a small scrap of ammunition. She kept a close hold on the letters, her fragile shield. His eyes burned into them, darting back as though called by some unwelcome orbit.

"Perhaps you do need a reminder, after all." He retrieved the knife, holding it delicately between his fingers. "*You* do not matter here."

Izaveta couldn't stop her feet shuffling back, putting some space between them. Behind her back, she reached for one of the jagged shards of glass, letting it bite into her palm. "You need me alive."

There was a marked shift in the air, the change from impending threat to present danger.

Izaveta swallowed, regretting drawing those eyes to her. They were oddly colorless in the light—a quality she'd noticed before but never truly understood. Not simply pale or bleached but shifting and ephemeral in a way that made her mind want to gloss over it. A small seam in his disguise.

"Alive, yes," he said softly, finally looking up from where she clutched the letters. "*Whole* is an entirely different question."

She didn't bother with subtlety this time. She had the smallest piece of leverage, and she couldn't miss her window. She threw the letters toward the guttering candle, a cascade of parchment eager to be consumed by the flames.

Kyriil lunged after them, knife forgotten. Izaveta used the edge of the workbench to push herself forward, grasping for his other hand. She slashed at it with the glass, a brief enough distraction to pull the ring from his finger.

Staggering back, putting as much space between them as she could, she put on the ring. She didn't feel the magic of it at once, though as a saint's relic it wasn't truly *magic*. More an invocation of the gods, just like that spell Sanislav had done to save Asya all those nights ago.

The palace, Izaveta thought desperately. She tried to picture it, the image slipping through her mind in jagged fragments of fear. She kept stumbling back until she hit the far wall, trapped again. Kyriil spun to face her, his expression oddly blurred. He didn't run toward her or bother with pursuit— perhaps he didn't have to when he had all this cascading magic at his fingertips.

Izaveta's other hand clutched around the ring, ridges digging in. *The Palace of Three Skies*, she thought. But she remained resolutely solid, the ring unmoving and ordinary beneath her touch.

Something stung her arm, and suddenly, the shadows were coming alive around her. Falcons tore themselves from the darkness and hurtled toward her—not solid yet clawing and sharp where their talons caught at her.

The memory of the palace fluttered in her mind, drifting further away through the pain and fear. She wouldn't get another chance. She could see that in the magic swirling around her, in the unforgiving burnish of Kyriil's eyes.

She couldn't get this ring to listen to her—perhaps an entreaty to the gods was useless from someone who had defied them so much.

Asya burst in her mind, more solid than the clawing falcons. Izaveta wouldn't get back to her, wouldn't be able to warn her. Wouldn't be able to make up for anything she'd done.

Then she felt it, that slight tug at the center of her being.

Kyriil came into view through the whirling wings. He wasn't rushing, the falcons slowing to a languid pace behind him, an expression she couldn't quite piece together in that snatched instant.

She didn't have a breath to wonder at it before her body was stolen into nothingness.

But that final blink imprinted itself on the back of her lids, his colorless eyes locked on to hers. She did know who he was then, surrounded by magic and the dark wings of falcons. The story behind why soothsayers saw the birds as portents of doom, the sorcerer who Queen Teriya had forced from her queendom in a moment of great triumph. The villain who snaked his way through every child's stories, deathless and unyielding.

Koschei.

Chapter Forty-Five

It took Izaveta longer to come back to herself this time. As if every time she was pulled apart, it was harder to re-form again. A thick veil of snow fell around her, obscuring the landscape in whorls of soft white against the dark sky above.

Panic threatened at the edge of her mind, a numbing cold beginning to creep in already. She still wore only a tattered dress and this storm was rapidly thickening around her. It would be utterly ridiculous to escape that impossible magic only to freeze to death in the wilderness.

A painfully poetic irony again.

Then the clouds shifted, and the muted light of the moons against the snow caught on something she recognized. Familiar but so unexpected that it took a moment for her mind to place it. The thin fractured outline of queenstrees, their pale bark blending perfectly into the snow-speckled landscape.

But she only let her mind focus on one thing. She had to find Asya first, before that imposter could reach her.

Izaveta slipped and stumbled through the deepening snow, her breath sharp and freezing in her chest. She couldn't be entirely sure she was even going the right way. With the cascading snow and mordant cold and her whirling thoughts, it was impossible to track a path. To know if she was getting closer to the palace or losing herself deeper within the wood.

And then there she was. Supported by another figure with a third bringing up the rear, three dark shadows that shouldn't have been recognizable. Yet it was unmistakably Asya, a bright splash of light against the battering scenery.

Izaveta ran, everything else flying away from her. Asya looked up, her brown eyes heavy as they caught on Izaveta. For a shuddering moment, that night flickered between them. Izaveta's confession into the screaming storm, the Firebird in all its fury. The truth of what Izaveta had done and what she would make her sister do.

Then Asya lurched forward, wrapping her arms so tight around Izaveta that she could almost believe she was holding together. For an instant, that was the only thing that mattered. The two of them alive and together—if not entirely whole.

"You're really here," Asya murmured, her voice thrumming through Izaveta as her grip tightened.

"I think so." Izaveta's voice felt less substantial, already being torn away by the wind.

"Then, it worked?"

"What—" Izaveta started to say, but as she pulled away, the words died in her throat. It was only then that she saw the blood.

"Asya—" She couldn't finish the sentence before Asya crumpled to her knees, hands slipping in the snow as she tried to hold herself up. The other two people moved forward—Izaveta had forgotten they were there, her world narrowing down to just her sister. She instinctively stepped between them, mistrust rearing up again.

"We're friends," one of them said, and when Izaveta still

tried to push them back, they grasped her wrist, firm but not unkind. "We're helping, my lady."

Izaveta blinked, trying to push through the anguish clouding her vision, and she saw she did recognize the dark-haired girl before her. Vilanovich, the strashe Izaveta had assigned to her sister, the one who had been so upset the night Asya had been shot.

Vilanovich leaned down to help Asya back to her feet, but couldn't seem to manage. "Dima, help me."

The other figure—Dima—reached an arm under Asya's shoulder, hauling her back to standing. Though Asya still didn't look quite conscious, her eyelids flickering and weight canting to one side. Vilanovich pressed an already-bloodied ball of fabric against the wound, a tiny impediment against the jagged red. It must have been a firestone blade, leaving Asya without the Firebird's strength.

"How are you here?" Vilanovich asked, stark gray eyes boring into Izaveta with something like accusation.

It made Izaveta bristle, some of that cold snapping back into her, piercing through her fear. "We don't have time for that now. What happened to Asya?"

"She was doing something to help you," Vilanovich said, the emphasis clear. "But the strashe caught up to us and one of them stabbed her."

Izaveta did not bother pointing out that was a nonanswer, providing no useful information, amidst Vilanovich's evident animosity. Izaveta could feel herself retreating now, her mind pulling back to that place of cold calculation where nothing could hurt her.

"We need to get her back to the voye," Vilanovich pressed.

"No." The word burst out of Izaveta before she had fully comprehended the weight of it, of that decision.

"But you're back now," the strashe said. "You can tell them the Firebird isn't a threat, the strashevsta—"

"Are the Azarovs at court?" Izaveta cut across.

Vilanovich stared at her, clearly not following the chain of thought. The expression rattled Izaveta, threatening to send her to that hollow place inside her.

"Are they?" she asked again.

"Yes," the strashe said. "But—"

Izaveta held up a hand to silence her. There was no time for coddling now, not with the threat of that imposter's magic looming over them. She needed the clarity now, the emotionless reasoning of her hollow heart, of her mother's scheming. If the Azarovs were at court, then the imposter already had a foothold there.

Izaveta may not know the extent of what was happening here—may not even understand its parts. But there was one certainty she could still hold on to, the only one she had left: when she had to protect her sister.

It was the only certainty she had left.

"Do you know of anywhere we could go?" Izaveta asked. "Somewhere away from the palace's reach?"

Vilanovich stepped forward, that accusation shining in her eyes again. "Asya needs help now, we—"

To everyone's surprise, Asya herself was the one to answer, her voice barely audible. "The Roost."

"No," Vilanovich snapped. "We need voye and—"

"You don't have to trust me," Izaveta said, more because they were the words she thought the strashe needed than because she meant it. "But believe me when I say the palace is not safe for Asya."

That seemed to be enough for Vilanovich, finally hearing the urgency in Izaveta's voice.

The soft thud of footsteps sent a sudden stillness through them all, a held breath before the onslaught.

Svedye. Izaveta wasn't ready yet, they needed more time.

But Vilanovich moved first, holding a saber as a makeshift crutch. "I'll distract them. You take her."

"No." Dima stepped toward his sister, unaware or not caring that he left Asya unsupported—Izaveta only just managing to catch her sister before she fell again.

"I'll lead them off," Dima said with a thrumming intensity, looking only at his sister. "You go."

"I'm not getting anywhere on this leg."

Now that Izaveta looked closely, she could see she was right. Vilanovich was listing almost as much as Asya, her face pinched with pain. She would not even make much of a distraction for the strashe—certainly not for that imposter—but it was all they had.

Dima glared at his sister. "They'll kill you."

Vilanovich's determination didn't falter. "They won't. Not without the Firebird."

"We don't have time to debate heroics," Izaveta interjected, but neither of them was listening.

"I can't let you do this," Dima said.

"Let?" Vilanovich stepped forward, still leaning heavily on her right leg but her eyes blazing. "After everything, you owe me this."

Some unspoken thing passed between the two of them, a history Izaveta had no part of. Something raw and jagged, still gaping between the siblings.

Dima whirled to Izaveta and Asya, imploring. "You don't want her to do this."

Asya shook her head, but it was hard to tell if the movement was even intentional, her eyes still shuttered and color leeching from her face with every breath.

Dima latched on to Izaveta, a fervent desperation that she couldn't help but recognize. "You know the Firebird doesn't want this. She won't thank you for leaving Yuliana behind."

Izaveta didn't hesitate, didn't allow herself to follow that path. What mattered now was keeping Asya alive long enough to be angry with her. "We're all dead otherwise," Izaveta said simply, a tacit acceptance.

Vilanovich gave a short nod, as if that decided the matter, but Dima still blocked her path.

"Then, I stay too," he said, reaching for a weapon.

Vilanovich looked like she was close to breaking apart. Her leg trembled beneath her, pain cracking through her voice—not just the raw pain of injury, but something older and far deeper. "I can't leave Asya unprotected, not like this. You have to help her."

Izaveta opened her mouth, a sharp reminder that they didn't have enough time ready on her lips, but Vilanovich grasped her brother's hand and pressed on. "Please, Dima. Do this for me. Do this and it's all forgiven."

Dima didn't back down and Izaveta could pick out the individual voices of the strashe now, far too close for them to waste any more time on debate.

"You lead them to the west," Izaveta said to Vilanovich, holding up a hand to preempt Dima's objection. "There's a hideout there, used by my grandmother during a coup and unknown to anyone outside my family. It's beneath Queen Katja's tomb. You can hide there and join us once the search lessens."

"Problem solved," Vilanovich said without a moment's hesitation, understanding at once.

Dima teetered still, and for a beat, Izaveta thought he was going to refuse, a kind of broken anger gashing across his features. But then he stepped out of Vilanovich's path, his expression closing off like the snap of a book. Neither sibling spoke, Vilanovich turning to Izaveta instead. "I'm leaving her with you because I know you will do anything for her," the strashe said, low and strained. "Because I can't right now. Not because I trust you. Don't let her down."

She didn't give Izaveta a moment to respond, turning to limp toward the oncoming strashe, a saber tight in her grip.

Izaveta was not a fool, she could see the fierce emotion in Vilanovich, the intangible thing that bound her to Asya. And Izaveta was sure Vilanovich understood what she was doing, the thin excuse she'd given to convince her brother.

They both knew there was no secret hiding place there.

Izaveta tugged Asya forward, staggering under her limp weight. "Help me," she snapped at Dima, still looking back at where his sister had disappeared into the snow.

He glared at her, anger in the tight set of his shoulders, but he took Asya's arm without complaint.

They were moving too slowly, Izaveta knew that almost at once. Even without Vilanovich and her injury, even if she managed to stave off some of the strashe, it didn't change that Asya could barely walk.

The dark silhouette of two bears flickered out of the pale landscape ahead of them and Izaveta cursed. On foot and injured, they had no chance against mounted strashe. She had to try for another strategy, to use her miraculous return from the dead to her advantage before the imposter or his spies could get near them.

The first bear lolloped forward, towering over her.

Izaveta squared her shoulders, reaching for imperiousness

while she stood bloodied and in rags, trapped by a storm. "I am Lady Izaveta and I command—"

But she broke off as the swirling snow parted to reveal the rider. Tarya, followed closely by Zvezda.

Izaveta almost sagged in relief. She couldn't say she trusted her aunt, but she knew Tarya valued the Firebird—the Firebird's life—above everything, and that was what mattered now.

Tarya's gaze flicked to Izaveta, the displeasure not shifting from her expression. "You evaded the price?"

The question made Izaveta feel oddly exposed, trapped beneath the weight of that again. "No," she replied, that hollow resonance booming in her chest.

Tarya held her eyes for a moment, ticking beats that they did not have the luxury of wasting.

"Come on," she said finally, reaching down to pull Asya up behind her.

Dima turned to Izaveta, his words almost lost to the whistling wind. "If we have bears, we can go back for her," he yelled. "Yuliana could ride—"

"We can't go back," Izaveta said, in a voice that echoed her mother's immovable command. "It's too late now."

Dima's jaw clenched, not bothering to try to hide the hatred he shot at her. "You would abandon her again?"

"I would do as she asked," Izaveta replied. "She knew the choice she was making. Unless *you* want to let your sister down again."

Izaveta may not know their history, but she knew when to dig her nails into a weak spot. And she knew they needed Dima with them still, they couldn't waste someone running back to get killed by the strashe too. The more people who could defend them, the better. A poisonous thought, perhaps, but a necessary one given the situation.

For an instant, she thought Dima might hit her—not the most absurd notion in everything that had happened. But instead he turned and heaved himself up behind Zvezda, gray eyes boring into Izaveta. "This choice is *yours*," he spat—more an accusation than acquiescence.

Izaveta ignored it as she pulled herself up behind Asya, balanced perilously between herself and Tarya. Her aunt barely waited for her to mount before urging her bear forward at a gallop.

Izaveta wrapped her arms around Asya, holding tight to the one solid thing. She could feel the blood staining her sister's side, warmer than the icy cold around them. Izaveta refused to look back, even when she heard the anguished cries of battle or the scrape of a sword. She'd said as much to Dima: they couldn't return now.

Asya would not thank Izaveta for this. But she was used to that, used to being the one who had to make the hard choice.

It definitely had nothing to do with that echoing space in her chest where a heart should be.

CHAPTER FORTY-SIX

Asya woke with her sister's name on her lips. Somewhere between a gasp and a shout, raw against her throat.

But it wasn't the phantom that had haunted all these lost days. It was her sister, flesh and blood. Sitting in a stout wooden chair, her hair disheveled and face pinched. But breathing. Alive. *Here.*

Asya couldn't stop staring at her, afraid if she blinked her sister might slip through her fingers again. She didn't look quite as she remembered. Her hair was pulled back in a simple plait, her eyes drawn, and she wore what looked like a set of Asya's hunting clothes. A strange reflection—who Izaveta might have been.

"Iza," she said softly, and her sister's eyes fluttered open. "I thought I'd lost you."

Izaveta leaned forward, elbows resting on her knees. "I could say the same."

Asya followed her sister's gaze to the slowly healing wound on her side. Firestone, Asya remembered that now.

It was an odd picture, the two of them. One that had played out before, Iza at Asya's bedside while Asya tried to piece together what had happened.

But it wasn't the same now, no matter how much Asya wished it could be.

She'd been so focused on her sister that only when she pushed herself up to sitting did the room begin to fill in around them. Familiar low rafters, the comforting warmth of a small fire, the oddly familiar confines of the narrow bed she lay in.

The Roost, where she'd lived with Tarya.

It felt so out of place against her memories, an overlay that couldn't hide what lurked beneath. Her own shashka running Commander Iveshkin through. The burn of that spell and the ease of Azarov's death.

She shook her head, hazy memories jostling against each other. How had they ended up at the Roost?

She opened her mouth to ask Izaveta just that, but the question that came out instead was "How are you here?"

Izaveta looked up at her—properly looked, for the first time since she'd awoken. There was something not quite right in that look. Something that made the relief in Asya's stomach turn sour.

"I—" Izaveta swallowed, some truth she didn't want to share shrouded in her eyes. "I'm not quite sure."

"But where were you?" Asya asked, an echo of hurt in her voice. She could see the lies gathering on her sister's face even now.

"I was in a tower," Izaveta began. "I don't know how I got there, but the Azarovs—" She broke off, catching herself. "I think they made some kind of bargain."

Asya didn't say anything as Izaveta told her story, each piece more confusing than the last. How she'd watched that curse spread within the palace, supposedly because of a crown. Letters she'd found that pointed to spies—those were hardly surprising—and a saint's ring that could travel through the skies.

"He..." Izaveta swallowed. "Whoever kept me in that tower, it wasn't Kyriil. He had magic beyond what should be possible."

Fear flashed in the depths of her brown eyes, an expression Asya was so unused to on her sister. An expression she didn't *want* to see.

"But how did you get here?" Asya asked instead, pivoting away.

Izaveta pulled a ring from her finger and held it out. "Saint Ilyova's ring. I stole it."

"It wasn't me, then." Asya's voice came out very small, suffocated by flashing memories of the ritual.

"What wasn't?"

Asya wrapped her arms around her torso, pressing down on the dull pain of the healing wound. "I've been trying to bring you back. To undo what I—what happened. Nikov helped me find a ritual, one to restore something that was lost. I thought it would reverse the price. But..." She trailed off, nodding to Izaveta. "I suppose that didn't work."

Izaveta leaned forward, her hand curling against her breastbone. Something unsaid again, something fragile that Asya didn't want to push against.

"*That* was the part you played," Izaveta murmured, making no more sense to Asya.

"What do you mean?"

"You—" Izaveta took a breath, squaring her shoulders as though pulling back into herself. "Oh, Asya. What have you done?"

"What have *I* done?" Asya repeated.

Disbelief and shock took a moment to permeate through Asya, transmuting into something else entirely. Until that very instant, she hadn't realized she was angry. There hadn't been any room for it, before. No way to grieve while also examining her sister's faults.

But seeing Izaveta in front of her now—not entirely safe but very much alive—Asya's anger kindled, sparking as her flames.

"*You* are the one who did this," she said, the words bursting out of some deep place inside her that she had no control over. "*You* decided to try your hand at magic you didn't understand, not caring what the consequences would be. Then you lied to me about it and tried to control everything, even when you had no right to. You made me—" Asya's voice cracked, something inside her cracking with it. "I thought I'd killed you. I could have."

"I..." Izaveta swallowed, eyes darting around. Looking for somewhere to land where she didn't have to face this. "I didn't mean for it to end like that."

"Your intentions don't change what happened. You killed our mother."

Asya saw Izaveta flinch, but she couldn't stop, her voice ringing hollow in her ears. If not for the traces of firestone still seeping through her veins, she was sure her words would have ignited. "And you lied to me. Over and over again, you lied."

Izaveta clasped her hands together, as if trying to hold herself together. She looked so small suddenly, not the fiercely protective sister or coldly calculating queen. But even that couldn't diminish the fury now it was ablaze.

"I told you in the end, didn't I?" It was almost a plea, fragile and uncertain from someone usually so unshakeable.

"Only when there was no other choice." Asya could hear the bitterness in her words. The poisonous anger and resentment finally bubbling through, all the pain of this past few weeks.

The grief that had carved out some part of Asya. A part she'd thought would come back if Iza did. Yet there was still a gaping fissure in Asya's chest, aching like a slow wound. Something taken she wasn't sure she could ever get back.

"I mourned you." The words splintered in the quiet. "You didn't even try to reach out to me. I spent all this time searching for you and you send a note to *Azarov*, of all people."

Izaveta opened her mouth and Asya could almost see the excuses collecting on her tongue. The lies.

"I did try, but—"

The door opened and Asya jumped. Dima ducked through, carrying a small water jug. Another discordant brushstroke in this familiar painting.

Asya swallowed. She didn't want an audience for this.

Then another piece shifted in her mind, memories slowly coalescing. She felt suddenly as if she'd been running at full sprint, forced to a stumbling halt. A realization just in front of her that she didn't want to touch.

"Where's Yuliana?"

Izaveta held her gaze now and Asya thought she could see that strange incongruity again. Like looking at her sister through slanted glass. "She stayed behind," Izaveta said.

"She—" Asya took a breath, scalding in her chest as the Firebird kindled. "You left her behind?" She looked at Dima next, incredulous. "*You* left her behind?"

Dima scowled. "The blame is as much on you, Firebird."

Izaveta grabbed her hand, pulling the conversation back to the two of them. "She wanted to stay, and with her leg, there was no way she could have run. It was the best—"

"Izaveta." The name came out as something closer to a curse now. "You don't get to make choices like that. How do you still not understand?"

Izaveta opened her mouth to reply, but no words came out. Asya wasn't sure she had ever seen her sister speechless. Her sister was the one who was meant to always have an answer, a way to talk herself out of things.

But she barely looked like herself now. A hollow desolation in the tight lines of her face that made her seem like a stranger. An uncomfortable inversion of the battering desperation of the Elmer, both sisters torn open and anguished.

Somehow, this was worse.

At least in the Elmer Izaveta had seemed sure, had felt substantial in Asya's arms. Now Izaveta looked unmoored. Ready to crumble to ashes again.

Before Asya could say anything else, the door opened once more and two figures stepped through. Oddly familiar in this space yet somehow still out of place. Tarya, followed closely by the spymaster, a scroll clutched in her hand. In that brief instant, something Tarya had said once rang in Asya's mind.

There was...one person I regretted leaving.

Tarya's eyes latched on to Asya, her disapproval as palpable as flames. "You're awake."

Asya felt herself wilt a little, reduced back to the child who had cowered in this house. She shot a glance at Izaveta, who said, "Conze Tarya helped us escape the palace." There was something ridiculous about Izaveta sticking so rigidly to titles and cordialities in the midst of all this, cramped in the small space of the Roost with destruction in their wake.

Asya pulled her eyes away from her aunt, looking to Zvezda instead, always a point of calm in turbulent waters. "What was happening at the palace when you left?" She couldn't quite bring herself to voice the second part of her question, the fear and hope catching in her chest at the thought of Yuliana left behind.

"It was chaos," Zvezda replied. "The strashe were scattered and unable to pursue, with the snow setting in and some of their own turning on them because of that magic." Her gaze flicked to Asya, a momentary reassurance. "Last I saw, Strashe Vilanovich was alive."

Relief burned in Asya's chest, almost painful in its weight. Though she didn't miss the unsaid echo. Yuliana had been alive when Zvezda last saw her. "How long has it been?"

"Two days."

The relief soured, smothering the breath in her lungs. A lot could have happened in that time, all choking possibilities. "Why didn't you try to wake me?"

"You had to heal," Izaveta said softly.

A small detail in the gaping mess of this.

"Was it a price?" Tarya interrupted.

Asya didn't look at her aunt, couldn't quite bring herself to care. "No."

Tarya didn't respond, did not rebuke Asya or fly into rage. But there was a slight change in the air, perhaps the most emotion their aunt ever showed—a shifting coolness, a detached disappointment. Asya gritted her teeth. She really should be used to that by now.

Izaveta stepped in, protective even now, even when Asya didn't want it. She nodded to the scroll in Zvezda's hand. "News?"

"Most of the same," the spymaster replied. "The palace is in disarray. That curse is spreading unchecked and Deryev is still calling on them to appease the gods and turn back to the Church. No one is truly taking charge, they were already one member short, and with Commander Iveshkin—"

"That was my fault too," Asya murmured, a shallow confession to empty air. The image of it replayed behind her lids. At least she'd given Azarov what he deserved. "I shouldn't have tried to be like you—" she shot a glance at Izaveta "—that way, people always end up dead."

Izaveta's eyes widened. "Commander Iveshkin is dead?"

"She's not dead," Zvezda said.

Asya's head snapped up. "What?"

"Commander Iveshkin is alive," Zvezda replied. "But gravely injured. The voye are seeing to her. And the young Azarov—"

"Kyriil is there?" Izaveta interrupted, her voice catching.

"He's calling for retribution for his father's death."

Izaveta glanced over at Asya, the weight of something unspoken heavy in her gaze. "Kyriil is dead."

Zvezda frowned. "My pakviye said only this morning—"

"An imposter stands in his place." Izaveta took a breath, chin raised as if steeling herself. "A powerful sorcerer. An immortal one. Koschei."

Asya stared at her, too much spinning through her mind. The vision she'd seen of the queen and the sorcerer, the ritual it had pushed her to perform. The falcons that had followed her since the Elmer—falcons that folktales said belonged to an ancient sorcerer. Her sister standing in front of her and talking of fairy tales as if they were real.

But she caught on to one thing, one certainty in all of this. "If he's there, then we have to help. We have to go back for Yuliana—for all of them."

"No."

CHAPTER FORTY-SEVEN

Everyone turned to Izaveta, the unwanted voice of reason yet again. But she did not back down, none of them had seen the sorcerer's power. It was easy for Asya to talk of being noble, of fixing their mistakes, when she had not truly seen what they faced.

"You can't just stride back into the palace," Izaveta repeated. "If Kyriil is there, then it's already too late. This sorcerer's magic is not something you can simply fight your way through."

"So you come with me," Asya pressed, an imploring note to her words. "You're the queen, aren't you? They have to listen to you. Even a sorcerer can't stand against all of Tóurin."

Izaveta hated that she had to squash that fractured hope, the belief that she could make a difference in any of this. "An uncrowned queen who vanished without explanation," she said. "I cannot reappear after all of that without knowing who is still on my side."

Asya's jaw clenched. "I forgot. Of course the most important thing here is whether or not you can still hold sway in court."

"That's not—" Izaveta bit out, forcing herself to hold on to her calm, to not let frustration get the better of her. Why couldn't Asya understand this?

"This isn't about what either of us *wants*," Izaveta pressed.

"It's about the most practical choice. You don't charge into a battlefield without knowing the numbers, without being sure of the lay of the land and the advantages we hold. Not if you want a victory."

"No, you don't, do you?" Asya said, her voice threaded with a hard anger. "Because the queen *doesn't* charge onto the battlefield, no matter what is at stake. She's happy to risk everyone else, to sacrifice those people in the palace now, as long as she can find victory in the end."

Izaveta flinched, her conviction momentarily cracking beneath her. How was she supposed to know the difference between pragmatism and callousness? How was she meant to know if she was making the hard choice for the right reasons, or if her hollow heart simply meant she didn't care?

"But *I* am not the queen." Asya's resolve did not flicker. "I'm the Firebird."

"Which is precisely why you mustn't go," Izaveta pressed, frustrated irritation cracking through her words. "He wants something from you. That's the only reason Vilanovich might still be alive. I saw Kyriil—" the name still stuck with her, too small but somehow more manageable "—run through with a knife and he brushed it off as less than a scratch. Even the Firebird cannot contend with that."

"Then what?" Asya snapped. "We hide here while the queendom crumbles around us, while the people we care about suffer? Every one of your points is all the more reason we have to act."

Izaveta's heart should have been pounding, but instead a cool surety was resounding through her. The certainty that came when she knew she had to protect her sister—even from herself. "You'd be walking into a trap," Izaveta said, holding on to that calm logic.

"What does it matter, when *all* of this is a trap? A cage

created by our roles—by the roles chosen for us. At least this way, I might be able to help someone else."

"This isn't about helping people or not," Izaveta replied. "You aren't any use to anyone if you're dead, or worse."

Asya's eyes narrowed. "Not any use to you?"

"That's not what I meant," Izaveta said hastily. Why did she always say the wrong thing to her sister? In every other situation, words bent to her, spinning to whatever story she wanted to tell. But with Asya, it all became tangled, that constant pull between what Izaveta had become and who she wanted to be. "You're—" Izaveta swallowed. "You're worth more than that—don't you see? You're—"

Worth more than me—but that stuck in her throat. A too-jagged piece of herself, one she couldn't quite drag into the light.

Asya turned away. "I wouldn't expect you to understand."

Izaveta opened her mouth, trying to find the words, even as her voice was fraying, all those neat stitches tearing apart.

How could Izaveta put into words that Asya was the one thing she had, the one *good* thing, and Izaveta was too selfish to lose her, no matter the cost? She remembered what the sorcerer had said. *You talk of love as if you could possibly understand it. Love is a destructive, vengeful creature.*

Perhaps he'd been right, love was destructive. The lengths it pushed people to, the prices Izaveta would pay. She'd never truly considered it before, the question of if her love could cause more destruction than help.

"I—I killed our mother to keep you safe." The confession, the jagged truth of it tore at Izaveta's throat. Almost an accusation, a reminder of all that Izaveta had sacrificed for Asya's safety. "All I ever want is to keep you safe. And I won't let you throw that away."

CHAPTER FORTY-EIGHT

Asya was shaking. Not with fear or grief but with rage. A rage born of the fire that had replaced her blood, of the destiny that had too often been ripped from her clutches. And no one—not even her sister—had the right to take that away.

"I didn't ask for that." Her voice shook too, the telltale tremble of the ground before a calamity struck. "I didn't *ask* for any of this. You took it upon yourself to decide what I wanted, what was best for me, without even deigning to ask me. Just as Mother would have."

There was something freeing in finally saying it. In letting all of these resentments come bursting out. "And you can tell yourself you did it for me, but that doesn't absolve you of anything. You cast that spell because you wanted to be in control." Asya could see the blow crack across her sister. But the twinge of guilt accompanying it was swallowed by her burning anger.

She was done being lied to. *Done* being used.

She held her sister's gaze for a fractured moment, expecting more of a rebuke. But instead, Izaveta's expression closed. That same coldness Asya had noticed before—as if there were something not quite right in this image.

"Your sister is right."

Asya had forgotten there were other people in the room, that Tarya watched on with her stolid impassivity.

Asya's voice steadied as she turned to her aunt, though she could feel her hands were still trembling. "I'm not going to use the Firebird as an excuse to abandon people."

Where before Tarya had stilled to pale stone, something crackled through her now. A terrible shadow of the Firebird that had once lived in her skin. "Your duty is not a mere excuse. I had thought you finally understood that when you took the price from your sister. Clearly, I was wrong."

But Asya didn't cower or tacitly agree as she might have once. "I *understand* that you've been happy to hide behind the Firebird," she said, voice dangerously low and threaded with sparks. "To pretend you can't take sides because that would mean making an actual choice. It would mean taking a risk with yourself. And you can't do that."

"You have always been too easily swayed by your mortal affections."

"This isn't about *mortal affections* or anything that simple. Yes, I care about Yuliana." She shot a look at Izaveta, sharp with accusation. "And Commander Iveshkin, and Nikov. But I also care about the people in the palace, the people of Tóurin who could get hurt because of something I played a part in."

Tarya didn't say anything. The silence stretching into a fragile, fractured breath. The former Firebird and the current silhouetted against the windows, ghostly flames snapping between them.

"Then, I have failed," Tarya said finally. "And I refuse to watch you risk yourself." She turned and strode out into the cold, any remaining fire extinguished. Zvezda started after her, something unspoken rupturing between them, but Tarya shook her head and the spymaster stilled.

Asya's fists clenched, her nails digging into her palms. She shouldn't have expected anything else, but it still hurt. Not the accusation, but the fact that her aunt could walk away now. After all they had been through, Tarya still refused to see the other way.

Asya turned to her sister, a cacophony beating in her chest. "I'm going back," she said. "Whether you're coming or not."

"With no plan at all?" Izaveta shot at her.

Asya raised her chin. "I have a plan. Zvezda said the palace is in chaos. We can use the cover of this curse to sneak in and free Yuliana—help as many of them as we can." She let embers kindle in her palms. She was done playing by the palace's rules, done being held hostage by what they wanted—and even a sorcerer had to pay the price of magic. She wasn't abandoning Yuliana again. "And I burn anyone who stands in our way."

CHAPTER FORTY-NINE

Izaveta was not quite sure what she expected, returning to the palace. The imposter styled anew as a king, strashe armed at every entrance. More of that impossible magic, ready to snare around them as soon as they stepped from the trees. Certainly, some marked transformation, something to show the great shift in power. The way so much had changed since she had last been here on the day of the coronation.

But it looked exactly the same. The light dusting of dawn fell across an unchanged and unmarred landscape, the palace as defiantly immovable as ever.

It was unsettling. That same uncomfortable sensation of the world spinning on without her. Spinning on, even as everything fell apart.

The veneer of normalcy shattered as soon as they reached the threshold to the entrance hall. No strashe stood guard, the door open and gaping as a cracked tooth.

Zvezda and Dima flanked her, both their weapons drawn, a strange procession for the returning queen. Tarya had stuck to her word and stayed behind, a presence that might have made all the difference.

Asya walked a little ahead, silent throughout their journey, and brittle in a way Izaveta didn't know how to address.

But they all froze when they reached the entrance hall, even Zvezda's surety faltering. Bodies lay strewn across the polished floor, the silver uniform of strashe dotted with crimson and mingled with the crumpled shapes of nobles. Those searing veins of ice, just like she had seen in the gardens, burrowing across their skin in deep fissures.

"It must be spreading," Zvezda said, her footfalls soft on the ringing marble as she moved forward.

Asya stared round, her face ashen, before alighting on Izaveta. "Did the sorcerer— Did he say what this is? Some kind of imbalance or a spell he cast?"

Izaveta shook her head, bile wrenching in her stomach. "He said I could stop it, that it was somehow our fault." She saw the concern flash across Asya's face, the same guilt she should probably be feeling and added quickly, "But I don't know how much of what he said was true."

That was a lie. Izaveta was fairly certain Koschei had not once lied to her—a lesson learned long ago: truths usually cut far deeper than lies. If she could feel that seed of truth in it, there was no reason to dismiss it.

But she didn't want Asya to shoulder that burden too.

"We should keep moving," Zvezda said, eyes darting around for any potential threat.

Izaveta quickly agreed, more relieved than she'd admit to be away from those bodies and the accusation they held. Zvezda led the way down a narrow passage, generally used by strashe or servants who needed to move unseen through the palace.

Izaveta didn't like following behind, unable to take entire control of their movements, but she knew she would hardly be useful if they encountered any sort of threat. They were heading for one of the Queen's Doors, one Asya had found that led to Zmenya's Tower.

It at least gave them some advantage of secrecy, the only reason Izaveta had not yet pointed out all the flaws in this barely formed plan.

Izaveta could practically hear her mother's voice, poisonous whispers chasing them. *Undignified behavior, not fit for a future queen.* Adilena would have likely already found a way to bargain with the imposter, to leverage this new magic to Tóurin's advantage.

The sound of clanging metal echoed and Zvezda held out a hand, blade at the ready. But before Izaveta could suggest they retreat and try for more care, Asya pushed forward, her flames ready.

"Asya!" Izaveta hissed, too late.

Three strashe surrounded a crouched figure, but they all turned at Asya's approach, eyes glinting and pupils reduced to pinpricks. The gleam reminded Izaveta of something—the translucent shard in the sorcerer's fingers.

Then something slammed into her from behind and the memory fractured.

Izaveta hit the ground hard, air rushing from her lungs as her chin cracked against the stone. It took her too long to recover, to orient her mind in what was happening. She only just managed to twist over onto her back when the person was on her, blood tracking down their arms where the frozen veins had clawed through.

They were unarmed, but hands clamped around her throat at once. Izaveta tried to push back, digging her nails into their wrists—but even as more blood trickled they did not relent.

Black spots bloomed in the corner of her sight, unconsciousness tugging at her. She could still see flashes of Asya's flames, hear the clang of blades, too preoccupied to offer Izaveta any help.

Just as suddenly as it had come, the grip loosened and her attacker slumped forward, eyes rolling back. Izaveta scrambled away, heaving to push their weight from her as her head still spun. Someone reached toward her and she threw up her hands, fighting back in the only primitive, desperate way she knew.

"Izaveta." The voice broke through the ringing in her ears, the tight pain of her throat.

"Nikov?" Izaveta's breath caught, for an instant the world around her was replaced by the claustrophobic walls of that cell, and an imagined Nikov leaned over her in her endless tomb.

But then his hand grasped hers and he helped her to her feet, the palace shimmering back into place around them.

He was clutching what looked like a candelabra, ornate and once beautiful but now dented from where he'd hit her attacker. Izaveta blinked, dragging air back into her lungs as she pulled her hand from Nikov's grip. The fight had subsided around her, the three strashe lying either dead or unconscious on the ground.

Nikov was the hunched figure they'd been attacking. If Asya had not hurtled forward, Izaveta surely would have left him to that fate.

A sour kind of regret curled in Izaveta's stomach—though she couldn't quite tell if it was regret at the actions or regret at how little she cared.

"You don't have to kill them," Asya was saying to Dima, breathing hard as the flames retreated back to her. "They don't know what they're doing."

"Willingly or not," Dima grunted, as if he had to force himself to address the Firebird. "It won't make a difference when they kill us."

Izaveta had to agree, but she did not voice it now. She was too aware of how heartless it would sound, especially in the face of her ineptitude.

Asya looked like she was going to respond, when she noticed Nikov. She hurried over to him and pulled him into a hug—a surprising connection Izaveta hadn't realized the two of them had made, another piece of her absence slotting into place.

"Are you all right?" Asya asked.

Nikov nodded. "A normal scholar's activities, you know." But even his humor sounded frayed.

Izaveta turned to Nikov too, taking stock of his disheveled clothes. Blood darkened the curls near his temple and a bruise was fading on his jaw. Standing this close, very aware of the way his breath filled the air—*real* and not imagined, Izaveta felt suddenly very exposed.

He had no idea, of course. He didn't know that she had turned to him in those desperate moments and spoken things she'd never uttered aloud before. But Izaveta couldn't forget it, a vulnerability that made her look away. "Why are you still here?" she asked.

He gestured around. "Leaving hasn't really been an option. But why did you come back?"

The question struck Izaveta as odd for a reason she couldn't quite grasp, but Asya answered at once.

"Yuliana. We're going to Zmenya's Tower."

"She's not there."

"Then, where is she?"

"In the cabinet room." Nikov frowned, as if realizing a moment too late he perhaps shouldn't have answered that, but responding to a query was just such a natural state for him that it had leaped free without thought.

"If she's in the cabinet room," Zvezda said carefully, "there's no way to approach with subtlety."

Fire blazed around Asya's fingers, that unmoving determination flinting in her eyes again. "Then, we go without."

Nikov glanced back at Izaveta, concern sharp in his features. "The cabinet has cloistered themselves there with the remaining strashe. They're all calling for the Firebird's blood. They think this is her fault."

Izaveta tried to grasp her sister's arm, to pull her back. "Asya."

Asya had already begun to walk forward, barely pausing at Izaveta's voice. "Don't say it again. I'm not changing my mind." A recklessness snapped around Asya, someone pushed too far, too many times. A recklessness that could still get her killed.

Everything in Izaveta was rigid, muscles pulled taut by inaction. There was nothing she could do to physically stop Asya, no way to make her sister listen to reason.

But at least she could stand at her side while this all crumbled.

CHAPTER FIFTY

Asya knew the way to the cabinet room well by now. She focused on that, on her careful steps, instead of all the things that might go wrong. On the fact that Tarya had stayed behind and her sister was questioning her every choice.

Foolhardy or not, Asya wasn't going to cower anymore. The Firebird wouldn't tremble.

She'd spent enough hours roaming the palace, even in early dawn light, to know that there should have been more people around. Strashe on patrol, attendants hurrying to make preparations, dedicants eager to get to morning prayers. The curse had so quickly turned the palace into a gaping mausoleum.

The quiet was eerie, eating at Asya's already-fraying nerves.

She knew this was a trap, that they were anticipating her return and had already cast her as the traitor here. None of that mattered. Even if they thought they were prepared for the Firebird now, armed with their firestone, they weren't ready for her full might.

And if Kyriil—or whatever name he went by—was using stolen magic, then he wouldn't be able to stand against the Firebird either. The Firebird had existed longer than the palace around them, longer than sorcerers and saints, and her truth couldn't be ignored. The price always had to be paid.

No one stood on guard by the huge double doors carved in looping whorls up to a facade of three gleaming moons. The strashe were distracted, as Asya had hoped.

She glanced over at Zvezda, Dima a little behind, readiness in the tight lines of his body. Izaveta hung back farther, her uncertainty clear. Nikov stood at her side, makeshift weapon still clutched in his hand.

"You should go to the Voya Wing," Asya said to Zvezda. "Make sure Commander Iveshkin is still safe."

But the spymaster shook her head. "I should stand with the Firebird on this."

There was something unspoken in the soft tone of her voice. Perhaps the memory of another Firebird, of the person Tarya used to be.

A slight swell of affection rose in Asya's chest. That these people were standing with her, even if her aunt was not. Even if Izaveta glared warnings at them. It solidified the certainty in Asya's chest, the blazing determination forged in flames.

The Firebird truly in her element.

She let the Firebird's wings unfurl as she pushed the doors open. A burning monster framed in the entryway.

The torches were extinguished, but Asya's own flames were more than enough to illuminate the stone-faced strashe lining the walls, to highlight the gleam of their blades. More than Asya had anticipated, but still not enough to withstand the Firebird.

The cabinet members stood arrayed around the table, all too agitated in their movements to sit. Other members of the court and clergy, people Asya vaguely recognized, waited close at hand as well, a tentative fear lingering over them all. The Azarovs stood at the center of it. Kyriil, the picture of grief for the father who wasn't his.

The strashevsta spoke first, apparently more confident with so many people between him and danger. "Firebird. You are bold to return to the site of your treachery."

"Perhaps she sees reason and has returned to pay for her crimes," Bishop Deryev said, chin raised and pious.

Asya barely heard him. Her focus had narrowed in, as if drawn by a Calling. All she saw was Yuliana, the curved blade of a znaya at her throat, framed by the far window. She was gagged, held frozen in place by that blade. But her eyes were vibrant as ever. Sparking toward Asya with the force of lightning.

Anger burned in Asya's veins. So predictable for the ways of the court, but it would make no difference against the Firebird.

"I'm sure we can speak reasonably," Bishop Deryev went on, as if he still mattered. As if Asya was even taking him into consideration.

They thought they'd found her weakness. That they knew her measure and she was no threat. But she wasn't bound by the same rules the rest of them were. Not anymore.

That was one thing Tarya had been right about.

The first hints of golden fire curled at Asya's wrists, so much more a part of her than her shashka had ever been. The flames so deeply entangled with her essence that she was made more of fire than flesh.

She walked forward slowly until she stood directly in front of the cabinet. Their expressions hadn't shifted yet. They hadn't felt the change, but they soon would.

No one gave a signal, but the assembled strashe moved as one into a defensive stance. She might have once felt guilty about them. They had played no true part in this, only doing as their duty decreed. The same logic Asya had used for so long.

But they had all stood against her far too many times. Backed the wounded animal into a corner. They could not pretend to be surprised when it lashed out.

She took a breath, calming as a Calling, and transformed.

The Firebird's sharp beak and burning eyes rose above her own features. Not a figure of protection now, but one of scorching vengeance.

The nearest strashe stumbled back, blades clattering to the ground. The one holding Yuliana balked like prey at the sight of a hawk, znaya falling loose at their side. They had not seen Asya like this. Had not seen Asya fully let go of her cares about their perception to stand against them.

And in their eyes, she saw a fear she remembered. That deep and immovable terror of a creature beyond the realm of understanding. It didn't make her hesitate or reconsider now. It spurred her on, playing the true role of the Firebird at last.

But something made her flames stutter. A strange shift in the air.

She had been so focused on Yuliana, on the blade poised at her throat, that Asya hadn't noticed Kyriil's slight movement. He moved like Tarya, a sliding shadow who only drew attention when deemed necessary.

But he caught her eye now, somehow separate from the roaring fire.

He wasn't looking at her like everyone else, with mortal terror at the unmatchable creature in their midst. But with a strange gleam of satisfaction. Almost *pride*.

Her flames snuffed out.

She staggered, their sudden absence throwing her off-balance. Not suppressed beneath the suffocating hold of firestone, or tethered somewhere deep in her chest.

Just...*gone*.

CHAPTER FIFTY-ONE

It took Izaveta too many shuddering breaths to realize something was wrong. She'd been watching the sorcerer, anticipating some move from him, so the abrupt sputter of Asya's flames did not immediately register.

Had someone hit Asya with firestone while Izaveta had been distracted? But no, there was no blood—no apparent wound, just her sister staring at her hands in a hollow disbelief. Izaveta's eyes snapped back to the sorcerer, everything tensing in anticipation. He was watching her now, a sparkling challenge in his eyes, as if daring her to understand.

This drawn-out waiting, knowing the executioner's blade would fall, but not certain when, unnerved her more than Asya's stillness. When he had all of that magic at his fingertips, why was Koschei still playing by the careful rules of court—not showing his true strength?

The answer skittered across Izaveta's mind, leaving cool dread in its wake: *because there's still something he needs.*

The rest of the room was teetering, strashe waiting for some trick from the Firebird and for her flames to surge again, not quite daring to charge yet. The very air was steeped in apprehension, the smallest spark ready to ignite.

Asya turned to look back at her, eyes wide and lost as nothing burned around her. Izaveta had anticipated magic or fire-stone, but this was something else entirely.

Izaveta had to pull this back under her control now, the only way she knew how. She marched forward, out of the un-settled shadows and into the clear light of the candles, squar-ing her shoulders as the familiar mantle of command settled over her. She glared at the line of strashe, not quite moving but tipping toward attack at any moment.

"That is quite enough." She heard how her voice echoed the stark lines of her mother's, but couldn't blanch from it now, not when it was her only asset.

The gasp that tremored through the room was almost worth this ridiculous risk, her name repeated over and over again in awed whispers. A return from the dead was certainly one way to command power—a step beyond the false assassi-nation attempt she had appeared to survive. This set her even further apart, not merely strong but a truly unending mon-arch, enough to make enemies forget their grudges and allies scramble back to her side.

"What happened?" echoed around, overlaid with "Where have you been?" and a cacophony of other questions too tan-gled for her to distinguish.

She let the wave crash against her, let their emotions run rampant while she gave herself a breath to form some strat-egy here. She gave Asya the smallest nod, a reassurance that this was wrested back into her hands.

A question broke over the others, sharp and unwelcome. "Did the Firebird attack you in the Elmer?"

Izaveta turned her icy gaze to the asker—Strashevsta Orlov in all his useless bluster. She let the distaste color her voice. "Of course not," she replied, cutting through the questions as every person hung on her words. "The Firebird performed her duty, as have I. It is no one else's place to question that. As you can see, I have returned, so we may now begin to untangle the mess you all made in my absence."

That left a ringing silence. Izaveta could see the annoyance on several cabinet members' faces, the uncertain shuffle of the strashe. It almost didn't matter what she said, she had their attention—based in anger or awe, it was hardly of any consequence now.

"But where have you been, Lady Izaveta?" asked Vada Nisova, long nails tapping against her arm.

"I paid the price for a spell," Izaveta started, rolling the words over her tongue as if to test their bitterness. "For the good of this queendom." A slight lie, but one she could not avoid in this moment, not if she wanted to pull them all back from that edge of violence.

"And what price did you pay?" This was Bishop Deryev, his eyes narrowed. Izaveta assumed he had managed to claw his way to power in the wake of Sanislav's downfall, the true actions of a devout man.

"Time," Izaveta replied, relieved to find her mind slid so easily back into this role. The role she'd thought she was leaving behind when she told Asya the truth, when she accepted she had to pay the price. "The days I have been gone from court."

"But what was the spell?" Deryev pressed.

Izaveta turned to him, her face impassive and irritation squeezed from her voice. Someone so new to grasping strands of power was always going to be loath to let them go. "That is a matter of utmost secrecy," she said with a glance back at Zvezda—the spymaster at her side certainly added to the credence of this. "There are traitors within the palace, as you have clearly seen." She swept an arm behind her, to the destruction left by this curse. "We must be careful with information until we understand the truth of this treachery."

"You talk of treachery," said a voice, silky and skeptical yet reverberating in the quiet room. Izaveta hadn't noticed him, standing back from the torchlight like a spider preparing its web. "An interesting notion for you, Lady Izaveta," Vibishop Sanislav finished.

Izaveta raised her chin. She knew Sanislav was a better political player than most, but she hadn't anticipated him talking his way out of the prison she'd left him in. "I see we truly are falling to destruction," she said. "I have barely been gone and already you are freeing traitors from the tower. Have you forgotten so easily the events of Saints' Night?" She scanned her eyes across the rest of the assembled people, pushing the weight of that accusation into every one of them.

Sanislav did not waver, and a flush of uncertainty crept through Izaveta. He had the look of someone who knew they held a winning card. She felt her gaze wanting to wander back to Koschei, to see where he stood in all of this, but she refused to look uncertain now, not in front of all these people.

"You're right, of course," Sanislav went on. "The attempted murder of a queen is a grave crime. Though not quite as grave as succeeding in that without consequence."

For a moment, Izaveta thought they meant the Firebird taking the price from her. Her eyes darted back to Asya, protectiveness lurching in her stomach again. But Asya seemed to realize the truth before Izaveta did—and only in her sister's eyes did the true meaning of his words permeate through.

Izaveta had never been queen and Sanislav, of all people, would certainly not refer to her as one.

A cold, sick dread began to spread through her veins. How could Sanislav possibly know that? And why would everyone believe him so easily? Even if it was the truth, a deep and ugly truth she had never wanted to claw into light.

"Ridiculous" was all she managed to say, too high and grating against the cavernous ceiling.

Sanislav turned so he was no longer addressing her but appealing to the court. "The Firebird came to me in an hour of regret," he said. Asya flinched back a few stumbling feet, toward Izaveta but not quite close enough. "She told me the truth of the price Lady Izaveta paid. She cast a spell that killed Queen Adilena."

Izaveta barely heard the gasps this time through the shrill ringing in her ears. She'd imagined this often, forced herself to picture it in moments of deepest guilt or fear. But spread in front of her now, the accusation she could not throw off when it clung so tightly to her, she almost felt unmade again.

Pieces of her unraveling as they were brought to light.

She could not quite look at her sister—could not look at anyone. She didn't need to guess at how Sanislav might have manipulated Asya to tell him the truth, that was, after all, his skill. She couldn't even blame her sister, not when it was fact.

Izaveta took a sharp breath, forcing herself to steady. "You would listen to the word of a disgraced traitor over your future queen?"

"Do you deny it?" Sanislav asked, too ready with the question.

Izaveta opened her mouth, and that brief moment of hesitation answered for her. The slight space in which she did not immediately dismiss it, the hard knot of guilt that had not quite yet dispelled.

She'd been so certain of this secret she hadn't even begun to contemplate she may have to rebutt it. So consumed with strategizing against the sorcerer that she had forgotten the trap she had so neatly laid for herself.

Asya took a step forward, positioning herself between Izaveta and the accusing eyes of the court. Even after everything, still standing at her side—a loyalty Izaveta deserved less and less with each passing day.

"It's not that simple," Asya said. "Izaveta didn't—"

"Did she not owe a price?" Sanislav asked, clearly enjoying his moment of triumph.

"She did, but—"

"Is the price for killing another not the caster's life?" Sanislav pressed. "It appears, Firebird, that you have helped your sister shirk the price." Sanislav was in his element now, enjoying the revenge he had no doubt been waiting for. "I assume that imbalance has caused the calamity tearing through the palace. Countless other lives so that you may ignore the very rules you set about."

"That is why you would not tell us the truth of it, Firebird," Vada Nisova cut in, her sharp eyes shifting to suspicion. A suspicion that crested across all of their faces, one Izaveta could hardly deny.

"No," Asya said again, struggling to grasp at words. "Iza," she hissed, shooting a look back at her, "you can explain."

But Izaveta did not bother to say anything, words scattered and useless at her feet. The truth, especially a painful truth, was always more powerful than any lie she could spin. Perhaps this was what Koschei had warned her about, her heart forgetting to care, even self-preservation thrown to the wind. But she couldn't get herself to say another lie, couldn't bring herself to spin this anymore.

Her silence was condemnation enough.

If Commander Iveshkin had been there, Izaveta might have

been able to appeal to her pragmatism, to sway some others to her side with her authority. But the people left here were all ones who Izaveta had betrayed or used, ones all too eager to watch her downfall.

Koschei finally spoke then, in the shaking determination of Kyriil's grief. "The answer is clear, is it not?" he asked. "Each as treacherous as the other, they have gone unchecked for too long."

"Indeed," Strashevsta Orlov said with the expression of one hungry to finally get their recompense—revenge for all the moments Izaveta had scorned him and Asya had dismissed him. "Arrest them both."

CHAPTER FIFTY-TWO

Perhaps because Izaveta had been waiting for that blade to fall, it did not surprise her when magic shot through the room before any of the strashe could move.

In one breath, she saw weapons ready to be drawn, Orlov's mouth caught in a shout. And then, quite abruptly, the air solidified. One moment able to move, the next, her limbs were caught against an immutable pressure. Asya's anguished cry crashed against it, smothered, even the stray hairs around her face were caught in it, suspended impossibly.

Izaveta's eyes strained, unable to look up from the point she had been staring at.

Then, just as quickly, feeling seeped back into her limbs and she sagged under the unexpected release. The room was bright as midsummer, sparkling sunlight throwing the other inert figures into sharp relief.

Confusion eclipsed everything else, and Asya mirrored her expression as she closed the distance between them. Two girls in a frozen landscape.

They stood now in a hall of strange, living statues. Arrayed all around them, caught midmovement. Faces twisted into yells, the sound sucked away and eyes unseeing. Zvezda and Nikov stood still at their backs, caught in this suspended moment.

A single movement caught her eye. Another living thing in this disconcerting sea of petrified mortals.

The creature she'd been waiting to strike.

At her side, Asya tensed, clearly trying to summon flames that would not obey. "What have you done to them?"

"They're quite all right." Koschei waved his hand in disinterest, watching her with a hunger in his colorless eyes. "We needed some privacy. I have been so looking forward to meeting you, Firebird."

Izaveta shifted, her body uselessly adjusting as if she could somehow hide Asya. A flimsy protection but one she'd never lose.

"Whatever this magic is," Asya said, her voice far more grounded than Izaveta's would have been, far braver as always in the face of the impossible. "Whatever you've done to the Firebird—" the slightest hitch there giving away the true fear below "—you will have to pay the price."

"I assure you, Firebird, I would never evade the price." He flicked his eyes to Izaveta, the unspoken accusation clear. "My magic is all accounted for in the balance. As for the Firebird's power," Koschei went on, enjoying his role as sole performer in this silent theater. "I have not *done* anything to that."

"Then what—"

"It's simple," he said. "What I gave, I can also take away."

Neither sister spoke, and Izaveta was sure Asya was wondering exactly the same thing. The Firebird's power had not been *given* by anyone, at least not in any of the history Izaveta knew. Was this simply more posturing, the sorcerer trying to throw them off-balance? There was still the lilting cadence to his words, a performance that had some purpose. A point he wanted to prove.

"What do you want?" Izaveta snapped, tired for once of these circular conversations, always dancing around the true threat.

Koschei's attention flicked to her, that same expression of mild inconvenience he'd worn when she'd driven a knife into his neck. "You already know the answer to that."

"The crown?" Izaveta said, reaching for comfort in the dripping skepticism. "It would hardly do you any good. What use is a scrap of metal?"

"That is for me to decide."

Izaveta could feel her sister's eyes on her, the questions that she again couldn't answer, but she kept her gaze steadily on the sorcerer. "It doesn't matter. I still don't know where it is."

His eyes narrowed, that predatory air sharpening around him again. "Would you stake your sister's life on that?"

Fear stuttered in her veins again, the one jagged emotion her empty heart seemed able to grasp. But she didn't let it seep into her expression, refused to stand in front of Asya and betray the power that gave him.

"Not much of a threat," Izaveta said instead. "When I know you need the Firebird alive."

He held her gaze, as if waiting for her to break, waiting for those fractures at her center to come apart. But Izaveta was well practiced at this—and she knew greed when she saw it. Koschei would not risk whatever he saw in Asya.

He dipped his chin, as if in silent agreement. "Calculating as ever, I see. Very well." Something shifted in the air, another breath drawn. A footfall behind them, frozen midstep a moment before, as Nikov was brought into this petrified tableau.

He looked around, motion suddenly arrested as he took in the scene.

"I warned you that this magic would spread," Koschei went on, though even as he seemed to be addressing Izaveta, his eyes lingered on Asya. "That if you did not tell me where Queen Teriya's crown is I would not be able to rectify this terrible imbalance." Repeating information for the sake of someone else, another part of this show.

"Imbalance?" Asya repeated, looking between the two of them.

"Of a sort," Koschei said. "But do you not want to stop it?"

As he spoke, a cold crackled through the air. Nikov let out a strained gasp and staggered back, cobwebs of frost spidering across his skin.

Asya moved first, always the quicker to act. She grabbed a saber from one of the motionless strashe, whirling to raise it at Koschei. "Let him go."

But even in the brief moment it took her to say that, the weapon in her hand melted away—metal turned to water cascading through her fingers.

"This is not my doing," Koschei said simply. "And I alone cannot fix it."

Nikov let out a low, choking sound, falling to his knees. Izaveta didn't let herself move, refused to run to his side even as some hollow memories in her heart screamed at her to do so. He looked like he was trying to say something, but icy veins tearing around his throat muffled the words.

Izaveta clenched her fists, trying to stop her mind from sprinting toward possible solutions. "I told you before," she bit out. "I don't know where it is."

"And yet I do not believe you." Koschei took a step toward Nikov and Izaveta mirrored it instinctively, wanting to put some barrier between them. "It is so hard to believe someone who lies over and over, isn't it?"

Yet it *was* the truth, for once. If there was some relic of Queen Teriya's, her mother had never deigned to tell her about it. Another of the queen's secrets she wasn't party to.

"Well?" the sorcerer asked. "You would not act to save the people of this palace, but perhaps you will act when it becomes more personal?"

"Iza," Asya urged, eyes wide and imploring. But Asya still didn't understand—even if Izaveta had the answer, it couldn't be worth it. Not if it would give this sorcerer what he wanted.

Maybe that had been his true purpose here, to force Izaveta to show her hand. To make Asya see the cold truth of who her sister was.

Izaveta looked down at Nikov, his lips turning blue as the dark depths of his eyes were stolen by crackling frost. "I don't *know*," Izaveta said again, desperation pressing into the words.

"I forget, of course." Koschei stepped back, hands clasped in front of him. "This is the wrong sort of motivation for one so heartless."

He nodded in Nikov's direction, commanding the magic around him like a dog, and the ruinous frost began to recede. Izaveta's chest loosened at last.

Asya's expression hardened as she rose to her feet and glared at Koschei. "You said you weren't in control of it."

He shrugged, a minor hint of apology. "I couldn't control it *before*. You changed that for me, Firebird. But it still depends on your sister's compliance."

"Izaveta says she doesn't know," Asya replied, with a fierce look back at her. "And I believe her. If you really wanted to help whatever this is, you would explain what you know instead of threatening and manipulating people."

Izaveta strode to stand at her sister's side, a swell of pride bursting in her chest. Even if she couldn't believe she deserved it, it had to mean something that Asya still stood by her. Still believed that some goodness resided in Izaveta.

As the spell lifted and Nikov drew in great shuddering breaths, Izaveta thought she finally caught the word he had been trying to say. Not so much a word, but a name, one that stuck strangely in Izaveta's mind. *Medvedev.*

But Koschei was unfazed. "He's alive, is he not? No true damage done."

He said something else then, perhaps some threat or further promise of destruction, but Izaveta didn't hear it.

Her eyes were locked on Nikov as he slowly came back to himself, the curse drawn away.

Of all the people in this room, he had chosen Nikov. A newcomer to the court, someone Izaveta had barely had time to know. Why had he chosen Nikov as her vulnerability, when he was one that made no logical sense? And he'd left Nikov alive, even though a death might have further proved his point.

He could have let Nikov die and told Asya it was simply the curse spreading.

Izaveta's mind was moving too slowly, usually so quick to let pieces slip into place. Because she didn't want them to. Did not want these fragments of information to fit together to form the picture coalescing in her mind.

"You didn't ask me," Izaveta murmured.

Medvedev, the ludicrous monk who had written about the stars falling from the sky to devour the mortals below. The one an imagined Nikov had mentioned in a dark cell.

"You didn't ask me," Izaveta said again, louder.

She was vaguely aware she'd interrupted something the sorcerer was saying, but she couldn't bring herself to care.

Nikov's face was perfectly blank as he looked up at her. "Ask you what?"

"Where I'd been," she said. "That was the first question every single other person asked. But you didn't." Try as she might, she couldn't stop her thoughts now. Now she was at the precipice, and any moment she would go tumbling over. "Because you already knew."

"Izaveta." He rose to his feet, his voice somehow just the same as he stood. "Let me explain—"

She couldn't even summon anger. She let out a laugh, cold and tinkling and devouring, that spread until she thought it might consume her. Her mother's phantom was laughing too, dignified as ever. Finally, something the two of them shared.

A low hiss told her Asya had realized too, followed by another *snick* of metal as she reached for a blade. Once, Izaveta would have wanted her own, a way to fight back when she was powerless and ashamed. Not with scraps of hard-won power but with blood.

But all she could find was laughter. The gods certainly had a sense of humor, at least.

"And I suppose this performance was for us?" Izaveta asked, her voice as sharp in her ears as a discordant note. Or perhaps a clash of blades. "A show of loyalty, so you could lead us into a trap?"

Koschei didn't say anything, content to watch this play out in front of him.

"Izaveta, *think*, that wouldn't—" Nikov began.

"No," she said in a low whisper—at least she thought she whispered it, but the word somehow seemed to reverberate through her skull, deafening. She didn't want to hear him say

her name like that, in the same casual way he had on Saints' Night. As if they could be familiar with one another, a mark of her severe lapse in judgment.

I believe once two people have stabbed one's sister in the heart, first names are acceptable.

Lies. All lies. Every thread of Izaveta's world was woven with them.

"You do not get to say that," she finished.

Nikov pressed his lips together, eyes finally rising to meet Izaveta's. She wasn't sure what she saw in them anymore, if there was guilt or triumph shining there.

And she still couldn't think of anything pertinent to say. Questions swirled in her mind, as they always did, drowned out by that echoing laugh. It had burrowed inside her now, a hollow remnant of her mother. Her mother amused to see Izaveta played for the fool again, with the one person she'd thought deserved her trust.

It made too much sense. Nikov had stayed in the palace despite all obvious reasons he should have left. There was no place for the Amarinth's envoy here now, and Izaveta should have seen that. Should have realized it if not for those lingering emotions that had let her believe he might have stayed for her.

"You lied to me." Asya's voice had found the anger Izaveta could not, and if she could, Izaveta was sure she'd be alight with flames.

Koschei stepped in then, smooth next to the jagged expression on Nikov's face. "It's never quite as simple as that," the sorcerer said. "Our sides are not so opposed."

But from Asya's glare, she didn't believe that any more than Izaveta did.

The air shuddered around them, as if the frozen people were beginning to press against the bounds of this prison.

"Alas," Koschei said with a calmness that belied the destruction wrought through Izaveta. "Our time wears thin. Do remember I gave you a chance to make the right choice before it gets so much worse."

CHAPTER FIFTY-THREE

Asya drew in a sharp breath, then another, terror hammering at the inside of her skull. A gaping emptiness inside her. No weapon, no power, just useless mortal flesh. Her mind couldn't wrap around what was happening. A constant presence since her mother's death, suddenly severed.

She felt the magic release around her. A breath unloosed. The room sprang back into motion, everyone oblivious to what had just transpired.

"Arrest them," the strashevsta said again, though the strashe still seemed hesitant to move. They didn't know how hollowed out Asya was, how she couldn't reach for anything to help the people she cared about. How too much was pounding through her mind to even begin to think.

"And kill the prisoner."

Those words punctured the haze in Asya's head. Sudden and bright among her tumbling emotions. She couldn't lose Yuliana too.

Her head snapped up. "No!"

Asya tried to reach for the Firebird again. Anything that might pull them from this situation—helpless, as all the people she cared about stood vulnerable.

But there was nothing there. No distant kindling or embers, no creature to reach for. As if their connection had been severed by a vicious hand. The thing she'd come to rely on, the comfort of flames, taken away when she needed it most.

And the strashe holding Yuliana was already moving. The blade ready to carry out that order.

Asya could see Dima running behind her, her own muscles readying too late. Her flames might have got there. The Firebird able to leap free and tear that znaya from the strashe's hand.

But Asya was too slow. They were all too slow.

She almost saw it play out in front of her. Her heart not ready for the blood that bloomed across the wall.

But Yuliana didn't fall. An arrow protruded from the strashe holding her, the spray of blood from their back.

The relief took a beat to pierce through her, the last-moment reprieve.

Asya whipped around. Tarya stood in the doorway, bow raised and expression immovable as ever. But it wasn't carved in her deep set of disapproval as Asya was so used to. Instead, a fierce determination crashed across her, the vengeful statue.

The room froze again, but with shock now rather than charging magic.

Zvezda's eyes were wide, her blade glinting as she stared at Tarya. "You're here."

Tarya gave a short nod. Not further explanation. But it resonated through Asya, the fact that her aunt had come back—that she had saved Yuliana's life without hesitation.

Asya caught Yuliana's eye again, the resolute set of her jaw despite everything. She felt Izaveta behind her, and the rest of their strange group, all the people who had stood beside her.

Flames or not, she wasn't giving up here.

Asya raised her stolen znaya and she felt some certainty return. *This* was something she knew.

The strashe moved then. A sea of silver and clashing blades, surging toward the predator suddenly reduced to prey.

Tarya ran forward, placing herself firmly on Asya's left while Yuliana stood to her right, a loose ring around Izaveta. A fragile line of defense, but all they had left.

Yuliana took Tarya's bow, listing heavily to one side but at least able to defend herself with that.

Asya's movements were clumsy as the strashe descended. All her careful training forgotten, her limbs suddenly feeling foreign and strangely empty. She managed to follow the rhythm of the fight, ducking and dodging the onslaught, but every motion was a concerted effort. Her focus dragged away by the aching emptiness. The absence as sharp as any blade.

And the strashe did not stop, even as Tarya and Yuliana cut them down, unyielding.

Asya was panting, sweat already beading icy on her forehead. The inescapable truth was beginning to form in her mind, reinforced by every blow—each one closer than the last. There were too many of them. Without her flames, there was no escaping this.

She looked around desperately, trying to push through the clattering confusion. The strashe had split their group, Dima and Zvezda fighting an unending assault. Their only hope was to try to carve a path through. To reach one of the entrances and flee into the narrow passages of the palace where fewer pursuers could follow.

Asya couldn't convey her plan to the others, so she just had to trust they would follow her lead.

Instead of trying to fight off the attackers, Asya switched tactics. Going for evasion, she ducked through the first line of strashe, under the clashing metal and flailing arms. She shoved a blade into Izaveta's hands, no time to explain anything. Her sister took it, gripping tightly even if ineffectively.

Asya felt rather than saw Yuliana and Tarya follow. Three ships attempting to carve through a battering storm. The brief flash of surprise from the sudden change gave them the advantage. And evasion was far easier when weaving through so many, as the strashe had to be careful not to hit their own companions.

Yuliana was out of arrows now, and even with Asya at her side, she couldn't keep up. Too much weight on her injured leg, and Asya could hardly stay still long enough to support her as blows continued to rain down.

Heavy chains—firestone or not, it hardly mattered—lashed out. One slammed into Asya's arm, sending her reeling into the nearest strashe with a sharp burst of pain. More chains flew out, ready to restrain the Firebird.

But Asya couldn't reach the Firebird. She was just a girl, desperately grasping for a chance. Trying to stand in front of her sister while enemies pressed in.

Chapter Fifty-Four

Izaveta saw a fleeting flash of opportunity through the clanging chaos around her. The strashe briefly parting to reveal Nikov, pulled back toward the edge of the room, not looking at the roiling fight in front of him. Not looking at what he'd helped to cause.

She gripped the blade in her hand—she'd never held a dagger like this, heavier than she'd anticipated but gleaming in its sharpness.

She pushed through, the strashe overlooking her in favor of the true threats behind her. They hardly needed to defend when Izaveta could barely raise her weapon. But that did not mean she couldn't use it.

She pushed free of the confusion, one strashe leaping after her. She shoved an elbow back, trying to throw him off, but the weight of the blade sent her staggering forward instead. He swung round, a fist catching the side of her head and sending stars spattering across her vision.

But the dagger had given her an idea. She let the weight of it guide her, adding momentum to her swing as the hilt crunched against his head and he dropped to the ground.

The world was tipped off its axis, the floor spinning beneath her, but she forced herself toward Nikov. She raised the point of the blade to his throat. "Move."

He opened his mouth to say something but she pressed forward. "I don't want to hear it. *Move.*"

He raised his hands, eyes shadowed as he backed along the wall, following the path Izaveta forged. The sounds of the fight behind roiled through her, fear pitching beneath her. But she didn't look back, there was nothing she could do there. No way to do more than Asya and those trained fighters. This was Izaveta's skill set, the one thing she could do—try to claw back any leverage.

She pulled on an ornate whorl of marble, gilt and glinting even in the dark, and a small door clicked open. "In there."

Shrouded by the dancing shadows and the turbulent yells, the two of them slipped into the narrow space. One of the Queen's Doors that led only out of the cabinet room, another secret way for the queen to move around in mystery—adding to her omnipotence.

Izaveta pulled the door shut behind her and darkness swallowed Nikov's face. It put a barrier between them and the danger, a moment for her scheming, even as she was leaving the others behind.

"Do you know who he is?" That question came naturally, the logical step in determining Nikov's part in all of this. The problem she was trying to answer without all its parts.

His face split, as if her words were carving him open. Izaveta felt he had no right to look at her like that, not when she had already been hollowed out. *Ripped* apart and pieced back together. "Yes and no." He shook his head. "I can't say."

"Can't or won't?"

"Does it matter?" he asked, every syllable ragged. "Do the

reasons behind all of this matter? Intentions do not change actions."

She pressed her lips together. A low blow. One that stung more than she would like to admit. She had clung to his re-assurances, his certainty that their choices defined them. Another lie.

"Is that all you can do now?" she snapped, anger finally breaking through the shock. There was a relief to it, something familiar and restorative. "Speak in riddles?"

He didn't respond, though Izaveta wasn't quite sure if that was because he had no answers or because he was trying to be evasive.

Part of her wanted to push him, to needle at this story until she finally had the whole truth. But it was pointless, because he was right, the intentions and excuses didn't matter. All that mattered was what an action *meant*, and in the grand scheme of things, it all came to the same end.

Izaveta turned away, glaring into the faint lines of light still limning the doorway. She didn't want to look at Nikov, to see that all-too-familiar face thrown sharply into new relief. She took a deep breath, then another. She should give herself ten heartbeats to sort through this, to reduce everything to pieces on a zvess board. Small and controllable, able to move into a solid plan.

But she had no heartbeats to count and even as the moments ticked by, Izaveta still could not quite catch her breath.

This had always been her strategy, her coping mechanism. With every barbed word from her mother, with every betrayal and twist of the knife, she'd been able to set them aside— just as the queen had always taught her. Carefully carving off pieces of her heart until she didn't have to feel at all.

But even without the jagged beat in her chest, she couldn't

set her emotions aside. It was divinely unfair that pain lingered longest, even as empathy began to fade.

Izaveta suddenly wanted to fold in on herself, to let out a breath and allow all those pieces fly away. They could just leave. Leave and let the court destroy itself. Let all the liars at each other's throats, trapped in this game forever.

But she couldn't let that happen to Tóurin.

The same question she'd asked Nikov in the tower—what she'd thought was her imagined consciousness. *What am I supposed to do?* The answer felt further away than ever, a thick sheet of ice between her and any kind of way forward.

"He has no heart," Nikov said, each syllable a great effort, as if he were choosing them with care. "And without a heart, he cannot die."

That trickled through Izaveta's frozen mind, familiar yet far away. Something she was certain she had once known, perhaps lost when she had haphazardly pieced herself back together.

"But if his heart were returned to him…" Nikov trailed off, eyes straining toward Izaveta as if trying to convey something else. Something her shattered mind could not quite grasp on to.

Izaveta turned the words over, trying to force them past the staccato rush of her pulse in her ears. She matched Nikov's calm, reducing this to a theoretical discussion. A mere question of translation, or the position of the moons. Not something that carved her open, not time running out as Asya fought for her life in that room. "Many of the things he has done should not be possible. So it is certainly not out of the realm of probability." She glanced back at Nikov, trying to maintain that calm facade. "And if it is true, where would you suppose he keeps his heart?"

"I can't say."

"How useful," Izaveta said, relishing the bitterness, letting it burn away anything else.

"But I think…" Nikov swallowed, knuckles shining white as he tried to push the words out. "I think I could take you there."

Izaveta let out a sharp sound, a pale impression of a laugh. "Forgive me if I don't like the idea of following you into another trap."

"A rather useless trap," Nikov pointed out. "To take you away from my master's stronghold."

A fist closed around Izaveta's chest, crushing her ribs. She didn't want to hear him speak like that, as if he was on their side. As if he had not just shown the truth of his betrayal. She wanted that change to show on Nikov's face, for him to close off and cackle at their misfortune.

But there was no sudden shift. The scholar who had felt like a tether and the traitor were one and the same.

"Fine," Izaveta said, though the word was so far from the truth it was sour on her tongue. "Fine. We find a way to get Asya out of here, then you're showing us where his heart is."

CHAPTER FIFTY-FIVE

Asya wasn't quite sure when she lost track of her sister, somewhere between one swinging znaya and the next. She spun around, a blow catching on her shoulder. But she couldn't see Izaveta anywhere in the crashing storm.

Another loop of chain lashed out at Asya. Her mind too caught in worry for her sister to duck in time. Then Yuliana was there, her arm flying out to pull Asya free.

They had nearly reached the doorway now, nearly rejoined Dima and Zvezda, more numbers that would give them some advantage here. A run out into the corridors of the palace where they could reduce the might of the strashe.

But she still couldn't see Izaveta. Surely her sister was fine—she'd used some moment to duck free. To leave them behind. The more practical choice, especially when protecting Izaveta hampered Asya against so many assailants.

But that didn't stop distraction holding her back from those last few steps.

From the corner of her eye, she saw a blade arc. The striking silver slashing a half-moon through the air, as if drawing the gods' eyes above them.

And then it plummeted, swooping down toward Yuliana's unprotected right side.

Asya moved too slowly. Without the Firebird to propel her, with her mind still distracted by its absence, her muscles weren't quick enough. She wasn't quick enough. Again, she would be too late.

But someone else moved too. Fleeting, as if Vetviya had granted her passage through the In-Between.

Tarya almost materialized between Yuliana and the strashe, her dagger poised to parry.

The angle was wrong, the momentum of the blade too certain. It sent Tarya's knife spinning from her hand, and Asya opened her mouth to cry out, too late. Her shout was a useless plea as the znaya plunged straight into her aunt's heart.

Asya couldn't hear anything. The chains latched around her, pulling her down so easily with the weight of what she'd just seen.

She vaguely knew people were talking, likely discussing her fate again, but the only sound was a discordant wailing that rattled in her ears. It crescendoed to a high-pitched keening, accompanied with that moment over and over again.

The blade plunging. The slight hint of surprise on her aunt's face, quickly wiped away. Emotionless once again in her final moment.

CHAPTER FIFTY-SIX

A terrible silence resounded from the other side of the hidden door, the silence of the graves in the queenstrees.

Izaveta drew in a breath, her hand reaching toward the door but not quite pushing it open. She wasn't sure if she was too afraid of what she might see, or if she simply didn't want to reveal herself—calculating an advantage again.

"Return the Firebird to her cage." Kyriil's stolen voice echoed toward them, soft but crisp as if he were standing behind them. "And find Izaveta. Justice cannot be ignored simply because of her title."

Even the walls whisper here, her mother had once told her. A warning to remain on guard, and certainly a poetic take on the phenomenon, but true nonetheless. Fyodor had taught her how it actually worked, the way the curve of the dome and angle with the wall amplified voices in an almost magical way so one could spy on the occupants of the room.

A little surreal to think of the two of them now, two ghosts showing her the secrets of a whispering wall.

Nikov's hand flashed out, grasping her forearm. He shook his head, a warning in the grim set of his mouth. She pulled out of his grip, scalding as a brand, and raised the dagger again even as her arm trembled. He knew as well as she that she was no fighter, but she hoped the murderous intent on her face was enough to keep him in check.

"You should take this chance," he said softly. "Leave now while he's distracted."

Uncharacteristically pragmatic words from Nikov, the same boy who'd spoken of the possibility in fairy tales.

Though as soon as she thought that, she realized she could not truly judge what was out of character when it came to the scholar. She had clearly not had the true measure of him. It was just as likely that he was trying to throw her off, to trick her into another lapse in judgment.

"He doesn't want her dead," he pressed. The sentiment gave Izaveta little comfort. Whatever he wanted with Asya, it was not good. "And you can't help her like this."

"If I needed unsolicited advice," she said, pleased to hear some of the bite return to her voice, "I would send my prayers up to the gods."

"The Firebird must pay for her crimes." That was Bishop Deryev, eager to be part of the conversation.

"She cannot die yet," Koschei said, commanding power in the room even if they did not all quite understand why. The people of court had always been good at gravitating toward power, taught at Adilena's hand just as Izaveta had been. "We must understand the nature of the imbalance, the role the Firebird plays in all of this. We have to be careful."

"See, he won't hurt Asya," Nikov murmured, words almost smothered by the whispering wall. "But you—" He swallowed, that tight restraint pulling over him again, as if he couldn't quite say it. Or perhaps he was simply trying to decide how to confuse her further, another facet of his performance. "He has different plans for you."

She ignored him. Why should he care what happened to either of them? He had no right to spout warnings and confusing half-truths in a semblance of helpfulness.

"Of course, the Lady Izaveta will still be held responsible too," Sanislav said, the vehemence in his voice cutting through her thoughts. "Strashevsta, begin your search. She must not be allowed to slip free."

His condemnation was hardly surprising, he would probably have handed her over without even being asked. But it was the silence in the wake of his damnation, no cries of defiance or treachery, that knocked the air from her chest. For all Izaveta's plans and manipulations, moving people around her like zvess pieces, there was not a single one left to stand in her favor.

A terrible certainty, something Izaveta did not want to face, crashed over her. She could not stay here. She could not help to disentangle this situation—to help Asya or Tóurin—without some kind of advantage. Something on her side.

Like the heart of this sorcerer with impossible magic.

You cast that spell because you wanted to be in control.

Asya was right, much as Izaveta wanted to ignore it, to pretend at good intentions. And now she was more out of control than ever, a puppet whose strings had been snatched by some unseen hand. Helpless as she watched calamity careen around her.

She stared at the door, eyes burning through as if she could see out to the court, see the poison that had taken root and would soon destroy it. What good was a queen who could not protect her own people?

Perhaps she never would earn her place as queen, perhaps it was not something she had ever been fit for, no matter what the gods said. But she could do this, could right some of the wrongs she had caused.

Even if it meant leaving Asya behind.

PART FIVE:

THE MONSTER'S LAMENT

Long ago, when the gods still wandered the earth, before this land
had its name, there was a young sorcerer who claimed he could
enchant anything. A bold claim in a time of such wondrous
magic—so bold the queen put him to the test. She dared him to
create a magic stronger than love. The sorcerer thought it would
be easy, spending all the time he could with the queen as he
worked on his spell. When he finally believed he had succeeded,
the queen called everyone to the demonstration and demanded
he use the spell on her. But he refused—for he could not destroy
someone he had come to love. Proof that his claim had been
arrogance, proof he had failed. So he carved out his heart, and
hid it away, where none could find it, even himself.

—"THE QUEEN AND THE SORCERER," AN OLD FOLKTALE

CHAPTER FIFTY-SEVEN

Izaveta kept the dagger dug into the small of Nikov's back as they moved back through the tight passageways of the palace, keeping to any lesser-known shortcuts. The saint's ring she'd taken from Koschei was still tucked in her pocket, but that felt too much an unknown entity. She had no idea how it truly worked, let alone how to get it to take her somewhere she'd never been.

So she pushed Nikov across the expanse of the grounds toward the bearkeep. The tight grip on the weapon in her hand felt like the only thing keeping her tethered here, stopping those poorly pieced-together parts from crumbling to nothing.

The grounds were devoid of life, the strashe mobilizing or dealing with some of that cursed magic tearing through the palace. It left a peculiarly empty landscape. The frozen land of the queen who had been arrogant enough to believe she could make a difference.

The bearkeep was just as empty, even the low snuffling sounds of the bears muted. Distant, somehow. Still, Izaveta moved slowly around the snow-flecked pasture to the warmth of the stalls.

A bearkeeper, busy sorting fish into various pails, stood between them and Olyeta's stall.

Svedye. Izaveta drew back sharply, pulling Nikov with her. Not an army of strashe, but the bearkeeper could still pose a problem—especially if Nikov said anything—and Izaveta's mind was too battered to come up with an adequate solution.

She closed her eyes, trying to count her breaths. To give herself a time frame to pull together and do *something*.

Beside her, Nikov strained, not pulling against her grip, but into it. As if holding himself back, lips pressed firmly together.

Evidently there was more to all of this, more Izaveta still did not understand. But she could not bring herself to care. Nikov had said it best: *Does it matter?* And in this moment, it did not. Understanding and information would not help her now, would not help Asya or Tóurin. Those lessons her mother had hammered into her had done nothing except ensure any sliver of Izaveta was crushed.

"Stay quiet," she muttered, relieved that she was still able to hold on to a veneer of command. Keeping the dagger pressed into his side, but carefully hidden—a more challenging endeavor than she had anticipated—she pulled him round the corner to face the bearkeeper.

"Good evening," Izaveta said, realizing at that precise moment that it was far too late for it to convincingly be considered evening, but she forged ahead.

His eyes widened almost comically at the resurrected queen. "I—I thought you—"

"We won't be needing your help." She did not elaborate—as soon as one provided too many unnecessary details, the lie was obvious, and she hoped that her presence should be enough to send the bearkeeper scurrying.

She moved toward Olyeta's stall with purpose, hampered only a little by Nikov.

But the bearkeeper followed her, composing himself. "Please, allow me, your grace."

Izaveta did not bother correcting the title, one she likely would never hold now. "No, we don't mean to be a bother."

The bearkeeper didn't seem to hear, desperate to please. "Are you traveling alone?"

Izaveta stiffened, drawing on any last dregs of her mother. "There are two of us, that is quite adequate."

"It's late," the bearkeeper said, eyes sliding to the sliver of night sky beyond the stalls. "And the snows come in fast this time of year—"

"We're not going far," Izaveta assured them, trying to push past while keeping the blade at Nikov's side.

But the bearkeeper's eyes narrowed on Nikov, concern lacing their face. "Are you all right?" Once, Izaveta's mere presence would have been enough to quell these questions. But she had long since lost any credibility, the heir who had returned from the dead and left her land in disarray. "Do you need water, or—"

"Help," Nikov garbled out, the word bursting from his lips as if from some far-off master. Sweat was pooling at his brow despite the chill night air. "We can't leave, we—"

"He's being humorous," Izaveta cut in, any semblance at control unraveling around her. "We should really be on our way."

"Are you sure?" the bearkeeper pressed, their eagerness morphing into something closer to suspicion. "It's no trouble, and you really shouldn't travel in this cold alone. I could fetch someone for you."

"No, I—" Izaveta swallowed, her mind coming up blank.

Before she could conjure an answer, before the bearkeeper could run for the strashe, something flashed in her peripheral vision. A flicker of silver, an echoing *clang* and the keeper dropped like a stone.

She stared between the bearkeeper's prone body and Nikov, the pail swinging absurdly in his hand.

"Why—" She broke off, realizing too late that she didn't want to know. A moment ago he'd been trying to give away her ruse and now he was helping.

All it did was add to the confusion consuming her like an unyielding mist. Was all of this just another trick? Another way to throw her off-kilter?

So she did not speak as she led Olyeta out of her stall and looped the harness over her neck.

She didn't even ask where they were supposed to go, simply inclining her head to Nikov in question. She didn't trust her voice, or her ability to see through lies. She wasn't sure there was anything she trusted, right down to the earth beneath her feet that could rupture at any moment.

"We need to head west," Nikov said with concerted effort again.

Izaveta could not even bring herself to utter the sharp retort of how helpfully specific that was. She was so tired of all of this. Of the performing and the scheming and the betrayals.

But she still had this one last task she could not forsake, these mistakes of hers she had to rectify. So she turned Olyeta westward, around the dying light of the Depthless Lake and toward the unknown expanses of the Undying Wood, with a traitor far too close behind her and only a blade she barely knew how to use between them.

CHAPTER FIFTY-EIGHT

Asya was shivering. The chill wind that whipped through the open dome tore at her skin, while the permeating cold of the metal cage sank into her bones. An unfamiliar feeling, one that brought a terrifying panic with it.

She hadn't realized how comforting the Firebird's steady presence was until it was torn away. Not just smothered by the firestone, pulled to an unreachable distance, but *gone*. It had been less than a full moon since the power had blossomed inside her, yet somehow in that time it had already become integral.

The bars of the cage felt like they were tightening around Asya with each breath. The scene beyond them shifting between the faint darkness of Zmenya's Tower and the claustrophobic fear of the Elmer. The helplessness stretching between memory and present, suffocating. Tarya falling and falling again.

Yuliana had tried to speak to her at first, tried to pull her out of those nightmarish memories. But even that wasn't enough.

Asya could see Yuliana's outline curled against the bars, her head bent in sleep. It was the only real thing around her.

Maybe Izaveta would come back. Maybe she had some plan that would fix all of this.

Asya remembered wishing for that once before with metal

tight around her, and it had come true. But she had no idea where Izaveta was now—what had happened in the cabinet room or if she knew where Asya was.

It was a foolish hope, Asya knew that. If Izaveta were here, then she'd be in a cage as well, just as powerless. Everyone who had stood at their side was imprisoned now, Dima and Zvezda held in some unknown place.

Imprisoned or dead.

Whatever they were facing, Asya should be glad that at least her sister was safe. That she hadn't been trapped by Asya's foolhardiness too.

But Asya wasn't the only one caught in this trap. A cage that spread much farther than the bars around her.

Much as she wanted to curl up in this cage and forget, to let the world slip around her while she crumbled, she knew she couldn't.

Too many other people were at risk here.

She stood abruptly, the floor of the cage tilting beneath her as the chain swung.

"Asya?" Yuliana said at once, her head snapping up. Not as asleep as Asya had thought, then.

"There has to be a way out." Asya ran her fingers along the latch, along each cold curve of metal. She didn't know what she was looking for, just that she couldn't stay here a moment longer. Couldn't stay still and slowly turn to stone.

"There isn't," Yuliana replied, a resignation in her voice Asya hadn't heard before.

But Asya pressed on. She couldn't let this small spark of hope die, not yet.

"If I had the Firebird," she murmured, clenching her fingers around the stubbornly immovable metal. "I could get this open."

"They open easily enough," Yuliana said, reaching one hand through the bars and grasping the latch. Asya had almost forgotten that Yuliana had spent far more time in here.

"It's a cruel trick." Yuliana maneuvered the latch with an awkward twist and the door opened. Even the sight of it made Asya's stomach lurch. Yuliana now stood looking over the empty abyss of the tower, the wooden platform much too far below for them to hope to reach it. "Freedom within your grasp but impossible."

Asya sagged, her forehead dropping against the bars.

Yuliana was right, it was a cruel trick. Close enough that a desperate prisoner might make the attempt, left maimed or worse, even if they managed to land on the platform.

With the Firebird, she could certainly make that jump. The risks wouldn't matter, not when it could heal her.

But she couldn't feel even the slightest spark. No soft rhythm of life that told her the Firebird was there.

"Is it gone completely?" Yuliana asked, the question falling heavy as a body to the base of the tower.

Asya flexed her fingers. "I don't know."

A fear clamped around her then—the thing she hadn't let herself wonder. *Was* the Firebird gone completely? What would that leave her as?

She looked up at Yuliana, her ragged breaths almost swallowing her voice. "What if it is? What if I never get that power back?"

"You don't need the Firebird to matter," Yuliana said.

Asya couldn't bring herself to reply. Perhaps, in an abstract way, Yuliana was right. But in the immediate, it made little difference to the crushing fear. The hollow space where the Firebird had lived, a protection she'd come to rely on.

A protection she wasn't sure would ever return.

CHAPTER FIFTY-NINE

"Are you going to tell me where we're going?"

It was the first thing Izaveta had said since the palace had vanished beyond the horizon behind her, a piece of herself winking out with it. Her question shattered the quiet, unspoken truce that had settled between them—delicate as new fallen snow.

Nikov sat in front, the dagger still trained on him, even though Izaveta doubted he would attempt to escape. Whatever game he was playing, it involved complying for now—which did nothing to put Izaveta at ease.

She felt the tightening of his shoulders, that same strain. "I can't."

"So I'm supposed to trust you to lead the way?" There was no bite to her words, none of the venom she would usually inject. Her well had run dry and now all she could do was scrape her fingers uselessly against the bottom.

"It isn't about trust," Nikov replied. "It's about a lack of other options."

There was an emptiness in his voice too, a resignation that resonated deep within Izaveta. They'd both given up on the swirling dance their conversations had once been, each fractured reflections of themselves.

The trees closed overhead, their bare branches like spindled fingers, making her chest constrict. Too many times, she had wandered into this forest blithely unaware of the true dangers they held. And now she was making the journey to an unknown location with a traitor.

The zvess board had been upended and she wasn't sure she could do anything to piece it back together.

Nikov was certainly right about that: she had a severe lack of other options.

She had not quite anticipated the cold. Leaving so quickly she'd barely had time to take a tattered fur rug from the bearkeep. It wasn't that same penetrating cold of deep winter, but it still seeped into her bones, numbing her fingers. The dagger was probably frozen into her grip by now.

A fluttered movement among the bare branches caught her eye, followed by another, and another. Scattered inkblots across the frozen landscape, as if the leaves had all risen to coat the trees again.

"Falcons," Nikov stated unnecessarily.

Izaveta let out a derisive huff. "I hardly think we need to worry about portents of calamity in the midst of one."

"No," Nikov pressed, desperation straining his voice. "No, it's more than that. They're—" He swallowed, as if choking on the words. "They're *his* birds."

The meaning of that glanced across Izaveta's mind, the idea that this sorcerer's power ran deeper than she'd even realized. But before she could process the magnitude of that, the nearest falcon let out a piercing shriek that made the hairs on her arms stand on end. And, as one, the falcons rose into the air—a darker shadow against the canopy—and dove toward them.

Chapter Sixty

Olyeta moved before Izaveta had a moment to react, the bear far better prepared than her. Leaping forward, Olyeta pulled them out of the path of the onslaught. The falcons let out a hunting cry, piercing as their razor-sharp beaks.

Olyeta plunged into the tangle of trees, the branches snapping behind them as more falcons dove. The reins slipped through Izaveta's fingers—not that she could have steered anyway. All around them was a blur of whipping branches and flurried wings, catching on her skin like invisible claws.

The falcons moved as one, anticipating their direction and soaring ahead to cut off their path where the sky opened up again.

The bear skidded to a halt, rearing up, her teeth bared in a snarl, but the falcons didn't so much as flinch.

Something caught Izaveta's arm, and a blinding pain flashed as a talon gouged into her flesh. She lost her grip, the solid bear vanishing beneath her, and plummeted down toward the frozen ground.

The air burst from her lungs and lights banged against her skull, rattling through her bones. For a moment, she didn't move, the sky whirling above her, as she tried desperately to drag in a breath.

Falcons flitted in the corner of her vision, and for several staggering breaths she couldn't tell if they were real or imagined. Flesh-and-blood creatures or phantoms sent to drag her back.

"Izaveta?" Nikov whirled, drawing Olyeta to a skittering halt.

My lady. The correction rang in Izaveta's head, even as she had no breath to utter it.

The cry drew the birds' attention. A teeming shadow that shifted its attention to Nikov and Olyeta.

Another wood, another falcon, flashed in her mind. The strashe who had died because of her on the hunt, because Izaveta had been too afraid to face her actions. She couldn't let that happen again—there were no pieces left of her to break, no room for any more loss.

Air finally filled her lungs again and she gasped, scrabbling to find purchase on the rocky ground and pull herself to her feet. Nikov was at her side before she managed to, throwing himself from Olyeta's back even as the falcons clawed.

"Did you do this?" she choked out, ignoring his offered hand. The sky above them was full of ink-black dots, circling higher as if readying themselves to strike.

"No, and—" His voice cut off, a strange breathless sound like a hand at his throat. "He'll—he'll know where we are."

He'll know.

After all she had seen Koschei do, the impossible feats of magic, this should not be a shock. Yet still she found herself struggling to grasp hold of the concept. The power of ancient gods and fairy tales somehow realized in front of her.

Izaveta dug her nails into the ground, trying to force her mind to calm. Reasonable, rational statements that she could rely on. If the falcons were a vessel of some sort, controlled by the imposter, then he probably relied on sight. Fyodor had always been sure to make her education well-rounded, and those small spells had been a vital part. The easiest spells, the ones that required the least magic, the least to pay, were ones that did not truly alter the fabric of the realm.

She'd only read about the spell, solely an educational interest at the time rather than a practical one, but she should be able to manage it. Not truly changing anything, just a twist of the light.

She took a deep breath. *Focus.* She had climbed down the side of a tower, traveled impossibly across the lands. She could do this.

Birch-tree roots. She turned, still on her knees in the icy mud. The roots around her were all captured in that same ice, but she scrabbled at the frozen layer, dragging several strands free.

Light from a moon-facing leaf.

That was more challenging, especially with the swirling cloud of black looming above them, blocking any hint of stars.

"Here," Nikov called, tearing a solitary leaf from another branch as if he knew precisely what she was doing.

She shot him a sharp glare, but practicality won out. She took the leaf, turning back to the ice-streaked dirt to prepare the spell. Fyodor's voice rang in her head, the calm cadence of his lessons on the best methods of crafting a spell. At least the pain of that grief had been long stolen by her price.

A flutter of feathers in the corner of her eye made Izaveta flinch.

Nikov's hand caught on hers where she traced the lines of the spell. "Think of the price—"

She pulled her fingers from his grip at once, ignoring the

faint spark of warmth. "You can't know what the price will be. I'll deal with it when it comes."

The same dangerous reasoning that had led her to the spell that started this all. She swallowed that thought down, grasping at another root, ready to twist it into the right configuration.

"I do know."

She froze, eyes turning back to Nikov, drawn by the odd certainty in his voice.

"An illusion spell will take your sight until the vision is done," he said, voice soft and earnest. "Right now it will, anyway."

Izaveta's dismissal of "You can't know that, no one can know that" died on her lips. She was hardly a good judge of when Nikov was lying, that had been thoroughly proved today. But all his lies had been clever—the sort of words she already wanted to believe. A lie that outlandish would benefit no one.

A sharp hunting cry cleaved through the air. Not just the call of a single falcon, but all of that teeming mass together. Ice leeched through Izaveta's limbs, the drowning threat of panic.

It didn't matter what the price was when that was the other option. "I trust Olyeta," Izaveta said simply, forcing the last birch root into place. "She can find the way."

"And you trust me to lead you? Let me do the spell, then—"

She shot him a dark look, her most practiced venom. "Then you can send a message back to the sorcerer?"

But even before she'd finished speaking, she had to concede that he was frustratingly correct as ever. If the illusion spell really did take her sight, however briefly, then she would be left at Nikov's mercy, unable to be sure where they were going. But she also could not trust him to do it, not when it was just as likely he'd find a way to twist it to his advantage.

Too many betrayals forcing her into a corner.

"We could do the spell together," Nikov suggested. "Then we split the price between us. Our sight would come back twice as soon."

Izaveta had never heard of something like that—not that she would admit it aloud. But Nikov would know more of it than her, and she couldn't see how a complex ruse would help more than simply running.

But still she hesitated. Was it lack of emotion or too much holding her back now? Her empty heart seeing the worst in everyone or the last of her hurt at his betrayal clinging on?

Another ink-black wing fluttered across the canopy overhead, drawing closer. She felt beady eyes on her, far more intelligent than a bird should be. They were merely watching, hunters confident their prey was cornered. Or waiting for another order from their master.

"All right," Izaveta said with an air of forced calm, as if she had some semblance of control over this situation. She readied Olyeta within arm's reach, hoping she was right that the bear would be able to lead them. "Mutual damnation, it is. We both do the spell."

Izaveta knelt for the dagger where it had fallen—precariously close to Nikov's own grasp.

"You know the words?" Nikov asked.

Izaveta gripped the weapon. "Of course."

In the edge of her vision, she saw a single, winged silhouette break free from the swarming mass above. It arced up, a blade reaching its zenith, before plummeting down toward them.

As if they'd all been waiting for just that, the other falcons reared.

"Send them to the Amarinth," Nikov said quickly, taking her hand in his again. "If you send them directly west, that's where he'll think we're going."

Izaveta didn't have time to process the meaning behind that or bother arguing the point. She slashed across the frigid ground with the tip of her dagger, cutting through the ingredients to send their power to Dveda. They said the spell in an easy unison, as if they had always been prepared for just this.

She felt the slight crackle of magic across her skin—nothing like the terrifying power of the first spell she'd done, the one that had killed her mother. This one was a mere trickle from the earth, a slight siphoning from so much more.

The soft light of the forest folded in on itself, and a shape stepped from the seam. Hardly more than a shadow, painted only with small specks of color, the illusion slipped into being. The hulking shape of a bear, two figures on its back. A rippled reflection in water that would fall apart under closer scrutiny. But it should be enough, especially in the confusion of the twisting forest.

The swirling falcons dove after it, changing their direction with an unnerving sharpness.

As they faded away, the illusion drawing them on, Izaveta felt the final part of the spell. The price, a soft nudge at her back. She'd not done a spell with a noncorporeal price before, something as insubstantial as her sight. But even as it nudged at her, she could feel she would also be able to ignore it if she wanted.

That basic tenet of magic: it could not take that which was not offered.

She could refuse it and bring the Firebird after her again, send the realm into turmoil again.

But that would help no one—least of all Asya.

Izaveta's gaze slid to Nikov, a deep gash slowly seeping red down his cheek.

He had come back for her. He could have simply ridden away on Olyeta, returned to Koschei and left Izaveta to the mercy of the falcons. But he hadn't. He'd come back.

His dark eyes were on hers, something oddly unreadable flickering there.

The darkness came so suddenly it made Izaveta sway. A rushing black that sent her mind tumbling back to coming undone. The Firebird's flames cleaving through her, tearing her apart at the seams, unable to fully coalesce again.

She reached out for where she remembered placing Olyeta, but her fingers caught only air.

Tightness closed around her throat. She had not anticipated the fear that would come with this price, the control wrenched from her grasp yet again. Could she even trust what Nikov said was true—that he had borne some of this price too?

"Nikov," she said, suddenly desperate for anything that could anchor her here, that could prove she was still substantial.

"Yes," he replied, a slight shuffling of feet to her right.

"Was that...?" she whispered, the cloying fear of the question somehow easier to voice in this darkness. "Was that really you in the tower?"

"It was." She felt the murmur of his breath too close to her and she pulled back, her foot slipping in the snow. "Well, I wasn't there in the physical sense," Nikov amended. "It was an apparition of sorts that allowed me to communicate with you."

"So you saw..." She trailed off, memories of herself in that lowest of places, all her weaknesses exposed. The ways she'd turned to what she had believed was her subconscious for comfort. It somehow felt like more of a betrayal than anything else. "Why?"

"Because he asked me to." Such a simple answer, laying it all out with that scholarly detachment as if none of it mattered, no more personal than any of Izaveta's games. "He wanted another way into your head."

"Effective, I suppose." Her muscles clenched, all the cracks smoothing from her voice, the threat of tears scalded away.

"I—" He broke off, that detachment leeching from his voice. "I tried to help."

Izaveta stepped back, away from his presence, which she could feel even if she could not see.

She did not allow herself to address the full meaning of his words. If she could believe any truth from him at all, or if this was some attempt at grandiosity to scare her away from even trying.

"We could wait to go on," Nikov said—voice too gentle, as if Izaveta really were fragile enough to crack. "With the price split between us, it shouldn't take too long for our vision to return."

But Izaveta shook her head—realizing only a beat later the futility of the gesture. "No," she said aloud. "We go now."

She refused to waste time on sentimentality, not when every moment counted. She could not be sure what was happening at the palace, what new power the imposter had conjured up. But she knew what she owed to the people there, to all the people across Tóurin.

She already felt enough like she had abandoned them—abandoned Asya. She couldn't now squander this small advantage.

Finding the warmth of Olyeta's fur, Izaveta hoisted herself back into the saddle with as much grace as she could manage when she was moving on memory alone. She felt Nikov climb up behind her, the light touch of his fingers as he got his balance.

Izaveta stretched forward, gripping tight to Olyeta's fur—partly to pull herself away from Nikov and partly to give her something solid beneath her touch. Something to prove she was still here.

"Which direction?" she asked.

"Continue northwest to the Undying Wood."

Izaveta tensed again. "But we're not going to the Amarinth."

"No," Nikov replied softly. In this proximity, with darkness pressing all around her, he felt suddenly too close. His touch was unexpected, a shiver of lightning across her skin. "What else is in this direction?"

"Plenty of things," Izaveta snapped, not bothering to bite back the irritation at this constant circular conversation. "Versbühl, Liljendäar, half a continent."

"But where would you find a myth?"

Izaveta was about to snipe at him again, when the answer fell into place. If this was all true, if the ancient sorcerer banished by Queen Teriya was somehow real—and had returned—there was one place he may keep his heart.

"The Skyless Hallows," Izaveta echoed. They were almost a myth too, the point where the mountain range that divided Tóurin from Liljendäar became unpassable. People who ventured in, eager to find its secrets, did not return.

Izaveta almost laughed again, the same jagged laugh that had tried to cut her apart. What better place to enter entirely unprepared with a traitor at her side and her vision gone?

CHAPTER SIXTY-ONE

The usual brightness of dawn was swallowed by the thick gray of clouds above Asya. She'd had her eyes closed, an attempt to block out everything around her more than to sleep, which she knew would be impossible.

But she jerked upright at the sound of footsteps.

Her heart lurched, briefly hopeful that her sister had returned. This might feel more possible with Iza here too. A little less like Asya had been cast out—away from her power, from her sister.

But she wasn't surprised to see the sorcerer ascending the wooden platform. He walked with a measured care, the cat stalking its prey. He reached the same place Asya had sat all those days before, when she'd still had some hope that she could help Yuliana.

He pulled on one of the levers, the chains shifting, and Asya's cage swung down toward him. She had to grasp the bars to keep herself from falling against them, her stomach swooping at the drop.

"I really have been looking forward to meeting you," he said when the cage steadied. "I'm sorry the circumstances could not have been better."

Asya didn't speak, watching him as some instinct screamed

at her to run. To attack, to *do* something. But there wasn't anything for her to do now, trapped and powerless again.

He stepped forward, so close she had to tilt her chin back to watch him. "The Firebird who can finally fulfill her true purpose. What she was made to do."

As he spoke, as the light shifted across the planes of his face, he seemed less and less like Kyriil. The voice was morphing into something else—something eerily familiar.

She'd heard him before. In those burning dreams and her vision. A voice drawn from the bowels of the earth, ancient and unused.

Don't you want to know what you were made for?

She had hoped that might have been Dveda. One of the gods looking down on her, hoping to help. A ridiculous plea, childish as clutching the icon her mother had given her.

All of that had been a lie. The idea that the Firebird had been chosen for something, that the gods had ever cared.

"That was you?" she asked finally.

He nodded. "That was the only way I could speak to you. My greatest creation and yet I could not set foot in Tóurin. Not while a Karasova queen sat on the throne."

Asya managed to force her feet to move then. Pushing herself to stand, muscles tensed to act. Instinct, so quickly learned since the Firebird had taken refuge in her skin, made her reach for flames.

But now, there was nothing, not so much as a stray spark skittering through her blood.

Emptier and more alone than she'd been before the Firebird rose in her. As if it had been a part of her even then, lying hidden.

Koschei stepped closer, his toes grazing the very edge of the platform as his colorless eyes bored into hers. "What I gave," he said with a tenderness that made her skin crawl, "I can also take away."

He'd said that before, in the cabinet room.

A lie or brash declaration. But Asya couldn't ignore the truth, couldn't ignore that the Firebird had vanished at his behest.

He seemed to read the question on her face before she could truly phrase it, before she could begin to understand the magnitude of what he was saying.

"You want answers," he said softly. "You want to understand. And I can help you with that."

Asya did want all of that, wanted it almost as fiercely as she needed to protect the people she cared about. An understanding of this duty, this burden that she had to accept.

But she was not a fool—not naive, no matter what her sister said.

"And what do *you* want?" she shot back.

His lips curled, subtle as the slowly curling edges of burning parchment. "You have already given me most of what I want. You set magic free."

She took a step back, her shaking foot struggling to find purchase on the pitching surface.

"I can leave you now," he said. "Trapped and without answers, on the precipice of despair."

She couldn't help a glance up at Yuliana, silhouetted against the dome now and too far away for her expression to be clear. Then back to Koschei, staring down at her with a magnanimous expression. A deity watching havoc wrought on the world at their feet.

He didn't say anything, did not offer her other options. He was waiting for her to say it.

"Or?" she bit out.

"*Or,*" he said with satisfaction. "I can show you the truth and you can take your rightful place."

She swallowed, her mouth dry as ashes. "And what price does that truth come with?"

"Consider this price paid." He looked down at her, a gentleness to his words that set Asya's teeth on edge. Speaking as if he knew her. "After all, you helped me so much already."

"And how can I know your truth means anything?"

"What does truth mean to you?" he asked. "You have surrounded yourself with people who lie. People who would use you and abandon you all while they spin their pretty falsehoods. But I think you deserve this truth. You can decide to believe it or not."

Her vision tilted strangely as he moved closer still. A shift in focus that caused the rest of the tower to fade to the background.

"You'll see soon enough I only want what is best for you. Best for all of us." He leaned forward, his hand reaching through the bars to hover at Asya's temple. She wanted to step back, to duck out of his reach, but her muscles couldn't seem to obey her. "I'm not the one who took your choices from you. Others may want to use you for their own ends. But only I can know your true purpose."

He pressed a finger against her forehead and a thick wave of shadow enveloped her.

Asya stood on the banks of the Depthless Lake again. A familiar scene was laid out before her—the same one she'd seen in the vision from the Firebird. The queen in a pearlescent robe standing before two bundled babies. The sorcerer stood opposite her already, familiar now in an intangible way. Koschei.

They argued as they had before, but there was a different cadence to the words now. The two of them spoke almost as equals.

"Arrogance," he hissed—though Asya heard the thread of frustration this time, trying to get through to someone any way he could. "You think you can—"

"I'm doing the ritual. My children will not suffer for this too."

She turned her back on him again, though Asya didn't even try to react this time. Something felt off about all of this, uncomfortable in a way she couldn't name. The flames erupted in Koschei's hand, roaring up. But they didn't leap to the queen's unprotected back as she'd expected.

Instead, they burned through the dusted snow to carve ritual symbols—reminiscent of the very ones Asya had done days before.

The queen looked up. "You'll help, then?"

Koschei's shoulders were slumped, turning in on himself. "I always would have, if you'd asked, Teriya."

"I know." The words were so small the wind almost swallowed them, a hushed admission.

Koschei knelt down next to the two bundles and pulled ingredients from thin air. Small pouches and vials all scattering around him like leaves. He shot Teriya a half smile, something familiar flashing between them. "You were never much good at sigils, anyway."

The scene flickered, the preparations for the spell readying as Asya watched and the moons above them began to set. Time passing in a breath.

The scene settled again, the ingredients arranged in a kind of organized chaos—a pattern and careful logic to them. A crown sat in the very center, not the same one Asya had seen her mother wearing, twisting whorls of silver and gold, ornate and imposing. This one was small and simple, fashioned like a young girl's kokoshnik, with only a single gemstone set into its point. The only sign that it was of any value.

"It's ready," Koschei said. He took a step back, taking stock of the mess he had laid out. Muttering under his breath, he counted through each one with meticulous care and a slight furrow to his brow.

It reminded Asya painfully of Nikov, a scholarly interest. Much more humanity than she'd seen in Koschei before.

"Bring them over," he said. Unusually imperious to address a queen like that, but the command had a softer cadence to it. A familiarity that spun between these two unlikely companions.

Teriya brought the two bundles over, still silent and serene as the sky above. The children she was doing this for—*twins*, of course.

Understanding permeated through Asya, so sudden she couldn't be sure if she'd come to it herself or this vision had forced it on her. This was the first set of twins, the twins who had first been split apart into queen and Firebird.

Teriya stepped back, tension knotting her shoulders though her face remained resolute.

Koschei seemed to sense her apprehension, moving to her side. "Teriya." He gripped her hand, reassurance in the gesture. "This will work, I promise you." There was an affection so vulnerable and open in his voice that Asya suddenly felt she was intruding. But even as she tried, she couldn't look away. This memory was guiding her perspective.

"I know," Teriya replied.

Koschei let his fingers brush across her knuckles as he

turned away, kneeling to address one item not yet a part of the strange pattern of flames. "The final step."

A wooden box, carved with a spiraling design Asya couldn't quite make out. He opened the lid with reverence and lifted the object out tentatively, as if it might turn on him at any moment. A dazzling warmth came with it, and small spates of light. A different brilliance to the Depthless Lake. Where those waters were a moon, this was a tiny sun. Bursting sprigs of golds and reds against the pale landscape.

A burning feather.

Not just set alight but made of flames. Like the feathered sparks that rose from Asya, somehow captured in a single instance.

Questions pierced Asya's mind, puncturing the serene calm of the dream. If these were the first twins, how did that feather already exist? The Firebird was created when the first twins were born—or so Asya had always been told. And what in all the gods' names were they using it for?

She didn't have a moment to examine them before she was caught up in the whirl of the spell. Koschei's chanting was low and rhythmic, captivating as a song. And familiar too... the same lilt of her Callings.

A spangled whorl of light wrapped around the two babies. There was something disconcerting about the sight. Beautiful yet terrible—a spider spinning the web around its prey.

Asya felt the sudden, desperate urge to stop this. This thing that had already happened yet dictated the course of her life. Ripping any choice from her hands.

But Teriya moved first, not trapped by the memory, lunging through the shimmering veil and into the heart of the spell.

Koschei's chanting broke off, eyes widening. "Teriya!"

She didn't look at him. A fierce determination was carved

into her features. The look of someone who had already made up their mind. She was murmuring under her breath, words too distant for Asya to catch. She moved to the center of the circle and pulled the burning feather from its careful perch.

"What are you—"

But before he could reach her, she plunged the sharpened tip of the feather into a pulsing vein on her forearm. Scarlet sprayed against the snow, bright as the lake. Teriya barely flinched, not so much as a hitch in her hurried chanting.

Koschei fell to his knees, body arching in pain. His guttural scream cleaved the air. He clutched at his chest, some essential part of him ripping away. Asya wanted to close her eyes, to scream at Teriya to stop. It was like watching the spell she'd cast from the outside.

But Teriya did not stop and Asya could not look away. The magic began to shift, so tangible it almost seemed sentient. An entity of its own with its own aims and purposes. Asya had never considered that—the idea that magic could *feel*, that its ephemeral nature could be more than just coincidence.

The feather flared, its light so bright it eclipsed the scene. And then it was gone, crumbling to burning ashes that slunk toward the two bundles. A gust of red sparks engulfed the nearest baby, a sprinkle of gold consuming the second. Just the same as Asya had seen all those years ago in a freezing cathedral in the ceremony that had determined her and Izaveta's fates.

The air settled, the tang of magic seeping back into the earth. Even in this fractured memory, Asya could feel the deep shift. A permutation that shuddered down to the very roots of the land.

As Asya watched, radiance ebbed from the lake. Not quite to the bare glimmer it was today, but still noticeable. *This* had caused the Fading. How or why, Asya had no idea. But Queen Teriya—the first of the Karasova line, exalted above all others—had started this slow destruction of her own land. And she had created the Firebird for her own aims.

"You altered the spell." Koschei's voice was hoarse, no accusation in the words. A deep sadness at not being trusted, not being *enough*.

"I wish you hadn't helped. That would have made this so much easier."

The only sound was the slow drip of blood from the still-gaping wound on Teriya's arm. "You know all magic must come with a price." She still wasn't looking at him, frozen in a suspended horror. "For this to last, to protect them for centuries to come, it had to be a true sacrifice."

He stared up at her, a painfully familiar look of betrayal cracking across his face. "And you sacrificed me?"

Koschei looked different now, thrown into a new light without the lake's full luminescence. Color leeching from his eyes, the planes of his face cast into sharp relief. Something feral lurked there—something monstrous.

"You should be honored," she murmured, and Asya could see she meant it. Really believed this to be a gesture of her love. "It means I truly cared about you."

"You didn't ask." Koschei's fingers clenched, digging anguished rivets into the snow. "I might have given it willingly. We could have still done this together, like we planned."

Teriya's lips tightened. "I couldn't take that risk."

She turned then, to the two babies—still eerily silent despite the commotion around them.

Koschei tried to rise, his shaking limbs collapsing under him again. "I'll tell them what you've done, I'll—"

"You will not be able to return to Tóurin. This spell banishes you—as long as a Karasova queen sits on the throne." She knelt next to him, tender, cupping his face in her hands. She turned it, so they both looked down at their reflections in the shining lake. "And we've now ensured that will be eternal."

He certainly looked monstrous in that moment—inhuman and unreachable. The clear villain standing opposed to Teriya's beautiful serenity. But Asya couldn't help a twinge of sympathy for him. Sacrificed and abandoned, in the end. A feeling Asya knew.

Perhaps it wasn't so simple to cast the monster in this fairy tale, not when the queen had claws of her own.

CHAPTER SIXTY-TWO

Izaveta had never seen drawings of the Skyless Hallows, save a few artists' imaginative renderings, which largely leaned on the dramatic, so she did not know what to expect. The snow had thickened as they drew closer to the mountains, cold clamping around the darkness that still consumed her vision, permeating easily through the threadbare rug wrapped around her shoulders.

When her sight finally did return, it was to a tapestry of darkness. The distant light of the stars overlaid by clawing branches. Everything felt so clearly in focus, her awareness of Nikov behind her fading away. They had not spoken beyond their initial conversation, their proximity too close for Izaveta to examine any of her more fragile thoughts. He'd told the truth, then. The price really had been shared.

The sky was clear at least, no threat of fresh snow to fall, which should be enough to stave off any hypothermia.

Either that or they would freeze to death, Izaveta supposed, examining the thought with a scholarly detachment that Nikov would approve. They could hardly turn back. Koschei knew by now that Izaveta had fled with Nikov, and he'd likely suspect their aim, even if those illusions had slowed him down.

No, there was no turning back. Izaveta would succeed, or she would truly become the frozen queen. An ice-cold corpse presiding over her ruined queendom.

She felt, rather than saw, when they arrived. Not only in the slight tension to Nikov's shoulders but in the very air. It had that same quiet, vibrating power the Elmer had, but it was thicker somehow, viscous with crackling magic. It trembled across her skin, settling like a layer of frost.

Olyeta skittered back, throwing her head side to side as if searching for the source of this strange sensation. Izaveta reached a hand down to stroke her flank, soothing. Olyeta did not spook easily. She had been well trained for a future queen, prepared for any eventuality. But this was far more than Izaveta could expect from her.

She pulled on the reins, speaking for the first time in hours. "We should leave her here."

Nikov nodded, his brows furrowed, a slightly pained set to his mouth. He hadn't spoken since they had left the falcons behind and reached this deeper snow. It struck her suddenly how unusual that was for him, to not even comment on the interesting nature of the landscape or speculate on accounts of the Skyless Hallows.

Because he'd been here before. The realization squeezed around her, a discomfort on her shoulders. He'd been here before and he didn't like it.

Her voice felt stuck, caught somewhere between wanting to berate him for not giving her more information and wanting to comfort him. She swallowed the hard lump of confusion. She didn't need that now, didn't need to think about the way she still ached to imagine Nikov here, alone and scared.

Instead, she slid down from Olyeta's back and Nikov followed with a soft crunch of snow beneath their boots. Izaveta pulled on Olyeta's reins, directing her away from this strange veil of magic. The bear complied easily, darting away from them and off into the distant, mortal trees.

"We'll be back soon," Izaveta called after her, her voice no more than a whisper. A prayer, more than a promise. Everything here felt like it was set at a slight angle, the ground off-kilter beneath her feet, her blood uneasy in her veins.

She turned away from Olyeta's shape, white fur vanishing into the snow, to face whatever lay ahead. It looked the same as the forest around them, clustered trees and bare branches, just like the forest that surrounded the Depthless Lake.

Yet everything about it felt *wrong*. A place mortals should not dare tread.

Izaveta stepped forward, careful, as if the ground were ice that might crack beneath her feet.

She opened her mouth to ask what they should look for, but closed it as the answer presented itself ahead. A tree—not any species that Izaveta could name—soared above all the rest. It had the same silver-white bark as queenstrees, with a slight sheen to them, almost like marble. But unlike the thin trunks of queenstrees, brittle and tall, this tree was as sprawling and expansive as an oak. Its roots reached out like spidered hands, mirroring the twisting branches above.

It had no leaves, yet somehow it seemed to rustle. A low whisper that gnawed at the back of Izaveta's mind, drawing her in.

And in the very center of the trunk was a tangled hole. As if someone had reached in and torn out the tree's insides, new roots like clawing veins desperately trying to heal over.

The perfect place to keep something one did not want found.

Izaveta paused, looking down at the sprawl of roots, spread

across the ground like the entrails of some great beast. They started only a few paces ahead, stretching a hundred or so more toward the trunk. Deceptively easy.

She knew the stories of this place, and Koschei would not leave something so precious unguarded. This was a threshold, a place between here and whatever was *there*.

Nikov put out a hand before she could step over the first gleaming root.

Izaveta arched a brow at him. "Are you finally going to provide some useful advice?"

"I think I should do this part alone," he said, something indecipherable flitting across his features. "You wait here."

She let out a bark of shattered laughter. "Yes, please go ahead so you can double-cross me again."

Nikov blanched a little at the sharpness of her tone, the flicker of hurt almost enough to make Izaveta regret it. *Almost.* She knew there was something else at play here, something she didn't yet understand that spooled between Nikov and the sorcerer.

But she didn't have any room for forgiveness now.

"You trusted me to lead you here."

She held up the dagger, her one contingency. "Well, as we both know, trust is conditional."

Nikov let out a puff of air. "Fine," he said slowly. "We'll go together. Just—" he swallowed, his mouth working "—be careful. You'll see…things."

"How specific." But the way he said it—such a simple statement—sent a cold fear clawing up Izaveta's throat, so she added, "What things?"

"I don't know," he replied, his eyes darting between her and the knotted roots. "It's different for everyone. You just have to remember it's not real."

"What did you see?" The question tumbled from her lips before she could catch it, her voice gentler than she liked. *Weak*, her mother would have said. *Vulnerable.*

Nikov did not seem surprised that she had guessed he'd been here before, only the slightest twitch of his fingers gave anything away. But he looked off before he answered, a slight skew to his words. "Just keep walking until you reach the trunk."

Another simple statement that sent trickling fear down her spine.

She gripped the hilt of her weapon—a weapon she could barely lift—but it made her feel she was doing something. Nikov had lied to her, had done nothing but lie to her, his ominous warning was probably another deception. An attempt to get her to turn back.

She did not truly believe that, but thinking it gave her the courage to take that first step.

There was a moment of pressure, as if she were pushing her hands against an invisible membrane. Then it gave way with a small popping in her ears, the snap of tension when lightning finally struck.

Her hands were shaking, but no longer because of the icy wind. The cold had evaporated. Though snow and frosted cobwebs still laced the trees around them, the air was warm. A slight breeze, almost like a hot breath on the back of her neck. It made her skin prickle, glancing around as if there might be someone else here. But it was perfectly quiet.

Even the strange whisper of the tree had vanished, as if taking that step had whisked her away.

She felt Nikov follow her, but didn't look at him. She did not want to see his fear, to have it ricochet back and amplify her own.

She had braced herself for monsters to rise out of the ground, for more falcons to sweep down on them with their talons bared. Or for the roots themselves to reach up and strangle them.

But nothing moved in the still landscape, and for a blissful instant, Izaveta allowed herself to believe that Nikov had been wrong. Lying or mistaken—whatever the reason, there was nothing to fear here.

It happened in the space of a blink, the pause between one breath and the next. Not like the shadowed illusions Izaveta had created, that forced themselves into being with effort, this figure stepped onto the earth as if she'd always been there. As if Izaveta had been walking toward her this whole time without realizing it.

Queen Adilena was dressed in the same clothes she'd worn the night she died, resplendent as ever. She seemed to carry her own light, not ghostly or ethereal. A welcome burst of sunlight in this darkness.

Izaveta stumbled to a halt, her knuckles white on the dagger's hilt. Something solid—something *real*.

Her mother stepped forward, a glittering smile on her face, and it was all Izaveta could manage to hold her ground.

"My dear," Adilena said, and the familiarity of her voice tore through Izaveta's chest. "I've missed you."

CHAPTER SIXTY-THREE

When Asya came back to herself, Koschei was gone and her cage had returned to the highest point. The light had changed above her, more time lost than she'd realized as the sky had shifted to night.

The vision danced behind her eyes. Teriya's betrayal and the real pain splintering across Koschei's face. How much of that had been true? It was easy to believe that a queen might have done that. Another person wresting choice from Asya's grasp.

She shifted, sitting up in the cramped space.

"Are you all right?" Yuliana asked at once, alert from her own prison.

Asya nodded slowly, pulling herself back to reality.

"What did he do?"

Asya took a moment to answer, still not entirely sure. "He showed me something."

She glanced up, Yuliana watching her with wide eyes, dark circles hollowed beneath them. It was not enough of an answer, but Asya wasn't sure how else to explain it. Too ephemeral in her mind to put into words. The moment that had started this all—the first lie.

But one thought solidified at the center of that. An un-burning ember.

What I gave, I can also take away.

Asya had wanted to believe this was the same as firestone. A forced wall between her and the Firebird that would wear down again. But what if it was more than that?

Could the Firebird die?

No. A small, defiant voice at the back of her mind. Beaten down by exhaustion and pain, but still pressing on.

Asya was the Firebird. If she was breathing, that meant the Firebird was still alive. That meant there was still possibility. The Firebird wasn't only defined by her magic, but the duty that had been placed on Asya long before any power had emerged. It was the only choice she still had, the only thing not forced upon her by someone else.

The choice to do what she believed was right.

She was still the Firebird, flames or no. That was what Tarya had taught her—that was what Tarya had died for.

Asya reached for the latch, twisting it the same way Yuliana had shown her. The cruel trick that would send most people to their deaths.

"Asya—" Yuliana's voice had a note of warning now. "Asya, what're you doing?"

The door swung open sharply, the weight of it tipping Asya toward the shuddering drop. She only just managed to catch herself in time.

"Do you feel the Firebird again?"

Asya shook her head. She looked down at the wooden platform, so small from this height. An impossible target.

She looked up instead.

Those chains snaked above them, up to the metal trellis that held them in place, just beneath the shattered dome of the tower. Zmenya's spire rose still farther, a single gleaming point against the sky.

Asya couldn't quite tell from the angle, but it looked like the trellis was too far below the dome itself to offer any possible way out if they climbed up. Then they would be stuck with only slick stone above and below.

Her eyes lingered on the trellis, on the chains that fell down below it.

There were still other cages hanging from them. Sanislav was no longer imprisoned, but his prison had not been moved. A glittering cage a little farther below them, and another following that, thick chains looping down to each one.

Not a clear or direct path—still not close enough to the platform for it to be feasible. But enough to slow the fall. She began to rock her weight backward and forward, to add some momentum to the swinging cage.

"I think I can do it," Asya said slowly.

"No." Yuliana heaved herself up against the bars, one leg still shaking beneath her. "Maybe with the Firebird, but without—"

Asya felt strangely calm about it. The clamoring panic fading away to a distant cloud. "If there's a possibility, then I have to take it. Too many other lives hang in the balance."

"And what about your life?" Yuliana pressed, a frayed edge to her words. A jagged pain that could tear at Asya's heart more surely than any blade. "There has to be a better way than this. *You* matter too, remember? Asya, please—"

But Asya didn't give Yuliana another moment to change her mind. The strashe's shout followed her as Asya plunged out into the air.

For a brief instant, it was almost like flying. A suspended breath, kept aloft by nothing.

Then she was plummeting down.

Her hands clamped around the nearest chain—far less solid than Asya had been anticipating. It shifted beneath her weight, slipping through her fingers with a burning friction. But even with the scraping pain on her palms, it did give her some control. More a curbed descent than a frantic fall. Her feet hit the bars of the cage hard, sending it swinging beneath her. Already raw and sweating, her hands struggled to grasp hold.

"Asya!" More a sudden outburst than actual calling for her.

But Asya couldn't stop now, not swinging perilously from this fragile perch.

There was only one other cage hanging beneath her, low enough to make the wooden platform *possible* if not entirely feasible.

Asya took a breath, wiping her hands on her already-filthy shirt.

This one was less of a jump and more of a stumble. Standing atop the cage gave her no leverage, nothing to push off when they were anchored so high up above. So when she tried to launch out into the air, the cage just swung beneath her.

It sent her just short of the chain—hand desperately outstretched as the air dragged her down. The final cage rose up below her, too fast and too solid. No Firebird to help soften the fall, no magic to heal shattered bones.

She braced at the last moment as she crashed into it with enough force to rip the air from her lungs. Her momentum tried to push her off, to send her rolling over the top and plunging down. She scrabbled to hold on, skin tearing again where she grasped at rough metal.

She couldn't quite get purchase, the untamed twisting of the chain and pitching cage beneath her too much to steady.

But she could see the platform, far closer now. Within reach below her—the smallest protection from tumbling down to the base of the tower.

Asya stopped trying to subdue the erratic movement of

the cage, still off-kilter from her clinging on to the side. Instead, she let herself go with it, followed the momentum as it swung back and forth.

Just as it reached its apex—the brief moment when the platform looked a little less terrifyingly distant—Asya let go.

A much less dignified fall, her balance uneven as she twisted through the air. She couldn't even tell where the platform was now, let alone where to reach out to grasp it. Just a whirl of colors around her.

At least she couldn't give Koschei whatever he wanted from her if she was dead.

Then she hit something solid, pain cracking through her bones. The platform juddered beneath her weight, a heart-thumping creak of wood as her knees smashed into it, letting her fall hard onto her stomach.

For a panicked moment she couldn't breathe. A ringing—more solid and overwhelming than church bells—resonated through her.

Then everything caught up around her. The sudden fall broken by just as abrupt a halt. Pain lashed through her in a wave, crashing from the top of her head down to her feet.

"Asya?"

Her name again, a whispered echo against the tower walls.

Asya rolled over by way of answer, the best she could do to show Yuliana she was still in—mostly—one piece.

She heaved herself to her feet, pleased to find they supported her weight. The heavy crank took her a moment longer, her stinging palms and torn-up fingers unwilling to obey. But then the mechanism shifted and the cage holding Yuliana came lurching down to the platform.

Asya meant to step forward to help her out, but she couldn't quite get herself to move. Her mind was still talking frantic inventory of her body, certain to find some repercussion for her recklessness.

Yuliana limped toward her, a storm gathering in her eyes. "How many times do I have to ask you to stop doing stupid things?"

Asya almost grinned, a heady relief at having survived. "Probably a few more times."

"This isn't just about you, you know."

It was only a breath later that the anger of Yuliana's words permeated that giddy haze. Asya hadn't been anticipating that.

Yuliana stepped closer, her voice a low rumble through Asya's veins. "You're not the only one who feels they have to fix things. Not the only one who can sacrifice themselves. Not the only one who wants to make all of this right."

"I—" Asya looked down, the words suddenly very small. "I'm sorry."

The lightest touch against her side sent shuddering starbursts along her veins. The touch was so at odds with the anger in Yuliana's voice that Asya thought she might have imagined it.

"Asya," Yuliana said again, softening to a whisper. One word that grazed against Asya's skin, sharp and bright and real.

Oh—it wasn't anger Asya had heard. It was fear.

"Don't do that again," Yuliana murmured. "Please."

Asya's lips moved, no sound coming out. "I can't promise that," she said finally. "I can't promise I won't do everything I can to help the people I care about."

She expected the words to fall between them like a blade. Another thing cleaving them apart.

But Yuliana didn't move. "Then, at least let me come with you when you do."

Asya held her gaze, trembling on the edge of a decision. It

wasn't like her sister's unasked-for protection, the help that far surpassed choice. It wasn't like Tarya's stoic preservation, the importance of Asya's value only on one axis.

This was an even footing. Someone who trusted in her choices, who trusted Asya to choose her own fate. Yuliana's hand reaching across a great divide and Asya's reaching too.

She nodded—a short, uneven movement. Not enough to express the sudden emotion pressing against her ribs.

Asya waited for Yuliana to step back. She waited for herself to move—to remind them that they had to go.

But she couldn't pull herself from this instant. This tiny world of just the two of them.

"Every time we get closer to each other again, one of us ends up in a cage," Yuliana said, a little breathless.

A small smile tugged at Asya's lips. "That's a beautifully poetic way of putting it."

"I mean it literally."

Yuliana's lips curved up in that expression that made Asya's heart jolt—the one where Yuliana looked almost surprised at her own laughter. Unexpected and delighted, all at once.

Asya leaned forward, her still-stinging hands running across the rough fabric of Yuliana's shirt. She gave a moment of pause, a moment for Yuliana to shake her head or pull away.

But Yuliana's arms moved too, hands tangling in Asya's hair as their lips pressed together. Not the devastating, drowning feeling of their last kiss. Yuliana pulling Asya from some abyss.

This was more—the two lost girls, the two girls desperately trying to fix everything, finally sinking into each other.

It was Asya who pulled away this time—not sharply, not carving that space between them again. Breath still mingling as she whispered, "I don't know what to do."

"You won't run," Yuliana said—no question, no judgment. Not asking Asya to be less than what she was.

"We can't."

Yuliana nodded in agreement. "We can't."

A burst of warmth at that *we*, the way their choices had become irrevocably intertwined.

"I don't have answers to any of it," Asya said, the words sharp in her throat. "I have no idea how to fix anything. But I think I know where to start. We have to help the others. Commander Iveshkin, Dima, Zvezda."

Yuliana held her gaze for a moment, Asya's heartbeat stuttering against her ribs. She could see the hesitation in Yuliana's gray eyes, the warring voice of logic—the soldier still ingrained into her, the one that said this was a foolish tactical choice.

But her voice was unwavering when she spoke. "Then, let's go."

Chapter Sixty-Four

All the breath left Izaveta's lungs in a rush, as if rebounding from a blow. She couldn't move, her vision consumed with her mother. Not the phantom that had dogged her since that terrible night, but as real as Izaveta.

"Don't look at it," Nikov murmured, his warmth suddenly at her side. "It's not real. It can't hurt you."

That was a lie. It *could* hurt her. In this oppressive space, Nikov felt less real than the queen.

But she clutched onto his voice, his reassurance, forcing her eyes away from her mother—*not* her mother, an illusion. She took another step forward, the effort suddenly immense.

Another image flickered into being, this one far less substantial. A memory, acted out in front of her like some grotesque play.

Izaveta stopped again, transfixed by the fluttering figures. Snow dappled the scene, a much younger Izaveta wrapped up in furs, her mother in only a dainty cloak. Candles dotted the night around them, small pinpricks of light. Music spilled out from the palace, a distant hum—tendrils of the festivities following the two of them.

It was a holy day, dedicated to Saint Dyena and her ability to capture starlight in her palms. The first holy day since

Asya had left, the first one where Izaveta had to step into her role as heir in front of the whole court.

Her mother had prepared her for weeks, going through lavish gowns and etiquette lessons and plans. Izaveta had felt special. A glittering gem in her mother's crown.

Adilena turned to her, the hint of a smile on her lips. "You did well tonight."

Izaveta's face flushed with pride. "Shouldn't we go back to them?"

Her mother spread her arms out to the sky. "That's the beauty of being queen, they will all follow me."

And soon they had, conze and bishops and vade, all whirling together in the flurrying snow. But Adilena danced only with Izaveta, a glimmering moment shared between just the two of them.

The scene shifted. Queen Adilena stood in the spiraling library, offering Izaveta a lifeline—a refuge. It spun away again, re-forming just as quickly. Izaveta was younger still, Asya at her side now as two small bears nosed their way forward. A ball of brown fluff that was Mishka and a spray of white that was Olyeta. Adilena watched on with that same smile, a gift for her two precious daughters.

A zvess board emerged in front of Izaveta, Adilena leaning across to correct her strategy. The first time her mother had thought Izaveta worthy of teaching in any real way, her mother sitting on the left-hand side as she always did, playing the red pieces—the side she claimed fitting for the queen. It was a shattered reflection of the final evening they'd spent together, the kaleidoscope light from the stained-glass window shimmering across the board.

The image burned in her mind for an instant, the glowing reflection of Queen Teriya and the Firebird.

The memories came faster, a transfixing blur. Some only a brief feeling, a remembrance of warmth, of affection.

All the between moments. Those glimpses of sunlight when her mother had turned her smile on Izaveta. When the queen had not been the monster Izaveta created in her mind, the cruel woman deserving of her fate.

Hot tears needled at the back of Izaveta's eyes, sharp and unwelcome.

She thought Nikov was speaking to her, but she couldn't hear his words over the onslaught. The lulling melody of her mother's voice, each syllable striking her like a blow.

It was an undoing. All the careful protections she had put in place being torn away, her armor peeled off piece by piece. And what if there was nothing underneath? A wisp that would blow away on the wind, leaving the world a better place for its absence.

She felt her knees give way, her hands scrabbling into the strangely warm earth as if she could find some way out.

The phantom of her mother stepped forward, the vision fracturing away behind her. "Don't you want to go back to that?"

Izaveta did. She wanted it so badly it almost cleaved through her, a desperate and pointless desire to be that little girl again. The one who had known nothing of betrayal and lies, who had no thoughts of murder. No blood on her hands.

"You still can," murmured her mother's melodic voice, enticing in all the promise it held.

"How?" The question cracked through Izaveta.

Her mother reached out, one hand cupping Izaveta's cheek. She felt so solid, warmth pulsing from her. With her other hand, Adilena found Izaveta's fingers, still loosely grasping the dagger. Adilena did not speak, but Izaveta understood her meaning easily enough.

Izaveta raised the blade, watching her reflection thrown back at herself in the gleaming metal. Her hair was a disheveled mess, her face pale and drawn and eyes empty. It showed her as she truly was—as she always had been beneath her posturing armor. Scared and desperate and alone.

She spun the dagger, her reflection rippling, her knuckles white as she pressed the point to her own ribs.

Another hand reached for her—Nikov, his face knotted with concern. His mouth was moving, though no sound came out. His outstretched fingers went straight through her, as if she really were no more substantial than smoke.

But something in that expression made her grip loosen. It pulled her away from the phantoms, away from the memories. There was another reason they were here, an important one.

Adilena sensed the change. Her grip tightened on Izaveta's face, morphing from gentle to clawing as she forced Izaveta to look back at her. She spoke in a low hiss, words as contorted as her expression. "The price should have killed you."

Izaveta did not flinch back. The venom was more familiar—less painful than the kindness. She simply nodded. "I know."

That was what she'd deserved for her arrogance, her wickedness.

But she still had to do this, still had to—

Then Asya stepped out of the shadows too, a cruel set to her mouth. The thing Izaveta had forced her sister to be. The sight sent her mind reeling back, curling in on itself again.

"You lied to me," Asya said, her words holding that same brittle edge they had on Saints' Night, after she'd realized only part of what Izaveta had done. When she had called Izaveta heartless. "You abandoned me and left me to this fate."

Her mother crouched next to her, crooning in her ear. "You claim you were trying to protect her. Yet you ruined her too." She pushed back a strand of Izaveta's hair, tucking it behind her ear. "You let your own people die rather than face your mistakes, rather than risk your ambition. *You* are a poison to this land."

The strashe from the hunt flashed behind her eyelids, the voye and conze and supposed friends Izaveta had used and discarded with barely a thought for the consequences.

And she had done it again, *again and again*, even returning to court after all of that. She had abandoned Asya to the whims of an ancient sorcerer—all because it had been the practical choice. Not the right one, but the one that served her own ambitions best.

Adilena read her thoughts on her face, finishing the damning accusation herself. "I loved you, I saw you better than anyone. I *made* you. And you killed me. All for a crown you're not fit to wear."

The tears were falling freely now as Izaveta tried to catch her breath. She scrabbled for the dagger again, hands shaking and vision blurring.

"Izaveta," said Nikov's voice, somewhere to her right—loud and sharp but somehow very far away. "It's not real."

But it *was* real. Even if her mother was not standing in front of her, flesh and blood, this was still real. Izaveta had done all the things they accused her of, and she deserved this pain.

She was a schemer, someone who could always think of some way out, some other option. Yet when given the opportunity, she had not tried to reason with her mother, or adjust her course in any other way. She had gone straight to that magic because she had wanted to. Because Izaveta had wanted to finally—*finally*—beat her mother at something.

Nikov reached for her again, saying her name like a low hymn. But even as she turned to him, his face transformed, twisting into an accusatory smile. "What more could you expect?" echoed his voice, laced with a poison she'd never heard before. "You used us all as pieces in your game."

Still more pressed in, all the wrongs she had caused, all the pieces she had sacrificed in the name of her ultimate goals. A cacophony of sins all ready to submerge her.

She couldn't do this. Couldn't hold the weight of this guilt anymore.

The point of the blade dug into the thin fabric of her dress, pricking her flesh with a bright bead of blood. The pain resonated with the ache already inside her, like calling to like. It took her a moment to realize she was the one holding the weapon, not her mother, not Asya or the hoard of accusing eyes.

Izaveta bent her head, waiting for the queen's final judgment.

"That's right," her mother whispered, painfully kind. "You have always known what you are."

Nothing. The answer resonated in Izaveta's head, so certain she was not sure if she had said it aloud. She was nothing, and to pretend at more than that was arrogance. To believe she could be more than that was further proof that her mother was right—Izaveta was a poison to this land. The fruit of a bitter legacy.

Something in that stayed Izaveta's hand, even as her muscles urged her to push the blade in farther, to end this pain. A tiny pinprick at the back of her mind.

What had Asya—the *real* Asya—said? Even in the aftermath of Izaveta's confession, proof of her sins strewn about them, Asya had not let go.

You're still my sister. I'm not giving up on you.

And neither would Izaveta.

She looked up at her mother, hair hanging around her in

sheets, blood and dirt and tears smeared together on her face. "No." A tiny cry against a screaming storm. She rose to her feet, a new energy pounding through her veins as she advanced on her mother.

"*You* made me into this," she spat, seventeen years of bitter resentment and desperation finally bubbling out. "You created this monster. You taught me to be heartless, to push everyone away. You cannot pretend to be surprised when the cornered dog bites."

Adilena's cold gaze cut into her, no crack in the regal mask. "Always shifting the blame. Always finding some clever way to shirk your responsibilities—your culpability."

"No." A single syllable that sent a tremor through Izaveta. A shuddering change that steeled her like a hammer forging a blade. "I won't become what you wanted me to be. I won't prove you right."

"No matter what," her mother laughed. "You know I always win. I'm always right in the end."

A new certainty, bright as the first rays of dawn, blossomed across Izaveta. She did not have to listen to this, did not have to allow her mother to keep manipulating her. Izaveta had done the right thing at the Elmer, with Asya at her side, and she would do the right thing now. Not for herself, not because she was owed any forgiveness, but because she would not let her mother's legacy be the ruin of this land.

She would not let it be the ruin of her.

With a wrenching scream, she raised the dagger high and plunged it through her mother's phantom. It split through the smoke, re-forming at once in its wake. But Izaveta was already moving, ignoring the clamor of voices, the sharp barbs of accusation.

Even the vision of Asya, face crumpled with grief, would not hold Izaveta back.

She strode toward the trunk, memories crashing into her like waves against a ship. But she was immovable, her course firm and set.

A last cry rang in her ears, her mother's dying scream, raw and guttural against Izaveta's skin.

And then it was gone. The clearing was quiet once more, serene and tranquil as if nothing had ever disturbed its peace.

She was breathing heavily, air battering against her ribs as if she had just outrun a storm. Perhaps she had. The dark clouds of her birthright, of her mother, were finally at her back. The dagger had tumbled from her hands somewhere in the haze of those visions, almost as if it had not been there at all.

But the bead of blood still shone bright against her shirt. A last reminder.

Nikov stood a little ahead of her, framed by the expanse of the tree, the gnarled hole in its trunk. He turned toward her as she approached and she half expected to see his smile—that one he gave away too freely, too ready to let others in. But his expression was tight, his jaw clenched and unwavering.

What had he seen in that hundred paces that felt like a lifetime? What memories and visions had come clawing back, haunted echoes she'd caught fragments of in his eyes?

Perhaps he was still entangled in them, their last tendrils refusing to let go.

Or perhaps, Izaveta realized a breath later, his hard eyes were because he now held the dagger in his hand, leveled at her chest.

Chapter Sixty-Five

A heavy quiet still sat over the palace. Even with the moons at their pinnacle, it felt strangely empty. Leaving Zmenya's Tower through the hidden tunnel, Asya didn't expect to see anyone, but even in the passages beyond, there was a strange stillness. The only sound was the shuffle of Yuliana's make-shift crutch, loud against the ringing marble.

They hadn't been in those cages long, but Asya couldn't imagine anything good had happened in the interim.

The quiet gave her far too much room to think as they crept toward the Voya Wing. Too much time for new fears to slink in, for her thoughts to wander to Zvezda and Dima, and then take a darker turn toward Tarya.

Asya was almost relieved when they came across two strashe on patrol, clearly unprepared to face any threats in the peace-ful hours of night.

Even with her still-injured knee, Yuliana disarmed the first strashe with impressive ease by leveraging their arm against the stone pillar—keeping too much strain from her leg—and then hitting them over the head with the crutch.

Asya was a little slower. She still reached instinctively for the Firebird—if not for its flames, then just for its strength to push her on

But there was nothing there. Trying to find a familiar foothold only to slip down slick nothingness.

The stuttering moment cost her. The strashe lunged forward, their blade carving through the air. Asya dodged a breath too late, the bright bite of the blade slicing into her arm. Blood splattered into the air. It was only a shallow cut, but the strange emptiness—no hint of the Firebird's sparking power to heal her—made her whole arm feel suddenly heavy.

"On your left!"

Asya spun, anticipating Yuliana's movements and snatching the znaya out of the air. The strashe lunged again, but now Asya brought up a blade to meet them. The shuddering weight of it sent her stumbling back into one of the polished marble walls, but at least kept the sword from her skin.

Orange torchlight danced above her head, a strange ghost of the Firebird.

Its glow illuminated her face and the strashe reared back, eyes wide and fearful. At least not everyone knew that Asya didn't have her powers. She used the hesitation to twist the znaya from the strashe's grip, mimicking Yuliana's quick blow to the back of the head with a slight twinge of guilt.

But Asya didn't have time to indulge in that.

She was going to move on when Yuliana held up the other blade, not quite the short, familiar weight of Asya's shashka but closer than the znaya in her hand.

"Switch?" Yuliana asked with the slightest hitch of a grin.

"I still don't understand your preference for znaye," Asya said, tossing the blade to Yuliana. She caught it deftly in her free hand.

"It's not my fault you're too short for it," Yuliana returned.

Only another two strashe stood guard in the Voya Wing—oddly deserted again. No sign of the medics making their way through late-night rounds or the constant movement of patients that Asya remembered.

These strashe fell as easily as the others—a trail of unconscious bodies in their wake that would alert anyone to their presence as soon as they were spotted. But Asya doubted stealth mattered here. Their escape would be discovered soon enough.

The door was unlocked and Asya pushed it open to the strangely familiar room. The place she'd been brought after the attack in the queenstrees. It felt so long ago now. Izaveta sitting at Asya's side, some hope left, even if it was thin.

Asya shook her head, dispelling the images.

Commander Iveshkin lay in a pale shaft of moonlight, a blood-soaked bandage tied across her torso. But, with a sagging relief, Asya saw the rise and fall of her chest. The commander really was alive. Not another casualty of Asya's mistakes.

Asya took a step toward her when another figure stepped out of the shadows. Mila, her interpreter, glinting znaya raised, had clearly been on watch for the commander.

"We're on your side," Yuliana said quickly, but Mila didn't lower her saber. Her eyes darted to Asya, cold suspicion in every facet.

"I know that might be hard to believe," Asya added, her voice far steadier than she felt. "But we need to get the commander to safety. That's the most important thing now."

Mila's jaw twitched, indecision teetering across her face. "You attacked her. They told me what happened. When your flames failed, *you* were the one who ran her through."

Asya held out a placating hand, but Mila recoiled as if it had been a lit flame. "Just let me explain, I—"

"The commander tried to listen to you," Mila said, a note

of pain threaded through her voice, "and look what happened. She's a good woman and you used her."

Asya's throat stuck. She couldn't entirely dismiss that. She *had* used Iveshkin, had put her at risk without even explaining the full truth. Fallen prey to the same hubris as her sister—just as Iveshkin had warned.

Asya opened her mouth, something like an apology trying to fly free. But before she could utter it, Mila screamed. A cry that rent through the air, clear as any warning bell.

CHAPTER SIXTY-SIX

"Stay back." Nikov's voice was low, soft as the unnatural breeze that swirled around them.

Izaveta still couldn't catch her breath, tangled in the on-slaught she had just endured. The terrain in her mind was shifting, new pieces slotting into place in configurations she still could not understand. But even here, in this desperate place, her pride would not let her utter the question. Whether this was Koschei's work or Nikov acting alone, it hardly mattered now.

Instead, she squared her shoulders. "You are no fighter."

"Neither are you."

A fair point, if this were a usual circumstance. If she were back in the palace and this conversation took place across the battlefield of court. But she had been pushed far beyond that, beyond the realm of politics and manipulations.

She launched herself forward. No thought of tactics or strategy, fueled only by a keening desperation. Nikov was right, neither of them were fighters, so surprise was her only ally. It gave her an opening, a heartbeat where Nikov had not been expecting her to act.

She grasped at the moment, ducking under his arm and jabbing her elbow toward him. A low grunt told her she'd made contact—Asya would have been shocked—and Izaveta dove toward the twisted heart of the tree.

She did not truly know what she was looking for, her nails tearing bloody as she scrabbled at the wood. She just knew she had to reach it first, had to—

A hand pulled her back. She stumbled, feet slipping on the uneven snarl of roots.

She slammed into the ground, teeth rattling. Then he was on her, one hand holding the blade to her throat, the other trapping her right wrist.

Her head spun, breath momentarily evading her.

Through the thundering race of her thoughts—of questions she still wouldn't voice, confusions she didn't want to examine—his eyes were a sudden point of clarity. The rich brown a strange surge of warmth in this landscape.

Skyless, this place was called, which seemed ridiculously mistaken, staring up at it like this. Broken by the tangled branches, the expanse beyond was nonetheless immense. Stars bursting across it in a bright dissonance of light.

She blinked, forcing her mind back under control. She could not let the caustic edge of hysteria overtake her.

Svedye, why had she let herself drop her only weapon?

"Let me up," she growled, her free arm shaking with exertion as she tried to push the blade away. But she was exhausted and drained, the usual sharpness of her mind deserting her, and apparently carrying books had given Nikov far more strength than it ought, because his grip didn't waver.

"Iz—" He caught himself, forcing out a huff of air instead of her name. "Don't make me do this."

"Can't you just—" Izaveta felt her voice break, a cracking through her core. "Just *explain*. Help me to understand what's really happening here. Whatever he has over you, it can't be worth this."

He held her gaze for a moment, and there was something wrenching in that look. A brokenness that resonated in Izaveta's chest, two people set on these paths and unable to turn back.

"You were the one who told me our choices defined us," she said, his words echoing back to her. "This one will define you."

He dropped his gaze, the blade sliding from her throat. "Yes," he said slowly. "It will."

She blinked, disconcerted by the sudden change. He stood abruptly, turning toward the tree.

Without the dagger to hold her in place, Izaveta tried to follow, but something tugged her back. A leather cord, the kind used to tie off scrolls of parchment, snaked around her wrist and under one of the tree roots, pinning her in place. He must have tied it in her brief moment of distraction—of vulnerability.

In that instant, she knew she could not let him do this. Whatever choice he had made, it would cleave the two of them apart. And even with everything he might have done, she did not want that.

He was facing the tree, muttering something too low for her to hear.

She tugged against the cord, swearing under her breath. "Nikov, don't—"

But she was too late, too late and too useless in this kind of situation. Nikov drove the blade into the tangle of branches at the heart of the tree. Even with the blunted, futile weapon, the bark gave way.

A scream ripped through the clearing, not so much a sound

as a *feeling*. The wailing lament of a dying beast, reverberating through the trees more solid than wind. Izaveta could feel it clawing at her, dragging her back toward some great unknown.

But Nikov did not turn away from his task, tearing away the last scraps of tree to reveal a deep hollow in the trunk. Not natural but hewn—a vicious gash through its very heart. And from its shadows, Nikov drew something out.

Silence fell with the finality of a blade.

Her breath caught, momentarily transfixed by the sight.

A tiny, ornately carved egg—like the ones kept above the grave markers in the Grove of the Fallen Queens. Pale as moonlight, wings and feathers were etched into the edges in delicate whorls. It reminded her of Saint Restov's blade, a faint glow that, rather than illuminate the world around it, seemed to drain it. Leeching power into its very being.

Nikov's shoulders tensed, as if waiting for something to happen. But the silence was absolute. Even the warm breeze had died, some deep rupture to the magic of this clearing.

She stared up at him, suspended in this moment. In this breath of possibility, where the die had not yet been cast. She couldn't reach toward him, not with the cord still cutting into her wrist, and even then, she was not sure she could have moved. She didn't want to be the thing to break the spellbinding, frozen silence in the air.

Nikov turned toward her. The small egg sent strange shadows shimmering across his features—shadows cast by no object, autonomous and somehow *alive*.

He held it out to her, his expression solemn beneath those churning shadows. "Don't let it break."

She took it with her free hand, tentative, as if it might collapse under her touch. But it stayed inanimate and quiet, only the slightest buzz against her fingertips betraying that it was anything other than stone. "But why did you—"

Before she could finish her question, Nikov staggered back. A web of smoldering black, like discarded ashes, slithered up his arms.

He looked down at it, momentarily intrigued, that look of scholarly inquisition. Izaveta could almost hear his light comment, *how curious*, before he collapsed to the ground.

CHAPTER SIXTY-SEVEN

Asya had thought they might have enough of a head start. A brief window of opportunity to escape, even after Mila's yell brought strashe running.

But Asya and Yuliana had barely made it to the entrance hall when they descended—as if they'd been waiting for just that moment. Silvered strashe interspersed with the bright red of Azarov's own guard.

Koschei stood in the very center, though it took Asya a breath longer to spot him. Her eyes wanted to gloss over him, to fill in the empty space he left. He still held the vague semblance of Kyriil. The bright golden hair and high cheekbones. But there was something else there too—the same otherworldly quality Asya had once seen in Tarya.

The strashe flanked him, oddly silent as he stepped forward. None of the assembled courtiers protested, none of them clamored to be the one in charge here. Kyriil's visage as grieving son had given the sorcerer some control here. Or maybe they could sense his magic now, sense that this wasn't someone they could cross.

Asya raised her blade, the soft *snick* of metal to her right telling her that Yuliana had readied herself too. But no attack came from the assembled strashe. They hadn't even drawn their znaye.

Perhaps they didn't need to, against such weakened foes.

"I won't let you harm her," Asya growled, angling herself in front of Yuliana.

Koschei's eyes flicked to her, bored. "Luckily for you, I'm not interested in your mortal worries."

A shadow moved behind Yuliana. Asya thought it was someone stepping from the dark recesses, another strashe ready to pounce. But as Yuliana tried to twist away, the shadowed shape adhered to her—fingers elongating to match her movement. Clinging tighter, even as she pulled away.

The same unnatural hum as when he'd held them all suspended in the cabinet room. A stolen, impossible magic. A shadow come to life, curling clawed, inhuman fingers around Yuliana's throat.

None of the strashe reacted. No one screamed or ran— not like when Asya's flames let loose. Just like before, when Azarov had decapitated that cursed strashe, Asya was somehow still the monster. The thing that had to be contained at any cost.

She tried to move forward, but Yuliana let out a sharp, choking gasp as the shadowed fingers constricted, blood beading where they met her skin.

Asya stopped. The message was clear enough.

She clenched her jaw, turning instead to the sorcerer. Flames felt alight in her veins even without the Firebird, a desperate and all-consuming anger at being cornered again. "What do you want?"

Chapter Sixty-Eight

Izaveta scrabbled at the leather cord, finally freeing herself, and fell to the ground with Nikov, trying and failing to catch him, her knees cracking against the solid earth. Rot festered along his arm, growing from where he'd touched the heart.

She still held the stone egg clutched in her hand, but no curse reached for her.

She looked from the delicate egg to Nikov. "You knew it would do that."

"You can't take something without a price," he gasped. "Not from him."

She didn't know where to begin thinking about that. Betrayals and salvations all tangled together, and she was entirely out of her depth in trying to understand sincerity. Not while that rot was spreading, creeping up his arm, a decay accelerating through his flesh.

Too many things at once, each bursting in her mind like falling stars.

Nikov's hands scrabbled at the ground, his mouth working. *"Go"* was all he managed.

She dug her nails into her palm, a sharp flash of clarity. She didn't know anything about curses, about magic this powerful, not beyond the folklore of her childhood. And that wasn't going to help her now, not with this curse snaring tighter around Nikov with every breath.

Izaveta pulled herself back to her feet, looking around with a ragged desperation. Surely there was something here—some way to negate whatever this was.

But there was nothing, nothing beyond the pulsing tree and tangled roots. That terrible helplessness washed over her again, the useless anonymity of someone lost and alone in the woods, unable to do anything for the person dying at their feet.

"I suppose this was your way of reconciliation?" she snapped at Nikov. "Get yourself killed in the process?"

But Nikov's eyes were unfocused, nails scrabbling at his chest where the rot was clawing toward his heart, no longer conscious movements. He couldn't reply—she wasn't even sure if he could hear anymore—but she couldn't let go of the anger. That was the only thing holding her together.

He was not allowed to die. Certainly not here, like this, with so many unanswered questions.

But Izaveta didn't have a good solution. Was that just because her heart wasn't in it—because it didn't care enough beyond achieving the goal of the egg?

What would her mother do?

Queen Adilena would leave him. Nikov had fulfilled his usefulness and was now a liability, in more ways than one.

Well, if her mother would abandon him, then Izaveta knew she couldn't. That was as good a test as any, do the opposite of what Adilena would have expected of her. Then, even if Izaveta could not count on her own nature, on the frozen space where her heart should be, she could at least rely on her opposition to Adilena's.

Izaveta looked back down at Nikov, the pale blue tingeing

his lips. She remembered being poisoned, remembered the suffocating fear. She couldn't abandon him to that, no matter what, not when he'd taken the egg so willingly.

"You learned from him, didn't you?" she asked. "So don't you know how to fix this?"

There was a terrible irony in the fact that Nikov probably *would* know more about it, would probably fall back on some academic treatise about the nature of curses. But he was silent and trembling, those black lines winding their way toward his throat.

Though, there was another place that might hold answers. The only place with more knowledge on magic than Vetviya's Tower. Another place that stood not far from the Skyless Hallows.

But it would mean going precisely where they'd sent those illusions, where Koschei's falcons had followed and where the sorcerer could already be waiting. Another likely trap, but one that Izaveta knew—even as her mind weighed the possibilities—that she was going to head straight into.

The Amarinth.

"You better not die before we get there," she said as she heaved Nikov to his feet and started the uneven walk back to where Olyeta waited. "Or I'll kill you myself."

CHAPTER SIXTY-NINE

Anger thrummed white-hot in Asya's veins as she studied Koschei. The strashe arrayed around him like a distorted halo, silver and deadly. He had taken the Firebird, taken any power from her. Now he was taking this too.

"What do you want?" she bit out again, hating the words.

He nodded to the short sword in her hand. She dropped it to the ground with a clatter, too loud against the quiet.

Koschei raised an eyebrow, holding Asya's gaze. "It's very easy to hold you in check, isn't it? But we'll fix that soon enough."

"Asya." Yuliana's voice was a low growl. "You know what I'm going to say. You—"

Koschei flicked a hand in Yuliana's direction and her words broke off at once. Not a choking, guttural sound, but an instant halt. As if her voice had been sliced away.

"No need for distractions," he said simply.

One of the strashe stumbled, clutching at their throat.

Asya looked back at the sorcerer, a creeping cold settling over her again.

He smiled, acquiescing to her unasked question. "As you know, the price must always be paid."

She looked at the strashe again, not just their silver silhouettes but beyond that. The one nearest her was missing an eye, the socket still dark with fresh blood. Another had pale gashes all down their left side, methodical and precise. The one nearest Yuliana still had a hand at their throat, scrabbling desperately for something that was no longer there.

They were not here to help with the capture. They were here as fodder. Fuel for this strange magic.

"It's crude, I know," he added, as if he were truly involving Asya in this conversation. "But only a short-term solution."

"Is that what the ritual did?" Asya asked, her voice thin as a dawning horror seeped through her. "Gave you the power to do this?"

"In a way."

He didn't elaborate and made no move toward any of them. A slow petrification spreading through the room, unyielding as any spell. The breathless moment of waiting.

"What do you want from us?" Asya asked, all the anger and frustration punctuating her words and cracking through the stillness.

He stepped forward, the shadows moving strangely across the sharp planes of his face. Not the usual shifting of darkness in direct relation to light, but a disconcerting animacy. As if the shadows clung to his skin, living things unto themselves.

"I showed you, didn't I?"

The vision flashed behind her eyes again. "Was it true?" she asked, not quite sure why that was the question to fly from her lips.

"It's how I remember it now," Koschei conceded. "It's been such a long time, I cannot promise it is unaltered."

There was a surprising ring of truth to his words. Asya knew well that she could not always tell when someone was lying to her. She was certain that Koschei could summon falsehoods more easily than his stolen spells.

"Teriya was only trying to help." Something Asya knew far too well.

Koschei let out a sharp bark of laughter. "Is that what you took from it? Teriya was trying to help only herself. She knew there was dissent in her court, that she was maybe weeks away from being ousted.

"We had planned to cast the spell together, even though I warned her." The words poured out of him, a confession centuries in the making. "It was supposed to give me control over magic so I could stand at her side and protect her. It was meant to ensure no one could harm her or her children. So we could run away to a life of our own when her queendom crumbled."

His lips twisted, a pain he still held on to. "But you saw what she did. She tried to go behind my back, but even with me right in front of her, she didn't change her mind. She altered the spell. Instead of protecting her so that we could live a peaceful life, she tore magic from this land for her own ends. She split it between her twins—the queen and the Firebird, able to ensure that the Karasova line would be eternal and unquestioned. Even if I was the price.

"Why do you think magic fades from this land?" Koschei asked, nudging her toward the understanding. "Why do you think you must take harsher and harsher prices with each passing moon?"

Asya's anger stuttered out, thrown by this change in question. "Because of what Queen Teriya did?"

All that time, all the people turning the blame on the Firebird—all the guilt Asya had felt. The terrible fear that those like Fyodor might be right. And the answer had always lain in the other half, the other side of the coin. The queen who couldn't accept accountability.

"Magic is only fading because of her interference, yes," he replied. "A part of it torn away from the earth, channeled toward her own means. Magic is not meant to be contained like that, and so it festers, it *changes*, demanding more and more as it drains away."

Asya thought of those two infants, so unaware in all of this. "And Izaveta…" Asya trailed off, not quite able to form the question.

"She may not know the full truth," Koschei replied. "But she is as complicit as the rest, happy to squander that magic for her own gain. Don't you see now? This is how it always goes with those who want power."

Asya did see. She saw her decisions torn from her grip once again. All choice and agency taken from her. A piece in another queen's game.

She shook her head, trying to dispel the lingering cobwebs of that realization. He was trying to confuse her, trying to find ways inside her head when none of that mattered. None of that changed the sharp truths of the present.

"All I want is to rectify the mistake I made in trusting Teriya," Koschei said, pressing forward again. "That's why I pushed you to do that ritual. You gave me back some of what I was owed, the magic that should have always been mine. I want to make up for my part in this and end the Fading—isn't that what you want too?"

Asya didn't reply at once. There was a trap in those words, a snare that would strangle her if she leaped too eagerly. "How?" she asked.

"We'll get to that," he replied, the light tone of a liar.

Asya was all too familiar with people who liked to claim

a higher calling while using it to justify their cruelty. Their mother had been adept at it, Fyodor and his order, General Azarov—all of them had thrived on it. Even Izaveta had fallen to it. Though Asya supposed she couldn't discount herself from that number, given what she had done. But look where that had led.

It only led to more destruction.

"If that is all you want," she said slowly, "why keep these prisoners here? Why hold the court hostage?"

"They of course may do what they wish, provided it does not impede our aims."

Our. The word felt possessive. Collecting Asya into his narrative.

"Then, why did you have General Azarov order me to kill the commander?" she snapped.

Koschei waved a dismissive hand. "General Azarov had a very narrow mindset. It made him easily exploited but unfortunately had some unwanted consequences." An elaborate way of absolving himself of any responsibility. "I do not care for the petty squabbles of court. The short-lived reigns of mortals. You'll understand my side soon enough."

"And if I don't?" Asya bit out. "If I still think there are better ways to fight for this?"

"You'll learn," he said with a casual nonchalance. "I'm sure of that. After all, we have all the time we need. Neither of us can truly die."

Asya felt his focus shift, the dangerous twinge in the air. But she couldn't move—as trapped as all those people had been in the cabinet room.

"But for now," he finished, "obedience will have to suffice."

Something glinted in his hand, conjured from the air in a

single breath. The price must have been wrought from one of the strashe around them, but Asya hardly noticed. It was too small to be a true weapon. Smaller than the icicles that dangled from the palace rooftops in late winter.

In that moment, Asya realized precisely what it was. Why the strange gleam of it looked familiar. She'd seen it in that strashe's eye when the unexplainable magic had clutched hold of them, frost slowly spreading in their veins.

It was only the smallest movement. The light brush of dust off a coat sleeve. But the shard of magic flew through the air with an eerie precision. Not toward Asya, but to her right. To where Yuliana still stood, held in place by shadows.

And Asya couldn't do anything as the gleaming shard pierced into the softer gray of Yuliana's iris.

The thin layer of frost spread across Yuliana's eyes, a glinting and unnatural shade of blue—just like that cursed strashe. But it didn't spread from there. Didn't encase her in magic the way it had the others, didn't leave her body frozen and contorted.

Asya took a tentative step forward. The air finally gave way around her, only her own dawning dread holding her back now. "Yuliana?"

But Yuliana didn't look up at her. The shadows holding fast around her neck slithered away. She didn't try to fight them now, didn't try to raise her sword to Koschei.

"I didn't lie to you before," Koschei said, entirely unconvincing. "I did not *cause* this magic to course through the palace. But thanks to your ritual, I do now have a certain amount of control over it. Instead of sending the victim into an immediate frozen rage and then death, it can be fine-tuned. It's beautiful, really."

Yuliana turned to Asya then, the movement unnatural. The

look in her eyes made Asya's heart lurch, the glinting shard of ice shining against her pupil.

It was a look that was jarringly, painfully familiar. The same way Yuliana had looked at her when they first met, when she had been playing the part for the order in the Elmer. As if Asya were her mortal enemy.

PART SIX:

THE LAST OF THE FIREBIRD

Can any power truly be considered a gift when it comes with
such a price?

—OLD TÓURENSI PROVERB

CHAPTER SEVENTY

Izaveta had never expected her second visit to the Amarinth to be like this, cold and broken, dragging a half-dead scholar behind her.

When she had come here with her mother years ago, they'd been greeted by a full retinue, scholars and attendants eagerly arranged by the massive circular doors. Water and strong svode had been waiting for them, bearkeepers ready to help the bears after the long journey.

Now the courtyard was dark and deserted, submerged in the flurrying snow. The wide domed building stretched up into nothingness, dense cloud pressing in so close that it felt unreal. But Izaveta couldn't feel the sharp crackle of Koschei's magic, and even against the thick gray, she would be able to see the black outline of his falcons.

Though they must be close by. Izaveta couldn't imagine them abandoning their watch so easily.

The circular doors she remembered being flung wide were shut tight. Nikov had lost consciousness almost as soon as Izaveta managed to get him onto Olyeta, but she'd felt the steady beat of his heart during the whole journey. The slight tremors that rocked through him as the curse clung tighter, dragging his will away. But all proof that he was alive.

A thin layer of snow dusted the doors, throwing the carvings into sharp relief. A twisting design of the stars, all centered around Vetviya's moon. She hadn't been able to see it in the bright light of day last time. A hidden beauty reserved for those who lived here.

She banged on the doors, not caring for propriety. She'd come all this way—risked too much—to worry about waking some scholars in the middle of the night. The knock echoed, a hollow beat against the night.

She couldn't hear footsteps or signs of movement. Just her own shallow breathing and Nikov's choking gasps.

Izaveta banged on the doors again, unrelenting, her palms smarting and eyes stinging. "Hello?" she screamed, her voice ragged. "Someone!"

One half of Vetviya's moon slid back, a small opening only large enough for a round-faced scholar to peer out at her, pink cheeks illuminated by soft light from below. He wore a sash of pale purple, the lightest shade afforded to full-fledged scholars of the Amarinth.

"Finally," Izaveta snapped, no shreds of cordiality left. "I need help with a curse."

"This is a place of research," the scholar replied in the tone of someone deigning to cater to an incompetent child. "Not somewhere to bring lost causes or charity."

Izaveta squared her shoulders, a cold fury solidifying through her. "Where else knows more about magic and curses than the Amarinth? What good is all that knowledge if you cannot use it?"

"We are not medics," the scholar said with a touch of distaste. "We cannot help. And even then, we could not risk bringing a curse like this within our walls."

Izaveta wanted to scream. A brief flash again where she

wished she had the Firebird's powers, the ability to burn things to the ground until she was listened to.

"He's one of your scholars," she pressed. "You can't just leave him to die."

But the robed man just shook his head. "Whoever he was, that does not change our ability to help."

Nikov let out a low moan of pain, his muscles contorting. Izaveta lost her grip on his arm and he jerked back into the door, head thumping against the wood. She tried to help him back up, ruin twisting across his neck as she watched, splitting and spreading like fast-growing tree roots.

"Just do *something*," she yelled, words tearing with the wind. "At least *try*, won't you? Doesn't he deserve that?"

The scholar's mouth thinned, an imperious twist as he began to speak, only to be cut off by another robed figure.

A woman wearing a heavy cloak, such a deep purple it was almost black, a thick golden chain hung around her neck, gleaming against the deep brown of her skin. She eyed Izaveta with a look of suspicion, directing her question to the other scholar. "What's the commotion?"

Then her dark eyes caught on what Izaveta was holding, the increasingly lifeless body.

"Nikov?" the woman breathed.

She slammed the hatch shut and pulled the heavy door open with a flurry of locks. Pushing past the other scholar, she reached for Nikov, gaze flicking along the lines of the curse, creeping closer to his heart.

Izaveta didn't have the energy to ask the questions bursting in her mind, to wonder at this scholar's intentions or look at the cold place in her chest that was nagging at her to leave.

"Can you help him?" No clever manipulations or maneuvers, no twisting of words or tearing at her flaws. Just a plea.

The woman finally looked up at Izaveta, no recognition on her face. There was something oddly reassuring about her, a point of calm in this rushing turmoil.

"I can try to contain it," the scholar said, voice even despite the absurdity of this all. "That's the most I can promise."

from her one by one. She didn't want to see this, yet couldn't get herself to look away.

"You say we want the same things," she said to Koschei. "That I should see your way of thinking, then you do this?"

"A drastic measure," Koschei conceded. "It seems I'm not as patient as I once was." His face darkened, real anger clouding it for the first time. "Especially not since your sister meddled—stealing away with my spy. Queens always taking what is not theirs."

He canted his head, an attempt at benevolence. "But I can give you something back."

Asya's breath ignited, the Firebird's return so abrupt it made her stagger. The steady beat of its wings in her chest came with a burning relief. A part of her had feared it might never reappear. That she'd be left in that emptiness forever.

A spark coiled around her wrist, comfort after the echoing cold. She looked up at Koschei, unable to glean what his intention was here. Even if the power gave her some relief, a comfort instead of an absence, that didn't make it a gift.

Just like the key Dima had offered her all those days ago. Possibility and damnation intrinsically wound together.

"Return the Firebird to her chambers," Koschei said, offering no further explanation.

Yuliana stepped forward at once, a curt nod to Asya as if this were the way it was always meant to be.

"Move," Yuliana bit out.

Asya's eyes darted around the hall. Even if Koschei wagered that Asya wouldn't risk the flames against Yuliana, there were other things she could do. Even if the strashe had no choice in this, she couldn't bow to the sorcerer's will so easily.

She spun, a bright relief to feel the flames coursing in her veins again, and let them fly free. A rearing outline of the

CHAPTER SEVENTY-ONE

Asya barely breathed as she watched Yuliana, waiting for this trick or illusion to shatter. For the act to break and Yuliana to come back to herself again. But even in the shadowed dark of this room, Asya could see this was no trick.

She turned on Koschei, her anger hollowed out by the resonating shock. "What did you do to her?"

The sorcerer gave a small shrug. "She sees you now as she always should have. The creature who destroyed her family."

Asya felt her insides wilt. A sudden frost through late-summer blooms. Could it so easily be erased? Everything that had grown between them torn away by a sorcerer's callous hand?

"Yuliana..." The name came out jagged. Closer to a choke than an utterance—something Asya didn't want to confirm.

Yuliana's expression didn't shift. That slight curl of disgust, held in check by her stoic immovability. "Firebird," she snapped, each syllable blunt. "Do not refer to me so personally. You have no claim over my name."

That hit Asya like a blow. A shattered mirror reflecting back at her, the memory of all those stolen moments twisted to something else. Everything felt like it was falling away below her. The people she had come to rely on each taken

Firebird, stronger now for its absence, leaped toward Koschei. She saw the briefest flash of fear in his eyes. The remembered expression of so many who had tried to stand in the Firebird's way, shadows and flames stretching out to claim them again.

But as the fire reached him, the whirling golds and reds of living sparks, it did not consume. Instead, the flames broke around him like waves around a rock. The strashe behind him had no such protections—but even as blistered flames reached hungrily for them, they didn't react. Not even pain could break them from whatever hold Koschei had.

Asya turned to run, to at least take advantage of this distraction. But Yuliana moved more quickly than should have been possible, unheeding of the swollen injury in her knee. She slammed Asya back into the wall with an inhuman strength. Asya's head hit the stone, stars dancing in front of her eyes. They mingled with the glittering shard in Yuliana's, a swirling and beautiful magic that Asya couldn't hope to reach.

Yuliana pressed her forearm against Asya's throat, pinning her in place. The Firebird leaped to her fingers instinctively, but the flames dissipated just as easily. Not from the sorcerer's power now, but from Asya's own hesitation. She couldn't use her power against Yuliana, not when Asya had seen what little her fire would do. It could likely flay the skin from Yuliana's bones, and even that wouldn't stop her.

A cruel gift for the sorcerer to return Asya's power only when he knew she couldn't use it.

"When are you going to understand?" Koschei asked, the wearing impatience of a tutor explaining the simplest concept for the hundredth time. "You cannot harm me with something *I* gave you."

Asya didn't bother to reply to him, didn't even glance over. She held Yuliana's gaze, as steady as she could manage. The storming gray fractured by the sorcerer's corruption. There had to be some of Yuliana in there still—some part Asya could appeal to.

But she found nothing. No hint of the Yuliana she remembered, the girl who had been scared to ride a bear. Who had held her close in her worst moments and not flinched away.

Just an endless, icy hatred.

"Return her to her chambers," Koschei said again.

Asya didn't try to fight it this time. Not when she could see there was no way out of this—no way that didn't leave her hands stained in the blood of the people she loved most.

CHAPTER SEVENTY-TWO

Izaveta sat rigid in one of the wooden reading chairs, tiredness lapping at her but unable to take hold. A sleepless night that seeped into day, waiting for news from the scholars while she jumped at every slight movement beyond the windows, sure falcons would descend.

She kept the stone egg clutched tight in her hands. It was not a comforting presence, more an unnerving specter. Unearthly eyes that she could feel roving over her, a power that would happily sink its fangs into her.

The scholar in the dark purple robes had not wasted time on introductions, not while she tore through every tome and apprentice within reach, but Izaveta gleaned from snatches of low conversation that her name was Eah and she had been Nikov's mentor. The one who had handpicked him from the candidates and raised him up to apprentice—until he vanished without a trace.

The waiting, the echoing silence gave her far too much space to think. To question if she had made the right choice here, risking everything to give Nikov the smallest scrap of a chance. To imagine where Asya was now, trapped with that sorcerer's unyielding magic, likely wondering why her sister had abandoned her. Why Izaveta had made the difficult choice once again.

It also gave her mind too much time to turn over the memories the clearing had shown her—the answer Koschei wanted. When her mother had first taught her zvess, in the cavernous space of the queen's chambers, where she'd told her how everything could be reduced down to this game and its pieces. The same place Izaveta had been avoiding since her mother's death, and the place it would make most sense to hide something of great importance.

Like a crown that had to be kept secret.

Izaveta didn't want the answer, not now. It presented her with a choice, one she felt entirely unequipped to make, not when she could barely trust the smallest of decisions.

Only when a clawing afternoon light spread across the room, greedily swallowing any lingering shadows in winter-bright clarity, was Izaveta allowed to go in and see him.

She wasn't sure what she expected, but it certainly wasn't Nikov sitting up on a plush sofa, chatting animatedly with one of the scholars.

The room was small—barely large enough for the seat Nikov was on, likely used for private reading and research, hardly an ideal sick bed. With Izaveta in the doorway, Eah and the other scholar took up the rest of the floor space.

"You're alive, then," Izaveta said, an edge to her words that she couldn't quite identify. Something between anger and relief.

Eah nodded, speaking for him, "I was able to contain it, indefinitely I believe, though the use of that hand may be hampered over time."

Izaveta's eyes traced down to Nikov's right hand, spidered veins of black still stark around his wrist. Not quite as burning as they had been, and no longer progressing farther up his arm. Izaveta watched one of the veins contorting, twisting itself to push against some new, invisible barrier.

"It's quite interesting, really," Nikov said. "One of Kovenna's old theories on the limitations of cursed anima combined with…" He trailed off at Izaveta's withering look.

Eah put a hand on the other scholar's shoulder, clearly reading the need for privacy, and neatly ushered them out of the room. The door fell shut behind them with a soft click, leaving Izaveta and Nikov in this tight, book-lined space.

Izaveta didn't sit. She did not even move from near the door, a strange feeling ghosting across her skin.

"You brought me to the Amarinth," Nikov said finally. "You wasted time on the detour and risked attracting his attention."

There was a hint of accusation in his words, a challenge that Izaveta didn't quite know how to face.

"You still had a lot to answer for." She had not meant to sound quite so callous, but at least it made her feelings clear. "A lot of lies to explain."

"I never directly lied to you," he said.

"No, you just carefully stepped around the truth. That always makes for the most convincing deceits." She clasped her hands together, trying to temper some of the anger in her voice. "I thought I was a good liar but you, *you* make me look like an amateur."

Nikov ducked his head, the fingers of his left hand tracing the darkened veins of his right. "I'm sorry," he said softly. "I tried to make up for it."

"By throwing yourself in the path of an impossible curse, all the while lying to me again?" Izaveta snapped, somehow his apology reigniting her rage again. "Honesty would have been more useful."

"Well, I couldn't offer honesty." His jaw tensed, voice raising to match hers. "So that's the best you get. I should have known that noble sacrifices were wasted on someone without a heart."

"Noble?" Izaveta scoffed. "I hardly think that counts as noble when it was only to assuage your own guilt."

"You'd know something about that, I suppose," he shot back.

Izaveta didn't even know why she was shouting, why these poisonous words flew to her lips so easily. She'd decided the moment Nikov gave her the heart that he was forgiven—that she did not have the right to judge anyone else.

But that couldn't stop the bitter tide of fury now, urged on by something she couldn't quite explain. "Perhaps if you'd not changed your mind at the latest possible moment, only when you truly had to, it would be easier to offer forgiveness."

"Next time I'll be sure to adhere to your criteria of what defines a noble-enough sacrifice."

"There won't be a next time," Izaveta yelled, a rushing wind unloosed. "Don't you see? You could have *died*, then who would be around to answer for any of this?"

"I thought I was going to," he replied, anger sagging out of him in a single breath. "That's what was meant to happen."

Izaveta's reply died in her throat, a sudden skittering stop after tumbling down a slope. The heavy weight of the words settled over her, the strange tinge of regret at his sacrifice not being permanent.

Her own words echoed back to her, a stark realization. *Perhaps if you'd not changed your mind at the latest possible moment, only when you truly had to, it would be easier to offer forgiveness.*

Just as she had in the Elmer, only letting her sister in on the truth when there was truly no other option. Only accepting the price for what she had done when it had already wrought so much damage.

"I know that feeling," she murmured.

Just as she had felt awakening after the Firebird's flames. She had expected an end, a neat closure to her story, a last desperate act that would at least cast her as heroic. And instead, she was still here, still here and still trying to find some way through. Not absolved of her crimes but endlessly laboring beneath them.

Death felt like the ultimate absolution, whereas living on required continued responsibility, being held accountable again in every different decision. Having to not make the same mistakes over and over again.

"I hoped you might," Nikov replied. And she could hear that fragile hope in his voice, the need for someone else who truly understood.

Slowly, as if the strings holding her up were finally releasing, Izaveta sank down beside him.

"Eah said you vanished," she said finally, no sharp accusation in her words anymore. "That you haven't been an Amarinth scholar for three years. So how did you appear at the palace, claiming to be their envoy?" She couldn't bring herself to speak the last part aloud but it rang in her head: *How did you deceive everyone so easily? How did you deceive me?*

"I want to tell you." He sat forward, resting his elbows on his knees. "I think... I think I can."

She raised her eyebrows, unspoken prompting. She wasn't sure she could speak again without cracking apart, too much of her dark and vulnerable self seeping through.

"Once upon a time—" Nikov began.

"Can you only speak in fairy tales now?" She sighed, the

admonishment easier to reach for. "It was endearing the first time but quickly grows tiresome."

"It makes it easier." He paused, a slight grin wiping the shadows from his face. "Endearing, you say?"

She restrained herself from rolling her eyes—a habit her mother had always hated in her. "Just tell your story."

The ghost of that smile clung to his lips as he went on, "Once upon a time, there was a boy who wanted to know everything. An impossible and highly improbable task, one might say." He took a breath and Izaveta could see him slipping into that scholarly detachment, see the way he pulled away from the story until it was something he could voice.

"But the boy wanted to prove to his mother that he could do what no one had done before. That he was worth as much as all the knowledge she had sought."

Izaveta remembered the last time Nikov had told her a story, the story of his mother who had chosen to stay in the Great Library of Kharur rather than raise him. She could see why pursuing this might have been his way of trying to reach out to her again, trying to prove that he mattered too.

"So he searched the library, reading every tome and scrap, trying to find the deepest secrets of magic. In an old book, encoded in a circular riddle, he finally found something: the final resting place of one of the most powerful ancient sorcerers. He knew the scholars of the Amarinth would not allow him to make such a perilous journey, so he did not ask permission. He just left."

Izaveta could almost imagine it. A younger Nikov, that same spark of certainty and mischievous smile playing at his lips as he slipped out, overladen with books and scrolls—any practical supplies left behind.

"The journey into the Skyless Hallows was far worse than

he imagined," Nikov went on. "But just when he thought he might die, he found it. And, to his surprise, he found the ancient sorcerer waiting there. The sorcerer said he was impressed at the boy's determination, at his relentless pursuit of knowledge, so he offered him a bargain: he would give the boy the gift of understanding magic, of knowing the truth of the prices and the Fading, in exchange for his help."

Nikov paused here, his hands weaving together, knuckles strained. "The boy was young and foolish and did not understand the true ramifications, so he accepted. The sorcerer held his end of the bargain, a rigorous and painful education that gave the boy all the knowledge he'd ever wanted." His lips tightened, the pain of that memory pulling at his features.

"But then the boy found out the truth of what the help entailed," he said. "That in accepting the bargain, he had accepted the sorcerer into his mind, and once that was done, there was no way to undo it. No way to break free of that control. It made it impossible for the boy to even share the knowledge he'd learned, trapped instead beneath that power."

Izaveta stared, so many pieces falling into place in her mind. Those moments when Nikov had seemed to so desperately want to say something, the sentences abruptly cut off. How he had to speak about his own life as if it were a story to even voice it at all.

"And the sorcerer now had the perfect tool for his revenge. He had been banished from Tóurin, but with the boy, he could work his way back in. He wanted—" Nikov choked on the words, sharp gasps of air. "He—"

Her hand flew out of its own volition, wrapping tight around his clenched fist. "It's all right," she said. "Just tell me what you can."

His eyes flicked up to her, a grateful flash of relief. "The boy did as the sorcerer bid, trying to work against him when he could. But the sorcerer suspected and so he came to watch over the boy himself once the mourning days started—when there was no queen on the throne. He took on the guise of the boy's father—"

"Ambassador Täusch," Izaveta murmured, another piece of this falling into place. "He really is your father."

"He was," Nikov amended. "Until the sorcerer killed him and took his place. But I didn't know until he turned up at the palace like that. And then no queen was crowned."

The cadence of Nikov's voice shifted, adjusting back into the air of a storyteller. "So the sorcerer seized his chance. The boy helped him manipulate the Firebird, push her until she believed there was no other choice than to do that spell." His words hitched a little, something close to guilt seeping in again.

"If you knew what that spell would do," Izaveta asked, "the power it could give him, why did you let Asya do it? She was not under his command, she could have stopped it."

"*Let* is a strong word," he said. "I planted it in the book as… as the sorcerer asked, but I tore the page. I tried to make the spell seem undoable. That's the only way I can work against him, by trying to work around what he says. I left those notes for you to find, hoping you would understand the code."

Izaveta reached into her pocket, to the crumpled parchment she'd kept with her in hopes it might hold some last scraps of information. The notes she'd hardly glanced at since her escape.

Hope everything settles now outside. They know you require immovable, immutable loyalty.

"You clearly thought too much of my intellect."

Nikov nodded to it. "Not a very elaborate code. Mikevesh's Cipher."

The first letter of each word: *he's not Kyriil.*

She let out a short, entirely unamused laugh that cut through the room like falling glass. She'd been anticipating something far more complicated when she'd first seen it, so she hadn't even bothered to think of a children's puzzle. "How helpful. It might have been more useful to spend your time stopping Asya from doing the spell."

"Perhaps," he conceded. "But I could only manage the smallest things, stepping *just* outside his instructions. And besides, that spell..." He trailed off, not the choking censure of Koschei's magic, but his own hesitation.

"What?" she prompted, a fragile breath trapped in her lungs.

"There was a chance it might give you back what you'd lost. And part of me wanted that too."

Izaveta rolled her eyes but couldn't quite ignore the echoing pang that sent through her heart—where her heart *should* be. Like a bell desperately trying to ring, only to find the metal warped and unusable. "Wonderful," she said, trying to press past the vulnerability. "So we have your sentimentality to thank for this situation."

He smiled properly then, the smile he gave away so freely— the one that made her breath hitch. "A simple *thank-you* would suffice."

She narrowed her eyes. "I'll consider it, depending on whether or not I'm alive long enough to say it."

She had meant to sound flippant, irrelevant to the grand scheme of things, but it hit like a suddenly discordant note. A thick silence descended over the small space, Izaveta trying to pair the detachment of the story with the real boy in front of her.

She had so many questions—intrusive, probably overly invasive questions—but the one that fell from her lips wasn't the one she expected. "Why didn't you tell me any of this?" She was surprised by the hurt that came with the utterance, echoing even through the cavity in her chest.

He didn't speak for a long moment, downcast eyes on his interlocked fingers. "Maybe because I didn't want you to see the worst parts of me."

Her hand went to her wrist, to the pale markings where the stratsviye had been. "You saw mine."

His shoulders tensed, as if anticipating accusation. That's what Izaveta would have thrown at him before.

She put a hand on his cheek, gently urging him to look at her—tentative enough for him to pull back. She wasn't even sure why she'd done it, except that she hated to see the humor drained from his eyes. The sparkling glint he held whenever he wasn't submerged in shame.

"You saw mine," she said again, fingers tracing down the soft curve of his jaw. "And you did not run away. The least I can do is offer you the same."

His hand shifted in hers, the tight fist opening so their fingers tangled together. A small point of certainty they could both cling on to.

"So what happens at the end of the story?" Izaveta asked.

They both looked down at the stone egg still pulsing in Izaveta's lap, the heavy truth of what it was.

"I don't know."

"I'll become like him, won't I?" The question was barely more than a breath, a light flutter that Nikov could ignore. That Izaveta could pretend she had not voiced.

He didn't quite meet her eyes. "Perhaps."

"A straight answer once in a while would—"

"We can't know for sure," he replied, his head tilting up to look at her. "There's hardly enough evidence to deduce a concrete theory."

"All right," Izaveta said. "Then, what's the working theory?"

Nikov chewed on the words, as if deciding the best way to describe her slow, impending descent into iniquity.

"It's not as dastardly evil as it sounds," he said slowly. "It's not so much that you will become a dark and twisted version of yourself. It's more like…you'll slowly forget to care."

Izaveta swallowed, trying not to show how those words rattled her. Indifference could be far worse than malice.

And she could feel some of it already—the way she had to remind herself not to leave Nikov to die in the Skyless Hallows, the way the pain of Fyodor's betrayal and death no longer felt like something that had happened to her but the distant story of another life.

How soon before she felt that way about everything—about Asya?

Izaveta got to her feet, a steely determination shooting through her at the thought.

"Then, I hope you're well enough to travel," she said. "Because I need to get back to Asya before that happens." Unspoken, the rest of the thought echoed in her head. *Before I stop caring enough to act.*

CHAPTER SEVENTY-THREE

Yuliana led Asya back to her old chambers. The same room she'd sat in when she'd tried to feel her Calling, where she'd sought advice from Tarya and where Yuliana had bandaged Asya's wound. Memories of the brief salvations she'd managed to find in the palace, all cast in the painful light of loss.

Now Tarya lay dead and Yuliana was warped into a shadow of herself. More ruin left in the Firebird's wake—in Asya's wake.

She'd hoped Yuliana might at least stand outside the door, far enough away that Asya could get her jumbled thoughts in order. But Yuliana let the door fall shut and stood rigidly in place, watching Asya.

"You're staying in here?" she asked, words grating against her throat.

"Yes," Yuliana replied. For the briefest moment, hope flickered in Asya's chest. "I don't trust you not to try something, Firebird."

The hope splintered to nothing at Asya's feet.

The door wasn't even locked. No heightened security or signs of firestone. Koschei knew he had her trapped.

Maybe that was the true point of this elaborate performance. For the sorcerer to show Asya how useless she truly was.

She turned her back on Yuliana, on the crushing weight

of loss, to try to take in the rest of the room. It was just the same as it had been all those—days? Asya wasn't sure, it felt like centuries now—ago.

But the palace was unmoving as ever. A fixed point in the roiling tides.

There was nothing more in here that might help her. Plenty of objects that could double as weapons, all useless when she wouldn't raise them against Yuliana. Held back again by those ties to humanity, all those bonds Tarya had warned her against.

Though Asya refused to regret them now. No matter how Koschei or anyone else twisted them against her. Tarya had decided what mattered in her final moments, and Asya was certain now.

But she was so tired. So tired of how much even the smallest morsel of fight cost her.

And even if she did kill Yuliana and escape—then what? If Izaveta had not found a way to stop Koschei's magic, then there wasn't one. And Asya couldn't do anything on her own.

She leaned back against the wall, watching the window through the corner of her eye. A sharp hope that her sister might emerge from the trees mingled with a terrible fear that she would. Wanting Izaveta at her side, but not wanting the risks it would bring.

"Don't think of trying the window," Yuliana said, apparently still watching closely. "Even the Firebird wouldn't save you from that."

The coldness of her voice made Asya's throat tighten. So at odds with the way she'd spoken in Zmenya's Tower when Asya had taken just that risk.

Asya wrapped her arms around herself, gaze caught on Yuliana again. A trap she couldn't pull away from.

"Do you know where Dima is?" Asya asked, a tentative nudge against the icy wall.

Yuliana's jaw twitched, the only slight hint of emotion. "Imprisoned somewhere too. All because you manipulated him."

Asya swallowed. She couldn't deny that. Not when so much of this was Asya's fault, all for letting her emotions show so easily.

She tipped her head back against the wall, arms tightening around herself. Sitting on the floor felt safer somehow, refusing to pretend anything was normal.

From this angle, Asya couldn't stop her eyes tracing over Yuliana, arms neatly clasped behind her. The rigid posture of a soldier. Asya couldn't even find comfort in the steady beat of Yuliana's pulse. *Alive*, yes, but there was no way of knowing how much of her was truly left.

Yuliana had been right, one way or another, they always had to face each other through the bars of a cage.

"I left notes for you," Asya murmured, almost unaware that she'd spoken aloud. "After the Elmer," she went on, a quiet desperation fueling her words. A need for *something* to crack through those bars. "I put them in places I thought you might be. In the queenstrees, all around Kirava. Near an armorer that makes only the finest znaye, no shashka in sight. Or next to the bakery that sells those lemon khvorost you used to like."

More than once during the mourning days, Yuliana had let slip her love of the thin twig-like pastries, in those moments where things had still seemed possible.

Yuliana didn't move, her eyes fixed carefully on a point above Asya's head. But even if she couldn't break through, it did help to remember. To expand her world beyond the dark confines of this palace. Beyond the sorcerer's control.

"The notes probably didn't make sense," Asya went on. "About Saint Ilyova and her bears, more proof they are holy creatures. I thought that way you'd know it was me but no one else would."

Asya felt the moment Yuliana's eyes drifted to her. A brief electrifying pulse like the tang of magic in the air. An odd expression wrinkled her features, a confusion.

Asya tried not to let her tone shift, tried not to show the tiny spark of hope that one look ignited in her. "I wonder how many people happened upon them and wondered why in the gods' names someone would leave strange messages like that."

Yuliana held her gaze, standing solid but somehow teetering. As if her lips wanted to lift into that surprised smile, but didn't quite know why.

Then she stepped aside sharply, her expression closing off, adhering to some unspoken command.

The door opened behind her and Koschei strode in. As he entered, he looked like Kyriil again. Asya supposed that must be the part he was still playing for the court—though why he was wasting his time on that, she had no idea.

But the image began to fall away as he moved closer. Not all at once, but imperceptibly. His features shifting and blurring so that he still looked like Kyriil from the corner of Asya's eye, but if she looked at him head-on, the visage was something else. Colorless eyes that pinned her in place.

Asya stood up, heart thrumming. She didn't know how to face this. It wasn't the twisted words and manipulations of the court, and it wasn't the straightforward combat of a fight. It was some confusing in-between, one where Asya couldn't even begin to predict the next move.

"You should get some rest," he said, the appreciative concern in his voice so real it was jarring. "You certainly need it."

"Hard to rest when so much hangs in the balance," Asya said, choosing each word carefully.

But he didn't reply. He walked on past her to the thick-paned window, peering down at the expanse of forest beyond. Asya wished they were there now. Even this would feel a little easier without the suffocating confines of the palace around her.

She took a small breath. No matter where she was, she had to try something. This could be her only chance. "I'm ready to hear your side of it now," Asya pressed on. "To hear how we can fix Teriya's mistakes."

He turned back toward her, something disconcertingly birdlike about the movement. A falcon encased in human flesh, talons still ready to rip.

"Is that so?" he asked, his inflection entirely unreadable.

He didn't say anything else, pushing the impetus onto Asya. Forcing her onto what he must know was uncomfortable terrain for her.

"Yes," she said, her voice thankfully less trembling than her insides felt. "If she is what caused the Fading, what has forced the Firebird to do monstrous things all these years, then we must undo it."

Koschei eyed her with his colorless look. "No matter the price?"

"No matter the price," Asya repeated, the words hitching a little as her mind took in the weight of them.

Koschei stepped back toward her. "Even if I asked you to burn out your dear strashe's heart?"

Asya didn't let her gaze slip to Yuliana. This wasn't a true command, this was him testing her. Trying to get her to show the lie. "If that's what it takes, then I would do it. The future of this land matters more than one life. The Firebird always knows that." She swallowed hard, hoping the emotion threaded through made her more believable. "I made that choice once already, didn't I? I took the price from my sister."

For a moment, she thought she might have convinced him. That she'd used enough of the truth to mask her deceptions. Then his face broke into a gentle, pitying smile.

"So sweet," he said with a crooning softness that made Asya's skin crawl. "But you don't have the talent for lying that your sister does."

"I'm not lying," Asya said, very aware that the desperate edge to her voice was deeply unconvincing. "I don't want the Fading to continue. I don't want magic to drain from Tóurin." She tried to stick to solid truths, to immutable beliefs that he couldn't claim to see a lie in.

"Perhaps," he conceded. "But I know you still question my methods. I can see your resolve is not strong. You do not truly believe me."

Asya's mouth was dry. "I do," she said, treading carefully on truths again. "I believe Teriya betrayed you and that she should not have done that spell. I believe—"

He slammed his hand against the wall, hard enough to crack marble.

Anger twisted his face, a sudden and jarring transformation from his placid humor. "Why is this still so hard for you to understand?" he hissed, the words low and guttural. A hint of the true fury that lay beneath his facade.

"I want to—" Asya tried, but he flung out an arm and a sharp gust of magic sent her crashing into the heavy desk. Wood splintered beneath her as pain cracked across her back.

From where she fell, breath sharp in her lungs, she saw a deep gash appear on Yuliana's arm. A wide chunk of flesh—

too deep a wound to hope heal on its own. The price torn from her for this stolen magic.

Yuliana didn't even flinch. The blood dripped down her side like rain, and she didn't acknowledge it at all.

Koschei took a careful step toward Asya, his face composed once more. "*Enough* lies," he said, in a cutting hiss that reverberated through the room. "The time for action is now. Your sister is the key to this spell and thus the only way to undo it."

Asya pulled herself to her feet, steadying herself on the splintered mess that had been the desk, her head still spinning.

"Once the line of Karasova queens ends," he went on, "then they will no longer be siphoning magic from the earth and the Depthless Lake can shine bright again."

Asya put a hand against the wall, something solid to grasp on to. "Once the line ends?"

"Permanently, yes," Koschei said with a relish that came of long, simmering revenge. "Your ancestors started this, one queen and her selfish actions. Do not let your own selfishness doom this land again."

The memory he'd shown her played out in her mind's eye again. The two young sisters at the heart of this terrible spell, binding it together without ever knowing. What the sorcerer said did make sense, even with the vengeance he brought with it.

Was that really the choice she would be left with again, a duty to this land or the love of her sister? She'd been forced into that once before in the Elmer, a decision she thought she could never take back. Two impossible choices balanced on a knife's edge.

"Well?" Koschei quirked his eyebrows, back to the casual conversationalist. "Are you still so eager to help? Or will you let your love for your sister blind you to the importance of this?"

Asya didn't say anything for a long moment. Too many consequences crowded into her mind, any decision here so pivotal. "I want to fix this," she said finally. "I can do what you ask."

"You will bring me Izaveta?"

"Yes."

He moved too fast for even her eye to follow. A sudden shudder in the air, then he was in front of her. He grasped her shoulders, leaning down to her height with patronizing ease. His nails dug into her skin like claws.

"Good," he whispered. "But since I still cannot trust your faith in me, I would remind you that far more hangs in the balance here."

Yuliana stumbled, as if the hand gripping her had suddenly loosened. She looked at Asya with wide, confused eyes—the real Yuliana in that sparking gray. It thudded through Asya like a resonating blow. Koschei stepped back, releasing his clawing grip so Asya could get a better view of his destruction.

"Asya?" Yuliana gasped. "You—"

Then those frozen tendrils clamped around Yuliana again. They spread from her eyes, frost cracking across her face like splitting ice. She fell to her knees, the spell still spreading, far faster than any Asya had seen before.

"Stop," she growled. She knew it was what he wanted her to say. Knew the point he was proving.

"Like I said, what I give…" He canted his head to her with a curl of his lips. He raised a finger, a father asking their child to pause, and the spell receded again. Back into just a glinting shard in Yuliana's eyes—and with it, any hint of the real Yuliana. "I can take away.

"And before you get into heroics, I know this girl is not the only thing you care about, is she?" His face curved into a sharp sneer, the planes of his cheeks less human the longer Asya watched. "She has a brother too, doesn't she? There's the spymaster who stood at your side, to her own detriment. Not to mention the commander I so graciously allowed to live. It would be a pity to have to reassess my mercy." He pressed forward, filling Asya's vision. "And let's not forget the little bear down in the keep. How much of him would I have to strip away before you finally saw my side? How long before you saw that the love you have for your sister is born from lies and treachery?"

In that moment, Asya was so acutely, sharply grateful that Izaveta had made the practical choice, that she'd not let even Asya know where she was going, that her knees felt weak.

"I don't know where my sister is," she said quickly. "There's no Calling to follow. No duty of the Firebird. So even if I agreed, it would be pointless. I could search for years and never find her. She's likely long gone."

She hoped it was enough to call his bluff. To place her still on his side while showing the impracticality of the task. To at least give her time to muddle through this.

But Koschei smiled, the gleaming edge of an assassin drawing a blade. "Luckily for you, I know precisely where she is."

CHAPTER SEVENTY-FOUR

The first falcon swooped low over Izaveta the moment she and Nikov stepped outside the Amarinth's neat grounds. The snow had stopped, leaving the landscape a hazy melding of gray and white. The falcon's wings stood out against it, followed by another two behind.

But they didn't attack, not like they had near the palace. The birds seemed to be waiting for something. An eerie tension that kept Izaveta on edge.

She held up Saint Ilyova's ring, the light glinting against its oddly muted surface. She'd left Olyeta in the warmth of the Amarinth's bearkeep—the bear had done more than enough work the past few days, and another journey would push her past the point of exhaustion. After all, the bear couldn't take the same rejuvenating draft Eah had insisted Izaveta and Nikov take before they left. It had burned against Izaveta's tongue, bitter as poison, but she had to admit the tiredness had fallen from her aching legs.

"You know how to use it?" she asked Nikov, gesturing with the ring.

"Yes." There was a serious slant to his expression that set Izaveta's nerves on edge. "He'll know where we are by now. He'll be prepared."

She could hear the slight undercurrent to his words, the offered escape route. The chance to listen to unfeeling calculation that urged her on. Marching back to the palace now was not the most logical solution, not with so little information in her arsenal. But, just as she'd thought in the clearing, she knew this was the opposite of what her mother would choose. And that made it feel right.

"Yes," she said, not letting any of that hesitation shine through. "But he doesn't know we have this." She patted her pocket, the carefully padded space for the delicate egg.

"You don't have to come," she added, regretting the words almost as soon as they'd fallen from her lips. "You can show me how to use Ilyova's ring and then stay here."

Nikov's lips quirked into a smile, a mere shadow of his usual exuberance but enough to quiet some of Izaveta's fears. "And miss out on all the opportunities for terrible calamity? I don't think so."

Izaveta gave a short nod, still not ready to voice the relief that gave her. Instead, she held out the ring, a small gesture of trust. "Take us to the Grove of the Fallen Queens." Far enough from the palace to give them some advantage, she hoped.

Nikov took her hand, a warm anchor in the icy cold, and they stole into unbeing together. Whispered away on the wind. The same fear didn't clamp around Izaveta this time, the terror that she might come undone to never pull back together again. Even if pieces were missing from herself, even with the vital part she knew was gone, she felt more substantial with someone at her side.

They coalesced back into the world in the quiet silver of the queenstrees, the snow blending seamlessly into the pale white trunks.

It made the dark wings of falcons stand out like spilled ink.

They didn't hold back now, no longer watching and waiting for whatever was to come next. The first one dove in a precise and unyielding arc toward Izaveta.

She ducked, curling over herself to protect the fragile casing of Koschei's heart—the thing she assumed the falcons wanted. But the birds only flew low enough to graze over her head, another leaving a shallow cut on Nikov's side.

Another swung low, talons brushing against Izaveta's arm—sharp enough to elicit a hiss of pain, to force her a few steps to the right. The birds continued like that in a strange pattern, as if testing some limit.

"What are they doing?" Nikov asked, swiping at another shallow cut on his cheek.

"They're corralling us," Izaveta said suddenly, still staring up at them. "Forcing us toward something."

The realization didn't help them much, as the volley of talons and sharpened beaks did not relent. A consistent and unnatural pattern that urged them on, any attempts to step out of line met with those sharpened talons—the frenzy swirling faster, too incessant for Izaveta to think.

Then, quite abruptly, it stopped, and the falcons' aim became immediately clear.

Asya stood a little ahead of her, a blazing trail of cinders crackling in her wake. There was something unfamiliar in her sister's expression, a cold-burning fire that made Izaveta hesitate.

Izaveta knew she should be happy, should be relieved to see her sister alive and free in front of her. But something was smothering that, some deeper shade of suspicion.

"How did you escape?"

Asya took a step toward her, that unwelcome look still lurking in her eye. "I didn't."

Izaveta felt her weight shift back, her body urging her to retreat. "Then, how are you here?"

"Koschei sent me to hunt you down."

"Oh" was all Izaveta could manage. She wasn't sure if it was the last of her heart finally forgetting, or just an inevitability, but no hurt came with the understanding. Just a heavy resignation, the blade Izaveta had been anticipating finally striking true.

"Did you know?" Asya asked.

Izaveta frowned, confusion momentarily eclipsing everything else. "Know what?"

"About the Fading," Asya pressed. "That it was caused by Queen Teriya. That magic only fades from Tóurin because she stole some to ensure the Karasova rule would be eternal."

Izaveta felt her jaw go slack. "Is that true?"

Asya didn't say anything, just watched her as if waiting for the act to finally slip.

"Asya," Izaveta started. "I didn't know that—how could I have known that? And I would never keep that from you."

But Asya's posture didn't relax. "There's plenty else you haven't told me."

"You don't believe me," Izaveta said heavily.

"When you lie about everything, it makes it hard to believe the truths."

She could hardly blame Asya for that, not after everything. But the hurt did come now—caustic and sharp in Izaveta's throat. Even for all the lies she'd told, for all the things she'd done, she had thought she could count on Asya to see some of the good in her still. And if even her sister had given up on her, then what hope was left?

"So that's it," Izaveta said, the question falling to a flat statement of certainty. "You've chosen who to believe in."

"No."

"No?" Izaveta asked, suddenly unsure on her footing. "Aren't you angry with me?"

"Of course I'm angry with you," Asya snapped. "But that doesn't change that we're sisters. It doesn't change that you're the person I care about most in the world."

Izaveta didn't know what to say to that, to the strange duality of that forgiveness. Something she still didn't feel she had earned.

"So you're not here to drag me back to pay for my crimes?" she asked.

Asya looked at her as though she had just started spouting Old Versch. "No, I'm here to tell you to run."

Izaveta stared at her sister, the words taking too long to string together in her mind.

"I can't," she said slowly. "What would be the point in fleeing?"

"Because then you'd be alive," Asya replied, as if it were obvious. "And you can't return to the palace anyway. He needs you for something, something that I doubt would be good for anyone."

"But then, if I run, he still wins." Izaveta realized with a jolt that she didn't mean that in the same way she might have before. Before, she would have meant that she could not concede to someone else taking control of the board. Now, she just knew she couldn't let his power run rampant, couldn't let that cruelty poison Tóurin, even if she was never queen.

"You've forced your protection on me when I didn't ask for it," Asya replied, clearly not sharing in Izaveta's revelation.

"So why won't you do this for me now? Why does it seem so easy for you to do the selfish thing until I'm the one asking?"

"Because I *am* heartless." The admission finally burst out of Izaveta, the last secret held between them. "Or perhaps I always have been. But that was the price. And now I can't trust any of my choices—any of my *thoughts*—because I keep forgetting how to care and it terrifies me."

Any anger in Asya's features loosened, giving way to a ragged guilt.

"You can't blame yourself for it," Izaveta said sharply, before Asya could voice any apology. "I'm the one who cast the spell. That was my choice. Foolish, impetuous, and arrogant, but my choice."

Asya took a step back—not quite a step so much as a stagger, the weight of this suddenly falling to her. "You said the price had been altered somehow. That we'd found some way to subvert it."

Izaveta pressed her lips together, this was precisely why she hadn't wanted to tell Asya. Seeing her sister's pain only highlighted the strange emptiness in Izaveta, last fragments of anguish ricocheting around the hollow place where her heart should be.

"I..." Asya trailed off, staring up at Izaveta with a lost expression.

"We can't just keep doing this," Izaveta said softly, reaching for her sister's hand. When Asya didn't pull away, Izaveta pressed on, "We can't keep protecting each other by pushing the other away, by burning everything else down. This is something we do together or not at all."

Izaveta half expected her sister to yell again, to force protection on her as she would have done.

But Asya nodded slowly, the unfamiliar sparks finally receding from her eyes. "All right. We do this together."

Even being reunited after their mother's death, there had still been some chasm that spread between them. Separation gouged out by loss and lies and pain. But in this moment—just as it had fleetingly in the Elmer—Izaveta felt they were truly the two of them again. Two halves of a whole, two sides of a coin. Two incomplete parts that never quite worked without the other.

Izaveta nodded. "And I have someone who I think can help."

She gestured to where Nikov had been hanging back, wisely giving the sisters that moment to themselves.

"*You.*" Asya whirled, flames snapping out in an instant, that vengeful fury bright in her eyes again.

He tried for a sheepish smile. "And here I thought Izaveta was the one I should be scared of."

Asya's jaw tightened, flames reaching out toward Nikov. She backed him against the thick-packed snow as rivulets of melted water flowed in the fire's wake.

"Sorry, sorry," he said quickly, holding up his hands. "My sense of humor has terrible timing."

Izaveta hurried forward, a hand between them—no fear of burning now. "Asya," she said, low and imploring. "It's all right."

"He's working for him," Asya spat.

"It's not quite as simple as that," Izaveta said. "Just as it's not always that simple for me." She hesitated. "Or for you."

That made Asya's fire flicker, a slight stutter of sparks as she finally looked at Izaveta. "*You* forgave him?"

"No need to look so shocked," Izaveta replied with faint indignance. "I'm a very forgiving person.

"And," she added. "He's more use to us alive for now." She winced as the words came out, colder than she had intended. The heartless thoughts once again.

But it seemed to satisfy Asya. With a last glare in Nikov's direction, she stood back, her arms falling to her sides and the flames dying with them.

"I am truly sorry," Nikov said, the shielding smile no longer on his lips. "I didn't want any of this."

Asya glanced over at him, but Izaveta could already see her anger ebbing. "I suppose none of us did," Asya said. "And you did warn me not to do that spell."

"I wish I could have tried to do more," Nikov murmured, that burn of shame back in his voice.

"No," Asya replied with a reassuring certainty. "No one forced me to make that choice. I did that on my own. You can't hold yourself responsible for someone else's actions."

Nikov's smile did return then, a little smaller and more tentative, but there.

Izaveta stepped forward, hoping the moment of sentimentality was done. "So if we're standing together," she said to Asya. "What are we doing now?"

"We have to find a way to stop him," Asya said at once. Izaveta loved how easily the right thing came to her sister, how clearly it was the first thought in her mind, even if she had none of the tools or planning to make it happen.

She'd been jealous of that once, wished she knew the same conviction. But now it was a relief, a heart Izaveta knew that she could trust.

"We found Koschei's heart," Izaveta said, lifting the delicate stone egg from the folds of her cloak.

Asya's eyes widened, sparks dancing across the dark brown of her irises. "Then, why haven't you destroyed it?"

"That wouldn't stop him," Nikov supplied, quickly shifting into his scholar voice. "It would ensure his immortality. With it gone, there would truly be no way for him to die."

"Then, why has he kept it all these years?" Izaveta wondered. "Why not eliminate something that vulnerable?"

To her surprise, Asya was the one who answered. "I think it's what keeps his revenge alive. If he destroyed it completely, then what use is his retribution? Teriya didn't just betray him, she broke his heart. And he can't let that go."

Nikov didn't say anything, his lips tight, as if the sorcerer's commands were pulling around him again. But he gave a sharp nod—as much as he could manage.

"So if we do a spell to return his heart to his body, he'll be mortal," Asya said.

Izaveta turned in the direction of the palace, a new determination solidifying within her. "And mortals can be killed," she finished.

Chapter Seventy-Five

What Koschei did not understand, perhaps what he *could not* understand without a heart, was that he'd presented Asya with the wrong choice.

He'd laid it out as a choice between two people she loved, between her sister and the survival of Tóurin. But that wasn't the truth of it, and she saw that now. Saw it the moment she'd set eyes on her sister again.

It wasn't even a choice between right and wrong.

It was a question of her being under someone else's control again—whether that be the gods or her mother or Koschei or even magic itself.

And Asya was done bending to someone else's will.

They didn't have much time, not with Koschei's falcons circling overhead, but they managed to form something that resembled a plan. Or, as Izaveta kept reminding them, as close to a plan as they could manage. It was better than when they last returned to the palace though, with only Asya's rage and desperate hope fueling them.

"I still don't know how you'll get close enough to him for the ritual to work," Asya said, crouched over the ingredients Nikov had hastily scrounged from their surroundings. "With that magic…" She trailed off, the others knew well enough what Koschei's magic could do.

"We have to give him what he wants," Izaveta said, as if any of this were truly that simple. "I know where Queen Teriya's crown is. We can use that to bargain—or appear to bargain. I doubt he'll attack when we hold something he's been searching for."

Asya twisted her fingers together. It wasn't much to rely on. "I can go to him first," she said. "I'll tell him you escaped me just before we reached the palace, but that I think you've gone after the crown. That'll give you some time."

Izaveta nodded. "Then Nikov and I can prepare the ritual and you can lead him into the trap."

They approached the palace in taut silence. It was oddly quiet again, no signs of that rampaging magic or searching strashe. A suspended kind of waiting. In the distance, the light of the Depthless Lake reflected the three moons above—a sliver even of Vetviya's cutting through the night. Asya wasn't sure if she was imagining it, but the light of the lake seemed to be flickering, a guttering candle ready to burn out.

The great doors stood open. A gaping mouth ready to swallow them whole. Once they were inside, they would go their separate ways. Izaveta and Nikov to one of the hidden tunnels that led to the queen's chambers, Asya to delay the sorcerer as much as she could.

Izaveta grasped Asya's arm before they parted. "Together, no matter what."

Asya nodded, surprised at the strength that came with that. The tightening threads of resolve that bound the two of them. "Together."

Izaveta pressed something into her hands. A faint tingle

against Asya's fingertips, strangely familiar. The egg, its pale stone soft in the illumination of the lake.

Asya tried to push it back. "You need it for the spell."

Izaveta shook her head. "Only once he's there. You can protect it better until then."

"But—"

Izaveta clasped Asya's hands around the egg, pulling away. "And it gives you leverage if something goes wrong."

Asya bit down on the arguments burning on her tongue and let her fingers close around the egg.

Nikov and Izaveta vanished into the dark, off to fulfill their role. But Asya had barely gone ten paces when she heard movement ahead of her.

She hesitated, flames curling at her fingers in anticipation.

"I know what you have."

A jarringly familiar voice.

Yuliana emerged from a narrow alcove ahead, the mocking silver of her strashe's uniform blending with the pale marble of the palace.

She drew her saber with a slick bite of steel.

Chapter Seventy-Six

Returning to her mother's chambers felt like stepping into the cold quiet of a tomb, a place that should be undisturbed, even if the occupant could no longer protest.

None of the candles were lit, but moonlight bled through the high windows, painting the room in muted hues.

The zvess board had been packed away, the pieces nestled into their narrow slots so that only the checkered surface gleamed in the faint light. So much had centered around that board in Izaveta's mind, the ultimate game that her mother always won. The show of her power.

The great window stretched above it, the intricate stained-glass portrait of Queen Teriya and her Firebird. As Izaveta looked up at it, she realized something. She had never been taught the name of Queen Teriya's Firebird, had never learned of her as a whole, separate entity. She'd merely been an afterthought to Teriya.

Izaveta might have believed that the queens wanted their power to be held above the Firebird's, wanted it enough to obliterate even a name from history. But in light of the vision Asya had told her about, another answer presented itself. That Firebird had no name, because it had not existed—not until Teriya made her bargain with Koschei.

Another lie of the Karasova legacy.

It didn't matter now, not with time steadily slipping away from them. Instead, Izaveta bent down to the zvess board—the same one she'd seen in that memory of her mother, the one that had jolted something loose in her mind. The narrow seam that ran around its base, and the side of the board Izaveta had never seen.

She'd asked her mother once if that was why Adilena always won—because she chose that side of the table. Her mother had laughed and said Izaveta would understand when she was older.

But Izaveta moved around to that side now, to see a small hinge hidden just under the board. Another of her mother's secrets that she'd taken to her grave.

Izaveta pressed it, her mouth dry. A part of her still expected this not to work, could not face the possibility of more lies. But, silent and well-kept, a small panel slid back.

A bitterness burned in her veins, even at this victory. Her mother had known all this time, had known the importance of Teriya's crown. Yet she had never deigned to tell Izaveta, even as she worked to find answers to the Fading. Answers that had sat across from her all along.

It hardly held the grandeur of the crown Queen Adilena had always worn, with its twisting whorls and glimmering brightness. This was barely more than a child's imitation, the fabric faded at the edges and beadwork coming unpicked in places. It felt ordinary too, no hum of magic or skittering power across her skin as Koschei's heart had held.

But it matched the one in the stained-glass window above them, and there was no reason for this secrecy if it were not the crown that tethered all this magic.

She lifted it carefully, almost afraid it might break. It was not only their leverage against Koschei but the connection Izaveta still had to the Karasova line, the magic that ensured their rule was eternal.

As she held it, a brief trepidation filtered through her. Perhaps she should have got Asya to do this part, should have trusted something that held so much power to someone who was certain to make the right choice.

"Ready?" Nikov held up the small bag of stolen ingredients, a sparse collection of herbs and salt, all surrounding the faded scrap of Saint Ilyova's bone she'd taken from the queenstrees. Hardly enough to stand against the towering magic of the sorcerer, even if the other pieces of the plan managed to hold.

But as long as Asya's delay had worked, if they had just a little time before Koschei was on them, then this would be possible.

"Yes," Izaveta said, in the easy imitation of confidence she'd long cultivated. "Let's make the preparations."

But Nikov didn't move, head downturned to the bag in his hands. "I think I should stay behind."

"Why?" Izaveta asked. Much as she hated to admit it, she did need him for this.

"I'm still bound to him," Nikov replied. "I can't undo that. If he commands me to betray you, I will."

She pursed her lips, teetering on the edge of this decision. Once, she might have questioned if this was treachery unto itself, an elaborate game that she could not yet understand. But no suspicion rose in her mind now, no calculating questions.

Now she just needed Nikov at her side.

"You've worked around his commands before, could you do it again?"

He shook his head. "In small ways, yes. Finding the tiniest loopholes in his words, and even that was near impossible."

"What does it feel like?"

Nikov's eyes flew to hers, clearly not the question he'd been anticipating. "It starts as an itch," he said, words stretched thin. "The smallest seed planted at the back of your mind, so subtle you might imagine you thought of it yourself. But the longer you ignore it, the more it grows. From a small inkling to an all-consuming scream."

His fingers laced together, knuckles blanching. "I experimented with it when I first made the bargain." That was such a Nikov thing to say, such a scholarly way to deal with the awfulness that it almost made Izaveta smile, a surprising fondness that had taken root. "I kept logs and records, theories to see if anything was manageable. To see how long I could hold out before it was unbearable, before I had to give in."

His jaw tensed, shame creeping in again. "It was never more than a day, even for the smallest commands."

Izaveta watched him, her eyes traveling from the familiar tangle of his curls to the soft curve of his jaw, the sharp tension in his shoulders, tightened by a shame he hadn't earned.

"I won't force you to stay and face him," she said, almost surprised at the words. "But I won't tell you to leave, either. Someone once told me your choices are what define you. Commands you cannot escape aren't choices, but this is. And I won't take it away from you."

Nikov's lips twitched, a shadow of a smile. "Sounds like a very wise person."

"He certainly thinks so." But she didn't reflect his smile. "You believe in me without a heart. And I believe in you now, whatever you decide."

He raised his eyes to her, his own humor fading. "Let's do this, then. Let's face him."

A panging echo of warmth rang through Izaveta's chest—

more painful for its absence. For her empty heart desperately *trying* to feel something more.

Izaveta ducked her head, grasping one of the vials to give herself something to do so Nikov wouldn't see the hollowness in her eyes. The empty space she couldn't get back.

But he didn't seem to notice, too focused on gathering his own work as he scrawled the first sigil in candle wax on the floor—faint enough that Koschei shouldn't notice it, not with his eyes on the crown.

"And not to worry," Nikov added, his usual lightness returned. "I'm truly a terrible swordsman, so even if he commanded me to kill you, I'm fairly certain you'd win."

Izaveta wasn't quite sure what made her do it. The way the moonlight suddenly caught the curve of his lips or the dark truths buried beneath his humor, or just the fact that part of her had wanted to since that first day they met, words dancing so smoothly around each other.

But before he could bend to draw the next sigil, she caught his hand, turning him to her. Crown still grasped in her fingers, almost an afterthought, she leaned in to kiss him. His lips responded, as ready to meet her as his words. It was a very different kind of kiss to the ones Izaveta was used to, where each person was striving for the upper hand, eager to claim some power over the other. This was as easy as their conversations, a dance only they knew, tinged with desperation. A finality that Izaveta didn't want to look at.

She pulled back, a little breathless. It was only the briefest stolen moment, a frivolous act in the face of what lay ahead.

"What was that for?" He grinned, still so close that she felt the movement against her lips. "No more information you need from me, is there?"

"In case we die," Izaveta said simply.

He let out a short laugh, somehow still smiling. Those freely given smiles that Izaveta realized she needed. "Ah, I was hoping for something less morbid," he said.

Izaveta tightened her grip on the crown, her cheeks a little flushed. She hadn't intended for that sudden vulnerability, or to allow a distraction to consume her. "Or in case the last memories of my heart vanish and I forget to care. One of the two."

"I'm beginning to regret I asked."

Izaveta opened her mouth to reply, a short quip on scholarly questioning, but it died in her throat.

The door now stood open behind them, the glancing light of torches illuminating the figure standing there, eyes alight even in the dark.

Koschei smiled. "Welcome back, Lady Izaveta."

CHAPTER SEVENTY-SEVEN

Asya held up her palms, the embers sputtering out in an attempt at peace. But Yuliana didn't lower her znaya.

"I'm on your side here," Asya said, subtly shifting her balance, edging toward the clearer path to her left. "I'm only doing as the sorcerer ordered."

Yuliana advanced and Asya's stomach dropped as the faint moonlight pooling through the windows caught on the strashe's face. The ice had spread beyond the small shard in Yuliana's eye. Now it fissured down her cheek like tear tracks, digging deeper into her with each breath.

"As am I," Yuliana said. "And he suspected you might be delaying."

"Please," Asya said slowly. "We don't have to do this. I did what Koschei asked, I brought my sister back here. We can go to him together."

Yuliana's mouth twisted. "More lies. I know what you have there. I heard what you're planning. A betrayal, even if that means my death. Though treachery comes naturally to you, I suppose."

"Yuliana," Asya tried, appealing to that girl she'd known. "You know that's not true. You know I wouldn't abandon you."

A cold smile distorted Yuliana's features. "The evidence

appears to contradict you." She counted them off on her free hand, voice raising with each addition. "You let them torture me in the Elmer and then left me at my brother's mercy. You left me locked in a cage because you were too afraid to use your power. You let your guard down and let Azarov maim me. You didn't even try to prevent *this*."

She pressed forward, sticking out her chin so the faint light caught on the frozen veins of her face. "Do you know what this feels like?" she asked, her voice dangerously low. "The way it tears at my insides, reshaping every memory into something jagged and broken. I can feel it crawling in my veins, feel the spell desperate to kill me. My body desperate to die. But it can't, not while the sorcerer wants me alive."

Asya stood frozen, unable to pull her eyes from Yuliana. Unable to rebuff any of these accusations.

"And it's not even a punishment for *me*," Yuliana spat. "I am just used and broken and discarded because of *you*."

Asya flinched, guilt seizing in her chest. Powerful and burning as the Firebird.

But it didn't consume her. Not this time. Because she knew Yuliana, the real Yuliana, would not blame her for this. Knew it with a rushing certainty that she hadn't realized she held until this very moment. Until she saw this distorted version of Yuliana trying to claw her way in.

Asya felt the change in the air, the moment Yuliana's body shifted from preparation to attack.

Yuliana lunged.

Asya almost moved too slowly. Her muscles still protesting against her, still so opposed to raising a weapon to Yuliana in a true fight. But Asya's borrowed shashka sang free, coming up to meet Yuliana's saber just before it could cut into the skin of Asya's shoulder.

Yuliana didn't relent. Her grace and speed heightened against Asya's reluctance, any remnants of injury forgotten to the spell.

Asya thought she had got to know Yuliana's fighting style in the days they had sparred together. Thought she knew the rhythm of parries and blows well enough by now. But the strashe had never fought with this intensity. With this burning anger behind her and no saving grace of dulled edges or forestalled blows.

Asya was on the back foot. Unable to truly attack when she didn't want to cause any harm.

Ducking under the lip of a towering statue, Asya hooked an arm around its base to whip around and get behind Yuliana.

The brief respite let Asya put some distance between the two of them. She let out a burst of fire, still not nearly to its full blazing light. The flames glanced off the gleaming floor, more alive than ever.

But Yuliana stepped through them easily, hardly hesitating even as the skin across her forearms scalded. The scent of burnt flesh was acrid in Asya's mouth. It made her stomach turn, and she couldn't quite dodge the next swipe of Yuliana's saber.

The blade bit into Asya's right shoulder, pain jolting down her arm. It took a wrenching effort to raise her shashka again. The Firebird roared in her veins, a snapping tongue of fire flashing out.

It twisted around Yuliana's wrist, trying to pull the saber from her hand. But Yuliana still didn't relent. The hand that gripped the hilt went an angry red, blisters bubbling on her skin.

It could peel back to bone and that wouldn't stop her. Only one thing would, Asya realized. The one thing Asya couldn't do.

Asya pulled the Firebird back, forcing its flames to subdue.

She had to run. To try to outrun Yuliana and reach Izaveta in time to finish the spell. Perhaps destroying the sorcerer would destroy his work too.

Asya ducked the next swing and launched herself down the passage to her left, the one that would take her to Koschei. The stone scalded beneath her feet, the Firebird urging her clanging footsteps on. Too loud to hear how close Yuliana was behind her.

Something slammed into Asya's shoulder, burying down to bone. The momentum sent her tumbling forward in sharpening agony.

It took her too many staggering breaths to put together what had happened. Then she caught the hilt of a knife out of the corner of her eye. She tried to pull herself to her feet, hands scrabbling.

A serrated kind of despair cut through her. She was already behind—Izaveta likely waiting for her even now. And here Asya was, trapped again by her own caring.

Footsteps crunched behind her. She managed to drag herself to her knees, arm screaming. She couldn't pull the knife out from this angle. A bright, jagged star of pain.

Yuliana loomed over her, spinning another blade in her palm. Asya had no other weapons, no hope of fighting with agony cleaving through her arm and no time for the Firebird to heal her—certainly not with the blade still dug deep.

Was that what Koschei wanted? To force Asya into this corner, for her to have no other way out but killing Yuliana or giving up? Either submitting to Koschei's will or destroying her own heart anyway? Another price she didn't want to pay.

Asya reached for her flames, a last desperate moment, and let them break free.

CHAPTER SEVENTY-EIGHT

Koschei took a slow step toward Izaveta, his disconcerting eyes hungry as they found the crown in her hands. Her pulse jumped, scanning the strashe lined out behind him for any sign of Asya. She was meant to delay him, to ensure the spell was ready before she led him here.

But there was no flicker of her sister's red hair, no hint of flames.

Ice seeped through Izaveta's veins. What had happened when she'd left her sister?

"I see you finally answered my question," he said with a nod to the crown. His gaze darted to Nikov, a disapproving slant to his mouth, and Izaveta felt the scholar stiffen at her side. "And my renegade pupil. A disappointment to the end, I see."

Nikov took a step forward, his hand twitching toward the still-waiting spell at his waist. "I brought her back to you. I got her to show me the crown. Isn't that what you—"

His words were cut off by some unseen force, an invisible hand that knocked him back into the zvess table with a juddering thump.

Izaveta easily saw the lie in Nikov's words, so it hardly surprised her the sorcerer did too. But she didn't move, keeping a firm grip on the crown, even as this all crumbled around them. The last sigil still needed to be drawn and the ingredients still sat in their neat jars, no use to her at all.

"As ungrateful as the Firebird," Koschei said dismissively, turning away from Nikov. "Though she'll see my side soon enough."

The slightest hint of relief. That meant Asya wasn't dead, that he hadn't got to her yet.

"I highly doubt that," Izaveta said, glad to at least cling to this anger. "I told you before, Asya is far better than me."

"And you were wrong then, were you not?"

No, she'd never been wrong about her sister, but she did not voice that now, not to someone who could never hope to understand it.

Koschei mistook her silence for assent, nodding to her with a benevolent smile.

He raised a single hand and the strashe rushed forward as one, either urged by that unseen magic again or simply by the strength of Koschei's command. Izaveta tried to fight back, to run or find some way through the tide. But it was useless— she'd never been a fighter, she was not made for this.

One strashe wrested the crown from her grip, her last vestige of hope, while another twisted her arm behind her back, holding her steadily in place. Out of the corner of her eye, she saw another drag Nikov from the wreckage of the zvess table.

"Take them to the throne room," Koschei said. "I believe it is time for a coronation."

The great doors to the throne room swung open to a frozen tableau, like performers in a play awaiting their cue.

Familiar faces lined the walls, a strange parody of a monarch receiving an audience. Strashevsta Orlov was at one end, his uniform crisp as ever, though a bloodied bandage wound around his hand. The cabinet members were scattered throughout, save for Commander Iveshkin, who Izaveta was sure would never have stood to obedience like this. Judging from their expressions, all caught between jubilation and terror, they knew something was not quite right with this imposter—that he was more than Kyriil.

Everyone was unnaturally still, only the slightest ripple of breath to show they'd noticed Izaveta's entrance at all, but she couldn't tell if it was fear or some greater spell that held them in place.

Koschei walked ahead, the strashe pushing her and Nikov after him. He did not sit on the high throne at the end of the room but stood carefully in front of it—somehow more possessive.

"As you can see," he said to the room at large, his voice echoing a cold memory of Kyriil, part of the pretense still held up. "Lady Izaveta has returned to the palace to answer for her crimes."

The strashe released her at the base of the dais, stepping away so that only she and Nikov stood in this great space carved before the sorcerer.

Izaveta's nerves urged her to retreat, to run before that terrible magic could be let loose again. But she held her ground. No use in turning back now. There was a strange comfort in that logic, in the knowledge that, one way or another, this was the end.

"Yes," she said. "I have returned, despite all the forces that would keep me from this throne." She looked to the assembled faces, hoping there might be some way to appeal to them, to bring numbers at least against this magic. "But not to answer for any false crimes. Whatever this man has told you, he is an imposter in Kyriil Azarov's place. We must not let him spread any more of his poisonous magic through Tóurin."

No one so much as murmured in response, though from the slight shuffling of feet, the tightly clasped hands, Izaveta was certain it wasn't a spell holding them in place. She could hardly blame them, even as her own disappointed desperation crested against their inaction.

What hope did any of them have in the face of this?

"No need to condemn me so soon," Koschei said, softer now, the words intended for only her. "I still plan to give you the crown you've so long craved."

Izaveta opened her mouth, the response taking far too long to form. Her mother would be so disappointed to see Izaveta tongue-tied in the one moment it truly mattered.

Orlov chose that moment to speak, a deep frown creasing his brows. "You cannot mean to crown her—we know of her treachery, we—" He broke off with a choking gasp.

The movement was so small, Izaveta might not have noticed it if her nerves were not so acutely attuned to the sorcerer. His fingers flexed, gaze not straying toward the strashevsta. Orlov fell to his knees, retching as if something was caught in his throat. Blood splattered the ground, followed a breath later by jagged shards of glass.

Glass that had been clogging the strashevsta's throat.

Fear, then, was what truly held them all in place around her, as unmoving as statues.

"But first," Koschei went on, as if there had been no interruption. "Where is my Firebird?"

Izaveta raised her eyebrows, false bravado coming more easily when it concerned her sister. "How should I know? If she is *your* Firebird, I would assume you kept a close eye on her."

Koschei ignored her, taking a prowling step forward.

"Nikov." The sorcerer spoke softly, an odd cadence to his voice, almost as if he was preparing to sing or recite a prayer. "Tell me."

Nikov's whole body went tense, bracing for a blow that had already fallen. He shot one glance at Izaveta, a desperate look that seared against her skin.

"I—" He screwed his eyes shut, a concerted effort to keep his voice in check.

"Nikov," the sorcerer said again, that soft reprimand of a tutor whose pupil has been caught slacking.

Nikov's teeth dug into his lower lip, hands tight around his own arms as if trying to hold himself together.

His explanation from before slid through Izaveta's mind like a knife. That was what Koschei was doing now, forcing him to listen to an order or else it would tear him apart from inside. This was precisely why Nikov had asked to stay behind, so that he would not be able to fall prey to this.

Perhaps Izaveta should have made Nikov leave—not for her own good but for his. "I—I don't know," he choked out. But the magic was clearly not satisfied, Koschei's unwavering gaze piercing.

Nikov sank to his knees, the bag of carefully prepared spell ingredients tumbling off his belt in a shatter of glass, his nails ripping at his own arms hard enough to draw blood. Izaveta saw the salt and powdered rosemary and sprigs of whitefern all discarded around him on the cold marble floor.

He was muttering something, too low for Izaveta to catch, the steady rhythm of a hymn only for himself. Izaveta sank down next to him, trying to grasp his hands, to stop him damaging himself any more.

He looked up at her, a fierce anguish lancing across his face. She caught what he was saying now, words tumbling

so tight together they were almost indistinguishable. "The ritual, we can still do it."

Izaveta shook her head. They had no sigils here to mark the space of the ritual, and the ingredients were shattered around them, glass shards digging into Izaveta's knees. She needed some way to get Nikov out of this—some words that would fix this. Words that had long since abandoned her.

Koschei stepped down from the dais, glass and herbs crunching beneath his feet as he loomed over them. "Do I need to ask again?"

CHAPTER SEVENTY-NINE

The fire blazed out of Asya, a flaming reflection of the Firebird itself. Too hot—more scorching than she'd intended, but tugged away from her on a tide of pain and desperation.

She'd thought it might make Yuliana stumble back. Might finally force the spell to pause for its own self-preservation. Or perhaps it would do nothing again, and Yuliana would just stride on through, heedless of her own blistered skin.

The flames had stretched beyond her control, pushed on by the Firebird. All her thoughts made too hazy by the blood dripping down her back.

Would it kill Yuliana?

She couldn't seem to get the flames to obey her. Too much whirling around her, emotions tangling with that terrible fear.

Then a scream burst through the crackling red—one that squeezed around Asya's heart. Pain so raw it scraped against the air.

It brought clarity to her mind in a flash. She snuffed the flames with a sudden hiss, drawing them back into herself with a gasp. Yuliana knelt in a circle of scorched earth. She clutched at her wrists, the old scars mingling with new burns.

"Asya—" Her voice was hoarse, burned but achingly real.

Hope stuttered in Asya's chest. In the sudden dim following the bright blaze, she couldn't see the shard glinting in Yuliana's eye.

"Asya—" Yuliana said again. "What happened—please— it hurts—"

Asya reached for her, pulled on by that imagined Calling. The notes that always drew her to Yuliana.

Too late, she saw the ice still glistening on Yuliana's cheek, the mocking pretense of the words. Yuliana twisted around her, pushing her to the ground, knife at Asya's throat.

Tears burned behind her eyes, sharp and foolish. She'd been too willing to fall for that. Her own hope turning against her.

Yuliana's knees pinned Asya's arms to her side—a useless precaution.

It was an eerie reflection of their first sparring match. But Asya had no extra blade now, no secret trick to force this into a draw. And she couldn't use the Firebird anyway, not when the flames wouldn't even hold Yuliana back.

Yuliana's face loomed above her, still contorted into hatred. The very expression Asya had feared so many times—all her guilt and self-loathing forced in front of her.

"And now what?" Yuliana growled, digging the blade deeper. "You won't even dare to summon your flames."

Even with the knife between them, they were so close now Asya could pick out the lines of darker gray in Yuliana's irises. The precise point where the ice shard corrupted her and had blown outward. Asya could still see that distant storm in Yuliana's eyes. The sparks of lightning that had first drawn Asya to her, when she had let herself be something other than the Firebird.

Perhaps this was all she was, though. A foolish monster who fell in love with a mortal.

So be it.

Ignoring the bite of the blade at her throat, she pushed herself up toward Yuliana. Not so much a thought or hope for escape, just a last desperate reaching. Trying to grasp hold of that lost girl again.

She kissed her.

The keen edge of the knife loosened at her throat. She felt Yuliana's lips part slightly against hers, a sharp breath of surprise. Even with the spell slowly poisoning her, Yuliana tasted just the same. The sudden static of a storm mingled with cloves and a glint of steel. Asya didn't push forward, hardly dared to move lest she break this. But Yuliana's lips pressed back against hers, a weight falling from the strashe as she relaxed into the moment.

A brief flash of familiarity. The Yuliana she knew, warm and real beneath her touch.

Yuliana lurched back, the knife falling from her fingers. The shard flickered in her eye, some hint of the girl Asya knew fighting back. The frost on her cheek receded, as if suddenly bathed in the warmest summer sun.

A fluttering hope lifted in Asya's chest—a childish wish that something so terrible could be undone so simply.

Then Yuliana's expression darkened. The ice cracked back across her skin, sudden and violent.

Asya didn't hesitate now. She couldn't. Not with so many relying on her, not with so much hanging in the balance. Yuliana—the Yuliana she knew—wouldn't want that.

The wall of flame that burst from Asya was unyielding and decimating. Born from so much pain she was sure it tore a piece of her own heart with it as it blazed through Yuliana.

CHAPTER EIGHTY

Izaveta could only watch as Nikov's gaze was drawn to the sorcerer, helpless as a mouse in a falcon's talons.

"She'll be here soon." The words clawed through Nikov's lips, unbidden. Only a small piece of the answer.

It gave him the briefest respite, a pause in the frantic tearing at Izaveta's grip.

Koschei canted his head, looking down at Nikov like a curious specimen. "And why has she not arrived *with you*?" He was clearly narrowing down his words, forcing any cracks closed, any possibilities for Nikov to step around the truth.

Putting a hand on his cheek, Izaveta turned him firmly so his eyes were on her. "Just look at me," she murmured back, hands clutching at his face—no care for propriety now, even on display in front of the court. "Just look at me, all right?"

Nikov nodded, teeth biting into his lower lip as if he could hold the answer back by sheer force of will. Sweat beaded on his forehead, muscles gnarled beneath his skin.

Izaveta had no idea how long he could hold out—what holding out on this answer might do to him. It was more than just a passing spell, it was something that had burrowed deep within him, something that would tear him apart if given the chance.

"It's an interesting power, isn't it?" Koschei said. "The longer one ignores the command..." He trailed off, eyebrows raised as he observed Nikov. "The more persistent it becomes."

Izaveta looked to the doors, for any brief flash of hope. Where was Asya? If the sorcerer was here then surely nothing else could have waylaid her this much, not unless something had gone very wrong. And without Asya there was no way to salvage this.

"He always did make things far harder than necessary." Koschei clucked his tongue like an impatient teacher, still watching Nikov's pain with detached interest. "We never had to be enemies, you know."

Izaveta didn't know what else to say, what else she could possibly say with Nikov trembling beneath her touch. A wasted education in lies and manipulations that would do nothing to help her now.

"Though that's probably why your father never saw much in you. Not enough vision," Koschei went on, his mercurial appearance shifting once more. The hints of Kyriil melted away, replaced by the stoic expression of Ambassador Täusch. "But we saw to that, didn't we?"

Nikov gripped her hand, a clamping vise, and murmured something—almost too low for her to catch. "Be ready."

Before she could respond, before she could snap at him to stop talking in riddles again, he lurched forward. Pulling out of her grip with movements jerky as a puppet, he grasped at the folds of the sorcerer's robes. "Please," he whispered. "Please take it away."

The slightest hint of a smile tugged at Koschei's lips. In that moment, a fleeting rush of anger flared in Izaveta, stronger than she'd thought was still possible, though perhaps rage

came more easily than affection. Anger that this man, whose smiles were so poisonous, could have claimed power over Nikov—who gave his happiness so freely. It caught beneath her armor, so unexpected she couldn't quite hide it.

Izaveta rose to her feet, not quite sure what she planned to do with nothing but her bare hands, other than find some way to make this sorcerer hurt.

Koschei must have felt her venom in the air, as his eyes flicked to her.

Before she could act, something moved in the corner of her vision, her body registering the threat before she did. A shadow tore from one of the courtiers, one moment a mere reflection upon the ground, the next startlingly solid. The courtier fell back, mouth gaping and hands grasping as if not quite sure what they'd lost.

It ruptured through the air toward Izaveta, rippling and re-shaping into something almost humanlike once more. Something with clawing hands that grabbed her upper arms tight, holding her back.

Nikov didn't seem to notice, whatever was twisting inside him too visceral for outside thought.

"You don't need to do any of this," Izaveta yelled, that new-awakened anger burning in her words. "You have your power, why waste your time with this display?"

The sorcerer's attention flicked to her, a less engaging side act to his current interest. "You know as well as I, power is only as great as you show it to be." He looked back at Nikov. "Now, Nikov, will you answer me? You know I grow quickly impatient."

Izaveta opened her mouth to speak again, to do something to delay this terrible inevitability. But Nikov's voice broke over hers.

"The Firebird has your heart," he gasped. It came out in a sudden rush, a dam finally broken by water too vicious to hold back. "And we were planning to return it to your body."

Koschei leaned down and grasped Nikov's right wrist, pushing back his sleeve to expose the trapped decay of the curse. Something rippled across the sorcerer's face, an ugly, living rage—gone in the next blink. It reminded Izaveta of that moment when he'd realized she had those letters, something so close to humanity that it still managed to cut deep.

When he spoke, that anger still lurked in the depths. A dangerous, twisting thing that made Izaveta's skin prickle. "You told her."

"You have to be very careful with your wording," Nikov spat, panting from the sudden release of his confession. "You made sure I couldn't *tell* anyone where it was. Not that I couldn't show them."

Koschei's free hand jerked—the sharpness of the movement betraying him—and that invisible force slammed into Nikov again. It sent him careening back across the slick floor, courtiers and strashe scattering out of his path until he slammed against the marble wall with a shattering *crack*.

A wicked-looking knife lengthened between Koschei's fingers as he advanced. Izaveta didn't see who bore the price this time, but she heard the ragged yell from the onlookers, the only sign they truly were more than statues.

Nikov sat up with a low groan of pain, red blooming across his forehead.

"What does it matter now?" Izaveta said desperately, trying to find any words to incite him, to get him to turn that anger back on her. "You've won, you've outsmarted us. Even if Asya has your heart, there is nothing we can do with it."

The sorcerer ignored her. He did not raise the knife as

Izaveta had expected, but held it out to Nikov, hilt first. A cold dread spread through her limbs at the gesture, the careful calculation of it. "Take it," Koschei said in that soft cadence again.

When Nikov didn't take the knife, Koschei leaned down and pressed it into his hands. Izaveta pulled against her shadowy captor, its claws wrapping tighter with each attempt, blood beading on her upper arms. She thought she knew what was coming now, the same sort of game her mother had enjoyed—that Queen Teriya had likely enjoyed too. The languid exhilaration of exerting power.

"Good," Koschei said. "Now stand up."

Nikov did as he said, gait unsteady and hands shaking where he held the knife. He looked wrung out, any last dregs of fight sapped from him by the blows.

If Asya were already here, if they'd managed to do the ritual, that blade would be enough to end the sorcerer. But now it was a useless prop, a cursed gift. And Izaveta could do nothing but watch, all her vain attempts at her own power scattered around her. Her own court held in thrall of the sorcerer's magic, already turned against her for her own actions. A failure she could blame no one else for.

"And now," Koschei went on, in the same hushed tone that slithered around the room. "Plunge it into your heart."

CHAPTER EIGHTY-ONE

Asya was running at full pelt. Time chased behind her, the jumping beat of her heart rushing in her ears. She was meant to reach the sorcerer first. Meant to guide him toward what they wanted, not be the one scrambling to catch up.

A scream, so familiar that it made her blood run cold. No, no, no—if Koschei had already found Izaveta, then Asya was too late.

She skidded around a smiling rendition of Saint Petrik and plunged after the sound. The Firebird pushed her on, as if it could sense some greater urgency.

The great doors to the throne room were swung wide to an awful scene, so unreal, Asya wondered if she'd slipped into a dream. People spread out in abject terror. A towering shadow holding her sister fast. A jagged blade trembled in Nikov's hands, poised over his own heart. His eyes strained, every muscle of his body taut as he tried to stop the knife from completing its path. And Koschei stood in the midst of it all.

"Stop!" Asya yelled, with no real thought or weight behind the command.

The sorcerer turned to her, an animated smile alighting his features. "Firebird," he said. "A pleasure to finally have your company. I was beginning to worry you might miss the excitement."

Izaveta tried to reach toward her, only getting a half step before the animate shadow pulled her back. Just like the one Koschei had used on Yuliana. That same stolen magic, prices cleaved from any mortal nearby.

"Stop," Asya said again. "Let them go."

Koschei spread his hands wide. "It's not I who holds them."

Asya gritted her teeth, words clipped short. "Release them from the magic you stole, then."

"Can you steal what was always rightfully yours?"

The Firebird churned inside her, irritated as she was at the circular reasoning. The useless words when she could see Nikov's resolve slip with every shallow breath.

Asya raised the small stone egg—their last vestige of hope. The only card she had to play, pulled from her hands again by her own heart. A desperate move by someone always too controlled by their own emotions, just as Tarya had warned her. Just as Koschei had suspected.

"Release them," Asya said. "Or I break it."

Koschei's face remained blank, though Asya thought she caught the slightest flicker. As if it had required conscious effort to maintain the semblance of indifference. "Why should I care if you break it? That only benefits me."

"You must have kept it this long for a reason," Asya said. "You need to care a little, otherwise even your revenge wouldn't matter. For all your talk of letting go, you can't let go of this." She was breathing hard, adrenaline speeding through her and sharpening her thoughts.

"Well?" she prompted at Koschei's silence. "Which do you choose—your heart or your prisoners?"

CHAPTER EIGHTY-TWO

Izaveta's breath tangled in her chest, trembling on the knife-edge of Asya's words.

Koschei was watching her sister with a careful calculation, and even a hint of admiration, as he said, "It helps you very little either way to stay the execution, you must see that."

Koschei was right of course, even without this magic holding them in place, there was no escaping this. Certainly not if they gave up the heart too easily.

"Asya," Izaveta murmured, a low warning. "You—" A tendril of shadow curled around her neck, pressing just enough to cut off her words.

But her sister didn't look at her, blazing eyes focused only on the sorcerer. "I give you your heart and you promise not to harm them."

Izaveta struggled against the choking shadow, warning words dying in her throat. Across from her, Nikov seemed barely aware of the proceedings, the tip of the knife jutting into his skin already.

"Very well," Koschei said. "I swear no harm shall come to them."

There was a deliberate inflection in his words, the same

trick Izaveta had used once before. He held out a hand to Asya in expectation.

Asya remained steadfast. "You first. Let them go."

With exaggerated grandeur, Koschei turned to Nikov. "You may lay down the knife. You are released from our bargain."

The blade clattered to the floor and Nikov slumped back against the wall, a red spot of blood blooming across his shirt. He met Izaveta's gaze, a mutual understanding flitting between them. An execution stayed but not escaped.

Be ready, he'd said, and it reflected in his eyes now, the smallest nod. The last ingredient burned in her pocket, the piece of saint's bone.

With another wave of the sorcerer's hand, the unnecessary performance of it all, the shadow holding Izaveta blew apart to wisps of dark smoke. She staggered forward, pulled by her own momentum, now there was no longer anything holding her back.

Too much given far too easily. A move only made when the opposing player knew they had the winning hand either way.

Asya held out the egg, but when the sorcerer did not move toward her, she acquiesced and strode forward, through the ruined remnants of their plan on the floor.

Koschei took the egg with a reverence that he could not quite hide, a gentle fear of having a great vulnerability so near to him, or the magnitude of his humanity laid out before him, the emotions that had first spurred his need for vengeance.

With a bitter twist, Izaveta realized she understood the feeling.

Asya had started to take a step back, slow and careful, when Koschei said, "I did think you might reconsider your allegiances. I only want magic restored to Tóurin. I want to cast spells without tearing the price from those around me. Far lesser sins, I think you'll find, than your sister's."

Asya raised her chin. "I know what she's done. That doesn't change anything."

"I assume you found your guard on your way in?" Koschei asked lightly. "Only one way you defeated her, I suppose."

Asya's jaw clenched, so tight Izaveta could imagine the cracks running through her sister.

Sick realization crested in Izaveta's stomach; that was what had kept Asya. That was what fueled Asya's burning desperation now.

"All the more reason to stand against you," Asya bit out. A rage-filled despair threatening to collapse on them all.

"It's hardly fair to blame me," Koschei replied. "When, if not for Izaveta, your strashe would not have been here at all."

Asya faltered, her eyes sliding to Izaveta. Izaveta tried to push as much as she could into that look, all the moments they'd managed to understand each other unspoken. She needed Asya to understand now.

"When you left the palace after performing the ritual," Koschei went on, that sickening realization spreading in Izaveta again, "your sister sent Yuliana to a nonexistent hideout. She pretended to offer safety, when instead she left your strashe to be killed, all to be sure nothing could slow her down. Yuliana *would* have been killed, if not for me." He trailed off, clearly enjoying the baited audience. "While your sister sent her to slaughter, I kept her alive."

Asya whirled on Izaveta. "You said she wanted to stay behind. But you lied to her—you left her behind?" Sparks burst across her irises, burning stars in a dark sky. "More than that, you tricked her. You sent her to die."

Izaveta took a half step back. "I had to—"

"She would be safe now," Asya said, her words tattered. "How could you do that? How could you make that choice?"

"I told you, Asya. With my heart gone, it makes every-thing—"

Flames blazed out behind her, so hot they seared against Izaveta's skin, her eyes watering at the brightness.

"That's hardly an excuse for all your past actions," Asya growled, stalking toward her now, a ragged grief shining in her eyes. "You said you would be honest with me. Is that honesty?"

Izaveta backed away and she felt Koschei follow, entranced by the discord he had concocted between them—finally forc-ing even Asya to reckon with who Izaveta truly was.

"Don't you care what you've done?" Asya pressed, the words sharp and burning as her flames.

"I tried, Asya," Izaveta said, a pathetic invocation. One that meant very little in the end. Her hand tightened around the saint's bone, the only thing she could grip. "I really tried to—"

"You *tried*," Asya panted. "And yet so many people lie dead while you get another chance."

Fire blazed out—not toward Izaveta, but toward Koschei. The flames didn't dare consume the sorcerer, too obvious a target, but instead the shattered glass and scattered ingredi-ents broken at his feet. In the same moment, Izaveta threw the saint's bone, the final piece of the spell.

The flames ignited it all, encircling Koschei in a jagged, crude arc.

Koschei reached a hand into his pocket to feel the fabric Nikov had slipped there while fighting the commands, care-fully marked in blood with the last sigil of the ritual.

Not the fluid deception they'd planned, but one wrenched from the hands of disaster. A scrambling and brilliant idea Nikov had managed to grasp, even in the midst of this all. Izaveta wasn't entirely sure it would work, not without the careful weighing and calculations, the ingredients jumbled together on the ground.

Koschei turned a vicious snarl on Asya and the Firebird sputtered out, clamped under his will once again.

But the sorcerer was too late. He already held the heart, the other pieces of the ritual spread around him, and that fire had ignited the spell.

A slight hum split the air, like magic darting to their aid. True fear burst on Koschei's face for the first time, the same fear Izaveta had felt at the Firebird, as light sprang toward him. Something between wind and water, both insubstantial and solid. Even haphazard as it was, the spell was working, mortality reaching for Koschei once again.

Then the egg flew from the magician's grip. A deep crack fractured through it as it tumbled to the cold marble floor, a resonating sound that shuddered through Izaveta's bones.

Koschei hadn't moved, there were no signs on his ashen face that his mortality had been restored. The light dissipated in an instant as quickly as it had come, swallowed by the air around it.

It was only then that Izaveta noticed the blood on Koschei's hand, faint specks from a shallow cut. It wasn't the spell that had lifted the egg from his fingers, and it wasn't magic Izaveta had heard in the air. It was a dagger. One that had flown through the room, so sure Izaveta had barely seen it.

But she could see the aftermath now. The egg broken in half on the floor. Nikov had said even the slightest crack could destroy the casing, could let the heart ripple away into nothing. This was far more than a small crack.

Koschei's heart was gone and with it, any hope of rendering him mortal.

CHAPTER EIGHTY-THREE

Asya stared in horror at the broken egg. All their sacrifices, all the risks they had taken in this throne room, and Koschei's heart was gone. Asya had finally managed to meet her sister's elaborate schemes and they had been destroyed by her fragile hope.

The deception had only worked because Koschei would so easily believe Asya to follow her heart past reason. And now the plan had been ruined by just that.

Yuliana stood in the doorway, arm still held aloft where she had let the knife fly free.

Her storming eyes were on Asya when she spoke. "I suppose you should have killed me after all."

The frozen veins had spread, splintering down her left cheek to clench hold on her neck.

Perhaps she should have killed her. Perhaps that would have truly been the kinder thing.

A jarring noise rang out behind her. Tormented and shrill, almost inhuman. Asya turned slowly, prey trying not to alert the predator.

Koschei's face was a marred mask as the sound escaped him. A desperate kind of grief mingling with a cruel excitement. It sent a shiver of terror through Asya. The kind of terror she remembered from seeing Tarya transform. The primal fear Asya had seen gathered around her. A fear that knows it cannot stand against this.

Whatever threads of humanity might have been holding the sorcerer back before were now severed.

Asya moved instinctively toward her sister, the two of them inexorably linked. At least standing together against this.

It seemed to take a conscious effort for Koschei to right himself. To pull the calm back around himself. As if the shattering of that final piece had torn something loose.

"It hardly matters now." His voice was high, a frayed edge to it as he stalked toward them. "An old relic. One that has no place now. No use holding on to sentimentality."

No one spoke, not even Izaveta. There was a fragility to this moment, something no one wanted to risk breaking.

"A rather nice trick," Koschei went on, not quite looking at Asya. "More than I might have expected of you, Firebird."

Asya inched closer to Izaveta. There was no way to protect all these people, but she could buy some time, even if her flames could not destroy the sorcerer.

Izaveta seemed to read her thoughts. She took a step forward, drawing Koschei's attention to her. A part of Asya still wanted to leap protectively in front of her sister. To not let her take this risk. But they'd agreed: together or not at all.

Besides, Asya was still the Firebird. This was still a duty she upheld even in the face of this. She owed protection to all these people.

"Your heart is gone," Izaveta said in that soft tone Asya knew to associate with careful manipulation. "The legacy of the Karasova queens ends with me. What use is there in holding on to this vengeance?"

His eyes snapped to her, wild and bright. "I would not expect someone who has always been heartless to understand the true price of love. Of *betrayal*."

Asya moved slowly to her left, small, shifting movements to put a little space between herself and Koschei. To give them a fighting chance.

Izaveta didn't rise to his tone, her words careful and compassionate. "I understand what it is to be betrayed by someone you care about. I've seen how power has corrupted. How it destroyed me and my mother before me. Don't let everyone else suffer because of that."

"Lies and lies and lies," Koschei said, an almost singsong quality to his voice. "You are exactly the legacy Teriya left behind. She'd be so proud of her ruthless progeny."

Asya turned her body slightly, trying to keep her eyes on the sorcerer while feeling for the press of people behind her. Nikov shadowed her steps, reading her intention in her movements.

"How would your legacy be any different?" Izaveta asked, proud anger finally breaking through. "Ruling this land in her place would not make you better than her. Ruling under fear and stolen magic would only be doing the same as her."

Asya let the flames build beneath her skin. She would only get one chance at this.

"I don't want to rule it," Koschei said, as if it should have been obvious. "I want to destroy it. To ensure her legacy is left in ruin. Any memory of her obliterated. Her queendom shall become a ruin of magic, a lesson to those arrogant enough to think they could control it."

The shock of those words, the way they swung what Asya had anticipated on its head, set the fire free a breath before she intended. A sweltering wall of scarlet and gold roared to life between Koschei and his silent audience.

"Go!" Asya yelled, gesturing toward the wide-open doors.

They were all slow to react, even with that burning wall in front of them. Embers reflected in the collected terror of their faces.

"Run!" Nikov shouted at her side. "Quickly—go!"

But none of them moved. Asya could see a few of them considering, even a few teetering steps. Not trapped in place with a spell—even stolen magic and forced prices wouldn't be able to maintain that—but held again by fear.

Asya pressed the flames toward them, hoping to at least spur them to action through self-preservation if nothing else.

But still they didn't move, even with golden tongues reaching toward them.

The flames crackled out behind her. A useless and wasted distraction.

Asya turned, holding golden sparks close to her fingers. Some small comfort.

"Surprised?" Koschei asked, some lucidity returning. "You shouldn't be. The people of this palace have always been able to recognize power when they see it. To recognize when they must bend." A slight smile tugged at his pale lips. "I suppose I have the lovely Teriya to thank for that. She trained them so well. On one side, they would fear the Firebird, and on the other, the queen. A perfect balance to keep them all in line without them even realizing it."

Asya met Izaveta's gaze, her own desolate horror reflected there. However unintentionally, their actions had led here. Asya's selfishness, her desperate need to have her sister back. Izaveta's mistakes.

And now there was nothing they could do to right it.

They couldn't even offer sanctuary to a court so steeped in lies and poison.

Koschei took a deep breath, tearing his eyes away from the shattered casing that had held his heart. "To business, then," he said.

Asya moved back to Izaveta's side at once, flames sparking in her hands once more. Her jaw was clenched tight, everything whirring too fast around her.

"So sweet," Koschei crooned, raising a hand like an admonishing parent. "But I don't need the Lady Izaveta quite yet." He turned to Asya so sharply she jumped back, again thrown by his jarring and abrupt shifts. "I need one thing from you first, my Firebird."

Her muscles all coiled, body readying itself before her mind caught up. But before she could even fall into one of her familiar stances, ready herself for some kind of attack, the pain hit her.

It tore through her like a living thing, wrenching bones from their sockets, twisting her veins into tight knots of snarled torment. It was like when the Firebird had first risen in her, that molding, re-forming transmutation. But there was no end to this, no bright burst of flame to finally free her from it.

Just a roiling, scalding pain as she was ripped apart. Not just bones and muscles tearing free, but thoughts and memories biting at their seams, desperate to somehow escape this.

The Firebird rose to her defense in an instant, the sudden agony pulling it free. No chance for Asya to think to suppress it or question what he wanted.

Agony clouded her vision as Koschei's blurred figure stepped toward her. He didn't raise a weapon, though, as they had in that ruined church. Instead, he reached out for her, flames unheeded, unafraid.

Those flames had felt solid to Asya before. They'd had brief flashes where the Firebird felt as corporeal as her own flesh. But only now did it truly feel like a real creature. A creature that Koschei was tearing something precious from.

Asya's throat was ragged, though she couldn't hear her screams anymore. She tried to pull the Firebird back inside her, back into the safety of her skin. But it was trapped in this agony too. Reduced to the base instinct of fear.

The Firebird's wings were spread wide when the sorcerer tore something from them. It jolted through Asya like a wrenched tooth, leaving a bloodied space where it had once been.

A violation of this beautiful creature, something unearned and unwilling.

The pain receded as suddenly as it had come, leaving her limbs aching and exhausted. Koschei held something carefully in his long fingers. A burning, crimson feather.

Asya was on her knees, fingers scraping against the marble beneath her. She didn't even remember falling. She felt Izaveta's hands on her, felt her sister's panicked breath.

Koschei glanced down at her, that strange affection on his face again. As if he were proud of the creature he'd made.

Asya lurched forward, her head unsteady but the Firebird already eager for revenge. Broiling fire readied itself at her fingertips, reaching out eagerly toward the sorcerer. Ready to reap vengeance for all he'd taken.

Then the Firebird was gone. No crushing weight of firestone, but that same terrible emptiness as before.

With barely a glance in Asya's direction, Koschei had taken away the Firebird again. Leaving only a ghastly isolation and a powerless girl facing down the monster she'd helped create.

The sorcerer turned to Izaveta, a hungry look in his eyes. He dipped his head in a mocking imitation of a bow. "Time for your coronation, my lady."

CHAPTER EIGHTY-FOUR

Izaveta grasped Asya's hand. It was the only thing she could think to do, a futile and childish gesture yet her mind had not produced anything else. No schemes or clever ways out now, just her and Asya prepared to be consumed by an inevitable tide.

Koschei gestured to the throne behind him with a sweeping wave. "Will you take your rightful place, Izaveta?"

Izaveta didn't move, fingers tightening against Asya's as if they could somehow save each other. "I hope you rot in the farthest reaches of the sky."

"Strashevsta." Koschei turned to Orlov, blood still staining his chin and crimson-edged glass scattered at his feet. The strashevsta jolted upright, jagged fear at drawing attention again. "Escort our young queen to her throne."

Orlov didn't hesitate or try to voice any complaints now. Gaze lowered, he marched toward Izaveta as if still on official business, the careful movements of a long-trained parade soldier.

"Don't even think about it," Asya growled. Even without flames burning in her eyes, she exuded a terrifying aura, a power that made the strashevsta falter. Nikov stood at her side, unarmed but equally protective.

But a flick of the sorcerer's hand and the two of them were thrown backward, hitting the floor with a resounding crack. Asya stirred first, blood speckling her too-pale cheek, but Nikov remained jarringly still.

Izaveta lunged toward them, instinct taking over again, but Orlov's hands wrapped around her.

He dragged her back toward the dais, oblivious to Izaveta's spitting threats.

All the weaknesses Izaveta could see in him now, the fear, the desperate need for approval and a more powerful hand to lead him, even memories of his hidden injury and graying hair did nothing to help her.

She kicked out, foot catching his shin only out of sheer luck. He hit her across the back of her head, bright falling stars popping in her vision and any fight sliding out of her as the world rippled around her.

He heaved her up the dais, feet barely touching the ground, and threw her onto the throne. Izaveta had never truly sat in it as queen, always the girl pretending, the girl wishing she could truly be in control. And now the foolish girl watching her own destruction.

She looked out at the assembled court, a perverse mockery of an audience to this coronation. Some of them stared back at her, but most had their eyes downcast, unable to watch but unable to intervene.

This court that was so used to seeing cruelty reign through a subtle hand or unwavering fist, that was so used to the way power was wielded stronger than magic, did not know how to stand against this. To them, was it truly so different to see a sorcerer grasp the throne than it was to see the Karasovas clutch onto it?

The twisted whorls of metal meant to mimic the Firebird's

flames, captured in the queen's throne, came to life. Still pale and gleaming, but somehow both fire and steel. They twisted around Izaveta's arms, a burning cold where they caught her skin, pinning her back in place against the throne.

Koschei ascended the dais toward her, the burning feather held aloft. He pressed it into her right hand, sealed in place by more of those enchanted silver flames. He stepped back to admire his work. "The heartless queen," he murmured. "The most important piece of my spell. A curse of this ruination could only be born from one without a heart."

Asya tried to push forward, the ground wheeling beneath her feet, marble panels morphing from solid to liquid, then back again.

"We made a bargain," Asya said, one foot catching in the strange marble sea beneath her. "I gave you your heart and you promised not to harm them."

"As I promise, I am true to my word." Koschei gave a benevolent smile. "But this is not harming her, this shall *preserve* her. To watch over a ruined queendom for eternity. Teriya's true legacy."

Still, Asya pressed forward, the anguish on her face splintering against Izaveta's resolve. "You claim to stand against all Teriya was, yet you lie just as she did. You go back on your promises just as she did to you."

The sharp *crack* this time was bone, accompanied by Asya's wrenching scream as she fell to her knees. Izaveta tried to throw herself forward, tried to rip against the impossible bonds, but there was no mercy there.

"No," Koschei replied. "But I am careful in how I word my promises."

Izaveta couldn't see her sister now, only Koschei in front of her and the dancing metal flames at the edges of her vision.

"And so we begin," he said simply. He lifted the tattered crown and placed it on her head, a mockery of what she'd once so desperately wanted.

There were no words to the spell as Izaveta had always been taught, no price that she could see—though it may have been wrenched from one of the onlookers—but she certainly felt the magic. Not snapping through the air, tingling and alive as it had been in that tower, but burrowing inside her.

Serrated veins of frost tore across her skin, bursting out from that empty place inside her. Not destructive but somehow fortifying, ensuring her place on this broken throne forever. The veins didn't stop when they had twisted across her body, jagged and burning cold, but spread from where her fingers touched the throne like ink blooming in water.

They cracked through the carefully polished floor, snaking toward any person they could reach and leaving an icy, acrid waste in their wake.

Izaveta's own poison leaking out into the land. There was something poetic about it, wasn't there? The gods laughing at their own dark sense of humor again. For all she could say she had tried, that she had always wanted the best for Tóurin, this was how it would end. She'd have the crown she had always craved, her reign eternal and unquestioned. A cursed gift again, the thing she'd once wanted warped beneath her touch.

The veins reached Orlov first, still standing close from his role in forcing her here. They consumed him in a breath, so quick his ragged scream of pain came out as a single ghastly note. Frost burst through his veins, spreading across his skin like fine summer ice. It contorted his face, a twisted mask of terror. A living and immovable statue.

Some people ran then, their instincts taking over or understanding finally breaking through that even compliance would not keep them safe. It was futile. Koschei did not even make a move to stop them, he didn't need to. The veins spread farther from Izaveta, dragging pieces of herself with them. Hollowing her out to an empty shell.

They consumed the assembled nobles and strashe alike, swallowing them as easily as Orlov and corrupting the ground they left behind. And still the magic didn't stop, cracking through the windows with a shattering of glass, twisting around the doors and reaching eagerly beyond.

This magic would spread across all of Tóurin—perhaps farther, she had no idea where Koschei's revenge might end. A burning and unending prison, so sharp with magic, it turned the air acrid.

Izaveta caught Asya's eye, the only other thing untouched by this spell. A curse that would tear them apart again, always forced to opposite sides. Different eternities of suffering.

I'm sorry, Izaveta thought. A useless apology now, but one she felt she had to make. So sorry that she hadn't trusted her sister sooner, that she'd forced herself into someone else—a person who did not care whose lives they ruined. She hoped Asya could feel her regret at least, even if Izaveta would never get the chance to voice it now.

CHAPTER EIGHTY-FIVE

Asya dragged herself forward. Through the pain clouding her mind she could only manage one thought. She had to get to her sister. Icy veins slipped under Asya's fingers, thickening like tree roots beneath her touch. The lifeblood of magic seeping through the land once more, but twisted to someone else's ends.

Every movement hurt, the comforting black of unconsciousness tugging at the edge of her vision. But even if it was to end in death all the same, Asya would rather die at her sister's side.

She managed to reach the edge of the dais, right leg dragging uselessly behind her.

She heaved herself up a step, trying to see her sister between the jagged shards of magic spiraling out. The color was draining from her eyes too, warm brown leeching away to nothing. That same spell that had consumed those strashe so many days ago—a mere preface to the final act.

Asya tried to pull herself up the next step, but her leg caught on the cracked floor and violent pain gashed through her again. A mangled cry tore from her lips, hot tears evaporating even as they spilled.

It drew Koschei toward her, away from the magnificence

of what he had created. He looked down at her, his features more indistinguishable than ever. Just his colorless eyes burning into her. "Don't worry, my Firebird, I'll heal you soon enough. Once all this is done. Then we can finally continue as we were always meant to."

She couldn't manage to speak, so she let out another guttural gasp—one that she hoped he could hear the venom in. She hauled herself farther, left leg scrabbling to find purchase. Her fingers grasped at one of the caustic veins of the curse, some purchase to help pull herself forward, even if it seared beneath her skin.

Koschei moved toward her, languid and relaxed. He didn't need to rush, not when Asya could barely move. He stepped on her hand, bones cracking beneath his weight. It dislodged her easily, sending her back to the bottom of the dais with another crumpled jab of agony.

"No interfering, Firebird."

A part of her knew this was pointless. Knew that she had no strength left, that she was too broken to do anything. No power of the Firebird to come to her aid now, just her own mortal body failing against this magic. But still she tried. Muscles determinedly pressing on despite everything.

This man had helped trap her into her role as the Firebird. Had killed and manipulated, all in the name of his own slighted heart. Had taken so much from Asya—so much that could never come back. She couldn't let him take her sister too.

Koschei kicked out, harder this time, his boot catching the side of her already-jangled head. Her grip slipped again, unconsciousness towering over her. Urging her into that dark, the peaceful quiet it would finally bring.

But she couldn't succumb to it. Not now, not like this. She heaved herself forward, the movement weak and futile.

"Why are you still fighting?" Koschei growled. "What do you still not understand?"

Why was she fighting? Asya wasn't sure she even knew. She wasn't even sure she *was* fighting him. Just that she had to get to her sister.

She tried to tug herself forward again, teeth gritted so tight she thought her jaw might crack.

Koschei reached out to one of the frosted statues beside him—Orlov, Asya thought through the lapping fog. The sorcerer drew the strashevsta's sword from its sheath, raising it above her. A shining fang of a blade unfurled beneath his fingers.

Koschei let his arms fall and the sword plummeted down into Asya. She felt the scream build and die in her lungs as the blade tore through them. Puncturing through flesh and bone all the way down to the stone beneath her.

Pinning her like nothing more than a fly. A nuisance.

"Stay *there*," he spat, each word punctuated by pain.

Asya still tried to move, but every breath was ragged, struck through by the gleaming spike. Even with her full strength, she couldn't have hoped to pull it free, and what little strength she had left was rapidly ebbing. Spilling around her in dark red blood.

After everything, was this truly how it would end? It didn't matter how hard they'd tried, it didn't matter all they'd sacrificed. They were still just instruments in another's hand, forced architects of the destruction of everything they cared about.

Koschei was watching her still, as if he could see the thoughts on her face. "Let it go, my Firebird." So soft, coaxing. "It will all be so much easier when you do."

It would be easier. So much easier to give in now. To do

what Tarya had always instructed her, to simply let go. Accept her immortal life alone, take the role Koschei offered her and let go of the pain.

Except that Tarya had died believing that might be wrong. Died for nothing, in the end. It didn't matter what Asya did now.

Asya strained her eyes, trying to at least glimpse Izaveta. To grasp on to the one thing that kept her balanced. But the angle was too awkward, the jagged spike tearing if she tried to move. She could only see as far as her sister's hand, the burning feather trapped in her fingers.

The same feather she'd seen in the memory of Teriya and the sorcerer. The ritual that had pushed them here. That had forced Asya and Izaveta onto opposing paths, tearing them apart at every chance.

Something burst in Asya's mind then, bright as new dawn sun. So sudden and clear she wasn't sure if it was her own thought or the Firebird's.

Queen Teriya had used that feather in the ritual to create the magic of twin heirs, to create the Firebird itself. But then where had the first feather come from?

It hadn't simply been a falcon's feather set alight or some trick. It had been the same solid yet burning thing that was now clamped in Izaveta's fingers.

That meant Koschei had not truly *created* the Firebird, it had existed before the ritual. Its own creature for centuries before—what else would have been keeping the balance of magic all those years?

Koschei hadn't created the Firebird, he'd merely bound it to a mortal.

CHAPTER EIGHTY-SIX

The realization burned sharp and bright in Asya's mind, so obvious she didn't know how she hadn't seen it before.

Koschei had control over the power he had given the Karasova line, over how she could wield the Firebird while it lived inside her. But if she could tear it free, unbind it from this prison Koschei had made, then perhaps it could stand against him.

A creature in its own right, the scales finally balanced again.

Now that she thought it, now she saw the ways the Firebird was trapped, it was easy to see the seams. To see the ways her bones had not been remolded into the Firebird when it had awakened within her, but had been twisted into its cage.

Asya could feel her mind slipping away, that blackness calling to her again. Without the Firebird in her bones, it would be a very final black.

But with the Firebird, it would be an eternity in this broken world.

Koschei seemed satisfied at her obedience, glad he had finally made her understand. He looked back to the spell spread around him, though no victory glowed in his eyes. Just a deep, inevitable resignation.

She squeezed her eyes shut, the decision easy, now that it

was in front of her. Koschei may have taken her flames, but the Firebird was still there. She imagined digging into those small cracks she'd found, the not-quite-smoothed edges where the Firebird's cage had been forged inside of her.

She stilled, concentrating. It was the very fabric of her own being, so intertwined that tearing it apart might tear her too. But she didn't care.

Koschei had taken too much, the spell he and Teriya created had taken too much. And now finally Asya could take something back.

"What are you doing?" The sorcerer's voice was high, nervous once again. She felt him reaching toward her, more spells circling around him.

She tore at those invisible, intangible seams within herself. The places where stitching had been laid in place so carefully it was barely distinguishable from flesh. And finally, with a last stitch unpicked, the Firebird rose from her.

Not part of her, but wrenching away. Ripping out of her skin. The flames burned at the edge of her vision, their heat scalding her as it never had before.

Koschei let out a stuttering yell, the most human sound Asya had heard from him. "It can't be let free—a power like that must not go unchecked—"

But Asya was done being nothing more than a weapon wielded by unseen hands.

With a sharp, gasping breath, the Firebird finally tore free.

CHAPTER EIGHTY-SEVEN

The Firebird blazed to life in front of Izaveta, the bright incandescence searing through some of the clawing frost, allowing her to look down once more.

The Firebird was not as Izaveta had seen it before. Not flames rising out from her sister, ephemeral and otherworldly. The creature exuded substance now, flames licking through the air, stronger than rain.

Eyes burned beneath the hooked mask of its face. No longer Asya's eyes but something else entirely, something sentient and furious.

Koschei scrambled back, staring at it like a treasured pet that had suddenly turned vicious. "That's—that's not possible."

The Firebird looked down at him, observing in the way a child might look down at an ant. Something so beneath them, it barely warranted acknowledgment before being crushed under their boot.

A low song trilled in the air, only the briefest echoing notes. The Firebird's call, Izaveta realized, its warning to the prey before it.

But Koschei didn't have a chance to move.

It consumed him. Not in the way flames might consume firewood, a slow burn to leave charred remains behind, but consumed with the same certainty that night swallowed day. The same swift and irrevocable inevitability of the passage from one day to the next.

The fire burned bright behind Izaveta's eyelids, a searing brand that she would never forget.

And then the sorcerer was gone, nothing left to even mark his grave.

But the damage he had wrought was still spread around them, Tóurin in tatters as he had wanted. All the assembled courtiers—even Nikov, caught midstep toward the dais—were frozen in that terrible spell. Magic burned too sharp in the air, suffocating as poison.

And the Firebird did not vanish, it showed no sign of sliding back into Asya's body—of returning to her sister as it should, returning to heal the wound tearing through her chest.

Instead, it remained hovering in the air before Izaveta, a massive, burning creature whose edges smoldered away to nothing. It was no longer moving in harmony with Asya, but a being unto itself—in fact, Asya wasn't moving at all.

Izaveta tried to stand, to run to her sister, but just like the rest of Koschei's magic, the throne still held her fast.

A useless victory, as his curse had already come to pass.

"You freed me."

The voice crept through the air, almost a physical thing. A presence that nudged against Izaveta's skin. She wasn't even sure she could call it a voice. It was to a voice what trails of ash were to a flame. A disconcerting, scorching shadow.

"Asya freed you," Izaveta croaked, unable to tear her eyes away from her sister.

Something sizzled in the air, a sharp tang, like lightning about to strike. That finally drew Izaveta's eyes up to the

Firebird. Its wings beat slowly, petering off into something insubstantial at the very edges.

Then Izaveta saw the things she'd heard—not the Firebird itself, but one of its feathers floating down toward her like a leaf on the breeze.

"For me?" Izaveta asked in wonderment.

The creature merely stared back at her, as if tired of the stupidity of mortals. "I pay my debts. A price is a price."

Izaveta just stared at the feather, hope almost too afraid to kindle in her chest. "Will it— Can it, really?"

The Firebird nodded, its sharp beak somehow disapproving.

Izaveta felt as if her lungs had suddenly cleared, the bonds already freed from her wrists.

It was true, then. The old stories of the Firebird, the tradition that Hunte Rastyshenik claimed to mimic. That if the Firebird gave a person one of their feathers, then that person could ask for one wish in return.

It suddenly felt like too much power, just grazing Izaveta's fingertips. She could do anything with that one wish, could restore Teriya's legacy and ensure the Karasova line ruled forever. Izaveta could twist the world to whatever she wanted, as long as she was careful. End the Fading or build herself an empire, tie magic back to her own blood again.

A dangerous temptation, one Izaveta wasn't sure she wanted, certainly not without her heart beating in her chest.

"Asya should have it," she said quickly. "Asya should decide."

The Firebird tilted a single wing down toward her sister, clearly in no state to make any sort of decisions.

"Can't you wake her up?" Izaveta asked, a desperate edge to her voice. This was Asya's territory, choosing the right thing, ensuring the good of all and not just her selfish needs.

"I could," the Firebird replied. "If that is what you choose in exchange."

Izaveta swallowed hard. This was too quick, she needed time—time to think this through logically, to question what her mother might have chosen and ensure she didn't follow the same path.

But the Firebird did not look patient, its discerning eyes burning into Izaveta.

"Can you undo this spell? Repair the damage Koschei did?" Izaveta asked, trying to at least determine the parameters of what was possible, to give herself a few more breaths to sort this through.

"I can."

"And that will return magic to its true balance, it will end the Fading?"

"Yes," the creature replied, no shift in her intonation, as if it mattered very little to her either way. "Without any threads of magic tied to your crown, balance will be restored again." It ruffled its feathers, a spray of sparks falling to the ground like dying stars. "I believe it will even return your heart to you. Another piece of magic that he meddled with, a price that should not have been altered."

Izaveta could hardly breathe as she spoke. "And Asya?"

"If you ask me to undo the magic he has done, it will not change her fate." Her coal-burning eyes drifted to Asya, to the blade still pinning her in place. "Magic is not killing her. Mortality is."

"You can't do both?" Izaveta asked desperately. "You can't heal Asya and undo this magic?"

The Firebird didn't reply. The answer seemed clear enough: one feather for one favor, nothing more, nothing less. The creature saw this as a debt to be paid, a promise to be fulfilled, there was no personal attachment here.

"But that isn't *fair*." Not fair that Asya should die when she had always tried to do good, when she had always believed the best of people. Not fair for Izaveta to be left to live on without her.

Izaveta knew that was a pointless argument, the Firebird and magic had no thoughts on fairness. No concept of what Izaveta was losing here.

"I will not wait forever."

How was she supposed to make this choice? She had always dreamed of control, of being the one to set the story. And now she had that wish too, yet it came with a price too high for her to pay.

In many ways, it was a choice Izaveta had made over and over before. The choice between power and her sister, between the good of Tóurin and her own selfish love for Asya. The awful fear of having to live without her.

She'd used each path more than once, neither leading to any kind of redemption.

All these decisions, the hard choices she had to make, tearing off pieces of herself. Would they just keep getting ripped away until she was nothing? A wisp that floated away to Zmenya's empty skies?

Her sister who had always seen the good in everyone, who had always tried to make things right not because of power but because she truly believed it. Or the land Izaveta had a duty to, the one the gods had chosen her to rule—not for power, either, but for the good of Tóurin.

Perhaps Izaveta would never know if she had made the right choice. Perhaps it would haunt her forever, the reasoning going around and around in her head to no avail. All things came with a price and that would be hers.

But she thought she knew the choice Asya would make. Even if it made Izaveta's skin want to tear away, the very fabric of her being unspooling.

"Undo the sorcerer's magic," she said, the words bitter and poisonous. Saving herself, saving the queendom—but leaving Asya to her death.

CHAPTER EIGHTY-EIGHT

She was dying.

Asya knew it in the too-slick spill of blood spreading around her. In the way the colors were sliding out of her grasp. In the way the pain felt like a distant thing now, something that belonged to some other girl in some other time.

Izaveta leaned over her, hair spilling across Asya's face. "Asya? Asya!"

Asya tried to ask her what had happened, if the Firebird had really burst free. But she couldn't get the words to form.

Yuliana knelt at her side, ice no longer cracking through the familiar brightness of her gray eyes. It made Asya want to smile, but the muscles in her face wouldn't listen.

"Isn't there anything you can do?" Yuliana was saying, a fractured pain in her words that Asya wished she could soothe away.

"Get the voye!" someone else yelled, the shout far away and echoing.

She tried to wave them off. To explain that she was fine, it didn't matter now. But no words came out, just a gurgling kind of choke.

Her hand managed to move, squeezing tight in Yuliana's, her sister's warmth on her other side. This felt like the most

Asya could have asked for. Even this, a bold hope for a monster and girl, intertwined then unloosed all at once.

A fitting end, to at least keep her humanity for these last precious moments.

CHAPTER EIGHTY-NINE

Izaveta stared down at her sister, her own heart thrumming in her chest again even as she saw Asya's stutter out. The unfairness of it cleaved through Izaveta once more, a ragged scream caught in her throat.

She looked up at all the onlookers, freed from the spell that had consumed them. The newly gleaming floors around her, all remnants of Koschei's magic undone. The world that would not have been possible without Asya's sacrifice. But the sword still protruded from Asya's chest, the pulse of blood slowing around her now.

In that moment, Izaveta was sure she must have chosen wrong, because there was no way the right decision would hurt this much. That it would rip her newly restored heart apart, tearing her sister from her with a terrible finality.

Her vision blurred in and out of focus, tears too afraid to fall because that would mean this was real. That Asya was truly gone and Izaveta had to somehow live on without her.

The broken halves of the egg that had held Koschei's heart lay a little beyond Asya, shifting and blurring like the rest of the world. All Izaveta's useless schemes discarded at her feet, her attempts at cleverness that had not mattered in the end.

Izaveta had made the difficult choice more than once, the

destructive choice, all excused in her mind by the promise of a greater good in the end.

And this was her price, her heart severed either way.

Izaveta's eyes widened suddenly, flicking up to the broken halves of that egg. The only substance that could contain a human heart, that was what Nikov had said.

She leaped to her feet, unconscious of the gasps around her. The heavy sobs of Yuliana against Asya's hair.

Izaveta had done the right thing for Tóurin. She didn't owe them any more of herself. Now she would do the right thing for herself. Even if it was selfish, she was the only piece at risk here. Damn all her talk of practical decisions, all her weighing and balancing of logistics. She had her heart back, and so she may as well use it.

She whirled on Nikov, tears tracking down his dirt-smudged cheeks. "Koschei taught you all his magic, yes?"

Nikov nodded, blinking in confusion.

"Did he teach you how to remove a mortal's heart?"

"Yes, but—" Izaveta's meaning dawned on him. "I won't take your heart to give to Asya, she wouldn't thank me for it. She wouldn't thank you either."

Izaveta knew that—knew that perhaps once she would have forced it upon her sister without caring about the consequences, as long as it meant that Asya lived.

"Besides," Nikov added. "The egg is already broken."

"Broken into two halves," Izaveta said, buzzing insistence swallowing her words. "A perfect vessel to split a heart in two. One part for me, one part for Asya."

Nikov stared at her. Izaveta was vaguely aware of Yuliana's silence at Asya's side, sharp eyes now on this conversation with a jagged hope. A hope Izaveta couldn't begin to examine yet.

"As a scholarly theory," Izaveta pressed, trying to break through to his logical side. "Is it possible?"

"Possible, yes," he said, brow furrowed and eyes worried. "But I wouldn't know the ramifications—we don't know what it might do in the long term or even if it would work at all."

"I don't care." Izaveta snatched up the two halves of the egg, the substance still warm beneath her fingers. "We have to try."

She held them out to Nikov, expectant, but he shook his head. "I need time to prepare, to try to configure some kind of theory—a plan. And her body might not last, I don't know what would become of her if we tried to put a heart into a long-dead body."

"Then, we don't wait," Izaveta said, no flicker to her resolve. "We do it now."

"Izaveta," he said slowly, softly imploring. She knew it was asking a lot—probably asking more than she deserved. But it wasn't just for her, it was for Asya.

Izaveta squeezed her fingers around his, the briefest touch. "Please," she murmured. "I've let her down so much. I made the hard choice once. I can't lose her again."

Nikov met her eyes, a painful understanding in their depths. He nodded.

"Get those ingredients," he said to no one in particular.

Yuliana moved at once, gathering them up in her hands even as they mingled with broken glass.

It only took Nikov a few minutes to prepare the spell around Asya, but to Izaveta's thundering heart, it felt like centuries. A drawn-out, painful torture to watch the terrible stillness of her sister's chest.

Izaveta sat on the lowest step of the dais, her hands clenched tight in her lap. She didn't want to feel Asya's coldness, the life ebbing further and further away with every breath.

"Removing it is easy," Nikov said, his tone falling to harangued scholar instead of terrified friend, his own way of coping. "It's splitting it in half that may be impossible." He laid out the last few ingredients, then picked up the pieces of the egg, unable to hide the slight tremble in his hands.

He knelt in front of Izaveta, the scholar fracturing momentarily to the fear beneath. The boy who had once pursued knowledge above all else, not understanding its price until too late.

"Are you sure?" he murmured.

Izaveta nodded. "Yes," she said, for once not lying in her expressed sincerity. "I trust you."

Nikov's throat bobbed, but he didn't question her any further. He closed his eyes, dark lashes fluttering.

Izaveta had opened her mouth to ask if she would know, when she felt it. She'd expected pain—perhaps similar to that terrible undoing after Asya had first taken the price. But it felt more like releasing a breath after breaking the surface of the water, something gently pulled away from her toward the humming egg in Nikov's hands.

It was only at the very last moment, as if her body had gone to take another breath only to find it stolen by the water, that a spike of fear pierced through. A moment where she forgot she could live without it, her blood stuttering in her veins and lungs seizing.

Then her heart was in Nikov's careful hands. A vulnerability Izaveta would never have imagined possible before, her mortal weakness laid out in front of her, far from her own control.

But it didn't scare her now.

She pressed a hand to her chest, no steady rhythm beat-

ing there. At least it took some of the pounding fear with it, tempered again by its removal.

Nikov was murmuring the spell under his breath, a low steady rhythm to keep the heart contained. His face was a picture of concentration, careful maneuvering as he held the two halves together, and then pried them apart.

It was those same strange wisps that had dissipated when the egg first broke, something between liquid and solid, yet somehow lighter than both. It looked brighter than Koschei's had, not wilted from the centuries of imprisonment.

That surprised Izaveta somehow. She had always imagined her heart a broken, blackened thing. Yet here it was, alive and surprisingly peaceful.

Nikov raised one half toward Izaveta, never breaking his careful concentration. As if he was carrying a cup filled to the brim with water and even the slightest hitch could spill precious drops.

Her half of the heart flooded back inside her with a sudden warmth, a renewed burst of fear for her sister. Izaveta didn't think it felt much different, certainly not like the emptiness of her heart being entirely gone.

Nikov turned to Asya next and Izaveta had to force herself not to lean forward and risk upsetting his balance.

A few strands of gold fluttered free as Nikov lowered the half toward Asya, disintegrating the moment air touched them. Izaveta saw Nikov's eyes straining, jaw clenched tight as he forced himself to continue the spell, to not let that slip worry him.

A few pieces of Izaveta's heart lost forever. A small price to pay if it brought her sister back.

Nikov held the half against Asya's skin, just as he had done for Izaveta.

For a moment, it didn't seem to want to flow into Asya. Izaveta's heart too brittle and broken to be accepted into someone like Asya. Nikov's soft voice coaxed it forward, urging it on into an unfamiliar home. Then it fell in a sudden rush, gold threads spidering across Asya's skin, sinking in when they reached her heart.

Izaveta flung herself forward then, reaching at once for the pulse in her sister's neck. But the blood was still beneath her fingers, no warmth rising to her skin.

Izaveta looked over at Nikov, a heavy sadness dragging at his features.

Perhaps it had been an impossible task, a childish fantasy for Izaveta to entertain. Or maybe her heart was simply not strong enough for the both of them, the two not as intrinsically linked as she had always believed.

Tears loomed behind Izaveta's eyes, still unwilling to fall. Unwilling to accept this failure again even as Tóurin rejoiced behind her. A hollow celebration, one that felt so frail without her sister.

The tears finally spilled free when Asya's brown eyes flew open.

EPILOGUE:

THE UNBURNING FIREBIRD AND THE HALF-HEARTED QUEEN

THE HALF-HEARTED QUEEN

Izaveta was sitting in her rooms, Lyoza curled up at her side, when they finally brought the news.

Out the window, the Depthless Lake shone brighter than the pallid winter sunlight, the fourth moon returned to its eminence.

The cabinet and other prominent members of court, generals and conze from far reaches of Tóurin, had been sequestered for the best part of three days, likely talking circles around each other.

Izaveta was actually surprised they'd come to a decision already, she'd been expecting at least a month of debate and counterarguments and ploys before they could reach a consensus.

Even knowing they were debating her future, deciding if she was queen or traitor, exile or commoner, she had not tried to sway them either way. She hadn't sent out spies or letters to persuade more cabinet members to her side, even when Nikov told her he had overheard a conversation between Sanislav and Vada Nisova.

Izaveta wanted no part in it, no more manipulations. She just let it happen, accepting their decision one way or another.

She wondered what had swayed them, if it had been the

miraculous return from the dead, or perhaps her sacrifice in front of all of them after Koschei's spell was broken. The test from the gods that Vibishop Sanislav claimed she had passed, neatly overlooking his own role in it. Commander Iveshkin had offered her support too, perhaps more convincingly than the vibishop.

Perhaps it was simply that the court was still fascinated with power they could not quite understand.

She supposed that hardly mattered now, though it would, in coming months when she had to find ways to make good on it. Had to find ways to persuade them to follow her in the changes she wanted to bring.

A role she'd so long coveted, that she'd thought herself chosen for, that now it was finally offered, she wasn't sure she truly wanted. But it was a duty she would not shirk, one she finally thought she understood the weight of.

She was still reeling, still not quite sure of herself, when the door opened again.

Nikov walked in, accustomed to eschewing the courtesies of things like knocking or announcing himself. He sat on the chair opposite her, reaching out one hand to stroke Lyoza.

"I hear congratulations are in order."

She looked up, not quite sure how to take that. "It would appear so."

He grinned, the smile so freely given even in moments when Izaveta had not deserved it. "Any last apologies to get in before you're crowned?"

She shot him a wry smile back. "I may have to amend the policy that queens do not apologize, given my history."

"Revolutionizing already, I see," Nikov said. "Next order of business should be separation of church and state. That would certainly garner some attention."

"I'll bear that in mind next time I want to give the vibishop a heart attack."

Silence lapsed between them, something unsaid that Izaveta couldn't quite understand.

"Well, I should leave you. I'm sure you have lots to attend to." Nikov stood up with a sudden formality that hung strangely about him. "I only came here to offer my congratulations." His chin dipped, eyes sliding down. "And my apologies too, I suppose, as I won't be able to attend the coronation."

Izaveta stood up sharply. "You won't?"

"I'm returning to the Amarinth," he replied, with a half smile that held none of the warmth of his usual ones. "It's where I should have been all this time anyway. I think I have some penance to serve."

Izaveta stared at him. He seemed to be waiting for her to say something, but no words came. So he just nodded to her, the hint of a bow, and he turned to leave.

She opened her mouth, wishing this was easier to say when his back wasn't to her. But even then, she couldn't quite form the words. Nikov had, quite literally, held her heart in his hands, he had reshaped it and offered her the salvation of her sister. So why was it so hard to say this? A sharp point of pride still holding her back.

"Stay."

The word was so quiet he could have ignored it, could easily have missed it and continued walking out of Izaveta's life. But he froze, as if he'd been waiting, hoping for just that.

"Stay," Izaveta said again and he turned back to her.

"We need more scholars in Vetviya's Tower again," she said quickly. "There'd be plenty for you to research. Perhaps not as much as in the Amarinth, but it certainly provides unusual opportunities."

"The Fading has ended," Nikov replied. "Is there still need for the tower?"

"There's always need for more learning, surely you must agree on that," Izaveta said.

"Is that the only reason you want me to stay?" he asked.

"Is a scholar's curiosity not enough for you anymore?" She smiled, but his expression remained serious, his own hint of vulnerability.

"Also for me," she said. "I would also like you to stay."

Izaveta went to Asya first, of course. Her sister was in the bearkeep, brushing Mishka down after returning from a ride. She'd been spending a lot of time with the bear—something about him demanding attention again.

Her eyebrows shot up when she spotted Izaveta, silk skirt trailing in the mud. Izaveta didn't know if it was her unusual appearance in the bearkeep or the growing connection between the two of them, the two pieces of one heart pulling together, but Asya seemed to know at once why she was there.

"What did they decide?" Asya asked, in the tone of someone prepared to go to blows if they didn't like the answer.

"I am to be crowned within the week."

Asya flung her arms around her, pulling her into a tight hug.

Izaveta pulled away, putting her hands on Asya's shoulders. "I have one condition of my queenship."

Asya raised her eyebrows in question.

"I need you to promise that you'll always be honest with me, whether it's a decision you don't agree with or a piece of news people think a queen should not hear. I don't want to let the power of the position take over me."

An odd expression creased Asya's face. "Do you still think you need that?"

"I hope not," Izaveta replied. "But I'd like the assurance there. The queen and the Firebird, still holding each other in balance."

"I don't think you need it," Asya said. "Not anymore."

"And if you're wrong?"

"I'm not." She pressed a hand against Izaveta's heart, the shared beat that bound them together. "Don't forget, I see into your heart clearly now. I know what you want and the work you will do for Tóurin. I know power may still be a temptation, but I also know you are stronger than that now."

There was such certainty in Asya's voice, a conviction and belief in Izaveta that made her want to believe it herself. A fragile and dangerous hope, but one she swore to hold herself to.

"Very well," Izaveta said. "Then, I have one other condition."

"A lot of conditions for something you claim to have always wanted," Asya grumbled.

"I don't want the archbishop to crown me," Izaveta said. "I want you to do it."

Asya's face split into a smile, boundless and unbridled. "I would be honored."

THE UNBURNING FIREBIRD

They buried Tarya in the Sunken Gardens, a quiet affair after the grand fanfare of the coronation. Asya didn't mind though, she doubted her aunt would have wanted any sort of fuss.

The only remaining mourners were Asya, Izaveta, and Yuliana—her hand still tight in Asya's. Zvezda had finally retired herself with a last whispered word to the tree that now marked Tarya's grave. A newly planted, purple blossoming oak that shouldn't be so vibrant this time of year.

Nikov had cast a spell on it to flower in all weather, so the Sunken Gardens was less gray and dead through the winters. He'd happily proclaimed that the spell only took a year of his life, to which Izaveta had protested at once. He'd relented and admitted it didn't require much, just renewal every year with a little of someone's blood.

"Do you think Tarya would have liked this?" Yuliana asked into the oncoming dusk.

· "No," Asya admitted. "Probably not."

But the Sunken Gardens seemed like the right place to remember the severe woman, as unbreakable and immovable as the plants here. The woman who had chosen her humanity in the end. Who had sacrificed it for Asya.

Asya could just imagine Tarya still sitting beneath the

empty branches of the tree, claiming no cold even when snow was building up around her. Even if Tarya might have said she wanted nothing frivolous, no unnecessary emotions, Asya didn't feel she was going against her aunt's wishes.

Tarya deserved to be remembered as more than the Firebird, more than another name in the Karasova line.

Asya swallowed, the thing she'd been trying to say to Izaveta for days rising up her throat again. She'd kept putting it off, as if she could simply pretend it out of existence, even as time sped past.

She shot Izaveta a sidelong glance. She still wasn't used to seeing her sister wearing the crown, her hair artfully twisted around the curling shards. She'd thought it would make Izaveta look more like their mother—or Asya's memory of their mother—but if anything it just made Izaveta look more grown-up. Serious and thoughtful compared to their mother's sneers.

A true queen to her core.

Yuliana caught Asya's eye, reading the thought on her face. Yuliana gave her a small nudge, a squeeze of her hand, and peeled away. Giving Asya the private moment with her sister.

"I have to tell you something," Asya said suddenly, the words finally breaking free.

"You're not staying, are you?"

Asya wasn't sure why she was surprised that Izaveta had anticipated this, always able to read Asya's silences. "The palace has never really been for me," she said gently.

Izaveta couldn't quite look at her, as if she needed a moment to get her feelings under control again. It was pointless now, though. Asya could feel them almost as keenly as her own through the pounding bond that tied them together.

"What will you do?"

"The Firebird was always meant to stand for balance," Asya said, putting into words the idea she and Yuliana had been hatching. "And I'd like to continue that, even without my flames. To find a way to ensure justice and balance in Tóurin."

She'd first told Yuliana of the idea the night before Izaveta's coronation. Asya had worried it was a silly thought, a foolish dream that she couldn't hope to enact. She'd told Yuliana about the boy in the Elmer, forced to bear the price for someone else's spell. And Vada Nisova had proved Azarov wasn't the only one to find that particular loophole.

But Yuliana hadn't laughed or pointed out the flaws. She'd simply sat down with Asya and begun to sketch out the logistics in that unerring, soldier-like way she was so good at.

"A noble goal," Izaveta said, a little stilted. "I can ensure you have all the resources you might require."

"I am coming back, though."

Izaveta looked up at her, as if she couldn't risk believing it. As if she still feared Asya might slip through her fingers. "Truly?"

"Always," Asya replied, putting a hand against her chest. "You can hardly be rid of me now."

And it was true—or perhaps as true as it had ever been, but now made into something tangible. Two sides of the same coin, two pieces of a tapestry, managing to cling on to each other through everything.

And now nothing could change that. No crown or sorcerer or duty. Two halves of a whole, together no matter what.

★ ★ ★ ★ ★

ACKNOWLEDGMENTS

It really is true what they say about second books, they're so much harder to write than the first one! This was true for *This Cursed Crown* for many reasons, not helped of course by the pandemic that we've all been dealing with since 2020. I ended up restarting the entire book more than once and still worried right up until this last draft that I might not have got it right for these characters who are so close to my heart.

But I can happily say now that I have made it through book two, and that is largely thanks to so, so many people behind the scenes.

The first thank-you has to go to my wonderful editor, Connolly Bottum, who stuck with me all through the difficulty of these drafts and still somehow believed in me and this story. Thank you as well to everyone at Inkyard Press for all your amazing work: especially Bess Brasswell for all your support, Brittany Mitchell for your amazing marketing, Laura Gianino, the most wonderful publicist, Olivia Valcarce for your enthusiasm and fantastic work on the final steps, and Jerri Gallagher for your wonderful copyediting once again. Thank you as well to Kathleen Oudit for the beautiful cover direction and Marisa Aragon Ware for the absolutely stunning illustration. You really outdid yourself with this one!

Thank you so much to the team at New Leaf, who have also worked so tirelessly, helping me through all the difficulty of this book. Firstly, to my agent, Patrice Caldwell, who has been an amazing champion through this, as well as her wonderful assistant Trinica Sampson. And to everyone else at New Leaf: Veronica Grijalva, Victoria Henderson, Kate Sullivan and Meredith Barnes.

Thank you as well to the team at Bookends who first helped me through this book deal and ensured this duology was published: Natascha Morris, Naomi Davis and James McGowan.

Huge thank-you to Katie Passerotti for reading every incoherent draft of this book and talking me through all the nervous breakdowns and fears that I would never finish it—I seriously couldn't have done this without you. To Tara Gilbert for all your late-night texts and encouragement. And to all my other writer friends who helped me through: Tiffany Lea Elmer, Briston Brooks, Tamara Mahmood Hayes, Zabé Ellor, Delara Adams, Anayib Figueroa, Peyton Austin and Kianna Shore. (You can thank her for Chapter Twenty!)

I want to also give a special thank-you to all the wonderful people who supported *These Feathered Flames* and really helped it find its readers during such a strange time: to all the booksellers, librarians, teachers, bloggers and online book people, I can't tell you how much I appreciate all your work! A special shout-out to Birdie (@birdienotabird), Chloe (@chloetheelvenwarrior), Landice (@manicfemme), Diana (@chasingchapters), Jacob (@a.veryqueerbookclub), Rachel (@bookworm_panda), Theresa (@libraryofsappho), Cait (@caitsbooks), Jaysen (@ezeecat) and Dalton (@cityveinlights) for helping to reveal the cover for *This Cursed Crown*—you're all so amazing, thank you!

Thank you of course to my family who helped me through all of this, especially to my mum and my sister Clemmie for helping me reach this finish line—and to my grandfather for very quickly reading a draft of this book to give me notes! Also to Lila Victor, surrogate sister, for the bookmark tassels of course.

There's always a fear that I've forgotten someone in the acknowledgments, and so the final thank-you to everyone reading this book—the fact that you've picked it up and stuck with Asya and Izaveta through this all means the world to me!